A SPARK IN THE NIGHT
WHAT DARKNESS HIDES
BOOK ONE

JMD REID

© 2024 by JMD Reid

All rights reserved. No part of this book may be reproduced, stored in a retrieval system or transmitted in any form or by any means without the prior written permission of the publishers, except by a reviewer who may quote brief passages in a review to be printed in a newspaper, magazine or journal.

The final approval for this literary material is granted by the author.

Edited by Poppy Reid

First Edition

This is a work of fiction. Names, characters, businesses, places, events and incidents are either the products of the author's imagination or used in a fictitious manner. Any resemblance to actual persons, living or dead, or actual events is purely coincidental.

PUBLISHED BY FALLBRANDT PRESS

www.FallbrandtPress.com

BOOKS BY JMD REID

What Darkness Hides
A Spark in the Night
A Gleam of Hope
A Heart of Pain

Shadows of the Dragon
Foundation of Courage
Lady Shadow's Ire
Guilt of Sacrifice
Sands of Loss
Wyrms of Regret
Madness of Light
Blood-Stained Shadows
Sailing the Ashen Seas
Lady Shadow's Promise
The Golden Trees Burn
Maelstrom of the Gods
Paradise Found

Jewels of Illumination
Diamond Stained
Ruby Ruins
Obsidian Mind
Emerald Strength
Amethyst Shattered
***
Jewels of Illumination Box Set

Mask of Illumination
Mask of Guilt
Mask of Vengeance
Mask of Hope
Mask of Betrayal
Mask of Redemption

The Storm Below
Above the Storm
Reavers of the Tempest
Storm of Tears
Golden Darkness Descends
Shattered Sunlight

The Storm Below Box Set

To my readers:
Thank you for allowing me to tell stories for a living

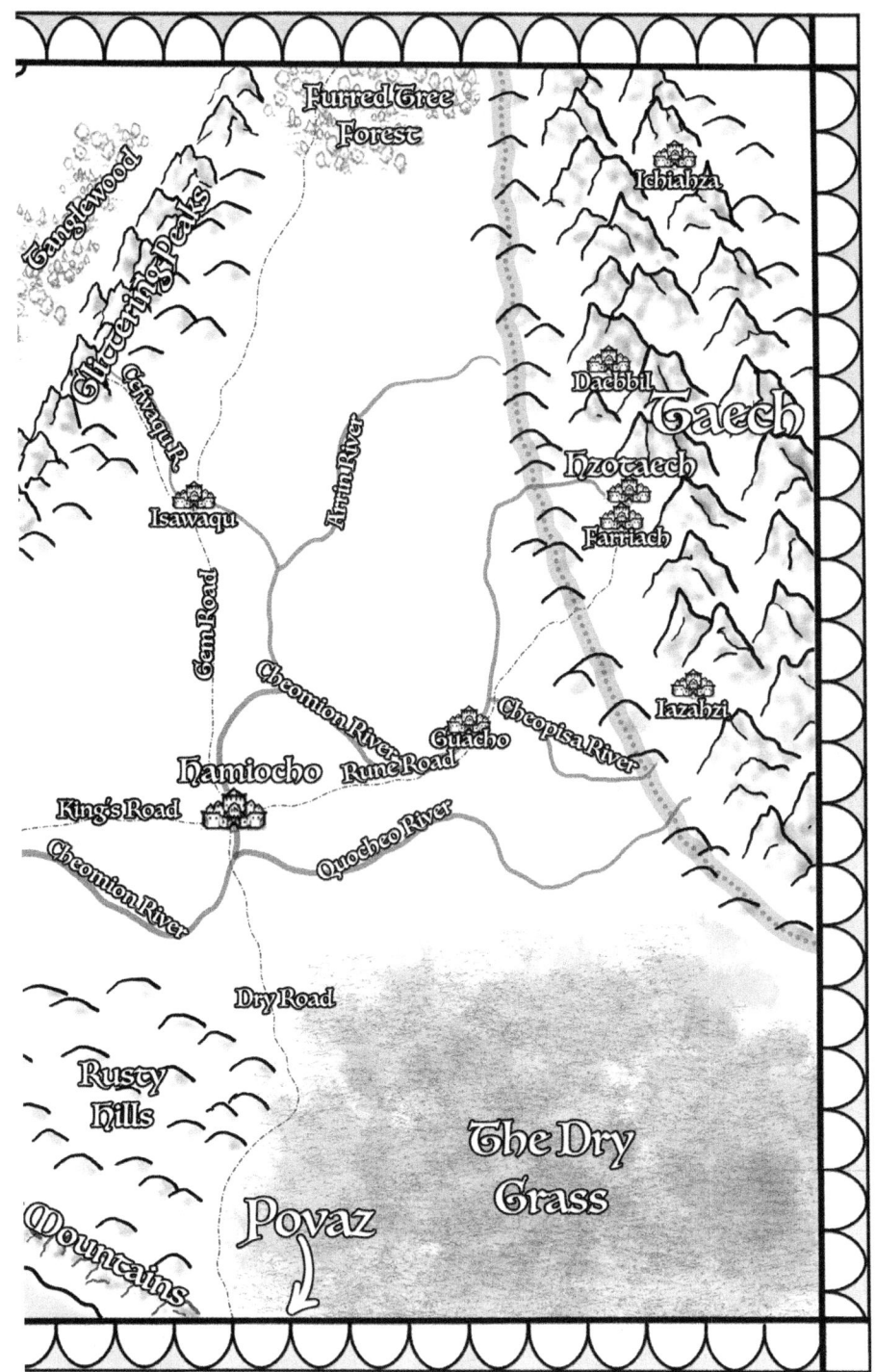

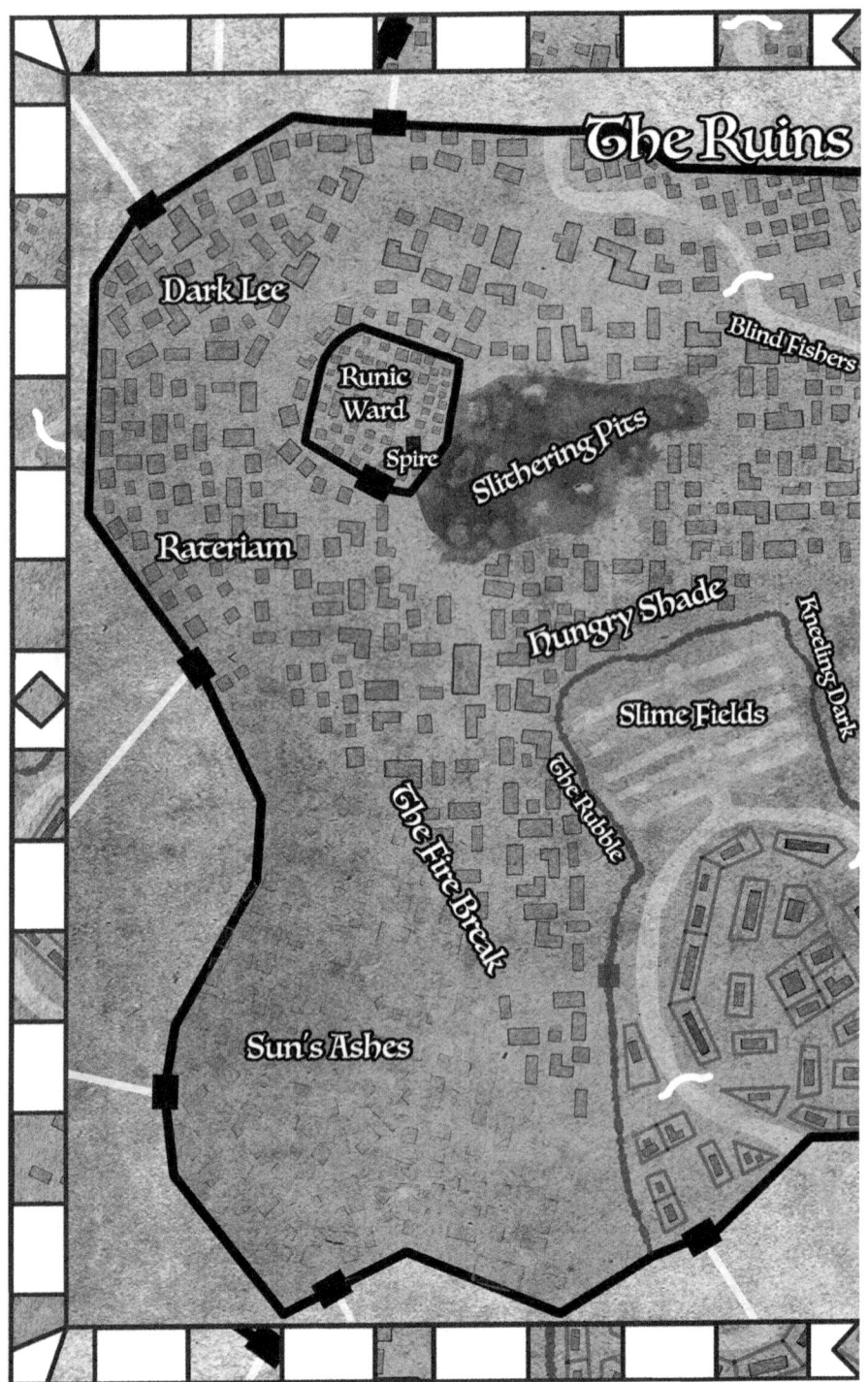

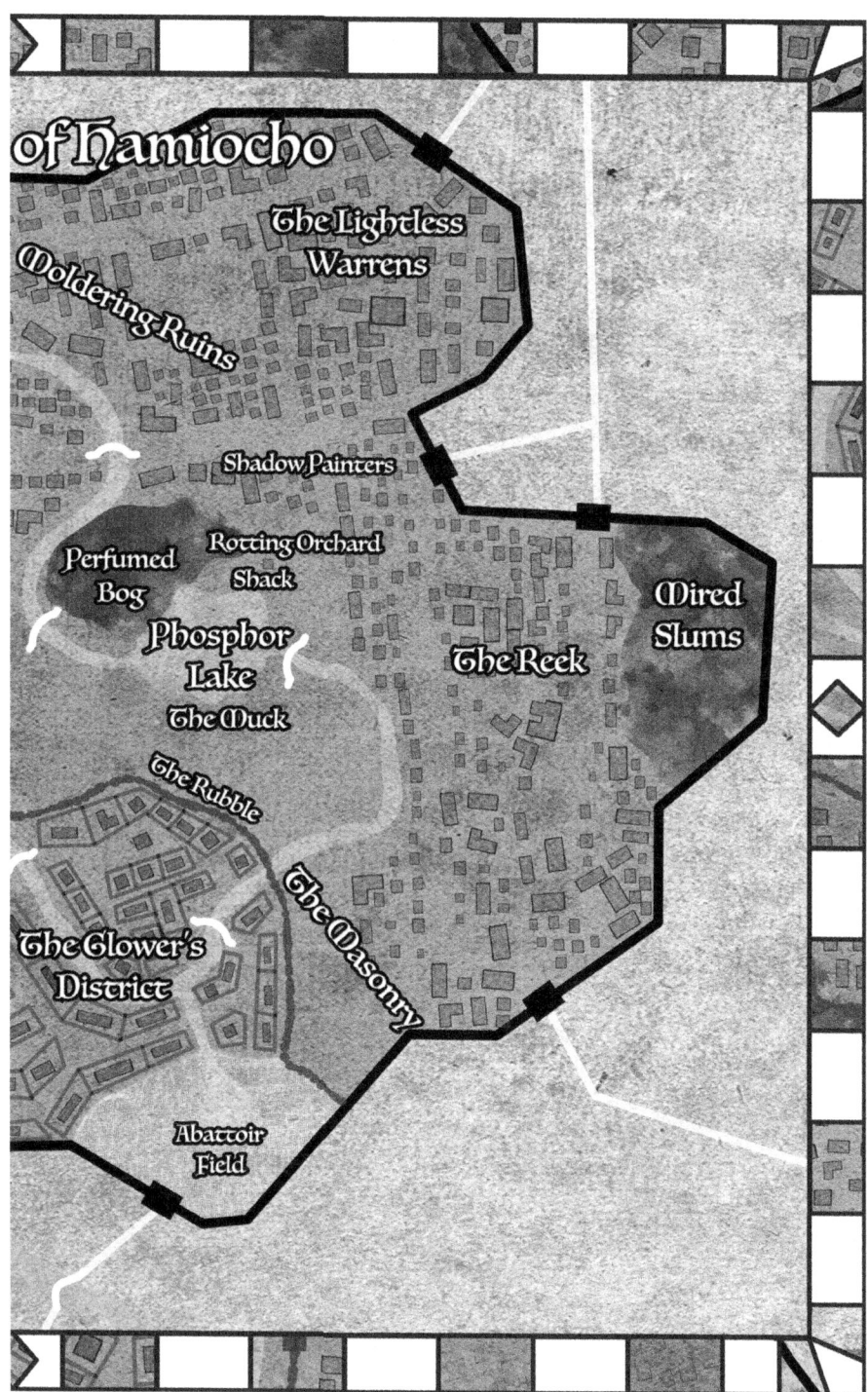

CHAPTER ONE

Ablisio was thirteen the day Death came for Hamiocho and the Darkfall plunged it into eternal night.

He could remember that moment with startling regularity in his dreams. He'd been a tall and gangly youth approaching his mother in height and resenting accompanying her to the market square as she shopped. Mostly because he had to keep watch over his younger sister, Amiollea. At eight, she clutched his hand as she stared at the bustling crowd. Here, the pale-skinned Povazian nearly outnumbered the native Karadrisans while a few of the tall and rune-stained Taechizians drifted about on their ethereal business.

Hamiocho lay at the heart of the world, or so boasted its citizens. It was the most prosperous city of the strongest nation, Karadris.

Ablisio and his family were Karadrisans. They weren't the rich lords and powerful merchants who dwelt in the southern section of town, but his father had a prosperous shop. A carpenter who turned out beautiful furniture to fill the appetites of those who gorged on the trade that flowed in all directions through the Crossroads of the World.

Or at least, the Crossroads of Karadris.

As his mother stopped at a spice merchant to purchase the savory delights that had traveled across the southern desert to reach them, his sister pulled at his hand. She wore a frilly dress of linen dyed a soft lilac, a matching bonnet framing her brown face. Tufts of her red hair, streaked with gold, peaked out and tumbled over her temples. Her yellow eyes, the same hue as his own, darted about the sights.

Beyond a pair of squat Povazian porters lugging sacks of heavy grain, she pointed at a puppet stand. Children gathered before it, mostly Karadrisan, but a few of the poorer Povazian were mixed in, their paler skin separating them from their betters.

"Come on," Amiollea said, tugging at him. "Puppets!"

"Mother doesn't want you wandering," Ablisio said, holding tight to her hand. Annoyance flashed through him. He had the same brown skin that characterized their race, though his hair was wholly bright red without the stray locks of gold. Their faces held similar features, same shape to the earlobes and angles of their cheekbones, though his nose was far bolder than hers. "Don't fidget."

She kicked him with the point of her leather shoe. Pain flared as the brown pants he wore did nothing to blunt her kick. He gripped her tight and grimaced. He yanked her against him, prepared to berate his little sister when a bright flash burst from the western end of the city.

His gaze shot up toward where it came from. Over the heads of the crowd of shoppers in the market and above the two or three-story, gray-stone buildings that made up their neighborhood north of Visgu Park, he stared at the Spire. It rose out of the heart of the Runic Ward, the quarter where the eastern Taechizians dwelled. Masters of the arcane arts of runes and magics.

The Spire was the highest structure in the city, standing on a large hill.

He could see nothing unusual that could have caused the flash. He shifted, wondering what that bright light was. He wasn't the only person staring off in that direction. Sounds erupted around him as bemused adults turned back to their shopping and stall merchants cried out their wares.

"Daggers made of the best Taechizian steel!"

"Fresh zucchinis plucked just this morning!"

"The best of Hamiocho's salted beef! Not an ounce of rot to be found. Cured in the best salt from Dahcho!"

"The puppets, Ablisio!" Amiollea stared up at him with petulant pleading quivering her lower lip.

"Ablisio!" their mother said. "Here, take this bag."

Their mother wore an airy dress of yellow linen that left her arms bare, the current summer fashion. She had a light scarf of silk wrapped around her head, hiding her golden locks. She held Amiollea's features matured to their full promise. She thrust out the sack at him, her fingers adorned with a few rings of silver and topped with moonstones; gifts from Father.

He snagged the bag of peppercorns from his mother while fighting to hold onto his sister. He was about to ask if he could let the brat go when the first screams erupted.

They burst out from the far end of the market, a woman screeching in agony that broke off into chilling silence. Then more frightened shouts erupted. Figures pressed through the crowd, racing from the outbreak of violence. Amiollea no longer fought to escape Ablisio's crushing grip. His sister pressed into his side, whimpering.

"Mother?" Ablisio croaked, fear drying his mouth, his words stiff.

His mother's ringed digits seized his wrist. Her fingernails, carefully filed and covered in a yellow glaze, bit into his flesh. Her face paled to a sickly tan as another scream cut off. Something ragged and bloody flew into the air held in a shimmering ripple, a distortion that soared above the terrified market square, trailing crimson and offal.

"We should . . ." Mother struggled to say. "We should go home and find your father. Yes. Yes. That's—"

The shimmer swept down to their right and plucked up a Povazian porter. Something sank into the squat man's chest, deep holes ripping into his flesh as if invisible horns had gored him. He bellowed as he rose in the air, massive rents piercing his body. He thrashed, his sack falling to the ground and bursting open to spill out barley corns. Amiollea sobbed and hugged Ablisio. He gasped, staring as the unseen Death ripped the man in half and flung his body in both directions. The legs struck a child, crushing the boy.

Panic burst in all directions. Karadrisans ran, crashing into each other. Ablisio couldn't think as he dragged his sobbing sister and stunned mother from Death. It swooped down again and again, ripping off heads. Tearing off limbs. No one was safe. A girl younger than Amiollea was wrenched from her mother's arms.

Fleeing Karadrisans knocked each other. A woman in a red dress fell on her face and cried out as a fat merchant stepped on her back. She struggled to stand only for more Karadrisans to trample over her in their mad flight. Ablisio was swept along the panicked flood, his mother clutching to his right wrist, his left hand holding Amiollea in a death grip.

The man racing before them, a laborer in a dirty jerkin, screamed as the boiling air swooped down and seized him by the head. A loud crack and the sound of wet meat tearing preceded his head popping off his body. His corpse flopped belly first before them.

Ablisio changed directions. He barreled into a woman and knocked her to the side as he dragged his mother and sister toward a tight alley running between two stone buildings. Laundry was strung between the windows above, creating a shadowed haven. His panicked mind gibbered to find safety.

"Ablisio!" his mother screamed moments before her fingers ripped from his arm, her nails leaving behind three bloody furrows.

He spun around to see her lifting into the air. Unseen claws pierced her stomach and chest, blood soaking her yellow dress. He stood rooted in horror as her face transformed into agony. Her silk scarf fell from her head as Death ripped her in half.

Blood splashed hot across Ablisio's face. He stumbled back and tripped over his little sister's leg. He fell on his backside. Amiollea sobbed and pressed against him as he stared at the two pieces of his mother.

The entity flung her away and surged for a new victim.

"Mommy! Mommy!" howled Amiollea as she huddled on his lap. Ablisio's arms went around her. He leaned against the wall, staring at the top half of his mother's body lying nearby, her face turned toward him, mouth open, yellow eyes unseeing.

He held his sister tight. She was the last thing he'd ever see in sunlight.

Like a vast sack had been thrown over the greatest city in the world, darkness fell upon Hamiocho. A great night so profound Ablisio couldn't see anything, not even his little sister trembling on his lap. He sat there, hot tears spilling through the blood drying on his face.

The world had broken.

~

Seven Years Later...

Ablisio awoke from his dream of his mother's death and the last vestige of normalcy Hamiocho ever knew. He was wreathed in comforting darkness. He couldn't see a thing. It was strange dreaming of daylight and color only to return to the present.

He breathed in deeply, his nose sorting through the scents around him. The foul decay of the Rotting Orchard was the most profound aroma. The familiar scent of home, the small hovel he had lived in for the last three years. Beneath the pungent scent of the moldering grove came the smell of two women. They were distinct to his keen nose. Seven years living in darkness had sharpened Ablisio's other senses. He could see with his fingertips and his skin, find his way by the drift of aromas filling his nose, or by his tongue tasting the air when he breathed through his mouth.

The earthy scent, mixed with his own salty essence, was Zhee's. His Povazian lover lay cuddled against him, the soft curves of her breasts pressed on his side. He could tell from her regular breathing that she still slept. The other scent, so similar to his own but with a lighter fragrance, was his sister's.

Amiollea's aroma was faint. Distant. He sat up and breathed in again while feeling the air currents shifting through the hovel. It was a storage shed for the produce harvested from the orchard that used to be here. All that was left was dead trees slowly rotting away. The shack's wooden walls were still sound save for a few places mold attacked. The door was open, changing how the air flowed through the room.

"I'm fine, Ablisio," his sister said, her voice drifting through the door. "I just needed to pee."

He could just smell the acrid scent above the other aromas. "I wasn't worried."

She snorted. "Right."

Zhee stirred at his side. Her hand went around his waist. A drowsy murmur came from her. His sister's footsteps padded across the mud before she entered the shack. Amiollea's movement shifted the flow of air. He struggled to picture her. She was fifteen now. No longer that sad girl he'd kept safe through the chaotic years after Darkfall.

You were easier to protect when you were too scared to talk back, he thought with annoyance.

"Are we going to the Kneelers today?" she asked as she settled onto her sleeping area. It was on the other side of the hovel.

A rumble rippled through his stomach. Survival in the ruins of Hamiocho meant doing things you hated. Venturing to the Kneeling Dark, where the closest dispensary lay, didn't number among Ablisio's favorite ways of acquiring food. He hated the groveling and fawning of the mucklings who dwelt in sight of the Rubble and the food contained within it. Whining, begging, and relying on others for survival.

Ablisio could only rely on Amiollea and Zhee.

He'd saved Zhee two years ago from a band of vile men. She had no one else, so he had watched after her with his sister. It had taken some time to learn to trust her.

Ablisio had believed the wages of trust were pain. Blood. Scars.

But Zhee had used a different coin to buy his trust. She had proved herself useful, dedicated to helping, and somewhere along the way, she'd wormed into his heart. Now he found such comfort in her and was glad he had ignored that instinct screaming at him to abandon her and leave her to fend for herself.

To hold onto that scrap of goodness and decency Darkfall hadn't squeezed out of him.

"We have enough dung to get a week's supply of algae," Amiollea finally decided. "We'll go to Kneelers. No point in climbing the Rubble and stealing from the Glowers or dealing with the Ratters."

Zhee shifted. He knew she was awake, but she wasn't speaking. Her stomach rumbled, too. He stretched out on his back and absently stroked her hair. It was matted and stringy, kept ragged and short. Staying clean was difficult in a city rotting more and more every day.

The Darkwall had cut Hamiocho off from the outside world. A barrier of darkness that followed the perimeter of the city's outer walls. None could leave. None could enter. Only, for reasons none could answer to Ablisio's satisfaction, the river flowing through the city could come and go. But those who tried to swim out either end found the same barrier.

They were trapped in the city walls, forced to adapt to a new life. He'd learned early on not to be picky about food. Favorite pets were eaten. Then rats. The rich merchants had seized the livestock pens and, through deals made with the Taechizian Runecarvers, kept their herds of cattle alive. It had been a month since he'd broken into a Glower's house, as the powerful in the city were called, and stolen a hunch of salted beef.

It was a risk breaking into a Glower's house. The Rubble had warning runes that sounded alarms and deadlier enchantments. Some runes caused pain. Others even killed, though those were few. Maybe even apocryphal. Year after year, more defensive runes sprouted on the wall, arcane mold closing up the holes thieves exploited, making it harder and harder to find a way in. Once over, you had to worry about the guards. Glowers had their own private soldiers to protect their houses and families. They would flood the unlit streets to hound any thieves.

But the risk was worth it. If you could get inside a house, you could find wealth.

If you weren't blinded by the *lights*. The Glowers used runed lamps to fill their homes with sorcerous brilliance.

Lights were dangerous in Hamiocho if you weren't indoors. They attracted Death. More than a faint glow from a rune attracted their attention. Even candlelight would send them swooping down to tear and maim.

No one knew why.

Was it a curse from the Creator?

Had the Runecarvers unleashed the demons?

Was it a plot by their enemies to destroy the heart of Karadris?

Those who had survived learned there was safety only in darkness. If you wanted light, you had to ensure it couldn't escape your home. It was said that the Glowers kept herds of livestock in a vast paddock roofed over by runic constructions and so well-lit *grass* grew.

But they held all the wealth in the city. They held the food.

"We'll go to the Kneelers," Ablisio finally said.

Zhee stroked his chest. He covered her hand and held it. Her head rested on his chest. He stared up into the dark. His sister didn't answer, but he could tell she was pleased by minute changes in her breathing and the sounds of skin rubbing on skin as she squirmed.

He liked making her happy.

"We'll go in a few hours," he said. "How long until noon?"

"Five hours," Amiollea answered. She possessed a good internal clock.

"Wake me in three," he said. "We'll kneel."

Pride was another thing that got men killed in Hamiocho. He couldn't afford to have any no matter how much groveling crushed his spirit. It wasn't just his life, but Amiollea's and Zhee's depended on him. Women who didn't have protectors were seized by any lowlife out there.

There was nothing sacred in Hamiocho any longer.

CHAPTER TWO

What are you doing up there, Maestro? Maegwirio wondered for, perhaps, the millionth time.

He'd never kept track.

The young man looked up the stairs of the Spire, the tower that lay in the heart of the Runic Ward in Hamiocho. It was constructed by his people a hundred years ago when they made their treaty with the Karadrisan. His people had supplied runic artifacts and the carvers to create them in exchange for their sovereign right to rule their mountains in their own way.

Maegwirio hadn't seen Taechiz in seven years. He had come to Hamiocho to be apprentice to one of the three Maestros of the Runes. Maestro Kozonio was said to have forgotten more about carving words of power than Maegwirio would ever learn.

He didn't doubt that.

Maegwirio had the misfortune to arrive in Hamiocho on the day of Darkfall. A mere hour before it, he had arrived at the Spire. A lad of only nine, two weeks from his home in the mountains of Taechiz, found himself entering the home of his new master. Maegwirio had trained hard for this day, pressed by his parents to learn all the runes and the Karadrisan tongue. He had even modified his name to help him fit in with the foreign city, adding the "io" suffix present on all male Karadrisan names.

Not that his bluish skin would let him blend in with the brown-skinned Karadrisans nor the paler-skinned Povazians who were used as cheap manual labor around the city. He would forever be marked with the blood of the Runecarvers; the magic stained his flesh. He was a conduit to shaping the world with his words.

He just had to learn.

"Of course, you arrive today," Eoxhinea had said upon his arrival at the Spire. She had been an older apprentice, sixteen or seventeen, a woman grown. She'd shaken her head at him as the heavy doors of the Spire boomed shut behind him. A tingle had run through the air, the awe of being here. "I don't have time to get you settled. The maestro needs all his apprentices."

"I'm his apprentice," Maegwirio had said in the trembling voice of a boy trying to act strong. He held his wooden soldier, painted with blue armor like a runic knight, tucked beneath his arm. It was a parting gift from his older brother.

"Technically," she'd said and held out her hand, a motherly smile crossing her lips. "Come on, let me show you to your quarters. In a few hours, we'll be back and you'll get to meet the others. You'll love Tzuzio. Soon, you two will be annoying us all as you race through the Spire playing tag."

"I wouldn't do that," he'd protested as she led him across the small entry room.

The tower looked bigger from the outside. Inside, it was cramped. A staircase spiraled up the outer wall. The next level was a kitchen, orderly and full of many runic devices from flameless stoves to cold boxes. The third floor held a dining hall. After that, the stairs wrapped past doors, each one carved with a name. He read the names of the four other apprentices, including Eoxhinea. Her braid of metallic gold hair, not too dissimilar from his own wild locks, swayed down the back of the gray toga she wore, her arms bare.

Finally, she stopped at a door with his name on it. She smiled. "See, you are an apprentice."

Young Maegwirio had nodded and dashed in. He had his own room. He didn't have to share with his older brother, who snored. He had a desk with its own ink bottle and quill, a small bed with a quilt stitched in runes, a wardrobe, and a trunk to store his meager possessions.

He smiled as he placed the soldier on the desk, standing proud and strong. A knight using the power of runes to keep Taechiz safe from anything. He had fantasies of learning the battle runes from Maestro Kozonio.

At the time, Maegwirio didn't know that he would never see the smiling, youthful Eoxhinea again. While he played with his soldier, Death and Darkfall came. Only his maestro had returned from the roof, bleeding badly from a deep cut in his side and needing the young boy's help in ministering to his wound with runic items.

Maegwirio had spent the next nine years hardly leaving the Spire. It was dangerous outside the tower. No light could be shed. People had to navigate blind. While the Runic Ward was one of the safer spots in the city, the Taechizian ex-patriots living in the quarter supporting each other through the chaos, many still died. It was estimated three-quarters of the most populated city in the world had perished in the first month of the disaster.

If I had arrived only an hour later, I would have seen what happened from the outside. If the world even still exists beyond the Darkwall. Maegwirio chafed to understand what had caused the calamity. At sixteen, he was tired of being in the Spire all the time. Being an apprentice to Kozonio had allowed him to study his runes and the delicate syntax of power even amid this disaster. But it was a confined life.

A prisoner's life.

Beyond the Spire, many eked out a horrible existence in the dark and rotting rubble. Everything festered. The scents sometimes permeated the stones of the Spire. No rain had fallen on the city. It sweltered, the summer heat seemingly trapped forever. The Cheomion River still brought in freshwater, but the Darkwall seemed to trap its evaporation, slowly turning more and more of the city into a mire. From those Taechizians who made the caravan travel to the Glowers to trade runic devices for food, he'd heard of sections of the city sinking into the muck.

Hamiocho was slowly dying.

Maegwirio had comfort for now, but there would come a day when they would all perish. He wanted to find out how to undo the calamity and break the Dark. He wanted to drive away Death and stop it from killing any who attracted its deadly attention.

Maegwirio wanted to understand what his maestro did at the top of the tower every day at noon. He knew a light flashed from the Spire from the maestro charging some sort of arcane device. He did not know why or for what purpose. Was it an instrument to study the phenomenon? Was it merely a beacon to give hope and mark the start of the next day, like he claimed? Even when he had the watery lungs for a week, he insisted on making the climb up to the top and working his craft.

The answers lay in the maestro's study.

It lay near the top of the tower. Maegwirio studied its door. It held the appearance of wood but had the color of steel. It was what his people called *opahzeokwa*. Wooden steel. The runes carved into the door had forever transmuted it. The frame, too, was of the same substance. The hinges were on the other side, impossible for him to attack. Written around the doorknob was the lock. Runes scribed so minuscule he had to bend over to get close enough to look.

It was the most complicated series of logic and power he'd seen. It consisted of twenty-three separate clauses all connecting each other, reinforcing the strength of the lock and canceling out any loopholes to get around it. The work was impressive. Maegwirio could barely link three clauses together with such grace and elegance.

It was poetry carved into metal and brimming with runic energy. Nothing could open this door. Not the strongest man nor the hottest flame. He couldn't affect any property of the door. The only way was to unravel the clues in the logic and work out the runic key that would fit it, the phrase that would cut through all the clauses and unravel the sentence.

It hurt his brain just studying it.

He wrote on a piece of parchment. He could easily reuse it again and again, using runes to wipe its surface clean of ink. No new paper entered Hamiocho. He had only the resources in this tower. Books that they had more than one copy of had long been wiped of words to use as journals to chronicle his progress in the runic arts.

As his maestro did his secret work above, Maegwirio worked through the logic of the complex sentence, searching for the weakness. The flaw. The lock that he could shape the right key to fit. He didn't have much time before Kozonio would return.

"I can take one, Amiollea," Zhee said, her voice light and winsome as usual.

To Amiollea, it sounded like the screech of alley cats fighting beneath her bedroom window when she'd been a girl. She hadn't heard a cat in so many years. A few must have survived. The smart ones who avoided their former masters' soup pot.

"I'm fine," Amiollea snapped. The younger girl swung both heavy sacks of shit over her shoulders. It was all human excrement, collected from the shadow painters' latrines. It was useful fertilizer. The slime farmers fed the vast pools of scum that kept the city alive.

Barely.

"My ol' gramma would say, why do twice the work when you can share the load?" Zhee asked.

I don't care what your ol' gramma has to say about any mucking thing! burned through Amiollea's mind. "I wouldn't want you to break a nail."

Zhee burst into mirthful laughs. Amiollea could hear the woman's large breasts shifting. She had left them unbound these days. Finding good cloth or leather was difficult. Most had rotted away by now. It was hard to keep things dry. Once the mold set in, they were lost. It had been four years since Amiollea gave up and started going nude.

Not like anyone could see her dirt-smeared body anyways. In the humid dark of Hamiocho, modesty mattered little. Her mother had the most beautiful dresses. Amiollea remembered that, but could not recall the last one she wore. She couldn't remember much of that last day in the sunlight. Or the dark ones that followed. Then, she'd been a scared kid slowing down her brother.

A burden.

He had protected her when many others would have abandoned her to snivel and starve.

"You are a silly one, Amiollea," Zhee said, bright and happy. She moved closer, the air stirring before her. Zhee's musk filled Amiollea's nostrils, intertwined with the scent of her brother. *His* was a comforting aroma to the girl.

Normally.

"Here, let me just take one," Zhee said, hesitating fingers brushing Amiollea's arm. Then, with confidence, slid up to the burlap sack. That fabric held out better than most, but was so itchy, so why wear it?

Amiollea didn't know what they would do when the last of their sacks failed. How would they collect the dung to trade for the algae? It was growing more expensive, too. The Slimers wanted more and more excrement to grow their crop.

We'll have to scrounge up more pots, she thought. They were not as easy to carry, but at least they didn't rot.

"I have it!" Amiollea snapped and jerked her arm away. "Carry the pots."

"Fine, fine," Zhee said. The Povazian girl had an easy hand. To Amiollea, it seemed like Zhee was too dumb to ever be offended. Her race was said to be slow-witted, all their brains found in their brawn or their breasts. "Ablisio, where are the pots?"

"Should be to your right," her brother said. He had three sacks and carried them without complaint. He was outside the shack amid the rotting trees thrusting out of the muck they lived around. Not many people entered the area.

That made it safe. Mostly.

"Found them!" Zhee called brightly. She hummed as she lifted them up. Amiollea didn't know what she had to be happy about. They had to pass through the Kneelers. Her brother hated groveling to the Slimers. Trading for the algae fed them, but he'd rather forage for his own food or for the supplies to trade with more honest brokers.

Not from the rich who hid behind the Rubble in their lit houses eating beef for every meal. Her brother would rather eat rat or catfish. They'd eaten dog and cat, and once had come across a mule that had somehow survived three years. They had feasted on its stringy meat before the rest had been lost to blowflies.

They hadn't been hungry enough to eat human, but more than a few had. Some killed to get their fresh meat.

Clay jars clinked as Zhee hefted them. She walked past Amiollea with confidence to follow Ablisio. They knew every step in and around their shack. It was their home. You didn't need to see to know it. With a grunt, she shifted the heavy sacks of shit and followed. Her bare feet sank into the mud. It squeezed between her toes and clung to her soles.

She'd grown used to navigating blind. She knew every tree in the Rotting Orchard by scent. Each had a minute difference in the acrid rot of their wood or the reek of the muck around them. She knew how the air flowed through them, so could recognize they were getting closer to the Perfumed Bog by the new foul aromas assaulting her nose.

She supposed the old her would have gagged, but cleanliness was something long forgotten in this place. It would probably be what killed them in the end. Infected wound, rotten food, poisoned fumes.

Out of the orchard and into the Perfumed Bog that lay on the north end of the Phosphor, she stepped with more care. A faint, blue gleam glowed to her left; the algae lake itself. It used to have another name, but she couldn't remember it. Most called it the Phosphor because of the radiance. It shed enough light to be dangerous to approach.

Death swooped above it and some said a monster dwelled in the center, creating waves that washed across the shore.

Desperation could drive people to muckrake the shores to risk gathering algae washed up by the waves before Death noticed.

Amiollea and her family knew the paths through the bog, placing each step with care. It was slow going, but it beat cutting your foot open and dying of rot, or stepping into the brackish waters and getting stuck in the mud. Things squirmed through the waters. Snakes hunting frogs. The slithering things were food, if they could catch them, but the snakes moved too fast and their bite could swell your leg up and kill you just as quickly as infection.

The air hardly moved in the perfume bog. The scents were a mélange of rotting vegetables, sour mud, serpentine musk, and amphibian sliminess. She knew each step she took. Her internal clock ticked away. An eagerness swelled in her.

"It's almost noon," she announced.

"I don't want you looking at the Spire," Ablisio said from the front. "You'll hurt your eyes."

"Yeah, because they're *sooooo* useful," said Amiollea. She rolled her eyes at the stupidity of his words.

"If you're ever thieving a Glower's house, you'll need to see."

"Like you'd ever let me do that," she muttered beneath her breath.

"I might die, Amiollea," he said. "You don't know what you'll have to do in the future."

An anxious hand squeezed about her heart. Life without her brother to watch over her? To keep the cannibals and the rapists, who often were one and the same, from her flesh? To find food for her? To make her laugh when the sadness overwhelmed her?

"My ol' gramma always said to stock your larder as if the worst winter ever approaches while hoping for a short one and a quick spring," Zhee said.

"My ol' gramma told me . . ." sneered Amiollea.

"What did your ol' gramma tell you?" Zhee asked. "You trailed off."

Amiollea closed her eyes, an unconscious gesture of frustration, and let out a low shriek. How could she mock a girl too stupid to recognize any insult? How could she drive the big-breasted leach sucking everything from her brother? Literally, some nights.

She used her mouth on his thingie.

"You're making too much noise," Ablisio said. "We're almost to the bridge."

Amiollea shuddered. Beyond it lay the Kneeling Dark, as the strip of the city between the river and the slime fields was known. A place of the most pathetic toadies and vile thieves who preyed upon those seeking to reach the Dispensaries and buy algae with dung or other valuables. They would rob you, maybe even kill you. If they did that, they'd either eat you or sell your corpse to the dispensary as fertilizer.

"Sorry," Amiollea muttered.

"You're forgiven," Zhee said, her tone rich.

"It's about to be noon," Amiollea added, eager to see the one thing that gave her hope that there was more than drudgery. She loved her brother, treasured every day with him, but life wearied on her. Fifteen, and she didn't see any end to their misery. They would all die sooner or later, joining the muck slowly swallowing the city.

She felt her brother and Zhee both look away by the sounds of their feet shuffling, the caress of their skin on skin, the stretch of tendons flexing muscles. She looked ahead boldly to the west and the distant Spire. It was on the far side of the city.

Three...two...one...

A bright light flared from the top of the Spire. It was blinding, so bright the pain stabbed into her mind. She refused to look away at the glow illuminating the tallest structure in Hamiocho. A gray finger thrust up into the darkness around them. The Light reflected off the top of the Darkwall, rippling around it like it sought to punch out and escape this foul place.

A single heartbeat of beauty.

Then it was gone. A blue stain covered the darkness. For a while, she would have some color in her life. It didn't matter where she looked, she saw the cerulean hue. The inverse light. She smiled in delight as her brother and Zhee straightened. The trio resumed their walk.

Ablisio sighed. "You looked."

"I did," she said cheerily. Her stomach rumbled. She shifted her two heavy sacks of excrement and knew, if they survived the Kneeling Dark, they would fill their bellies with stringy algae and live another day.

Another chance to see beauty.

CHAPTER THREE

The door opened at the top of the tower. Maegwirio rose, the thrill of illicit activity racing through him. He slipped down the stairs to the kitchen where two plates and two bowls were set out. Thick, green algae filled the bowls, steam still rising from the beef broth he'd cooked them in. It was a thin broth, but it added some flavor to the algae. On the plates were hunks of grilled steak cooked on the flameless stove, a slab of stone with runes carved into it that would heat up.

He sat at his table and opened the book beside him. *On Logic and Constructs* was one he'd read many times; a time-honored treaty on preparing complex rune sentences. He still needed to master it to unravel the lock.

"Maegwirio," the maestro said as he limped in, pain spilling across the pale-blue features of his craggy face. His hair still had strands of his original bright gold, but most had tarnished to a dull gray. What little remained. It grew wispier by the month. His shoulders were bowed by age, his left hand gripping his cane of wooden steel, carved in the manner of the Great Serpent of Iazahzi, the vast white snake that wrapped about the top of the mountain and froze, forming its eternal snow-capped peak.

"How is your hip, Maestro?" he asked with concern as the older man limped across the room.

"Feels like I have a rusty nail driven into it," he grunted. A smile flashed across his face. "So the same as always. And I see you have not been idle."

"Easy to make the same thing every day," Maegwirio said. "Just like it's easy to have the same conversation every day."

"Mmm, true." The older man sank down with a low groan. "We do run out of things to talk about. Unless you have made progress on your thesis."

"I still have not quite figured out how to link more clauses," said Maegwirio. "I study, but unless I'm just copying directly, I can't ever make the logic as eloquent as I need. My word choices always feel so clumsy. Blunt."

"Blunt can be good when you blow down a wall, but to be a maestro, you must have—"

"The finesse of a red-spotted hummingbird hovering in place before the yellow-blush honeysuckle. I must insert my beak into the narrow well of the flower to reach the nectar without disturbing the deadly toxin coating the bright petals."

"I have used that example before, huh?" the maestro said. He plunged his spoon into the algae soup and pulled out a large, stringy wad of it. A long tendril of the boiled green reached down to the soup. "And the one about the ants crossing the fly trap, careful not to disturb the triggering hairs?"

"And the one about the bat flying through a cave without crashing into a stalactite. I've heard them all, Maestro."

The older man nodded. "Well, I'll try to think of a few new ones or risk boring you to death."

"There is one thing we could talk about," Maegwirio said with a casual air. He cut into his steak. The meat was cooked all the way through. He didn't like the way the Karadrisan nobles ate their meat nearly bloody. Whenever one of the powerful men who controlled the food in Hamiocho visited, a rare event, he had to be careful on how he cooked their supper.

"You are as obvious as a red-breasted robin singing for a mate in a lilac tree," he said. "You are not ready for what it is I do up there."

"And when will that be?"

"When you can finesse your runes." The maestro chuckled. "You're . . . ?"

"Sixteen."

"Sixteen . . ." He chuckled. "Well, I don't expect you to master them for another decade. It takes a certain way of thinking. A deep understanding for how the runes and the words they represent connect to create their effect. It is intuitive. It is something you can only learn through time."

Maegwirio glanced at his maestro. "Do you have the time for me to learn?"

"Of course I do." The older man straightened. "Why, I haven't felt this good in weeks. I'm breathing as strong as a bullfrog croaking on a summer eve."

"That's a new one," Maegwirio said as he swallowed his disappointment.

"See, always something left for me to teach."

He plunged his spoon into the algae. He slid it into his mouth, the broth adding flavor, but unable to disguise the faint taste of grass it always seemed to have. He didn't so much as chew it as swallow it whole. It slithered down to his belly.

"We're running low on meat and algae," Maegwirio said. He stirred his spoon through the soup, the thick algae slowly closing behind the path, leaving only a thin scar. "I could carve any failing runes for the Glowers you'd have to attend to."

It was how they survived. The rich—the Glowers, as Maegwirio had heard they were called —fought to preserve as much normalcy as possible. They kept their stone houses in good condition, lighting their interiors with runic lamps. Without the skill of the Taechizian carvers, Hamiocho would have died out years ago. The beef came from the Abattoir Fields, a large, artificial pasture with a roof created fast through runes before the grass died. The Slime Fields were another such roofed area where the Chemosh River had been partially diverted to grow the algae in safety. The clothes, the utensils, and the comforts of the powerful depended on the Runecarvers.

The runes kept them alive, and they kept the rest of the city alive. Barely. The one thing runes couldn't give them was enough fertilizer to feed the algae. He didn't like to think about what the green scum fed upon, but he also didn't want to die.

"You know I can do the runes properly, Maestro," Maegwirio continued.

"They pay for me to do them."

"I am trained by you. I can carve every single rune as well as you can, and they know it."

Maestro Kozonio shook his head. "They won't trust the work."

"Oh." The apprentice's shoulders slumped. It was counterproductive to his studies to venture in the caravan across the city, but he wanted out of the Spire as badly as he wanted to find out what his maestro did on the roof. That door to the roof was warded as tight as the office, the same logic used for both locks.

"But nothing says you can't come with me," the maestro added. He leaned back in his seat, studying the youth. "You're, what, fourteen now?"

"Sixteen," Maegwirio said, his heart bursting with excitement. It flooded through him. Not only to leave the Spire, but the Runic Ward. "It's been seven years, Maestro."

"Has it . . .?" A distant look grew in the old man's eyes. "Sometimes, it seems like just yesterday that they were all alive."

Maegwirio swallowed, his exhilaration killed by the change in the older man's mood. He never knew what to do when the silence descended. He just spooned his algae while his maestro stared into the past.

With a heavy sigh, the older man cut into his meat. "Yes, you can come with me, Maegwirio. I can introduce you to Lord Achogear and the others. Let them get used to you. In a while, well, they might accept you in my stead. I don't need to traipse across the city. Dangerous out there. Last time, those Sun Ravagers tried to rob us. They called us poisoners."

"You didn't mention that," Maegwirio said, a chill rippling over his skin. He remembered that night three years back when the crazed cult had set a fire in the southwestern quarter of town. They tried to create an artificial sun to replace the one lost. Many had died from flames and smoke. More from Death. The soldiers had torn down dozens of buildings to create a firebreak before the flames reached the Glowers. The flames reached so high, they struck the dark dome above them, giving shape to the construct imprisoning them.

"Shame they didn't all die in their fire," muttered Maegwirio. "Especially their leader."

"Cinder . . ." Anger shadowed the old man's face. "He's preaching again, or so I hear." He shoved a piece of meat into his mouth and spoke around it. "Whipping up his rabble. Glowers fear another assault on the Rubble. It'll be dangerous when we go. You don't have to."

"I have to," Maegwirio said. "I'm not afraid."

"Most youths aren't." The old man shook his head. "Fear is your best friend. You can't always trust it, but you should definitely listen to it. Keeps you alive. Keeps you sharp. Tells you when you're doing something stupid."

THE FLASH DIED DOWN behind Emmait, plunging the world back into darkness.

He shifted the thick coil of hemp he'd stolen from the Glowers. Stealing into Lord Achogear's house filled the young man with satisfaction. It had been his home as a boy. He'd lived with his mother in the servant quarters in the basement.

She died on Darkfall, and Lady Achogear didn't need to waste food on a Povazian whelp. He was thrown onto the streets, plunged into darkness. Scared, alone, lost, he crawled across cobblestones. Men and women stumbled about.

The smart ones moved through the dark as blind as him.

The ones with lanterns or candles discovered Death didn't care what title a man possessed or how wealthy was a woman's husband. The entities killed without caring.

The frightened boy, only eleven, had crawled into an alley to hide. The darkness suffocated him. He'd never experienced such utter black before. There had always been a little light. A rune glowing on a device shedding a pale, blue glow. The starlight or moonlight peeking through the high, narrow windows at the top of the small room he shared with his mother. He clutched his knees to his chest and sobbed, missing her.

He'd never known his father well. "You look like him," his mother had always whispered. "It's in the eyes and ears. Especially your eyes. Yellow as the sun."

Emmait had little need for his father. The bastard had thrown him into the darkness.

It was there, crying in the dark, that a whimpering, snuffling sound found him. A wet nose brushed the back of his hand. A wet tongue licked him. The boy's crying stopped as he felt the furry, warm body of a puppy. He pulled that dog into his lap and laughed as the tongue bathed his face, lapping up his tears. A little tail wagged with excitement.

The dog gave him something to protect. To defend. Emmait had stopped being a boy that day. He'd become a man, struggling to survive in the ruins. Many would have eaten the puppy in the coming months. Hunger had gnawed at Emmait's belly, but he couldn't eat Sun, as he'd named the dog. They suffered the belly pangs together.

Sun had grown. Now a full-grown dog padded at Emmait's side, muddy fur rubbing against his naked leg. Lean and dangerous, Sun had saved Emmait's life more times than he could count. As keen as his nose had become, as sensitive as his ears had developed, as much as he could "see" by feeling subtle air currents on his skin, Sun was better.

Ears sharper.

Nose stronger.

When Sun froze, so did Emmait.

Their bellies were both full. They had filched salted beef out of the cupboard when they found a length of runic rope. Made from wound strands of algae which were then transmuted into hemp, it would fetch him more food. The salted beef would keep fresh for weeks yet. He could hold off eating it for as long as possible if he found other sources.

The ground began to slope. The air shifted and swirled through the narrow streets of this section of the city. The cobblestones were mostly clean of muck. He stepped his bare feet with care. His soles were toughened, but he didn't want to cut himself. He listened for any strange sounds. In buildings, he could hear people moving about, scrounging. Any wood would have been long since stolen away. These structures were made of stone, the only reason they still stood.

Mostly.

The scent of bricks flared in front of him. Then he felt the start of a rubble pile. It was fresh. He didn't remember it being here. He edged around it, feeling ahead with his feet sweeping over the cobblestone until he was past it.

The sounds of the Sluggish Waters grew. The river had another name, but people didn't bother with it. The sluggish current oozed through the city. The air grew wetter. He could smell something almost fresh. They were north of the Phosphor and near the city wall. In the domain of those who lived off the Chemosh.

The Blind Fishers.

They knew the secret of catching catfish from the river and guarded it jealously. Emmait had no idea how they did it. He'd once tried fishing in the river, but he never had a bite. Whatever their methods, they always had a catfish or two for trade if you had something.

He approached their camp, hearing movement. "Ho!" he shouted in the dark. "It's Emmait!"

"You got that mangy mutt with you?" a voice shouted back. "Five fish for him."

"You know that's insultingly low, Drahio," Emmait answered, a smile on his lips. "Be serious."

"That's easily that mutt's weight in fish," he said. "He's not going to get any fatter. The older he gets, the stringier he'll be."

"I like my meat tough," Emmait said, his hand sliding through the matted fur. "I have rope. Thirty lengths. Rune created rope."

"Thirty?" Drahio laughed, his voice echoing through the dark. Others chuckled around him. "What Glower's cursing your name right now? That's quite the expenditure of food he had to spend on it."

"Lord Achogear. He was more than generous to donate it to me."

"His charity is legendary," Drahio said with mocking solemnity. "You keep accepting it, and he'll want to speak to you face to face and make sure you're enjoying all the comforts he's been providing."

"He can try." Emmait smiled. "It's not my fault he keeps the same idiot in charge of his guard. The man couldn't stop a fat cat from napping before the fireplace."

"Well, thirty lengths. That's worth three catfish. Fresh caught just this morning. Lively ones."

"Gutted?"

"You want the guts, too?" he asked. "Afraid they're already cleaned and added to the offal pile. Why I'm offering three catfish."

"Four," Emmait said. "I want to eat tomorrow, too."

"You mean your dog wants to eat tomorrow."

Emmait laughed. "He does like that. What do you say?"

"Fine, fine, because I like you. I will let my children starve so you can have *four* fish and live like a rich merchant."

"You don't have any children to let starve," Emmait called back.

"No," the voice said, growing sad.

Emmait winced. He hadn't meant to wound the man. "I have the rope here. Let's trade. I have a long walk ahead of me."

Water splashed. Then footsteps slapped through the mud. The scent of fish oil, that slimy aroma, made his mouth water. Sun panted. Emmait scratched between his dog's ears. They would eat well today.

A rare blessing in Hamiocho.

Drahio stopped a few lengths away. Emmait unslung his rope and tossed it into the dark before him. The man managed to catch it after it bounced off his body. He marveled at the feel of it. The air shifted and the sound of fish scales rasping announced they were extended before him.

He snagged them up, the four fish all hanging from stone hooks thrust through gills. The Blind Fishers craved those, too. They weren't the strongest and could snap and drop your fish into the muck. Emmait didn't see how those were strong enough to catch one of the heavy catfish, but how else did they do it?

"Survive another day, Emmait," Drahio called. "Watch for the Kneelers. They're getting . . . aggressive."

"The Ratters said the same thing last week," Emmait said. "I think it was last week."

"What does time matter in hell?" The Blind Fisher chuckled as he retreated into the dark. "Keep that dog fat and healthy for me. I'm looking forward to the day of eating his succulent flesh."

"Only if you can get past his teeth to slit his throat."

"A problem I hadn't considered."

Emmait turned and headed up the street, Sun at his side. Their catch filled the air with the pungent scent of fish oil. Any scavenger with a good nose would sniff them out. He rubbed at his dog's fur and said, "Safety."

Sun sniffed around. Emmait waited, not moving save for shallow breaths. He focused on his skin, sensing how the air moved now that he was beyond the Blind Fishers' defenses. The scavengers lurked out here.

They would think him an easy meal.

Sun's sniffing grew fainter as he padded away from Emmait. He stood alone in the dark. His hands held the cords dangling the catfish. He was aware of what he wore around his neck. The dagger in its sheath. A new blade. Something else he'd stolen from Lord Achogear's home a few days back.

A good steel dagger was too valuable to trade even if it wouldn't last long out here. Metal corroded fast, so he had to use it while it lasted.

Footsteps echoed from his right. He focused his hearing in that direction. He felt every hair on his body standing up, sensing the air currents flowing through this part of town. He concentrated on any minute changes. He breathed through his nose, sorting through the reek for the musk of other humans, but the fish was too pungent.

His heart thundered in his chest. The cold surge of exhilaration pumped through him. If scavengers came, he'd be ready. He shifted his grasp of the fish from his right to his left hand. He found the hilt of the dagger, ready to draw it.

The footsteps came closer.

He drew the knife.

There was no mistaking the sound of a sharp edge rasping against a leather sheath. The footsteps paused. Emmait held his blade low, turning slowly in the mud to face the source of the noise. Someone lurked in the darkness. Man or woman, it didn't matter. If they came for Emmait, he would make them regret it. Even if he died, he'd leave them bleeding.

The tension squeezed through the muggy darkness. The stalker's breath quickened. Feet shifted in the muck, the squelching sound almost screaming in Emmait's ear. The moment was fast approaching. Decision. Who would attack first? Who would charge forward through the dark and risk a fatal trip before reaching the other?

Emmait gripped the knife's wooden handle. Runed wood. Valuable in Hamiocho.

The footsteps retreated.

Emmait didn't relax. He kept track of the figure moving through ruins, his ears pricked for more trying to sneak in from behind. Maybe this one was an obvious distraction while the rest sneaked up behind Emmait. He shifted slowly in place.

Quick footsteps grew closer. Familiar ones.

Sun rubbed against Emmait's left thigh in the darkness, brushing the fish. He sighed. He had nothing to fear with Sun around. His dog would alert him to any scavengers thinking to creep up and steal what was his.

He sheathed his knife and grabbed a fistful of Sun's fur. The dog's warmth bled through the dirty coat. He held on as Sun led him to the right. He fixed that in his mind. Keeping one's bearings was a skill you learned in Hamiocho, or you died lost and confused. Soon, Sun led him through a broken doorway into a room with a brick floor. The wood of the building smelled rotten. Mold and mildew.

He bent down and tossed one of the catfish to the side. Sun went for it, attacking the morsel and tearing at its flesh. Emmait laid the other three fish across his naked lap. They were already gutted, but now he would flay them.

"Don't choke on the bones," Emmait said to his dog as he began cutting the fish by feel. His stomach rumbled. He'd already digested that salted beef. He would relish this feast. He would gorge on the succulent fish and forget about the darkness for a little while.

CHAPTER

FOUR

Zhee hated crossing Treacherous.

It wasn't the original name of the bridge crossing the Sluggish Waters, just like that wasn't the river's true name. Those didn't matter. Things had more practical names now. Descriptive. And Treacherous described the rickety bridge.

The white-painted bridge, or so Zhee dimly remembered from a lifetime ago, had faced the festering atmosphere of Hamiocho bravely for a year. Sadly, it had lost the fight and surrendered to the rot. The paint had come off in places, letting the wood beneath soften and decay. Crossing it was a careful balance of steps placed just so. A path couldn't be memorized because the bridge deteriorated more and more with every day.

But it was the fastest way to the nearest dispensary.

Ablisio led the way, the wood creaking beneath his weight with his every step. Below, the dark waters gurgled as they swept around the mooring. Zhee feared the river slowly ate at those thick logs, hastening the day that Treacherous would collapse while they crossed it.

She winced as she heard Ablisio take another step. Her man was fearless, a good quality to have in a city consumed by darkness, but also a bad one. He would do the risky thing to procure them food and protect them, but it would also be what killed him.

We're all dying here, she thought as she touched her belly. Her flow was late. That wasn't uncommon. Sometimes, she was late by a week or more. She had been so regular before Darkfall, but since then, it happened.

It didn't mean she was . . .

She pushed that implication from her mind. She didn't need to worry about tomorrow when they had to survive today. And that meant crossing Treacherous *twice.* She took her first step onto the bridge as Ablisio kept crossing. He moved too fast. He wasn't taking the time to test the boards.

"Go faster," Amiollea muttered as the girl stalked past Zhee.

"It's not safe to go faster," Zhee said without taking insult from the girl. She understood Amiollea and didn't mind the sister's jealousy. Zhee understood why Amiollea was suspicious. It was true Zhee had used Ablisio to stay alive all these years, but that didn't mean she didn't care for her man. That she didn't enjoy the pleasure of being his woman.

There were few joys to have in this world, and Ablisio was one of those.

Zhee hoped he loved her back, but she didn't pretend that things weren't what they were. She had offered her body to Ablisio to ensure he protected and fed her. He had never asked for her to lie with him, but she wanted to make sure she was useful to him. They both got something out of it. And at first, after Ablisio had saved her two years ago, it had been that basic.

That transactional.

But she'd shared her life with his and had grown to know both brother and sister. She was glad that she'd met them.

Maybe it was love she felt for Ablisio. She wasn't sure, but she knew she didn't want to see him—either of them—get hurt. She wanted all three of them to return. She could put up with Amiollea's barbs for that very reason. She wouldn't fight back because it would be bloody. Not physically but emotionally.

The only way for Zhee to win was to make Ablisio drive away his sister.

Zhee wouldn't do that because it would break him. *Besides, he'd side with her over me.*

Ablisio might love her back, but she knew he would choose his sister.

Zhee understood why. She could handle being second in his heart. She could even handle just being soft and curvy which provided Ablisio a few moments of comfort in the terrible world of Hamiocho.

Maybe that was the best Zhee could expect from a man in this terrible place.

But she was pretty sure he loved her.

The bridge creaked beneath her feet. She winced, waiting for the snap of wood and the sudden plunge into the river beneath. She didn't know how to swim. She pictured vanishing beneath the dark, sludgy waves for an eternity, gasping, moaning, unable to see which way was up and down. No scent. No feel of air. No hearing.

"Muck and misery, you're a slow sow," Amiollea muttered. "We're across already."

"Sorry," Zhee said with a bright smile that hid her pounding heartbeat. "It's like my ol' gramma said, better to take twice as long instead of dropping the soup and ruining supper."

Amiollea muttered with mocking tones in the dark.

Zhee took another step. The wood creaked worse. Her heart beat faster. She could feel how rotten the boards were beneath her feet. Fear whispered in her mind that Ablisio's and Amiollea's weight had weakened them. That they would snap beneath her feet. She shifted her weight, the board flexing as she planted her foot down on the next.

A low whimper rose in her throat. The entire bridge shook. A small tremble like it shivered. Was this it? She had her eyes squeezed shut like that would matter. She edged her foot forward, feeling the next board. It was mush. The wood gave beneath her probing toes. She pushed past it to find the next plank, all her weight on her left leg.

A loud groan rose before her.

A strong hand grabbed her arm. "Zhee, it's okay. It's still solid. You're fine."

Ablisio held her. He pulled her along, his footsteps creaking. Her bare feet slid over the rough wood, feeling for weakness. She could do it alone, of course, but she went faster with him guiding her. She smiled even though he couldn't see it. She smelled him over the dirt and mud and reek of Hamiocho. That scent meant safety and comfort and even pleasure.

He'd never hurt her.

Her next step brought her to soft mud, and she groaned in relief, shifting the clay jars she carried to hold the algae. Squishy, wet muck squeezed between her toes. Feeling the soggy ground had never felt better.

She let out a long breath.

"Good, can we go?" Amiollea muttered. "I'd like to eat today."

Ablisio didn't say anything but before he let go of her arm, she felt his thumb caressing her. Maybe she imagined it, but it sent a rush of warmth through her. He might not love her, but he did care for her. He valued her for more than just the pleasure of her body.

The trio crossed the mud and muck of the Kneeling Dark. There were small pockets of walls, remnants of the building's foundations left behind when the Rubble was created. The runed wall guarded the rich and their food against the poor and the starving. The barrier lay before them, the northern spur that encircled the Slime Fields and the source of the algae that would keep the small family alive for a few more days.

"They're smart, the Glowers," Ablisio had told her once, perhaps a year ago. They lay together, limbs entwined while Amiollea slept on the other side of their shack. "They give us just enough food to keep us from being desperate enough to surge over the walls and take it from them."

"But they make us pay for it," she'd answer.

"I know." He stroked a finger across her cheek. "That's the part that's really brilliant. We're too busy scraping and scrounging for things to trade for that food, or killing each other over it, that we don't have the energy to do anything else."

"It's terrible. Why do they do it?"

"Why does anyone do anything here?" he asked.

She waited in breathless anticipation for his answer.

"Fear of dying. They want to live another day."

His words had stung her. It made her wonder why they shared pleasure. Was he rebuking her? He didn't need to bed her to survive. If they stopped, he wouldn't have any problems feeding himself. In fact, if he abandoned her and Amiollea, he would have an even better chance of surviving.

The pain faded as she had realized then that people could do things in Hamiocho that had nothing to do with survival. They did things for murky reasons like love. It was the moment the idea blossomed in her heart that she didn't lie with Ablisio only to live another day.

She did it because she wanted to give them both solace from their terrible lives. It was one of the few escapes from misery. Not just the sex, but the kissing, the talking afterward, and the intimacy that they shared.

The intimacy that necessarily excluded Amiollea.

No wonder she hates me so much, Zhee thought as they crossed the Kneeling Dark.

People moved around them. She knew they wouldn't attack until after. If they even did. Those who dwelled here begged for food from the dispensary. Sometimes they were successful. Other times, they would steal from those crossing. That could be dangerous for everyone. Would the ones around them take the risk today?

Or had they robbed someone already and had the algae they needed?

The grassy scent of the dispensary led them to it. The smell of algae differed from the other reeks of Hamiocho. She shifted the clay jars in her sore arms and winced as one pressed into her naked breast. She wished they weren't as big. It wasn't like anyone could see her, and her lower back might not throb so much.

A new scent filled her nose. Metal. The jangle of chainmail echoed before them. The armed guards of the dispensary shifted in place at hearing her family's approach. A sword rasped from a leather scabbard, the tip ringing for a moment.

"We have shit!" shouted Ablisio.

"Who doesn't?" asked the guard. "I squatted one out just an hour ago."

"Enough for food!" Ablisio added. "Lots of it."

"Good for you, darkling. Got you some algae. You can squat it out in a day or so and come right back." The guard laughed, his armor jingling.

Working here was how he earned his dinner. No one used money any longer. Very few things had value outside of food. Sharp blades, sacks, strong rope. The guard would be paid in algae with a stipend of meat. If he had a family, they probably worked the Slime Fields inside the wall, lit by the glow of their crop and shielded from Death's greedy eyes.

They passed the guard and soon reached the dispensary. It was a building that had light in it. She knew that much. The workers would take your offerings in there, tally things up, and return with the food.

There wasn't much to do but wait.

She leaned against the building, the stones cool but rough against her naked back and buttocks. She could hear Amiollea darting back and forth with too much energy. Ablisio joined Zhee at the wall, his shoulder touching hers.

"I want to find a better way to feed us," he said. "I don't like crossing that bridge. Too dangerous. One of us could be hurt."

"You don't want to try foraging around Phosphor Lake? Gamble on being a muckraker and hope you escape Death?"

"No." He sighed. "Wish we had a cat."

"How long has it been since we had rat?" she asked.

"Maybe a month. When we found that rope somehow kept dry in that chest."

Zhee smiled. The three of them had feasted on the rats. The Ratters didn't like to part with their quarry. They and their wives lived on the other side of the Runic Ward in a vast maze of old buildings where the rats festered.

"Better than algae," Ablisio said.

"Unless you're going to turn cannibal, there aren't many alternatives." Zhee hesitated. She lowered her voice. "Are you planning on going over the Rubble again?"

"Maybe. Find some salted beef. We could eat off that for a few weeks."

Before she could answer, the dispensary's door opened. Their clay jars were set down in the muck before the door slammed shut. Amiollea darted over to them and groaned as she lifted one. The way her feet smacked in the hard-packed dirt sounded louder.

"We're going to eat!"

Zhee carried the other jar with the algae. It was enough for the three of them for a few days. Ablisio led the way out into the dark, not carrying anything but his truncheon out. A length of ironwood he'd stolen from the Glowers years before. It didn't rot or rust, protected by the runes.

It had weight.

She could feel the covetous presence as they moved from the dispensary. The denizens knew they had food. They slithered in around them. Mutters drifted out of the dark to Zhee's ears. She caught different stenches. Some reeked of stale sweat, others of old shit. One had the acrid reek of piss like he constantly urinated on himself.

Ablisio marched on with powerful steps, thudding his truncheon into the meat of his thigh. A staccato warning to those in the dark. Like the hiss of a viper before it sank poisoned fangs into your foot.

Let them listen, Wise Owl, she prayed to one of the totem gods of her people. She didn't know much about her people's faith, only what she could remember from her parents and gramma. Her mother had sewn clothes in their small home in the old Povazian quarter of the city while her father had worked as a porter, hauling heavy loads on his broad back for rich Karadrisans. He hadn't been too religious, but her mother had prayed to Wise Owl and Clever Fox and Crafty Tortoise.

Clever Fox, show them intelligence to ignore us, she added, not really sure what a fox even was. Her parents had left Povaz when she was a toddler.

Ablisio paused. Amiollea sighed.

The shift in the air, the presence of men moving, spilled around them. Footsteps slapped the ground. She tensed and set down her jar as the attacker rushed in. Ablisio roared a mighty bellow in answer.

Zhee flinched against impending pain.

CHAPTER
FIVE

The attack rushed in from all sides.

Ablisio gripped his ironwood cudgel, the weight familiar. He had battered the skulls of would-be robbers a dozen times. The cold pit in his stomach flared to life with the ferocity of a spark falling on summer-dried grass.

The feet smacked through the muck. Five or six men. Desperation reeked around them, stale and old, a mix of shit and piss and hunger. He shifted his stance, his heartbeat seeming to slow. He didn't know it, but his useless eyes flicked out across the black.

Zhee fell into a ball behind him. He heard her curling up to protect herself. Amiollea didn't. She stood near him, her feet shifting. Through the battle fire, fear cut through him. She would get herself killed if she fought.

"You don't have a weapon, Amiollea!" he barked moments before the enemy was on them. "Get down!"

The air rushed before him. Ablisio swung his cudgel in a brutal, horizontal arc. He struck an arm. Bone snapped with a loud crack. A scream of pain burst from the robber's mouth. His momentum still carried him into Ablisio.

He twisted his body so his attacker stumbled back. As he did, he struck the man in the back, feeling the heavy thunk of striking a skull. The attacker crashed into the muck, groaning.

More attackers followed.

～

I won't be useless like Zhee, thought Amiollea as the Kneelers came to rob them.

The Povazian could cower, but Amiollea would fight. There were too many for her brother to handle. He needed her. She wasn't a child any longer. She wasn't that little girl sobbing in his lap covered in their dead mother's blood.

A figure rushed at her, his foul reek filling her nostrils. His footsteps heavy. He grunted, breath labored already. She stretched her right foot out to her side and smacked the mud. A loud, wet smack. The attacker changed directions.

Air whooshed by her as he swung at the emptiness.

A smile burst across her unseen lips. She lunged her hands out and found his wrist. She gripped it, feeling the tensed muscles. He held something in his hand. Maybe a stave or possibly a sword. She darted her head down like a feral beast and sunk her teeth into the meat of her attacker's forearm.

"Mucking bitch!" he screamed as she ripped at him. Whatever he held fell with a thud to the mud as she savaged his flesh. The salty taste of his life filled her mouth. "Get off me, slut!"

His off-hand slammed into her temple. The blow snapped her head back and tore a hunk of flesh from him. She stumbled back, little lights flaring through the darkness, mixing with the blue stain left by the Spire's flash. Spitting flesh, she stumbled into the prostate Zhee. Gasping, Amiollea tripped over the cowering girl. She rolled and bumped into an urn full of algae, rattling it.

Amiollea scrambled to gain her feet. She dug fingers into the slimy ground and pushed to her feet. Sounds smacked the muck behind her. A foul reek filled her nose while currents of air washed over her body. Strong arms seized her and pulled her back into a man's wiry form.

"Ain't you a squirming quim, eh?" he growled as she felt his staff stiffen against her buttocks. "What a delight you'll be."

"Stick your prick in me, and my quim will tear it off!" she howled, thrashing like a catfish in the net.

∼

Amiollea's shouts animated Zhee.

Despite the fear coursing through her veins from the grunts and smacks of Ablisio's fight, she couldn't lie here any longer. She had to get in the fight and protect Amiollea. Something thudded to the ground. A man growling in pain, the scent of blood spilling through the air. Something smacked on the muck and scrabbled out.

A hand searching for something.

A weapon?

She thrust her arm out, her fingers sliding across the filth, searching for it. She brushed a piece of wood and seized it. Thick and splintery, awkward to hold. She went to rise when the attacker brushed her head. He seized her hair and yanked her up to her knees.

"What we got here!" he growled. "The other slut? You smell Povazian. Got dem big udders, do ya? And I bet ya got a sweet mouth. Open wide. Got somethin' for ya."

She snarled, fear beating through her heart. She didn't have to do that any longer. Not when she had a weapon in her hand. She slammed the plank before her. It cracked hard against his leg. The snap of a knee joint twisting sent vicious joy through her along with his howl of pain. His fingers sprang from her hair.

She gained her feet.

"Muck-covered bitch!" he snarled. The air rippled before her.

His fist landed on the peak of her right breast. Pain exploded through her bosom. She screamed, tears springing in her eyes. She swung her plank down a second time, cracking across the crown of the bastard's head.

The meaty thunk filled her with another surge of satisfaction. He groaned and staggered before collapsing on his belly with a splat. She spat on him, the triumphant fury muting the pain throbbing across her breast.

"No!" Amiollea shouted, thrashing.

Zhee whirled around to help the girl.

~

"Amiollea!" snarled Ablisio as he fought. He could hear his sister being pulled away and smelled the lust oozing off her violator.

He wanted to save her, but he was fighting for his life. Two men attacked him, swinging haymakers in the dark. He fought with every sense he had. His arm hairs warned him of an attack striking at him. His nose smelled the fetid stench wafting from the men. His ears picked up their footsteps and ragged breathing. How their stances changed. The way they inhaled sharply before attacking.

Fear and rage animated his attacks. He had to get to Amiollea. His soul screamed with terror for her that he channeled into his blows. He twisted his shoulders so an attack whisked by. He slammed his cudgel in a hard riposte. A solid blow. The loud crunch of a collarbone snapping. A screech of pain from the bastard.

The enemy wept in pain.

"Amiollea, I'm coming!" he growled. "Fight!"

"I'm coming!" mocked the foul robber to his right. "She somethin' special to ya! Gonna enj—"

Ablisio's cudgel took the braggart in the throat. The crunch of cartilage cracked through the air. The man dropped beside the sobbing thug. Ablisio whirled and charged at the sounds of his sister being carried off, heedless of where he stepped. He wouldn't let anything happen to her. Mother told him to watch her.

The last thing she ever asked.

A hand snagged his leg. Tight fingers jerked him off his feet. He slammed into the muddy ground hard. His head struck something solid buried beneath the muck. Pain throbbed through his skull. Lights flashed.

"You broke my arm!" spat a man full of pain. "You gonna squeal for that. You don't got a quim, but you got somethin' nice for me."

Ablisio kicked out behind him, striking the rapist in the face. He snarled and threw himself on Ablisio's back. The pair rolled and thrashed in the muck, Ablisio throwing elbows to knock the bastard off. Despite having a broken arm, the kneeler had desperate strength, gripping Ablisio's right wrist and preventing him from swinging his truncheon.

He grabbed the man's broken arm and twisted. Bones ground together. The kneeler snarled and thrashed on him. His head slammed down, striking Ablisio in the forehead. Fuzzy pain washed over his thoughts.

Ablisio's grip loosened as the world spun around him.

The man's howls of pain cut off with a loud, wet smack. He fell limp on Ablisio. He pushed the body off and smelled Zhee's welcoming scent. She panted over him. He pushed himself to his feet, swaying for a moment, his head throbbing.

"Save her!" Zhee shouted.

Fear cut through the fuzzy fog on his mind. His sister was out in the dark. He could hear her squirming and thrashing. Her would-be rapist's voice rasped, saying vile words. Ablisio's blood boiled as he charged out at them.

"You're going to die slow if you touch her!" Ablisio howled as he ran across the wet muck.

"Touchin' her right now," the muckling said, his voice sounding like rusting iron scraping together. "Gonna take her before you to prove it!"

He slowed as he reached them, listening. His sister thrashed and snarled, her skin rubbing against the rapist. Her legs kicked and smacked muck. Arms slapped into a body. Ablisio raised his truncheon for the swing and hesitated.

He could miss her attacker and hit her hard in the head. He might kill her.

Ablisio's fear tightened as the man struggled to dominate his sister.

∽

"No, no, no!" Amiollea hissed. He was so hard against her as he struggled to get his manhood between her thighs. Her legs thrashed. "Ablisio, brain him!"

"I'll hit you!" he spat back. He was there, just out of arm's reach.

"Ah, he cares for you," sneered the rasping man. "But you'll care for me more once I'm in you."

"I'll tear it off!" she hissed and slammed her heel down into his shin.

He cackled.

She reached behind her to claw his face while ignoring how filthy his hand felt pawing at her breasts. She raked fingernails down his face, tearing flesh. She wouldn't let him take her.

"Don't worry about me, beat his head to a pulp!" she shrieked. "Kill him, Ablisio!"

"Take it!" her brother snarled.

She didn't understand what that meant until the wind washed over her. The man stopped for a second, struggling to understand what her brother had said. She thrust her arm before her and seized the thick end of the cudgel, warm with muck or blood.

Howling, she swung it over her head to hit her attacker. The handle cracked into his skull with a satisfying thunk. He grunted and loosened his grip. In a burst of speed, she sprung from him. She struck Ablisio's solid form, spun, and landed on the muck on her side.

"Kill him!" she shrieked as her brother surged forward.

~

Zhee focused on the injured attacker.

"Please, please!" the kneeler moaned. "My shoulder. He broke my shoulder."

She swung the plank hard. It slammed into the side of his head. His cries cut off. He fell back onto the mud, landing with a wet splat. She panted, her breast aching from the punch, sweat pouring down her body. She stared off into the darkness.

"Kill him!" screeched Amiollea.

Then she heard a loud impact and Ablisio snarling like a beast. Blows stuck again and again. A man squealed like a pig in the abattoir. The sounds of a creature who knew its death approached.

The thug at Zhee's feet moaned. She cracked her plank hard into his head again. She felt the side of his skull cave in this time. His body spasmed. She spat down at him before she staggered toward the sounds of Ablisio's primal rage.

Flesh tore. The other man screamed.

"This is what you wanted to stick in my sister?" Ablisio bellowed.

The monster choked on something. A hot surge of satisfaction shot through Zhee. Vile men like these, those who took instead of asked, could all die like that. Limbs thrashed in the muck. The man's strangled squeals echoed through the dark.

Zhee reached Amiollea, following the sounds of her ragged breathing. She touched the girl's shoulder.

Amiollea flinched.

"Are you okay?" Zhee asked, her voice soft.

"I'm fine!" she snapped. "Don't let up, Ablisio! He's still alive!"

"Not for long!" he replied, voice rasping.

Zhee stood with Amiollea in the dark, listening to the rapist's final gurgles of life, a cheap commodity in Hamiocho. Spilled as easily as emptying one's bladder in the latrine.

Her hand drifted to her belly. Her flow would come. It had to.

This wasn't the place to raise a child.

CHAPTER SIX

After eating the catfish, Emmait hung up the remaining fish from a creaky rafter. He formed the knot deftly by touch to secure it. He felt drowsy from gorging on the succulent flesh, his stomach aching from the feast. Fish oil and grease coated his fingers. He held them out to Sun, smiling as the warm tongue bathed them, cleaning up the last remnants.

He leaned down and stretched out on the mostly clean floor. It made a nice, if hard, bed. Sun snuggled up beside him. The dog rested his muzzle upon Emmait's stomach. He idly scratched the dog between the ears as sleep called to him.

He didn't dream in color any longer. He hardly remembered what color was. Even when he snuck into the Glowers to rob them, the sight of hues other than black startled him with their vividness. In his dreams, everything was shades of gray.

He played in the backyard with Eoblugio. Unlike Emmait, Eoblugio had the brown skin of a full-blooded Karadrisan instead of the paler hue of his own skin. They were in the garden, Eoblugio dressed in finer clothes of velvet instead of the cheap linens Emmait wore. That didn't matter to the two boys. They were stalking through the gardens, a pair of wolves sighting their prey.

Acenisea played with her dolls at a miniature table. She wore a refined gown of soft gray. It might have been pink or yellow; he couldn't remember. Acenisea was younger than the boys, a bright smile on her lips. Emmait didn't think of either the noble girl or boy as his siblings.

He was the bastard.

The mistress's whelp.

Eoblugio glanced at him as they crouched in the flowering bushes, staring at their "prey." They were mighty steppe wolves, the largest predators in the world. Capable of attacking caravans. One girl playing with her dolls was no match for their tenacity.

The two boys nodded.

Pounced.

Eoblugio led the way, bursting out of the bush and snarling like a feral wolf as he landed behind his sister. She shrieked and whirled about in a flare of braids. Emmait followed, crouching beside Eoblugio. The girl fell off her chair and quickly burst into tears. She rolled over and stood sobbing in place, rubbing at the stains on her dress. Her nurse swept over, a stern woman who fixed Emmait a hard stare.

"What are you surprising Miss Acenisea for?" she demanded. "Well, Emmait?"

"It was Eoblugio's idea," Emmait stammered, wilting like the Drylands in summer. "He said we should play wolves."

The woman snorted. "Think I don't know which of you leads the other into mischief. I'm going to have a word with Lord Achogear about what you've done to his daughter. Have you strapped for staining her pretty dress. She just received it, didn't you, moppet?"

The girl nodded, her face buried in the woman's midriff.

Emmait always got the blame. Always took the strap. He was Lord Achogear's child, and he wasn't. Whenever Lady Achogear saw him, her lip curled in a snarl and she hissed vile words about his mother. Words Emmait wouldn't understand until years later.

He didn't understand then why his father hated him. As his dream shifted to another memory, he was crouched at the door to Lord Achogear's study, peering inside. His mother sat on Lord Achogear's lap, the pair kissing. His hand had half-unbuttoned her dress and pressed into her bodice. Emmait knew he should look away, but he couldn't.

The hurt of outrage rooted him to the spot.

Lord Achogear loved his mother enough to kiss her, but the man wouldn't say a word to the boy. Emmait complained to his mother all the time, and she would just comb his hair and say, "Living here is better than on the street. You can be strong and endure it."

He would shout back, "How can you love him when he hates me!"

"Because I love you more," she'd answered. The statement baffled him. He loved Sun, but he wouldn't hurt his dog. The dream grew more and more of a quagmire of painful moments. The sludge that trapped him in humiliation. Being switched by Lady Achogear because Eoblugio stole sweets from the kitchen. Forced to go without supper because Eoblugio spilled juice on Acenisea's dress or pulled her hair or cut off the head of her doll.

Pain heaped on pain heaped on pain.

And through it all, his mother kissed Lord Achogear, not caring.

A low growl rescued him from the torment. He sighed as the dreams faded. Color and shape and images were all swallowed by the dark. He opened his eyes and felt Sun standing beside him. Emmait brushed the dog's coat, the fur bristling.

His heart burst into frantic activity. The cold energy surged through him. His hand shot to his chest and found the hilt of the knife. He drew it slowly, carefully, as the sounds of men moved about in the house.

Footsteps crept closer and closer.

He forced himself to breathe slowly as he moved with care to his feet. He struggled not to make a sound. Over the scent of catfish oil and muck, the reek of the men assaulted his nostrils. One was familiar. The figure who'd almost attacked him.

Idiot! Emmait snarled. *Why did you sleep here? You should have gotten farther away.*

The men entered the building from all sides, creeping through the other rooms. They *knew* he was here. He counted footsteps. Five of them. Their breathing grew ragged with excitement. One of them inhaled deeply and let out a long sigh of hunger.

Sun darted from Emmait's side. Claws scrabbled across the floor. A growl proceeded the savage rip of tearing flesh. A man screamed in pain and crashed to the ground. Sun mauled him, the horrible sounds echoing through the building.

The other men froze for a moment.

With growls of their own, they rushed in.

Air whistled. Emmait dodged to the right. Something slashed past him and struck the floor with the ring of cast iron. His dagger slashed where Emmait pictured the attacker to be standing. He struck a firm belly. His knife ripped across skin and muscles. The man gasped. Blood spurted hot over Emmait's hand, filling the air with a coppery, salty scent. His blade cut so deep, it caught on the hip bone, jerking the weapon out of his hand.

Something wet splatted on the floor. The man screamed in horror and dropped to his knees. He scrambled to pick up something that sounded wet and slimy. Before Emmait could recover, the man collapsed on his side, whimpering in pain as he died.

The air swirled and watched over Emmait's back. Emmait turned but not fast enough. Something struck his left shoulder. His arm went numb as the blow sent him stumbling. He turned and currents washed across his face. He threw himself backward to dodge the next blow.

The attacker growled and rushed after Emmait.

The wounded youth slammed into the wall. It creaked. A groan ran through the building.

"Get this mucking dog off of me!" howled another enemy.

The attacker with the familiar scent rushed at Emmait. So he bent his legs and ducked low before pushing off the wall. The attack slashed over him and struck wood behind him. He slammed his uninjured shoulder into the man, his right arm wrapping around an emaciated form. The two fell to the floor in a tangle of limbs, desperate hands scrabbling at each other.

Claws scratched on stone. Sun rushed across the darkness. A man screamed. The dog tore at the bastard's flesh as Emmait rolled on the floor, struggling to gain leverage on his opponent. Their dirty, naked bodies rolled over each other. A bony elbow slammed into his stomach again and again. He found the man's face and gouged an eye with a thumb.

"Bloody bowels!" the man howled. "Plague-ridden muckling, I'll gut you for that!"

Emmait kept pressing his thumb into the man's eye. It popped. A viscous liquid poured over his digit. The man snarled, thrashing. Emmait rolled him over, getting on top of the man. He slid his hand down to the throat, squeezing it.

The man picked up something wooden that scraped across the floor. Emmait had a moment to react. Not enough time. The cudgel slammed into the side of his head. Light flashed. The blow threw him off the man. He rolled into something warm and wet.

"Where'd you go, muckling?" spat the man. "Gonna kill you and then that dog! Ahgrio, get in here and help me!"

"Not gettin' my balls ripped off," a retreating voice called.

Emmait squirmed, struggling to think, his thoughts sluggish from the blow. He pushed back across the wet and warm things spilled on the floor. They were like snakes, ropy but covered in sticky blood. Still fresh from . . .

The man I disemboweled.

His hand shoved behind him, realizing what must be near here. He searched and found the body. The attacker stomped toward him. Heavy wood smacked into a palm. The man was over him, moving. Emmait pictured him raising his cudgel. Another blow to the head would finish him. He had to find it.

He brushed a hard handle.

With a scream, he ripped his knife from the corpse and lunged upward. The cudgel fell at the same moment. It cracked across his back as he rammed the knife into the robber's heart. Hot blood spilled over his hand as he drove the shocked man back.

"You . . ." croaked the man, his cudgel falling from his grip and spilling over Emmait's throbbing back. "What you do that for?"

The man fell to the ground, ripping the dagger from Emmait's hand. The man groaned. The other man gurgled as he died, strangled by Sun's tight jaws. It was how the dog liked to kill. Disable his prey then go for the throat. Not to rip out their windpipes, but to choke them.

Emmait found the body of his attacker and swept over bony ribs for his knife.

"Just . . . just . . . wanted to eat somethin' good," the man croaked.

Emmait seized the knife and ripped it free. A fresh spurt of blood splashed on the dying man's chest. Emmait winced at the bruise across his back and listened to the man's final, gasping breaths. Died for a few fish. Emmait grunted, his head pulsing now. A nauseated writhe twisted through his guts.

Sun tore into a body, ripping off flesh and gobbling it down. Emmait didn't stop his dog as he lay back on the floor, his nose filled with the scent of blood. The delicious aroma of the catfish followed. He closed his eyes against the headache, his skull pounding. He ignored the wet tears of Sun's grisly feast.

Emmait didn't eat men, he was no cannibal from the Reek, but meat was meat for his dog.

"I'd be lost without you, Sun," he said as he stared up at the blackness. He burst into wild laughter at what he said, his mirth verging on a cackle.

He was lucky. The only one in Hamiocho who had the Sun.

CHAPTER SEVEN

Emmait woke up to Sun's hot tongue lapping across his cheek.

He groaned, head throbbing. The side of his head felt tender. He breathed in, smelling drying blood and cooling bodies. He struggled to recollect the fight. Blurs of the frantic fight in the dark filled his mind. Fragments of action. Of thudding impacts. Rolling on the floor. He didn't remember lying down and sleeping.

"Must be alive if you're just licking me," he muttered.

A hot tongue ran across his mouth, tasting of Sun. He ran his hands through the dog's mangy coat and sat up. He shook his head. Pain skittered across his temple like water skates dancing across a pond, but the rest of him felt fine. He probed at his temple, finding a swollen knot in his hairline but no open wound.

No risk of infection.

He patted his chest and realized his dagger was missing. He searched around the room and found the bodies of the men. They were all naked with nothing worth salvaging on them. One had been feasted upon by Sun, flesh torn. He wiped his dagger clean on the chest of one of the corpses before sheathing it.

He rose on unsteady legs. His hand swung wide as he searched for the catfish he'd hung from the ceiling. He could smell them close. He brushed one, the scales warm and not as slick as they should be, the oil drying even in the humid muck of Hamiocho. He sniffed it.

Smelled fresh.

A growl rumbled from his belly. He had an empty stomach and a full bladder. He pissed on a corpse with some satisfaction.

"How long was I asleep?"

Sun didn't answer.

Emmait felt like he hadn't eaten in a day. He headed for where he remembered the exit. He crossed the floor on bare feet, stepping through puddles of tacky blood. He was about to step out when Sun stiffened beside him. A low growl rumbled from the dog's throat.

He concentrated as he stayed still, trying not to breathe. The distant sound of jangling metal reached his ears. It was a sound he'd only heard inside the Rubble. Soldiers. The armed and armored men who served the Glowers. They patrolled the dark streets around the well-fed homes to keep out thieves like him.

They shouldn't be here.

"He bought three catfish," a voice said. "Had 'em in the building over here. Him and his dog."

"You sure he had a dog?" a gruff voice said. "Don't be telling me tales, muckling."

"'Course I'm sure. His dog ripped off ol' Ismio's cock. I heard him howling 'bout it."

"Where is this building?"

"He's gone by now," said the muckling. Had one of them escaped? Emmait couldn't remember clearly. "He'd be dumb to stick around—" The man yelped. "Over there!"

Fear bubbled through Emmait. Why were the guards out searching for him? He'd stolen from Lord Achogear's residence a dozen times, and the selfish muckraker had never bothered to send his soldiers out beyond the Rubble. None of the Glowers did. They kept them close at hand. The only soldiers outside the wall guarded the dispensaries.

Emmait needed another way out of this building. He struggled to remember the attack. The five men had come at him from different directions. It meant there was more than one way in here. He moved back slowly, holding the catfish close to his body. Sun moved with him, slinking back as the heavy tromp of boots and the jangle of chainmail swelled in volume.

The soldiers would have rune-enchanted gear. Metal that wouldn't rust. Boots that wouldn't rot. The men were clad in wealth that would tempt the wretches in Hamiocho, but the soldiers had the skill and gear to beat back any muckling. They might make as much noise as a parade, but they still lived in the dark like the mucklings they fought. Their senses sharp. Only their masters stayed in their houses, safe from Death and able to use runed lamps, pretending that the world hadn't ended seven years ago.

That nothing had changed.

They would do anything to maintain that fantasy.

Emmait's hand clenched on the cord holding the fish as he felt the air in the room. A current flowed through it, leading out the way he'd entered. Which meant there was an opening behind him. He retreated back on silent feet for it, the skin on his back alive, detecting the minute changes in the flow of the breeze. He changed the direction of his backpedaling, aiming for the exit.

"In here," the man said. "Door's about . . . Right here. But he's got to be gone. We ambushed him yesterday. He killed my friends."

"Someone's certainly dead in here, Captain Fhaaghin," a young voice said. "Stinks worse than the abattoir."

"My friends," the guide said sadly. "We just wanted some fish. He had three of them. He could have shared."

Anger flared in Emmait. They had come in to murder him, not to ask for scraps. He tamped down his emotion and slipped out the back door and onto the muck. The jangle of metal clattered around him. The soldiers were spreading out slowly to surround him. He was downwind of them, the airflow carrying their stench to him.

He had to keep it that way. He moved north into the ruins. He didn't know these streets that well. He clutched his food to his chest. He wasn't about to give up his next meal to these bastards. He edged across a road and felt an alley opening. He moved toward it on silent steps, glad the armor made so much noise.

"Do you know where he would go next?" the gruff man, Captain Fhaaghin, asked. It sparked memories in Emmait's mind.

A Povazian guard lounging on the porch eating a pear. His broad build filled out his chainmail. Juices ran down his chin. He grinned at Emmait and tossed the fruit at him. It was the first time he'd eaten one.

"Huh, muckling?"

"Don't know where the thief comes from," the man said, "but he likes to trade with the Blind Fishers."

"He's come a few times I can remember. Always gets fish. They like what he brings. Good scrounging. Rune-made rope or wood. Talk to them. They're down by the river, catching their fish. They fish themselves, I hear. Swim out into the water and catch dem catfish in their mouths."

"Like they're otters," said Captain Fhaaghin.

"What's an otter?"

"Never mind. Give him the jerky."

Emmait moved down the alley. This gave him an idea. He had killed those who lurked in this neighborhood. The guards would never think to look for him now. He only passed through here. He slid his hand along the building as he retreated to a door. The guards started moving, armor jingling.

He twisted the latch and shouldered the door. The loud groan sent his heart pounding. Blood surged through his veins as he waited. The guards kept tromping toward the Sluggish Water. He stepped into the house, Sun padding in with him, and smiled.

He'd camp here for the day, let these guards wander off through the ruins, and find something new. Lord Achogear's ego must be stinging to send his men out into the dark. He wondered what he could steal next time.

Ablisio chewed on the algae. It had a stringy consistency, not as slimy as it was two days ago. It already had a bitterness to it. In a few more days, it would be inedible. But they would run out before then. He gulped it down, hating how it caught between his teeth.

He hated having to deal with the very men who profited off his misery. In a few more days, they'd have to return to the dispensary with another collection of excrement, or he'd have to find another way to feed his family. Nothing to trade to the Ratters but his sister and Zhee. The Blind Fishers didn't trade in women, only useful goods, but the Ratters were fat. They profited from selling to the Runecarvers for supplies.

Not that Ablisio would sell his sister or Zhee. He wouldn't even rent them. He'd have to find a way to earn his food that didn't mean groveling to the muckrakers who profited off the rotting corpse of Hamiocho.

Could he brave another thieving raid? He'd almost been killed last time. The runes on the rubble were getting harder to slip over without triggering an alarm. The guards knew the streets better so when they chased you, they could easily surround you and kill you. He'd been lucky last time to dodge that spear thrust and get past the guard before the others penned him in.

Dare he risk Phosphor Lake?

Zhee approached, her footsteps a little heavier than his sister's, and her scent earthier. Richer. She filled his nose as she settled down beside him. She pressed up against him. Warm and soft and plump in so many nice ways. He slid his arm around her, the tension relaxing from him. She smiled and rested her head upon his chest. Her hand idly stroked his stomach.

Amiollea made a disgusted snort from her side of the hovel. "If you two are going to boff, I'll go count the trees."

"Don't go far," Ablisio said as Zhee's soft touch stirred heat in him. The burdens of worrying about their future faded in him.

His sister stepped out, her footsteps stomping with an angry tenor out into the Rotting Orchard. How he would love for Amiollea to stop being such a brat about Zhee. She was an aide to their survival. Helped him relax when he was stressed. Her presence lessened his worry. She gathered excrement with Amiollea. Zhee could watch over his sister when he did something risky like rob other mucklings. She also had her ideas and insights that helped them survive.

She comforted him in ways different from his sister, and not just the pleasure she gave, though that was what interested him now. He found himself kissing her, pressing her down. Her softness inviting. She squirmed and wiggled in such enticing ways. Her hands stroked his skin, igniting heat.

Soon they were gasping together. He tried not to be loud—they were vulnerable right now—but it was hard to care when the need built and built in him. He had to spill his seed. He held her tight and loved how she whimpered beneath him.

Her breathy passion swelled his own.

The moment arrived.

Hot.

Fiery.

They collapsed into a tangle of limbs together. He held her tight, coming down from his pleasure, enjoying the feel of him. He ended up on his back, her head lying on his chest. He stroked her matted hair. His own was getting too long. He'd have to hack it short again with a sharp rock.

"What's weighing on you?" she asked, her voice soft, a whisper that wouldn't carry to Amiollea lurking outside, keeping watch while not wandering too far.

"How do you know something's weighing on me?"

"I can see it."

He snorted. "No one can see here."

"In my heart." She slid her hand over his chest to rub over where his heart labored. "I can feel it like currents of air across my skin or scents in my nose. You're thinking of doing something reckless."

"How long can we live like this?" he asked.

"What choice do we have?"

"I don't know. Things need to change. Something bold. A way to upset the comfortable. In chaos, there's opportunity. I think my pa told me that."

"Mmm, that sounds difficult," she said, her hand stroking down to his stomach and lower. She wrapped around him, stroking him.

He smiled at the way she touched him. He felt complete with her. "There has to be something better for Amiollea than this. For all of us. We're going to drown in the dark, choking in the mud. No one will care once we're gone."

"I'd care if you died," Zhee said. "So would Amiollea."

He grunted.

"She just needs to grow up a little." Zhee kissed the side of his cheek. He felt himself responding to her strokes, rising to her touch. "Mmm, you're going to be bold, huh? Going to take what we need?"

"Yes," he growled, a reckless bravado settling on him. "I'll do what it takes. Things have to change."

She slid on him, rubbing on his hardness. He awakened passions in Zhee, and she swelled them in his. She kissed him as she slid down his body. Her breasts were soft on his chest. His hand stroked her back, caressing her.

He would be bold for his sister and Zhee. He had to be. There was no hope if something didn't change.

～

Amiollea wanted to throw up at the sounds coming from the hovel. "A second time?"

It was bad enough hearing their moans drifting out of the hovel once. She pushed away from the rotting tree, sick of it. Being bold sounded amazing. To go out and seize something for them, something better, was a plan she supported.

But not if it made Zhee so . . . so . . . Povazian.

"Big-tittied cow," she muttered as she heard their passion building a second time. "I can be bold, too, brother. Idiot!"

She couldn't stand it. Listening to them made the algae in her stomach roil. She marched away from their home, drifting north toward the edge of the rotting orchard. Beyond lay what used to be the market area. Where their mother had died. It was now the home of the Shadow Painters, the strange, half-mad ascetics who created paintings on the ground or the walls of buildings. You had to sweep your hands over them to feel the subtle texture of the paints and imagine what they created.

They were big, though. It was hard to hold any portion of the image in her mind.

Sometimes, she liked to explore them while her brother wasted his energy atop Zhee. When she'd locate a new painting, she'd stroke over them, following the brush strokes. She delighted in how the ascetics could bring something to life in her mind through just simple lines. Last time, it had felt like a bird.

She vaguely remembered those flying through blue skies.

None of the birds had survived Darkfall.

As she reached the Shadow Painters' territory, she drifted near the tower she sometimes climbed to watch the Light.

Noon was a few hours away. She glanced to the east, staring toward the Spire out of some innate sense of direction. Part of her ached to go right up to the Spire. To see the Light up close. She bit her lip. To go to the Spire would mean staying away from the hovel for too long.

Her brother would be furious.

Still, it would be such a bold thing to do, to sneak off alone. Dangerous. But she was skilled at walking silently. Her brother had taught her how to survive when it had been only the two of them. He'd turned a crybaby girl into a lean stalker.

She craved to see the Light up close. Ablisio could spend his day rutting on that seed-sucking parasite, but not Amiollea. She didn't get what was so great about what they did. Sounded like a lot of grunting for a few moments of gasping.

There was better use for her brother's energy.

Irritated, she decided to do it.

She marched west alone.

If her brother wanted to waste his strength and time, she would waste hers doing something better. Naked and alone, not a weapon on her, she made her way down the street. Her feet moved over the cobblestone, feeling their familiar pattern. She left behind her tower and passed someone in the shadows painting a masterpiece.

This street would take her to a bridge which crossed the Sluggish Waters upward of Treacherous. Instead of leading into the Kneeling Dark, it led to the Blind Fishers. They didn't bother with women. Some said they had families living on islands in the center of the river, the men only coming to the western shore to trade.

Others said they mated with the fish and sold their children.

Either way, she had no fear of them. Those who lurked in the ruins beyond were predatory, but she wouldn't have any fish so they would have little reason to rob her. Not that they would even detect her. She would be a shadow. A whisper. Her brother had taught her to move without a sound. She would slip through and enter the Slithering Pit. It led right up to the Escarpment, the cliff that ran along the east and north side of the Runic Ward. The Slithering Pit was one of the low points of the city, half-flooded and haunted by vipers.

But she didn't fear the snakes. She didn't need to if she was bold.

She soon reached the Fisher Bridge, a much sturdier structure than Treacherous. It was too far north to be worth the detour when hauling food back and forth from their home. She crossed it without incident.

She tensed now. Her ears were keen for any sounds as she moved up the street. She knew much of the city well. Her brother never wanted her to get lost. Together, they had explored it, creating mental maps. It was something her old self would never have imagined being able to do, but when survival mattered, Amiollea always surprised herself.

As she crept through the ruins, the scent of drying blood caught her nose. She swallowed. Violence a day or two old. Were the perpetrators nearby? She paused for thirty or forty heartbeats, listening, smelling, and holding her arms out wide to feel the air moving over her naked body.

She weighed her eagerness to see the Spire up close and the fear of being captured...

Excitement won.

Despite the doubts creeping into her mind, it was too late for her to sneak back. She'd already been away too long. Ablisio would be mad at her no matter what, so she might as well make this act of rebellion worth it.

Besides, she'd be fine. She was skilled. He'd taught her how to survive. Nothing bad would happen to her.

She repeated the lie over and over as fear tightened her cold belly.

∽

Emmait was ready to leave the neighborhood near the Blind Fishers. The guards hadn't bothered searching beyond that one house. He'd eaten his catfish and rested while his headache faded. Now with a good night's sleep behind him, he was ready to implement a new idea. A revelation he'd had.

If the guards were out here, maybe it was the perfect time to steal a haunch of salted beef from Achogear's house.

He'd just left the building when Sun let out a low growl, barely audible. He froze, his head cocking right and left. Soft footsteps moved up the street. The person was skilled, hardly making any disturbance. The air shifted and his scent reached Emmait's nose.

Mud, algae, and something . . . feminine. A woman moving alone. That was unusual. Women who didn't have protection found it one way or the other, whether they liked the new source or not. Only the Glowers played at marriage.

Out here, things were far more direct.

How much could I fetch for her? he wondered.

Ratters always wanted new women. They had both the means to pay for them and to support them. This woman would become the third or fourth "wife" to a rat-catcher, tanning little hides and spreading her legs a few times a week in exchange for food.

Emmait slipped out into the dark. She was heading west toward the Ratters. How serendipitous. He didn't have to grab her right away. Why haul her farther than he had to? With his hand resting on Sun's fur, he moved through the dark street after the female, following her faint, exciting musk.

CHAPTER
EIGHT

"Where did she go?" Ablisio snarled as he stomped through the mud of the Rotting Orchard outside their door. "That dumb little twit!"

"She probably hasn't gone far," Zhee said. She stood in the doorway of the shack, feeling the currents of air across the front of her body created by Ablisio's passing back and forth.

For a while, she had been feeling good. They had made love twice, and both times she'd found her release, something she'd never experienced before Ablisio saved her. He knew her body, how to touch her. She wasn't sure it meant he loved her, but he cared for her.

Of course Amiollea wandered off, Zhee thought, annoyed.

The sour musk of fear spilled off Ablisio. Zhee struggled to picture him in her mind's eye. He was Karadrisan, which meant he had brown skin, darker than her own pale Povazian flesh. His hair was shaggy and in need of being cut again. She knew the shape of his body, the hardness of his muscles, the breadth of his chest. She imagined the contours of his face, nose bold, lips full, jaw square.

He felt handsome to her touch. She had never seen him in light save the softest glow found on runes protecting the rubble, and then only for fleeting moments as he scrambled over the makeshift wall. He always left her behind as he thieved his way through the Glowers District.

Now she imagined his face tight, brow furrowed. He stomped past her and struck one of the trees. It gave a mournful creak before toppling over with a loud splat onto the mud. Broken branches snapped. The scent of rotting wood filled her nose.

Wise Owl, where has she gone? she thought. Then it occurred to her. A flash of insight delivered to her by the totem spirit. "She's going to watch the Light. It's nearing noon, yes?"

"Idiot girl," Ablisio said. He swallowed, as if gulping down his anger, and went still. "You're right. I lost track of time for a while."

A pleased warmth ran through Zhee.

"She'll come back once the Light blossoms," Zhee said. She exited the shack and moved toward his scent, the sound of his breathing. She hugged him from behind, pressing against his back. She kissed his shoulders, tasting him beneath the grime. They should risk bathing again. Going down to the river and slipping into the dark waters. It made noise, never a good thing, but it was so refreshing. "She just wanted to be alone."

"Not safe to be alone."

"You go off alone all the time," Zhee said.

"I'm not a little girl!" He turned in her embrace and gently pushed her away. "Out there, she's asking for a predator to snatch her up. If she's lucky, she'll be sold to a Ratter. If she's lucky! Those foul, shit-eating mucklings will pass her around their camp until they're tired of using her."

"I'm aware of that fate better than you," Zhee said, keeping her voice flat. She hated thinking of those days. She had survived them. "But she's smart. She'll be careful. And she's not far. Just beyond the grove."

"You know where she is?" Ablisio said, his tone almost accusatory.

"When we go gathering," Zhee said slowly, "she likes to go there. I let her think she slips away from me and trail after her. I keep your sister safe."

"Where?" he asked.

"The Shadow Painters."

"Oh." She could feel the tension relaxing out of him. No one was harmed by them. All they cared about was their art. Maybe they were mad, or maybe they were still devoted to the remote god of the Karadrisans. He was so remote, he didn't even have a name. Unlike Povazians, Ablisio's people didn't pay much attention to their souls. They cared more about the here and now.

They didn't have Wise Owl to soar over them or Clever Fox to scout for them. No Cautious Toad to lead them to water or Suspicious Viper to guide them through danger.

Are the spirits able to help me here? she wondered.

"She'll come back after the Light," Zhee said. Her hands absently went to her stomach and rubbed in slow circles. A touch of fear rippled through her. "She'll come back. You taught her well, Ablisio."

"Hopefully she won't make my mistakes," he grunted.

She smiled for a moment before the unease returned. She couldn't be pregnant. One more day. Her flow would come tomorrow. It had to.

Ablisio's fingers brushed her arm and trailed down to her hand. She took it, feeling his strength as they waited for the flash of light that would announce noon. Her heartbeat quickened. She could feel the moment arrive.

The strange brilliance spilled like a flood from the Spire, a beacon in the madness.

∼

AMIOLLEA STOOD at the bottom of the escarpment after crossing the Slithering Pit. She wasn't sure if there were even vipers still living in there. It was a low point in the city, a depression that had flooded early on. She'd crept across muddy streets, the water up to her waist in places. She made her way with care, keeping her bearing. Something important to do in unfamiliar territory.

She'd gone slow to minimize the noise she made and kept her ears peeled for the sounds of others. Mucklings avoided the Slithering Pit. No one liked wading through foul water and risking deadly bites of the rumored vipers.

But she'd done it.

At the top of the cliff above her was the Runic Ward. The Spire lay in there. What would it be like to witness the Light from down here? It was almost time. She could feel her internal clock ticking away with her heartbeat. She rested her hands against the cliff, staring straight up at the black above.

Were Death circling above her? Were the murderous spirits swooping and gliding over her head waiting for the light to illuminate her and take her? There were times when a mad impulse would seize her to spark a light and be seen. To reveal the world around her for one last moment before Death took her.

Some did that, no longer able to take the black. They made fires to draw Death to them. She knew one man who had a sword and had tried to fight the unseen entity. She remembered how he'd screamed exactly like her mother had. All Amiollea had seen was the bright fire stabbing her eyes with pain even from two or three blocks away.

Her brother had hauled her away at a run.

Then there were the Sun Ravagers. The mad cult had set the southwestern section of the city on fire. It was a poor slum full of wooden structures. They had created a blaze so bright, the entire city was illuminated. The flames leaped up into the dark. Death had killed many that day, and others were lost to the flames.

The followers of Cinder had tried to make a new sun to save the city.

She'd spent three days hiding in a building with her brother, both too scared to leave until the last of the flames died.

"Now," she whispered.

The Light flashed above her. It spilled out across the sky, the pain of its brilliance stabbing into her eyes. She screamed and ripped her gaze away, shocked by the intensity of it. She could still see it burning across her vision. She buried her face into the crook of her arm, staggering from the shock of the blessed illumination.

The agony reached into her mind. She gasped and shuddered, tears rising at the corners of her eyes. The bright blue smear across her vision made the pain worth it. She lifted her head and smiled at the *color* in her world.

It would be there for hours. Longer. She smiled as she leaned against the escarpment. The slick rock felt cool against her skin as she flicked her eyes back and forth, watching the color smearing across the dark. She wanted to cry out her enjoyment.

Seven years living in the dark city kept her from doing that.

She was about to press off and back home when she heard noise. It echoed from her left. Around the escarpment. A loud groan echoed. The clatter of metal. The rattle of chains. She had never heard such a sound in her life.

I shouldn't, she thought as she strolled along the escarpment. The ground rose steeply in front of her. She found a street, the cobblestones worn by the flow of water down it. She moved up it as the rattling stopped.

She frowned as the sound shifted. She heard men talking. They weren't speaking her language. She grinned with delight when she realized who they were.

∼

EMMAIT HAD BEEN ABOUT to pounce on the girl when the new sound burst through the silence.

It had shocked him. He ducked down with Sun as if he could be seen. He was lucky to find this strange, perhaps mad, woman after the Slithering Pit. He thought he'd lost her in the flooded ruins, forced to move slowly so he wouldn't make much noise and to detour around deep patches of water.

He'd feared that she even had been leading him into a trap by venturing into one of the most dangerous sections of the city. Emmait had followed the barest hint of sound and trusted Sun's nose. Flowing water was a problem, but standing water wasn't a hindrance to his dog's sense of smell. Not if the trail was fresh.

Still, they only found her when she screamed out in pain. The girl had looked at the Light. He cringed when it had flowed over him. This close, it had lit up the ruins around them, shedding white everywhere as it spilled across the world. He waited for the whispered wind that announced Death's presence.

It hadn't come.

Now the girl moved toward the loud sounds. Her footsteps echoed on cobblestones. She hiked up a slope. They must be near the southwestern edge of the Slithering Pit. Emmait hesitated, debating if he should keep following her.

He didn't like the sound of rattling chains coming from the Runic Ward above. He stayed clear of the blue-skins. You'd have to be mad to do anything with men who had magic. It was said they could speak a word, and you'd burst into flames or turn to stone.

Better to rob the Glowers than to have anything to do with the Runecarvers.

Now his quarry hurried toward the sound like she recognized it. Had he been tracking a blue-skin this entire time? He couldn't have. She smelled like a muckling and moved with the confidence of one.

How many rats can I get from selling her? he wondered.

His belly rumbled. The catfish already felt like a lifetime ago.

Emmait followed her on silent steps, Sun at his side. He stroked the dog's fur as they climbed the slope.

※

Excitement rippled through Maegwirio. It was the day of the caravan. He was finally allowed to travel with them to the Glowers. He waited at the base of the Spire, listening to his maestro trumping down the stairs after doing . . . whatever he did on the roof to make the Light. The old man had his walking staff with him. The runed wooden steel thudded on the stone steps.

"I can feel your impatience," Maestro Kozonio said. "I am coming."

"Sorry, Maestro," Maegwirio answered, shifting in his cow-leather boots. He hardly had an excuse to wear the well-made footwear.

The old man came around the corner, leaning on his staff. He took each step with care. Maegwirio felt the age weighing down on the maestro. He bit his lower lip. Concern flooded through him for Kozonio's safety.

"Maybe you should stay behind," Maegwirio said. "I can handle the runes. I know them well enough to impress the Glowers."

"I'm fine. Just the stairs tiring me. I'll be better when I can stretch my legs."

The maestro crossed the entrance room to the makeshift lightlock. It was something every lit house needed. You couldn't just open your front door. If light spilled out, it could be enough to bring Death on you. To prevent that tragedy, they had a small room with no lights. With the interior door closed, no light could spill out into the dark.

A nervous flutter of trepidation washed through Maegwirio as he closed the interior door. He both enjoyed and loathed going out of the Spire. He savored the freedom of leaving his home more than he hated the oppression of a world without light. He could get so lost out there. He could stumble over a hazard he couldn't see, make a wrong turn and get lost, and the entire time he'd feel the weight of the black pressing on him.

He didn't know something lacking any substance could have weight. He just felt the pressure on his shoulders whenever he stepped out into the oppression. He waved his hand before his face, trying to see it.

"Maestro Kozonio," a respectful voice said after the pair stepped out of the Spire.

"Is that you, Eddakwio?" asked the maestro.

"Indeed," the warden said. He was a man who spent all his time in the dark. Most Taechizians didn't know more than the most rudimentary use of runes if at all, but they could serve the community in other ways.

"Good, good, you're going to make sure I don't trip and break my hip like Fiaxhazio did last time."

"If I did that, who would make the runes to ease my swollen joints?" asked the warden. "Xhaegio?"

Both broke into laughs. Maegwirio forced a chuckle, not wanting to be excluded from their jovial camaraderie. He didn't know any Runecarver named Xhaegio living in the Runic Ward.

"Hello, Eddakwio," Maegwirio said when the laughter died off.

"Is that Maegwirio?" Eddakwio asked. "Your voice sounds deeper. You shaving yet?"

"I've been shaving for years," Maegwirio said, his cheeks warming.

"But now Maestro Kozonio thinks you are a man. Ready to brave the wilds of the dark. To step out of our walls and face the hungry hordes of mucklings."

"Hordes?" he asked. "There are hordes?"

"Certainly," said Eddakwio. His strong hand landed on Maegwirio's shoulder. "Which is why you'll want to stick in my shadow."

"How will I see it?" muttered Maegwirio. "There are no shadows in Hamiocho."

"Exactly! So you better be good at spotting them." The warden laughed.

That makes no sense, thought the youth.

"Make a wrong turn out there, and you'll find yourself the newest wife of a rat-catcher," the warden added. "Or the next meal for a starving band of mucklings."

"They don't really eat flesh, do they?" Maegwirio asked, craning his neck and staring sightlessly in the direction of the walls. "And I'm a man. I can't be a wife."

"The Ratters don't care much about that," said Eddakwio. "Not when they find a smooth-faced boy."

"I shave," he protested.

"Don't mind Eddakwio," said Maestro Kozonio. "He grew up wrestling bears, so he doesn't have the keenest sense of humor."

"Truly?" asked Maegwirio. "You were a runic knight? I wanted to be one of you when I was a boy." The defenders of his mountain home had ignited his imagination as a boy. Mighty warriors, armored in runes, who rode upon the mighty bears of Taechiz.

"Aye, I was a knight. Bears have better senses of humor. They never complain if your jokes are bad."

"Bears can't speak."

"Exactly!" Eddakwio chuckled again.

Already, Maegwirio felt better knowing a runic knight who'd once worn the enchanted armor and wielded an ensorcelled blade. He would stay close to Eddakwio as they crossed the city to the Rubble and their meeting with the Glowers.

A loud grating sound split the darkness. The rattle of chains clattered. The gates were opening. The former knight's hand on Maegwirio's shoulder tightened for a moment before he pushed the youth forward toward the sound.

The weight of the darkness didn't feel so heavy today as the warden led them to the gate that led out into the part of the city known as the Rateriam. It was the first neighborhood of Hamiocho the caravan would pass through. And the safest.

Assuming he didn't get snagged by any Ratters looking for a bride.

They don't take youths, do they? he wondered as they joined the others who were going out into the lightless city.

~

It's Runecarvers, Amiollea thought.

She realized now what she'd heard as she crouched by a wall. The gates to the Runic Ward had opened. Even before Darkfall, it had a wall built around the neighborhood separating the Taechizian quarter of the city from the rest. The blue-stained people were the masters of carving runes and working magic. They kept to themselves. Even after Darkfall, they could have lived with the Glowers.

She'd heard about caravans. The Runecarvers traveled to the Glowers to trade their magic for food.

She crept to the top of the hill and listened to the milling men. They talked in their language. It sounded alien to her ears, like the chatter of birds made with the tongues of men as they waited to travel to the Glowers for food, unafraid of any mucklings.

Who would attack...

An idea nibbled in the back of her head. The caravan would return with both fresh and salted beef. They would bring back enough food to feed their quarter for a few weeks or longer.

Her brother wanted to be bold, but could they be *this* bold? Could they dare steal from the Runecarvers? There had to be weaknesses to exploit. Most of the Taechizians lived in homes sealed from the outside. They weren't at home in the dark. They would have their guides, but if someone carrying a pack of food could be separated...

Picked off from the herd...

Intrigued by this possibility, she crouched in the dark and waited for the caravan to depart. Her brother would be impressed if she delivered an opportunity to steal a haunch of salted beef. They could live off that for weeks.

~

Runecarvers...

Was the muckling girl here to rob them? Did she know some way to get value out of their caravans? If she had the confidence to do that, was Emmait missing something about her? Curiosity itched at him.

If she could get value off the Runecarvers, either food or enchanted goods, it would be worth investigating. Maybe he'd figure out how she stole from them and do it himself.

Maybe it was something safer than stealing from the Glowers.

He rested his hand on Sun's neck and waited, listing to the Runecarvers. They were loud, not caring who heard them. They were confident in their guides and protection. In the runes they stitched into clothing and stamped into the metal.

He crouched with patience. What else did he have to do but survive?

What else was there?

CHAPTER NINE

"She's not here," Ablisio hissed, keeping his voice low.

Fear fueled the anger bubbling through him. Where had she gone? He'd waited for her to return after the Light flared, enduring beat after agonizing beat of his heart. Each one drew his skin tighter and tighter and tighter until he couldn't stand the pressure.

Now he felt on the verge of tearing apart.

So Zhee had led him to the tower Amiollea liked to watch the Light from.

"Where else could she be?" he demanded as they stood atop the tower.

"I don't know," Zhee answered out of the dark. He felt her nearby. "I truly don't know."

"Did she hurt herself? Did we miss her in the dark?"

"We didn't smell her, or any blood."

"And if mucklings found her?" His voice was ragged, raw and bruised. "Huh, Zhee? What if they took her?"

"She wasn't taken."

"You don't know that!" He wanted to shout at his full volume, to fill this tower with his fury. Too many years of caution kept his voice low. A rasping growl. "How can I take care of her if she runs off?"

"She's growing up. She can't remain your little sister forever. You have to—"

He sprang at her and grabbed her arms, cutting off her words. His hands slid down her greasy skin as he stared toward her unseen face. "She will always be my little sister! Mother told me to watch her. To not let her go."

"Ablisio . . ." Zhee whispered. "She'll come back. We just have to wait for her to return to the shack."

"Wait!" He ripped away from her. "While my skin feels like it's about to rip to shreds? She's out there. Somewhere. Alone, Zhee! How can we find her?"

"Give her a chance to come back." She touched his shoulder. "A little while. She's just . . . rebellious."

"Rebelling against what? Staying alive? Does she want to die?"

"No, she just wants to be her own woman. She doesn't have a place—"

"No place? Her place is with me."

"That's not what I mean." Zhee sighed heavily. "She's turning into a woman. She's starting to . . . need things."

Ablisio fell silent. Contemplating *that* churned his stomach, too. He didn't want to picture his sister heaving beneath some filthy muckling, giving herself to his lusts in exchange for food. "She doesn't need to do *that*. I provide food for her without needing *that* from her."

"Is that what you think I do?" Zhee asked, her voice tight.

"Isn't it?"

She let out a hissing screech, so unlike her. She moved. It sounded like she picked up something before the air shifted before him. He had the barest warning before the mud splashed across his arm and his face. Some got in his eye, stinging.

"Muck and grime, Zhee!" he growled, wiping at his eye. "What was that for?"

"I'm not your whore, Ablisio."

His face warmed with embarrassment. "I didn't mean it like that."

"Oh, you meant it. You said it. The *only* reason I spread my thighs for you is so you'll keep me safe and feed me. That's it. Can't there be another reason? I can't *enjoy* it. Can't *enjoy* being with you?"

"Well, I mean . . . Isn't that how this started?" he muttered.

"I thought we had gotten past that. But if that's all I am, you can stumble around in the dark by yourself."

She whirled around and marched down the tower steps.

He cursed beneath his breath, bewildered by what she was saying. What she meant. More? Her footsteps were heavy. Dangerous. He rushed down the steps and out the tower after her, feet smacking against the mud. He caught up to her and seized her arm.

"Zhee!" he hissed.

"So I am just your whore!" she spat as he jerked her around. "You won't let me leave!"

"You're not my whore," he growled, confused and angry at her for twisting his words. "You're not my prisoner, either. I just . . . I don't want you walking alone through here."

"Why?" she asked. "Afraid someone else will get to use me? You won't have my plump body squirming beneath you?"

"I don't want you to get lost and hurt like—" He choked back the words. *Where are you, Amiollea?* "It's not safe to be alone."

"I don't need your protection all the time." Zhee tried to jerk free. "Not around here. I know this area. It's our home. We're safe here. Your sister is just sulking. She's jealous."

"Of what?" he asked, confused.

"Of me!" Zhee burst into weary laughter. "You're the only man in her life, her protector, and she no longer has you all to herself. She has all these burgeoning feelings with no outlet. It's why she hates me."

"She just thinks you're useless," Ablisio muttered then hastily added, "Which you're not."

"I've heard her opinion many times. I'm just a leach sucking on your cock."

"You're not a leech!" He struggled to understand what she was saying. Zhee had always ignored Amiollea's antagonisms. It was like none of Amiollea's barbs could penetrate Zhee's skin. They just . . . bounced off her.

"What am I to you?" Zhee asked after a few moments. There was something in her voice, a waver of emotion.

"You're . . ." He frowned. *What is she?* "You're Zhee. You're . . ." He didn't know the words to say what he felt. She wasn't his wife, right? She was the woman he . . . lived with. His brow furrowed. "I like you. You're warm."

"I make you feel good," she said.

"Yeah. Is that so bad? I like it when you make me feel good. And that makes me want to keep you safe. Protect you. You're like . . ." He couldn't say she was like his sister. Not with the things they did. "I don't know. You're something to me, Zhee. You're comforting. You're my . . . woman. I care for you."

"Really?"

"Yeah, really." He hesitated, suddenly worried about what she would say. "And you?"

"I care about you."

He smiled. "That's good. Sorry. I just . . ."

"I know. I'm worried for Amiollea, too. That girl might not believe it, but I care for her. Like she's my little sister, Ablisio. And I don't know where she is, but I want to believe that the Wise Owl is watching over her and Clever Fox is guiding her back to our hovel. She just needs to get out and relieve her frustration. You know it's hard for her when we're together. It reminds her just how alone she is."

"But she's not alone," Ablisio said, stung by those words. "I'm here. You're here."

"But you're not all *hers*. And she's needing that more and more. Someone to be hers. Someone she can hold and kiss and love, and it can't be you."

"What do we do about that?" he asked, swallowing. He didn't want to drive his sister away, but if he had to choose between her and Zhee . . .

"Do you know why I don't fight back when she says those awful things to me? Even when it makes me want to rip her filthy hair out, I hold back. Do you know why?"

"No."

"Because I know I'll lose." Her words quivered. Cracked. Broke. "I'll lose. You'll choose her over me. So I am trying so hard to avoid any conflict, but her frustration with me is growing, and she is as stubborn as you. I'm going to lose you, Ablisio."

He smelled something salty and realized she was crying. He pulled her to him, holding her in the dark. She pressed her face into his chest. Hearing her fear . . . All he could do was rock her as she clung to him, her emotions pouring out of her.

"You're not going to lose me," he said even as he feared what choice he would make if Amiollea gave an ultimatum. Amiollea was his sister. His flesh and blood.

But Zhee was someone he didn't want to lose, either. They were both important to him. He would rip himself apart if he had to choose. What could he do to bring Amiollea around? How could he get her to accept Zhee so he wouldn't have to ever make that choice?

"I'm just so scared," Zhee whispered. "I don't want anything to change, but it's going to. I can feel it. Everything rots and spoils in this city."

⁓

THE CARAVAN DEPARTED.

Emmait counted the footsteps of two dozen or more men moving in the dark. Some clanged with metal, others had the whisk of cloth. *Clothes.* He couldn't remember the last time he had worn anything. Years. Six or more. One of them sounded old, joints stiff and walking with a heavy staff.

They spoke in their language, incomprehensible to his ears. He could hardly detect the muckling girl as she slipped from her hiding place to trail after them. He squeezed Sun's fur and followed his mark. He and his dog drifted through the darkness as the possibilities bubbled inside of him.

Would she slip behind one of the stragglers and lift something from the blue-skin? Emmait had vague memories of pickpockets, thieves who did that in crowded marketplaces. Perhaps the muckling girl was one of them. If the Runecarvers were as deaf and blind as the Glowers, she might be able to approach them in all the clatter.

Could he do the same?

It sounded like such an interesting possibility. To move in among the group. Some of them stumbled. These were men who didn't often move through the dark. They were slaves to the lights in their shuddered homes.

One person *could* slip among these blind cows and steal any delicious baubles. Who would notice anything with all the cacophony they made?

It almost hurt his ears.

He had to find out if he could do it.

In a whisper, he commanded Sun, "Stay."

It was time to find out just how close he could get. Exhilaration pumped hot through his veins. He moved off into the darkness, eager to discover the senses of these Runecarvers.

∼

Amiollea felt wicked as she stalked through the dark after the Runecarvers. A mischievous grin. A cat's smile. She remembered cats. Distantly. She stalked behind the caravan with the exuberance of a kitten stalking a grasshopper in her family's back garden.

They have no idea I'm behind them!

Despite her playful mood, she stepped softly. She went slowly to probe with her feet before her. Cautiously, searching for threats that could hurt her or even make her stumble. She could not make noise. Even with her careful pace, she kept up with them. They tripped and cursed in their musical language.

Blue-skinned Runecarvers.

Moving like this reminded her of one of the stories Ablisio told her in the first days after Darkfall. Of daring girls who snuck through ruins and moved without making a sound. Who knew how to step on mud with care. Who could slip through rotting vegetation with hardly a rustle. Amiollea had tried so hard to emulate those princesses.

Strangely, she couldn't remember her mother ever telling those stories. The princesses in Mother's stories were all graceful and beautiful and well-behaved. They gave chaste kisses to their champions who went out to slay monsters or waited at the tops of towers to be rescued.

She liked her brother's stories better.

Now she was Princess Amiollea. These Runecarvers would head for the Rubble, the vast wall around the Glowers. The food was beyond there. They would trade for it. As blind and deaf and bumbling as these Runecarvers were, she wondered if she could walk among them and just *take* something.

Her stomach growled. She ignored her empty belly.

She licked her lips and kept after them as they left the edges of the Rateriam beyond and descended toward the arcane walls. They moved through ruined buildings. The streets here were dirt-smeared cobblestones, easy to traverse.

They must use the same route every time. Keep it clean. Ablisio is going to be so proud of me if I bring back meat.

As her excitement mounted, she heard a noise behind her. Someone was out there in the dark.

∽

It was surreal moving blind through the dark. Maegwirio had gone from residence to residence in the Runic Ward. Those were short journeys through the impenetrable dark. This was a trudging sojourn. He took step after step with no idea what was before him. Feet smacked on cobblestones around him. His stomach lurched with each step, and he was grateful to the guides moving among the stumbling sheep.

The guides were the nimble goats leaping from craggy peak to craggy peak.

Maestro Kozonio hobbled at his side, his walking staff clicking on the ground.

Maegwirio tried to maintain a sense of adventure, but the impenetrable black wore at him. The intangible murk possessed a terrible weight. It almost smothered him. No air moved. Just humid warmth swirling around him. Terrible stenches rose from every direction. Sour and overripe and foul. A mélange of rot and decay and festering filth.

How do people live out here? he wondered. *Moving blind, slinking through the muck. How do they not go crazy?*

He found himself tugging at his robes, broiling in his cloth. He looked around in a futile gesture to see *something*. He didn't know where they were.

How far they had to go. Sounds echoed around them. The guides were talking, joking.

To them, this was routine. Monotony had numbed them. He ached to have their ease with the black. He rubbed at his arms. Sweat poured down his face. His hair clung to his scalp. He glanced at every sound.

What is it like to be cool? he wondered.

Hamiocho now had only one season: muggy. He only had distant memories of his boyhood in the mountains of Taechiz. Running through alpine meadows in the summer, skiing across the high snow in winter. The air crisp and sharp. Glacial-caped peaks rising in every direction, thrusting at the sky with such majesty. He pictured Atzuchaeb Hzachit, the mountain rearing over Farriach, the city where his family lived.

It was said the mighty Chemosh River had its source from the majestic peak's glacier.

He ached to see the mountains again.

Instead, he was trudging through the dark. As much as he wanted to leave the tower, he missed the simple fact he had light. He could see around him. All he had out here was his imagination, and that fed his growing fear. He populated the empty black with watchers. Desperate men wanting to raid the caravan. It didn't happen much. They learned that Runecarvers' blades were sharp and the guides knew how to use them.

His shoulders itched. The more he thought about eyes, the more he felt them on him. He kept turning his head to spot them. He had the queerest idea their eyes would gleam. A soft shimmer that would let him spot the attack before it came. He rolled his shoulders to soothe the growing itch.

"We're halfway there," Maestro Kozonio said. "The first time is almost the worst."

"What's worse than this?" asked Maegwirio.

"The second time, when you know what it's like out here and have to face it again." The old man's hand brushed Maegwirio's sleeve. He slid down to squeeze the young man's hand. "You are doing fine. It's normal to be nervous."

"Thanks." He drew comfort from the wrinkled grip.

"True," said Eddakwio. "My first time out here, I kept smelling piss. Turned out, Fiaxhazio had piddled himself."

Fiaxhazio roared from the other side of the party. "Then why were your pants soaked and mine were dry, huh?"

"I fell in a puddle," Eddakwio said with mirth. "So, your pants still dry, Maegwirio?"

"Still dry," he said and smiled. The laughter rippling around him released the tension. He wasn't alone in the darkness.

That was the most important thing, he realized. So long as he could hear the others, know they were just within arm's reach, he could endure not seeing. They were all as blind as him. All they could do was stumble on together.

He took a bold step as the warden laughed at a new joke. Maegwirio strutted. Every one of them had made their first trip, and now it was his turn. He was trusted enough to come. No longer just an apprentice.

It felt good to—

The wardens' laughter died. The silence that fell on the party squeezed about Maegwirio. He stumbled as he bumped into Porresio who had stopped before him. All the young man's new confidence evaporated. He peered around, wondering what had the guards spooked.

Then the shouting began.

CHAPTER

TEN

Emmait froze with the Runecarvers. He was nearly on them, only two steps away from their flank. Every muscle tensed as he sensed something had changed. Boots shifted. What threat was out here? Had they detected him?

Not as blind as I thought. The pressure on Emmait's heart squeezed. He had to breathe but they might hear—

Shouts erupted around the caravan. Emmait jumped in shock, spinning in place as bare feet slapped on stone. Noise burst from every direction. Metal rasped on leather as the guards drew their swords. They shouted in their language.

Emmait grimaced. He was in the middle of an ambush. Some band of mucklings was shouting and whooping, making noise from every direction. It was a confusing cacophony of sounds echoed around him. Too loud for him to pick out what was going on.

A screen of noise to deafen his sharpest sense.

How did I miss them? Emmait demanded of himself.

The attackers and the guards clashed. Metal clanged. Men screamed. The coppery scent of blood tickled Emmait's nose. Heavy boots thudded at him.

He darted right, ducking as a sword swung over his head. He drew his knife from the pouch dangling around his neck, not sure what to do.

Men shouted and died. Footsteps thudded around him. He turned to his right at the clink of metal, raising his dagger before him—

Someone slammed into him from behind. Emmait and the stranger both gasped. They hit the ground, the robed Runecarver thrashing atop Emmait, shouting in hoarse fear. He rolled over, shoving the figure off. His hand tangled in the leather strap of a satchel.

Emmait ripped the satchel from the man. The scent of tanned, oiled leather filled his nose. The pouch smacked into his thigh. There was something valuable in there. He gained his feet and struggled to get his bearings.

"Get the food!" someone screamed.

Idiots, they're going to the Rubble.

Fighting was all around him. He chose a direction and darted ahead, his dagger clutched in one hand, the satchel flapping behind him. A body thudded to the ground to his right, a meaty thunk followed by the scent of hot blood.

~

Maegwirio felt his satchel ripped away and didn't care.

He rolled from the muckling attacker and bolted to his feet. His heart pounded fear through his veins. The cold spilled over his mind. He couldn't think. He just had to get away from the muckling who wanted to kill him.

"Maestro!" he shouted as he rushed blindly ahead.

Someone screamed to his right. A meaty thunk echoed as metal struck another body. Shouts boiled around him. He couldn't make sense of it. He couldn't find his maestro. Death swirled all around him. He struggled to think.

A greasy hand grabbed his arm.

"Got you, blue-skin!" a man hissed in Karadrisan.

Maegwirio lashed out of pure panic, slamming an elbow in the direction of the muckling. He felt the crunch of something breaking followed by a squeal of pain. Maegwirio wrenched free of the attacker's grip and darted away.

He ran into the darkness. He couldn't see anything before him. His screaming heart pumped frigid fear through his veins. His boots smacked on cobblestones. Sounds echoed around him. Shouts. Screams. Pain. Agony.

"You broke my nose!" the muckling snarled behind him, voice stuffy. Nasally. "I'll gut you!"

Oh, no, oh, no. Where is Eddakwio? screamed through Maegwirio's mind.

Footsteps scrabbled behind him. He put all his strength into his runn—

CRACK!

He struck a building wall at full force. Lights burst across his vision. The dark world swam around him. He spun, dazed, and crashed into the man chasing him. His spinning arms struck the attacker in the side, sending him off-balance. Maegwirio fell onto the cobblestones as a loud, fleshy thud echoed.

"Muck and shit!" snarled the attacker.

Maegwirio struggled to move. His entire body felt fuzzy. Something hot and wet spilled over his temple and clung to his hair. It dribbled over his nose and reached his lips. It tasted hot and salty. He shouldn't be tasting that.

"Where'd you go?" the muckling growled. Staggering footsteps, sounding woozy, stumbled off in another direction.

Have to move, screamed through Maegwirio's thoughts. *Get up. Find Maestro Kozonio. Get back to help.*

He didn't know which way to go. He groaned. Acid gurgled in his stomach and burned his throat. He wanted to sick up. He stood on tottering feet. The world spun around him. He couldn't see anything, and yet he knew it whirled like a child's top. Bile crept up his throat.

He stumbled to his right. His feet dragged over the cobblestones. More warmth poured over his head. He could smell his blood. His thoughts battled with a foggy haze settling on his mind. He heard something moving before him then he gasped and tripped on a loose stone. He stumbled forward, struggling to keep his feet beneath him.

His dizziness overcame him. He fell forward. But not into the ground. He struck someone who gasped with a feminine shout. His arms tangled around her body. His face pressed into greasy, warm skin.

"Help," he croaked, confused.

∽

Chaos boiled through the fight around Emmait. Runecarvers ran in every direction. The mucklings had a strange smell about them. More ash than mud. And something else. A scent that tickled his nose. Acrid, almost like the potential of fire.

Shouts came at him from every direction. It was a bewildering array of noises. He didn't know where to go. People were tripping over each other. Shouting. Dying. Metal plunged into flesh with a sickening, wet sound. Weapons clanged. Swords swished through the air.

The Runecarver guards swung their blades in every direction. Emmait had to thread his way out with the satchel. He didn't know what it contained, but it had to be worth this. Now he just had to get out and back to Sun.

He felt alone without his dog.

He chose his direction, hearing a lull in the violence. He crept ahead, not fast. That would make noise. That was Death. Someone collapsed paces to his right, spasming on the ground. Someone ran before him.

"Poisoners!" snarled one of the mucklings. "You're all poison!"

"Strike it!" another shouted. "Now, now!"

Strike what? thought Emmait.

His toe brushed a body. He stepped over it. A staff thunked to his right. Wood on stone. Metal jingled, too. Emmait discerned two sets of footsteps, the armored one heavy, the other light. Almost frail. An image of a grandfather blazed in Emmait's mind, his mother's grandfather who always had this look of disgust when she visited to bring medicine for his joints.

Emmait edged past the pair. The guard stiffened and snarled something in the Runecarvers' tongue.

The air rushed. Emmait jumped back. The sword slashed before him. The guard rushed at him, boots heavy. The man had instincts. Cold fear slithered through Emmait's guts as he backpedaled before the swishing blade.

Air gusted. Swirled. He pictured the guard swinging diagonal slashes, first from the right, then the left. Right. Left. Right.

Emmait seized his moment and darted left. He rushed by the guard, slashing low with his knife. He struck thick, leather pants. His blade bit into the tanned hide but didn't penetrate. The man grunted and pivoted. Armor jangled in front of Emmait. A second guard. He ducked, but not soon enough to avoid a fist striking his head.

He stumbled to the side and tripped, rolling through hot blood pooling on the ground. He gained his feet, the guards rushing in. Armor jangled in that telltale way. Emmait rolled to his right. The blade struck the cobblestones.

Sparks flared from the impact for a moment. To someone who spent his life in darkness, it was enough to illuminate his attacker. A split instance to see the tall guard clad in a coat of linked chains, his face fierce.

His neck exposed.

The light faded and Emmait twisted on his feet. The guard had his scent. He knew the dark. Running was foolish. Emmait didn't know this area enough to have a sense of where he could escape. He had to kill to live.

Boots shifted. The attack came.

He ducked low and felt the blade whistling over his head. He smelled the Runecarver's armor. The rustle of his chainmail. He pictured the figure from that mental image. He focused on the size and shape as the guard shifted to recover from his miss.

He clutched the stolen satchel in his off-hand and thrust his knife for the guard's throat.

The blade slammed into something fleshy. A gurgling gasp burst from the guard. His blood gushed hot over Emmait's hand. It coated him in the man's life. Dying, the guard slammed his left fist into Emmait's head, throwing him back. His blade caught in the man's throat, bound on the vertebrae, and wrenched free of his hand.

Emmait fell on his back. A moment later, the guard fell, too. His sword spilled from his grasp, the cool metal skittering into Emmait's hand. He felt the sharpness of the edge on his skin. He snagged it up and gained his feet, grinning at his prize.

"Strike it!" shouted from a muckling.

A spark flared. Something sizzled before flames caught on a torch held by a naked man.

Terror struck Emmait.

～

THE RUNECARVER SPOKE in his native language. His arms, covered in *cloth*, hugged Amiollea's naked body. His face rubbed across her chest. She staggered beneath his weight pressing on her slender frame. She felt something warm smearing across her skin and smelled his blood.

Why did you have to trip into me? she thought, fear beating through her. Shouts echoed on the road ahead, the fight raging. The air reeked of spilled blood and bowels.

Her hands pressed on his head to push him off her. Blood spilled from a gash on his forehead. He gasped in pain as she prodded his wound. Her fingers slid over his brow to feel a nose. A large nose. Who was this bleeding man?

"Where you'd go!" a muckling snarled in the dark. He staggered in her direction. "Break my nose? I'll gut you!"

His footsteps grew louder. Her instincts screamed at her to abandon the Runecarver to his death. He hugged her tight. Though she couldn't understand his words, she recognized the tone. He begged her for help. She furrowed her brow as a weight pulled at her selfishness.

Her brother wouldn't abandon someone.

She hissed, "Come on! You have to stand."

"A woman!" the muckling said as he rushed in their direction.

She shoved the Runecarver to the side. His arms slipped from her. He groaned as he hit the ground. She shifted her feet, listening to the steps rushing at her, picturing the attacker in her mind. The muckling moved erratically. He weaved. His voice sounded slurred. The scent of blood grew stronger. The air moved as she visualized the approaching person. Thin, like her, but with muscles toughened by the dark. He had long legs, and between them...

"Haven't had a woman in a bit. Getting hard to find, they are! Ratters got 'em all."

Her hand lunged out for his weak spot. She struck his belly and slid down into matted hair. She found his cock and squeezed hard. He roared in pain. She ducked before he even threw his punch. She yanked hard on his manhood as her foot kicked out, striking the back of his calf near his ankle. She hooked him. He fell back, off-balance, while she gripped his manhood in a crushing hand.

Flesh tore. Blood spurted. The man screamed like a woman.

She threw his severed flesh at him with a great deal of satisfaction. He thrashed on the ground as she spun around and found the scared Runecarver. She didn't know what was happening with his people.

Were they winning? Losing?

She bent down. "Hey, hey! I'll help you!"

She grabbed his arm. He muttered something in his language. His hand grabbed her waist. She pulled him up. He leaned against her, smelling . . . clean. Fresh. There was no mud on him, just the salt of sweat and the dry aroma of cloth.

"Thank you," he muttered in her tongue as she led him a way from the fight.

"Come on." Footsteps thudded around them. "And be quiet. We're still in danger. We need to get—"

Bright, red light flared behind her. She gasped at the flicker of flame. It wasn't a muckling who had attacked the Runecarvers. It was the Sun Ravagers. The mad cult led by their insane prophet Cinder. One of them had lit a torch. He stood in the center of the Runecarvers. Everyone with any sense screamed and ran from the brilliance.

"THE SUN IS BORN!" howled the man. "IT EXPOSES YOUR EVIL, POISONERS!"

She glimpsed an old man hobbling toward the shadows, leaning on a walking stick.

The soft whisper rustled the air.

Panic surged through Amiollea as Death descended. Shadows danced before her. *Her* shadow. She was in the light. The cultist shouted in exultation. His torch rose into the air. His rapture turned into pain. Amiollea whimpered like a child. The Runecarver leaning against her cried out in fear.

"Run!" he shouted in her tongue.

They ran, leaning on each other, stumbling down the road. A sickening, wet tear ripped through the night. The torch fell to the ground and sputtered on the cobblestones. Something heavy crashed to the ground.

More men screamed.

∽

Emmait pissed himself.

Death ripped the Sun Ravager in half, the cultist's body falling with his torch amid the scattering people. Light painted Emmait's flesh. He could see the leather satchel held in his left hand, the sword and the runes carved into its blade lying on the ground to his right. The air whispered above him.

He spotted a dark alley.

Ran.

He pushed an old man out of his way, throwing him to the ground in his mad flight for safety. Screams erupted behind him. His piss poured down his thighs as half a body crashed into the ground before him, a Runecarver torn apart by Death.

The torch sputtered behind him.

"Sun! Sun!" he cried out, wanting to hold his dog. He needed Sun.

He raced into the alley and into the welcome embrace of darkness. He plunged between the building and onto a dark street a block away. He dove behind the building, curled up his legs, and rocked back and forth.

"Sun! Sun!"

The light went out. He was alone in the dark. All alone. He pressed his face into his knees and sobbed in relief. He hadn't died. The light hadn't killed him.

He'd escaped Death once more.

CHAPTER ELEVEN

Terror whipped through Maegwirio as he ran with the muckling girl. He held her hand as they raced down the street. He could see the buildings rising around them, faintly outlined by the red flickering behind him. His thoughts grew sharper through the throbbing pain in his head.

They fled the light and the screams.

Be safe, Maestro, he thought. his boots smacking on the steps.

He gripped the girl's hand as tight as he could as they climbed up the hill toward the Runic Ward. The light dwindled. The buildings turned into shadows. She jerked him to the right. He gasped, his arm nearly wrenched from its socket. He stumbled after her as they plunged down an alley into pitch blackness.

He couldn't see anything and yet she kept running, heedless of any hidden dangers.

She veered right and didn't run into a building. He realized they raced down another street a block away. He couldn't figure out how she knew they were out of the alley. A stitch formed in his side as he wheezed for breath, his robes clinging to his body. Sweat poured down his face, overwhelming his eyebrows and stinging his eyes.

He wanted to stop, but fear wouldn't let him. He didn't stop running.

Death had come. He'd heard the stories, but the reality of hearing the whispers and seeing people ripped apart by *nothing* terrified him. The reality of it was so different from those who had given muttered accounts. Seven years ago, these entities had killed Eoxhinea and Maestro Kozonio's other three apprentices.

Today, they killed people Maegwirio knew. Maybe even his maestro.

He clutched the muckling girl's hand as the hill grew steeper. He ran half-bent over, panting. He wasn't sure how long they had run, but he couldn't go on much longer. His legs burned. He finally stopped, pulling her short.

She hissed and tugged at him, her breath coming fast, hard. "It's coming for us," she whimpered, fear thick in her voice. "We have to get back to my brother."

"What?" he asked. "Your brother? One of the attackers?" A jolt of fear shot through him.

She was a muckling.

"My brother isn't one of those madmen!" she hissed, anger devouring the fear in her voice. "Those were Sun Ravagers."

"Why would they attack us?" Maegwirio struggled to think. "No one attacks us."

"Normal people fear Runecarvers, but what do the Sun Ravagers fear?" A shrill laugh cackled from her. She sounded his age or younger. "They set a quarter of the city on fire."

"I remember," whispered Maegwirio. "I saw it burning . . . from a window in the Spire." He had turned off the lights and opened the shutters to watch the blaze almost in a daze.

"You've been on the Spire?" She sounded so excited, which made her feel even younger. "Do you make the Light?"

"No." He struggled to catch his breath. "I don't. My maestro does that."

"Maestro?" She said the word slowly. "I don't know what that means."

"My . . ." He sought for the word. "My teacher. He's the Runecarver educating me."

"You're an *actual* Runecarver and not just Taechizian?"

"Yeah."

She grabbed his hands, her warm breath sweeping across his face. "Why does he make the Light? Why at noon every day? What's it for? To give us hope?"

Her words spun around him, giving him a strange sense of vertigo. He breathed in and smelled her. She stunk of muck and sweat. He had no idea how long it had been since she'd bathed in clean water. Her hands smeared grime onto his, but there was something feminine about her. Girlish in the way her words spilled out. Breathy.

"I don't know why," Maegwirio admitted. "He won't tell me. He locks the door behind him. He's done it every day since Darkfall. Maybe he did it even before Darkfall. I don't know."

"You don't know?" she asked. "I don't remember seeing it as a girl, but that first day in the dark, scared and hungry with my brother, I remembered how it lit up the night. It was miraculous seeing light that didn't bring Death. It made me think of my mother and how happy she must be to see me from up in heaven."

He swallowed, hearing the pain in her voice. His hands tightened on hers. The back of his throat tightened. He didn't know what to say now. "Well . . . I mean, if he does it at noon, maybe no one noticed it while it was daylight."

"Maybe," she said. Her tone brightened. "If you tell me about being a Runecarver, I'll take you back to the Runic Ward."

He swallowed. "But what about the others? My maestro was in the party. They were fighting before . . ."

She shuddered. "I don't know. It won't be safe to go back. The Sun Ravagers might still be around. Everyone ran. Your maestro . . ."

He stiffened under her words. His maestro couldn't be dead. He needed to learn more from the wise man. And whatever he did atop the Spire was vital. Maegwirio didn't have the skill to do it. To even understand it.

I can't even get into his study.

He was torn. He wanted to go back, but how could he find anyone after the attack? They would be stumbling in the dark. Lost. He wasn't even sure where he was. But if he went back to the Runic Ward, he could get help. Searchers who could march out into the night and find the Maestro and any other survivors.

"Take me back," he said, tightening his grip on her hands. "I'll answer any questions on the way, but we have to go quickly."

"Okay." She paused. He thought she was shifting. "I think it's this way."

"You think?"

She ripped her hand from his, and he could almost feel her stiffening. "It's this way. We came down a slope. We're a block over from your path, but that shouldn't matter. Don't you know the way back?"

"No," he said. "I don't understand how anyone finds their way through Hamiocho blind."

"Your eyes are a crutch. They make you weak. Without them, you have to learn other ways to see. I can feel you moving on my skin. I can smell how close you are. My ears are picking up echoes. We have buildings around us, but there is an alley to our right. The sounds don't echo back from there as much."

He stared at the darkness where he thought she stood in awe. "You can do all that?"

"If I couldn't, I would have died a long time ago. Come on."

She padded ahead of him and began asking her questions.

∼

"You have to know the mechanics of language," Maegwirio was saying to Amiollea. That was the Runecarver's name. Maegwirio. It sounded both familiar and foreign at the same time. It ended like a proper Karadrisan name for a boy with the "io" suffix, but the first part contained strange sounds not found in her tongue. "Know it better than you know yourself."

"Okay," she said, frowning. "What does language have to do with carving runes?"

"Runes are words," he said. "They are . . . not quite pictures. They're too simple designs for that. More the idea of pictures."

"Idea?" She shook her head as she led him through the Rateriam toward the Runic Ward. Her fear bled away as curiosity took over. He padded beside her, his movement strange. She could hear his skin rubbing on the cloth. It made a rustling sound. It had been so long since she'd worn clothes. She'd long forgotten about modesty.

Now she was reminded how naked she was beside Maegwirio. He was a boy. Her age. There was something . . . titillating about walking with him. A tingle she couldn't quite place the origin of danced across her skin. And there was this heat stirring in her nethers. It was similar to that uncomfortable heat she felt when she heard Zhee and her brother.

"How to explain this . . . ?" Maegwirio said. "Drawing them is pointless. We'd need somewhere with light."

"No place around here like that," she said. "No muckling has light. We all live in the dark. Must be nice growing up in the Runic Ward."

"I didn't grow up in the Runic Ward. I just arrived in Hamiocho a few hours before it happened. Bad luck, huh?"

"No one has good luck here," she said. "It's a cursed city. Now explain why runes are words. I thought they were little carvings."

"You know your letters?" he asked.

"I know *of* letters, but why would I learn them? Even if I didn't live in the dark, I didn't come from a noble house. My father knew how to write. A little. And to read. I've seen some things. Scratches on paper."

"Letters represent sounds," he said. "That's what an alphabet is. Like what you Karadrisans use for writing. Take your name, Amiollea. It's made up of eight letters. A M I O L L E A."

She didn't know that. She said her name slowly, "Aaammmiiioollleeaa." She could hear the different sounds. Some of them were the same, like the "ah" at the beginning and the end, and the two "L" sounds rolled from one to the other.

"So Maegwirio has . . ." She struggled to count. She could hear the "M" at the beginning, then there was this vowel sound that wasn't familiar to her. Maybe an "A" but not quite. It was like two sounds blending from one to the other. Next came that strange combination of "j" and "w." Was that one or two letters? "I don't know."

"In your language, it has nine," he said. "In mine, it is made up of one rune. *Aegwi*."

"Only one rune for nine letters?" She frowned. "And you left off the 'io.'"

"That's not part of my name in Taechizian, which is Maegwim. We often adopt Karadrisan gender suffixes to our names to make them more palpable to your ears."

So that's why Zhee's name sounds wrong. She should be Zhee. "Povazians don't do that," she said.

"No, they don't," he admitted. "But that's their decision. Our people made ours. So, runes represent words or ideas. The rune in my name, *aegwi*, means 'light.'"

"And where does the 'mmm' sound come from at the beginning and end, Maeju . . . Maejwi . . . Maej?"

"Maej?" he asked, amused.

"Your middle is hard to say. I feel like my tongue is going to curl up in a ball."

"The M at the beginning and end were added by my parents, decorations for the rune. We use a simplified rune to mark those letters that are placed about the central rune. They're . . . helper runes, like your alphabet."

"So you need a separate letter for sky and water and river and mud and blood and man and woman and all that?" she asked, her brow furrowing. "Where Karadrisan needs . . ."

"Twenty-two, I believe."

"That seems so much simpler," she said.

"You have to know how to *spell* those letters to make words, so there is still some learning. But the fact ours are pictures is why runic magic works." The excitement bubbled out of him as they moved through the dark toward the Runic Ward. She felt fairly safe with a blue-skin in the Rateriam. She'd heard the Ratters didn't want to anger their biggest customers. "Letters are symbols that represent sounds, but runes represent *ideas*. And ideas are what give shape to purpose. It is the will of the carpenter that planes the wood into a staff, the will of the stonecutter who fashions the brick for the wall, and the painter who decides on the colors to adorn the canvas. A Runecarver is no different. We impart our will through which images we draw, and those images tap into the Energy that flows from beyond this world."

"Energy?" she asked, frowning. "I don't know that word."

"It's the potential to do work," he said. "Beyond the reality of this world, a metaphysical plane exists. It's full of boundless potential, the embodiment of creativity. And like all potential to do work, like the energy you take through nourishment that lets you walk, it can be used if you know how. I can tap into it to reshape reality."

Her stomach gave a noisy rumble. "Don't talk about nourishment. I haven't eaten in days."

"I guess no stealing food from us thanks to the Sun Ravagers."

Guilt rippled through her. "Just a little. I have to survive out here. I don't get to live in the safety of the walls and trade runic goods to the *Glowers* for food."

"Don't they trade food with you?" he asked, sounding shocked. "The algae they grow in the Slime Fields or the meat they raise in the Abattoir Fields?"

"They make us pay steeply for algae. It goes up every week it seems. More and more shit."

"The algae needs excrement to grow," he said. "Perhaps there is a supply issue driving up the price?"

"Why would that do that?" she muttered.

"Well, it's a simple law of economics . . ." He trailed off and chuckled. "You don't even know what economics are."

"I know lots of things!" she hissed, trying to keep her voice low. Her cheeks burned, fueling her flare of anger. "Do you know how to tell how sound a building is by knocking on its wall? Or how to learn a new part of the city without seeing anything? Can you smell the difference between clean water and foul? You'd probably get the bloody bowels and shit yourself to death in a week!"

He chuckled instead of getting offended. "True."

"Economics." She snorted. "Doesn't sound like something that keeps you from getting killed in Hamiocho."

"No, it wouldn't," he admitted after a moment. "Survival hones what is necessary."

"And learning to draw pictures isn't necessary." She declared it with such confidence that it must be true.

"Those pictures are the reason any of us are still alive. Without runes to light the fields where the food is raised, the grass would die. Without it to purify the algae grown in the pools, it would be poisonous to eat. You would have starved to death six years ago without them."

She winced. "Sorry."

The cloth of his outfit rustled, and she pictured him shrugging. "We come from different places. We've had different ways of surviving. I lucked out being the apprentice to Maestro Kozonio. I'm hoping to learn all his secrets so I can keep us alive for years to come."

"Can this really keep going for years?" she asked. "My brother doesn't think so."

"It has to," Maej said. "Doesn't it? What's the alternative? We all die."

She shuddered and kept walking, her head lifted to feel the currents of air washing over her cheeks and forehead. They were changing. Something blocked the flow ahead. "We're near the Runic Ward. We're coming up on the wall. The gate you came through will be to the left."

This strange pit formed in her. She had just met this Maej, and as much as he had her emotions tossed to and fro with his causal comments, he knew about the Light. And he had access to good food. To clothing. He had so much that she lacked.

"It's a shame we're here," she said, hearing her voice echo back, reflected by a large surface before them. "I would like to learn more about runes."

"There's a lot to teach. You have to make arguments," he said. "Logical explanations to make the world change. To convince the energy to do the work at your direction. The really powerful stuff, which probably includes the Light, requires multiple clauses all working together in harmony. You have to make it elegant. I'm not so good at that yet."

"That was all sour mud spilling from your mouth," she said, "but it's interesting. If you were to draw a rune, you could change anything. You could make a stick into metal."

"Sure," he said. "If I could see, of course."

She bit her lip. "They won't let me pass, will they?"

"Probably not," he said. "Our people don't trust outsiders. Not even before Darkfall."

"You trusted me."

He paused and then she felt her hand reach out. He missed her arm and landed on her hip, his fingers sliding over her stomach. This strange, nervous heat ran through her. Did he want to use her? To take her? Maybe he would give her runic items or food if she...

There was one thing her brother never would allow her to trade, but she was a woman now. Fifteen, if she had her count correct. She had breasts. She'd heard Zhee and her brother enough. Her stomach rumbled. If she could get wood from Maej or food...

His fingers moved a little lower as she thought through her decision.

"You're not wearing clothes," he gasped, ripping his hand away from the edges of her pubic hair. "I didn't mean to try and touch you there. I'm so very sorry. I was looking for your hand."

Amusement bubbled through her. He didn't want to take from her. Then she blinked, realizing she was considering giving it to him. Well, he was a sweet boy and not some brute who tried to force her out in the muck.

"Here," she said, taking his hand. It was warm and so clean compared to hers. She flushed, feeling the dirt and grime on her body now. She suddenly wanted to run away, but he held her so tight.

"I could meet you outside the walls," he said. "There's a side door around the corner overlooking the Escarpment. The ledge is wide enough to stand on. No one uses it. Say, an hour after Light tomorrow?"

"You want to see me again?" she asked in shock.

He laughed. "Isn't language amazing? You still use a phrase like 'see you' even in the pitch black. But, yes, I'd love to talk to you. I can tell you about runes, and you could tell me about what it's like out there. It doesn't sound pleasant."

"It's not," she said, her voice soft. She considered it. *I can convince him to get me food. Runic items. Other things. I could learn about the caravans.* A warmth fluttered through her belly. *And it would be wonderful to speak with him again.* "Could you bring me something you made? Something runed. Like, I don't know..."

"A knife?" he asked. "I could shape one out of anything and turn it into steel. It's easy."

"You'd do that for me?" she asked in shock. *That's so valuable.*

"Sure," he said. There was this innocence about him. Tears suddenly stung her eyes. "After Light." He swallowed and squeezed her hand. "If my maestro survived... If he didn't, there might never be the Light again."

Horror washed through her before she beat it down. No, no, the Light had to happen. It was one of the few things good in the city. "He's alive. You'll see. The Light will be back."

"The Light will be back," he said, squeezing her hand.

She squeezed him back. "So I'll be here. Tomorrow. An hour after Light."

"Good. I am glad I met you, Amiollea. The universe must have thrown us together for a reason."

"Yeah," she said even as she regretted releasing his hand. She swallowed. "The wall's near us. Just walk forward. You'll find it. Go left. Bye, Maej."

～

MAEGWIRIO FELT the smile on his lips as she said bye to him. He liked that she called him Maej. He'd never had a nickname before. He flexed his fingers as she walked away. The heat of her slowly bled from the skin even as her aroma lingered.

It was pungent, to be fair, but there was something beneath it. Something exciting. He swallowed at the fire stiffening his loins. He hoped she would show up tomorrow. Giving her a rune-made dagger was a small price to pay to "see" her. It wouldn't even take much work, just cut up some old leather and use the runes to transmute it into steel. Then a few other runes to sharpen it. An afternoon's worth of work.

She sounded like it was a priceless treasure.

Maybe it was. He felt the darkness around him as the fact he was now alone sank in. Fear for Maestro Kozonio, Eddakwio the Warden, and the others flitted through him. People he knew were dead while he'd been chatting with a pretty girl.

Guilt flushed through him. He stumbled toward the wall, hoping he went in the right direction. The confidence he had walking in the dark vanished without her there. He waved his hands before him, sweeping them out as he felt for something. He struggled to understand how she could just *sense* things around her.

She knew the wall was over—

He brushed the smooth exterior of melted stone. It was runed together to form a thick, impenetrable wall. It had steel in the center, a barrier created in case the Karadrisans ever turned on his people.

He felt the old runes, the will imposed by Runecarvers long moldering in their graves back in Taechiz. He followed the sweep of the wall, keeping his right hand on it, his robes rustling. The noise sounded so loud to his ears now. His footsteps were even louder. He cringed as he wondered if he was being noticed by the mucklings. Those that lived around here were the Ratters, he reminded himself.

They respected Runecarvers.

We buy enough of their rats, he thought. The Glowers gave plenty of food, but only to those who did work. There were many Taechizians who relied on the Runecarvers' generosity to keep them fed. His people didn't abandon each other.

He never realized that the Karadrisans did do that. And what about the Povazian laborers who were imported by the thousands to carry heavy burdens and build the grand homes of the rich? Had they been thrown out into the dark?

It wasn't right. Runecarvers could be doing something for everyone. They could ensure all had food. Maegwirio never realized how insulated his people were from what was truly happening in the city. They relied too much on what the Glowers told them.

Maybe we should be paying attention, he thought.

Just as he was about to follow that line, he brushed something. Metal. Smooth. The gate. Relief surged through him. He banged on it and shouted in his tongue, "It's Maegwirio. Hello! I'm out here alone!"

"Maegwirio?" a voice asked. A loud clang echoed. Then the gates swung inward, pulling away from his hand. "Just you? Where are the others? What happened?"

"We were ambushed," Maegwirio said. The shock of saying those words aloud made him tremble. Now he was safe, and panic fell on him. "I don't know if the others are alive or dead."

Someone guided him into the guardhouse which was black as night. But there were people around him. More and more Taechizians gathered while he drank cool water and struggled to relate what happened. He left out Amiollea, some instinct whispering that the elders wouldn't be happy he was meeting with a muckling girl tomorrow.

An hour later, as a search party was readying to go out, shouts echoed. The gates opened and cheers erupted. Survivors returned. Maegwirio gained his feet, struggling to listen for the tap-tap of his maestro's staff.

He struggled to filter out the other noises. He was certain Amiollea would have heard everyone coming, but he was blinded by his eyes. He didn't know how to see with his skin. How could he when he wore clothes? The heat of her smooth belly and the brush of her nether hair filled his mind for a moment.

He pushed down the memory, focusing on the sounds.

"He's here?" a voice croaked. "Maegwirio? He made it back?"

"Maestro?" the young man gasped in relief. He moved out into the crowd, jostling into strangers. They parted for him. "You're alive, Maestro?"

"Because some muckling knocked me to the ground," his maestro said, his voice cracked. He sounded ancient.

Maegwirio seized the old man in a strong hug. Thin arms returned the embrace.

"That saved me like poor Eoxhinea had on Darkfall," the maestro continued. "The man beside me was caught in my place." The horror in the old man's voice stirred those memories of Death whispering from above, the unseen claws ripping and tearing.

"We saved all we could," snarled a Karadrisan voice in their tongue. "Lucky we came when we did. Saw that light blazing and went running, knowing someone needed help."

"Who's that?" asked Maegwirio.

"Captain Fhaaghin, commander of Lord Achogear's men," the maestro answered. "They were out in the ruins hunting a thief. They were tracking a runed dagger he stole. We found it in Eddakwio's throat."

Something lurched inside of Maegwirio. "He's dead?"

"Muckling hit him where his armor didn't protect him." Bitterness twisted the maestro's words. "They all deserve to have their runes destroyed!

Sun Ravagers are going to suffer for this. Captain Fhaaghin and his men are going across the Sun's Ashes to deal with them. They want to find this thief."

"Good," said Maegwirio, reeling from learning the former runic knight had died. *How did I survive when Eddakwio did not?*

He helped his maestro back to the Spire. After preparing them a meal of algae and rat meat, he found his thoughts not drifting to his stolen satchel nor to the Sun Ravagers who wanted to kill his people. He wondered about a muckling girl crossing a city all by herself surrounded by peril and unseen dangers.

CHAPTER
TWELVE

Hours had passed. Hours.

Ablisio's pacing before the hovel had worn a furrow into the mud. He couldn't stop marching back and forth. Too much time had passed. Something had happened to his sister. One of the piss-drinking savages had seized her and made her his whore.

Ablisio had failed his mother.

The thought burned a pit through his stomach. He felt the acids leaking out. He clutched at his side as he stared sightlessly into the murk of darkness. Reflexively, his eyes twitched at any noise his sensitive ears picked up. Zhee stood behind him, so tense her worry almost radiated like heat from her.

What would he do without Amiollea?

Her presence had kept him strong when the darkness fell. Holding her small, trembling form on his lap forced him to stay in control. He couldn't forget the terrible panic he'd felt when first surrounded by a night so deep he couldn't see the tears spilling hot down his sister's face. How could he not forge himself into a weapon to cleave through the black and keep her alive?

He'd had no choice but to figure out how to survive. To move without sight. To see with his skin and ears. To open up his senses. All for his little sister, and now she was lost.

How would he find her?

Just as panic almost overwhelmed him, he *sensed* her.

Amiollea.

The pad of her soft footsteps on mud. The scent of her rising over the fetid rot of dead trees thrusting out of the mud in some mockery of their former glory. She returned to him. He listened for the sound of her steps.

Firm. Confident.

"Ablisio!" Her voice rang out of the darkness, bursting with girlish exuberance. "I—"

"Where in the muck and slime have you been?" he growled and marched at her. "What shit-infested pool did you crawl through?"

He couldn't stop the anger bursting out of him. He didn't want to. He had *worried* for hours and hours. He had twisted and tangled and mangled his insides with stress over what had happened to her, and she returned with such flippant ease.

"Ablisio?" she gasped, recoiling.

He found her by following the air shifting around her body. He gripped her arms and breathed in deeply. He smelled her scent, but there was something foreign. A trace of blood. Not hers. And a male's scent he didn't recognize. Too clean to be a muckling. She gasped as he hauled her right before him. He felt her breath explode on his face as he stared down at her.

"Tell me, Amiollea," he growled. "Where were you all day while we were terrified you'd had your head bashed in? Or some shit-smeared muckling had made you his doxy and was passing you around to all his crap-brained friends?"

"Ablisio," she gasped, squirming. "Not so tight."

"Tell me!" he shouted, a shout louder than he'd made in years. "You think you can just slink off whenever you want! That you can traipse around this fetid mire and nothing bad will happen to you?"

"I was careful," she muttered. "I just wanted to see the Light."

"That damned Light is death!"

She flinched in his arms. Her entire body trembled, and he smelled the hot tears. "I-I-I . . . I just wanted . . . t-to get away . . . or a bit . . ."

"Get away from what? Safety?" The pain in his belly fed the fire. "From me? Are you an idiot?"

"No!" she sobbed. "I just . . . It's this . . . and then . . . I found something! Something we can use. Or someone!"

"That male I smell on you." His hands tightened on her arms. He ignored how she squirmed. "Don't tell me you let some slimy Ratter at you? Do you think I'd trade you for food?"

"I met a Runecarver!"

Her words smacked through his anger. "What?"

"A Runecarver." She shuddered. "I was by the Runic Ward."

Zhee groaned behind him.

Amiollea stiffened in his arms. "Yes, I went that far. I wanted to see the Light up close. It was glorious, Ablisio. You might want to just spend all day rutting on your whore, but I don't want to hear that. So I left. Went for a walk."

"Across half the muck-filled city? Death kills us all, how stupid are you?"

"I'm not stupid!" she shrieked. "While I was out there, I found an opportunity. A way to get things. Resources. I met a Runecarver boy. He was nice. I saved his life."

So shocked, Ablisio forgot about his anger and didn't even interrupt her as she talked about stalking a Runecarver caravan. It was the most blitheringly stupid thing he'd ever heard. Dangerous. The blue-skins had magic. Enchanted weapons. Unknown devices. No one could be safe around them. They were worse than the Glowers. The Runecarvers kept those rich, pampered, clean bastards alive. The blue-skin bastards ignored the rest of Hamiocho, leaving the mucklings, including his sister, half-starved and crawling through the rot.

It was a miracle every day Ablisio and his small family hadn't died of disease.

Amiollea's voice quavered as she described the Sun Ravagers igniting the torch.

Memories sparked in Ablisio's imagination. Death whispered. Flashes of Darkfall burned through his mind. The horror of his mother rising into the air, unseen talons thrust through her body. Her screams as it ripped her in half.

"He agreed to meet with me," Amiollea finished. "Tomorrow. He's going to give me a knife!"

"In exchange for what?" Ablisio asked, clammy with sweat. "For you to fall to your knees and please his cock?" His stomach churned at the thought of his sister doing that.

"No!" snapped Amiollea. "He's not a degenerate like all the other *men* in the city."

"Are you calling me a degenerate?" Ablisio asked, cheeks warming. Zhee had taken him in her mouth many times.

"No, no, you're a man." She sighed then muttered, "Not your fault that big-titty leach latched onto you."

He ignored her snide words. What would he do if his sister ever made him choose between herself and Zhee?

"He just wants to talk," Amiollea continued. "Learn about the outside. He's interested. And he's from the Spire. His maestro *makes* the Light. He's going to teach me things and . . ." She drew in a deep breath. "There's going to be more caravans. If we're careful, we can steal from them. They have guards, and they're skilled in the dark, but we're better. They don't have special defenses on their goods, either. If we sneak into their midst, we can grab sacks of food. We can steal meat, Ablisio. Salted beef! Enough to last us weeks. I think they use the same route. They walked it like it was familiar. You wanted to be bold. This is it. Our chance to make things easier for ourselves!"

Ablisio swallowed. He didn't want to reward her behavior, but . . . His stomach rumbled. Salted beef. Real food like they ate before everything fell apart. Not algae. Not slimy fish. Not even stringy rat. He just had to let his sister out of his sight.

It was such a risk. Runecarvers . . .

"Will you let me meet him tomorrow?" she asked, such trepidation in her voice.

What did this the boy want with her? A Runecarver interested in a muckling? Of course, he wanted her body. Probably would laugh to his friends about the dirty slattern he used outside the wall. The idea of some man pawing over his little sister, of abusing her trust, sickened him.

"No," he said coldly.

"But, I prom—"

"No!" he snarled louder. "I'm not letting you cross half the damned city so you can trust a stranger to give you a knife. Maybe he seemed nice when you were helping him return, but how do you know he won't try to harm you?"

"Because he wouldn't," she protested. "I just know it. Not every man in Hamiocho is a vile pig. You're not."

"I thought you said I was like all the others. You all but accused me of taking advantage of Zhee."

"You don't do that!" she hissed back. "She takes advantage of you. Please, Ablisio. We need food. The algae won't last much longer. Do you want to go to the dispensaries with sacks full of shit and hope the price hasn't gone up *again?*"

"I'd rather muck around Phosphor Lake for algae and risk Death than lose you." He put his hand on his sister's shoulder. "And that's what will happen!"

"Ablisio?" Zhee whispered behind him. "You can't do that."

"*I* will do what it takes to keep you both alive and safe." He pulled his sister to him and hugged her. "I'm not losing you, Amiollea. I'm not failing Mother. You're not going."

She squirmed in his embrace, struggling to break free. She screeched, vicious and vile. "I hate you! I'm grown up! I can take risks, too! I don't want to lose you, idiot! Let me help! This is safer!"

"No!" he growled and released her. "I've kept you alive this long. I know what I'm doing."

She hissed a sound of pure frustration before she marched from him and into the hovel. He heard her sit. Her sobs echoed from inside. They resounded through the small shaft. He wanted to keep up his anger, to be strong, but her pain dug at his resolve.

Zhee padded up to him.

"I won't let that little bastard use her," he growled.

"She wants to use him. It's different."

"I'm sure you know about using men," spat Ablisio. He winced the moment the words came out.

"I do," Zhee said. "I used you in the beginning. We used each other." She touched his arm. "She doesn't want to use him *that* way. She's . . ."

"What?"

"Nothing." There was something in Zhee's voice. Almost amusement. "You need to give her some room. Some independence."

"She doesn't understand. I'm not always going to be there to protect her." How long could anyone live in this terrible place? The things he had to do to keep them alive . . . "She has to be smart for when that day comes. She won't get it by trusting this Runecarver."

"You're wrong," Zhee said as she broke away and headed for the hovel. "I trusted you. It worked out pretty well for me. You can't be the only good man left in Hamiocho."

"It's not this pissant. He just wants to drain his berries."

"You can't keep her on a leash forever."

Of course, I can!

He turned to face the darkness. He'd have to be vigilant. She couldn't be allowed to go off on her own. He or Zhee had to be with her at all times.

CHAPTER THIRTEEN

Fur ran across his fingers.

A hot tongue bathed his face.

Thoughts returned to Emmait.

He rose from the fugue of terror, his fingers buried deep into Sun's coat. The dog's hot tongue slathered across his cheek, lapping up grime and tears. The shocking return to sensate awareness rocked through Emmait. He trembled, his chest heaving. The last he remembered was the whispers of Death swirling through the blazing light the damned mad cultist unleashed.

He'd fled the Runecarver, clutching his stolen satchel. He had felt it swinging from his shoulders. Then he'd collapsed behind a building. He must have wandered without knowledge through two miles of the city to return to Sun. Stumbling without awareness.

The tragic possibilities that could have befallen him in such a state frightened Emmait as much as everything else.

He clutched Sun, hugging his dog tight. He luxuriated in the warmth of fur. The comfort of the tongue now licking at his ear. He shook, ragged sobs bursting from his raw throat. Choked sounds of masticated grief. He'd never come so close to Death. Never come so close to the chthonic horror swirling in the sky of this cursed city.

Holding Sun proved he lived. He found hope as he clutched tighter to his pet. His dog yelped, squirming. Emmait gasped, releasing his grasp. His hands planted on the dirty stones he sat upon. He brushed something metal with his fingertips as Sun sprang back, claws scrambling. After a moment, the dog darted back in and nuzzled into Emmait's chest.

"Sorry," Emmait said. He drew breaths down his ravaged throat. His voice sounded worse than a file grinding off rust.

His fingers brushed the metal again. Cool steel. A sharp edge. Not his knife. He had shattered memories of planting that in the throat of one of the Runecarver guards. Then he'd snatched up a blade.

The guard's weapon.

He found the hilt and lifted the sword before him. The coolness radiating from the metal from it brushed his cheek. It disturbed the air before him. His left hand slid down the blade, exploring the weapon. It was as wide as three of his fingers and possessed a crossguard hilt. He felt runes inscribed in the blade along a strange furrow down the center of the weapon. The blade narrowed to a chisel-like point. It felt light in his hand. Balanced. The pommel had ornamentation on it, feeling like three trefoils around a disc.

"A runed blade," Emmait said in awe. Not just a knife. This was a weapon that would never dull or rust. It would get dirty, but it could be cleaned with ease. He could buy himself a harem of Ratter women with it or be fed by the Blind Fishers for life.

Or until they slip the blade in my guts and use my innards as bait.

The sword was one of the most valuable objects in the city. Too valuable to ever trade. In most fights, a rotten chair leg or a piece of shattered masonry acted as a weapon. This would inflict real damage.

Sun stiffened. A low growl rumbled from the dog.

Emmait straightened and turned his attention, struggling to get his bearings. He'd left Sun near the Runecarvers' gate when he went off on his own. Sun always waited patiently for his return, so he was confident that must be where he was. Out of the darkness came the growing sound of footsteps. A column of soldiers. Armor jingled. There was a difference to this sound. A change in the style of armor some of the guards wore. There were more guards than the Runecarvers had with them.

Glower soldiers sent to help the Runecarvers after the attack?

He crouched low, breathing shallowly through his open mouth to minimize any noise. Sun stood ridged by him. The gates opened on squeaking hinges. Shouts and cries burst from the city. Sobs and exultation. A reunion. Cheers. And the wails of grief. Emmait shifted at the sound of community. For seven years, he'd had only Sun.

No one else.

In the muck, it was hard for anyone to care about anyone beyond how they could help *you* survive. From Runecarvers, he heard genuine sounds of delight mixed with the real pain of loss. He knew he should leave, sneak off before they realized a muckling lurked so close to their gate, but their commotion echoed through the emptiness inside of him.

His mother rose in his mind. Always smiling. Always happy in the silks and jewels given to her by Lord Achogear. Though she'd showered Emmait in affection, she'd also shared her love with *him*. Still, Emmait had found a home in the household even if he were the bastard. Up until Darkfall came and he became a burden. Something useless.

A castoff.

These were the sounds of people who'd never been thrown out. He listened to their celebration. It drifted away from the gate into the heart of their closed community. Their little paradise above the rest of the muck.

The one place no thief had the bravado to risk. Emmait certainly wouldn't climb their walls. Those walls were covered in death if you didn't know how to use runes. Alarms would resound. Lights would illuminate you.

Death would come.

As the sounds drifted away, he realized the soldiers remained near the gate. In fact, they were walking out of it, their armor jingling. They were talking with someone, their voices becoming clear as they approached Emmait.

"How are you going to find the Sun Ravager thief now that he's lost the dagger?"

"Take the war to the Sun Ravagers," answered the familiar tones of Captain Fhaaghin. The head of Lord Achogear's guard *still* hunted Emmait.

They could track the dagger? His hands tightened on the sword. *Do they know I have this? Do they assume it's lost?* The urge to throw down the treasure seized him for one wild moment.

"If this thief's one of Cinder's, we'll force that crazy bastard to release him," continued Captain Fhaaghin. "We'll also teach him and his vermin not to attack the Runecarvers again."

"We would be most grateful. The caravan will be setting out tomorrow. Early. Expect us."

"I'm sure the merchants will. My boys and I are heading out into the Sun's Ashes."

Nasty laughs echoed from the soldiers. Emmait swallowed. He lived in the Sun's Ashes. It was his favorite place to lie low. Many thought it was cursed after the Sun Ravagers had set it alight. It didn't help that Cinder and his followers haunted the westernmost end of the city beyond the ruins, listening to the madman preach his insanity.

Wanting to stay far away from Captain Fhaaghin and his men, Emmait decided to go east to Phosphor Lake. Maybe he'd hide in the Perfumed Bog or the Rotting Orchard. Perhaps even farther east in the Povazian Slums. It was near the Reek where the dead were first collected after Darkfall. A stinking, rotting charnel pit haunted by the foulest of the mucklings.

Cannibals.

The soldiers marched out. The gate closed. Emmait listened to them departing as he decided on his course. He would cross the Sluggish Waters and get as far from those guards hunting him as he could. As he waited for them to depart, he opened the satchel he stole, hoping for food.

He smelled something dry. It crinkled. He reached in and found paper. He frowned at such a useless item. The satchel itself was valuable, but he was hoping for more. He reached deeper and found a glass container. He opened it; took a sip.

Gagged and spluttered.

A bitter, iron smell filled him. Ink? He dumped it out. The vial was small, but maybe he could come up with some use for it. Last, he found a quill made of metal with a sharp point to it, but it felt too flimsy to be a weapon. He sighed, his stomach rumbling. He tore off a piece of parchment.

You're made from plants, right? Dim memories of a life in the light rushed up to him. He popped the piece into his mouth.

It had a bitter flavor. He grimaced as it dissolved into pulp in his mouth. He kept chewing it anyways. Then he tore off a large chunk and chewed on it. It sucked up the moisture from his mouth. A raw thirst beset him.

He had to find water and wash out the ink.

He headed down into the Slithering Pit to search for clean water while eating pieces of parchment.

∼

MAEGWIRIO FOUND comfort in cutting the piece of leather. Focusing on his task kept his memories away from the chaos of the attack and the terror of the torch. He had never feared a flame until he heard the whispers of Death in the air.

Keeping his promise to Amiollea seemed a better use of his mental energies.

His maestro had retired to bed. Maegwirio should have been in his own. A second caravan would head out early in the morning to finish their mission, but he feared closing his eyes right now. It was better to follow the stencil he'd traced of the very knife he now used to cut the leather.

He sat at his workbench before a heavy desk, battered in spots by dropped objects and gouged in others by slipped tools. Shelves surrounded him, full of all manner of materials held in small containers of ceramics. Each had a rune painted on them, identifying what they held. From types of cloth (wool, cotton, linen, more), to metals (iron, various alloys of steel, nickel, more), to different woods, clays, muds, and plant fibers.

He cut the tanned cowhide with care, the smooth surface sliding beneath his fingers. He finished cutting out the shape of the blade, a triangular section of material. He set that to the side before he molded clay into a handle. He kept shaping it until it was about right and turned it into the wood with runes. From then, he shaped it with a knife to finish it off.

A good Runecarver needed to be an adequate craftsman. Maestro Kozonio preferred wood so Maegwirio knew the art well. He worked, the shaving landing on the table. The runed knife had no problem cutting through the wood. It wouldn't dull; the Runes of Intensification gave it a razor-honed edge.

He hummed as he worked, something he remembered his mother doing when she painted sitting before her easel. Her brush flowed, creating an ordered picture out of the chaos of smeared linseed oil paints on her palette.

He found comfort in the memory. He wondered how his family was doing. If they still prospered in Taechiz. Did the world even still exist outside the Darkwall? What if they were the only ones who'd survived, or if this catastrophe had befallen more of the world than just Hamiocho?

He retreated from such dark thoughts.

Instead, he pictured his mother humming as she painted while he carved the handle.

Even if he suffered in the dark, the rest of the world must still have the light.

Maegwirio finally finished shaping the handle and brought it to the leather blade. He fit the leather strip into a groove he cut in it. First, he used Runes of Incorporation. They had to be drawn finely. He didn't have much room to work with. He produced a slender-bladed instrument with a narrow, metal handle.

He carved a simple declaration.

"*Ahzorrox kwaeb wif zopapazin soriakwif.*" He carved each symbol, using the flexible verb *iakwif*, which meant "to unite," in the future maintenance tense to join them. It formed the final ideograph in the sentence. He had the meaning fixed in his mind and pressed his will into the runes.

His runes tapped into the potential energy waiting beyond this reality and channeled it. He didn't hear any change, but he could feel the bending of reality. He picked up the shaped handle and the leather rose to it. The two materials united into one impossible object.

It was a simple joining. Something he'd mastered several years ago. It didn't require supporting clauses that all affected each other. A simple sentence. Object. Subject. Verb. The next one would require two clauses, more advanced work.

He rose and moved to the shelf with the metals. He examined the runes until he found a good alloy of steel. A carbon-iron mixture with an additive of nickel. Perfect for knives. He plucked out a sliver of the metal and returned to the worktable. He placed it on the blade and carved a set of runes on the hilt.

"*Abbefi kia chifabbeoched zotteg, ye eokwa xhahzorrox iak zopar koll.*"

This argument would turn the leather and wood into metal, using the sliver as the guide for what type of metal. If he didn't have that, he'd have to write out all the properties of the metal including the percentage of various base metals. It would be a long sentence, multiple clauses that all had to reinforce each other and make a logical progression. If he messed up his grammar or syntax, it would fail.

He hadn't here.

The power rushed into the dagger and washed like a wave, transforming it into the gleaming sheen of steel. The soft texture of leather vanished. The pale grain of wood vanished beneath a metallic sheen. He picked it up, the united parts cool in his hands. The blade, however, needed work. It still had the dull thickness of leather.

It was more the idea of a dagger.

Runes of Incorporation were no longer needed. He had to shift to another category. Runes of Destruction. He had to strip away material to form a sharp edge. It was a delicate sentence. Complex, but within his skills. He had done this sort of work before.

"*Yoziti rarrisoll akeddef xhon ab kwutzix, kwaeb agw zip ras zottedi akwal, un chebbil.*"

Metal sheared off the knife as if an invisible blade slashed toward the edges, shearing off the material again and again, working with care. Maegwirio felt that touch of awe. It was easy to forget when by drawing delicate runes. He had to make every stroke perfect. He couldn't rush. The applications of runic magic were vast.

The limitation was time.

It took so long to learn. To form the runes with the right precision. It meant the child wouldn't be able to help around the house or farm, forgoing chores and learning crafts that would help the family to study the esoteric. It was an investment that had to be paid for upfront. Their instructor, even one of the three maestros, had to be compensated for their time because training apprentices took away from their ability to produce their own crafts.

Making even a knife took time.

It took even longer to scratch the runes into the metal now that it had turned into a solid piece of steel. They weren't elegant runes. He certainly didn't acid-etch it. He just had to be careful. It took strength and a steady hand.

The blade shaped, he brought his diamond-tipped stylus to the metal and began carving his next argument using Runes of Intensification.

"*Omab edge zorarris sorran.*"

With that, it would never lose its edge. It would be sharp until the end of eternity.

Lastly, the most important one for the climate of Hamiocho, he used a Rune of Adaptation. This dagger was made of steel, but steel could corrode. So he had to prevent rust and oxidation. The metal would be inured from the elements.

"*Latzen zorarris soraeghil.*"

It took an hour to scratch that last sentence. The muscles in his forearm burned from the strain of scratching into the metal. The noise echoed through the workshop. His eyes were bleary from the strain, but he kept his focus up long enough to make the last inscription and allow the potential energy to flow through his words.

Now the blade could sit in the most brackish water and not pit and rust.

He leaned back in his chair and fought a yawn. His mouth opened into a wide cavern, eyes squeezing shut. As he did, the door opened. His maestro peered in, his eyes blurry. His wrinkled fingers held the door handle tight.

"Have you been in here all night?" Maestro Kozonio asked.

"Making a knife," he said. "I wanted to practice. Maybe have something to show the Glowers I have the skill to make quality items."

"Are you offering this as a trade?" asked Kozonio as he leaned in. He glanced at the shavings of the knife and the leather. "Interesting methodology."

"I didn't want to use any resources that couldn't be spared," he said, flushing. "You know, it's just practice."

"Excellent practice." The maestro picked up the blade. "It's not the most elegant blade. The weight's a bit off, but it's good. Looks sharp. You made fine runes. Good control on the scratches." He placed his free hand on Maegwirio's bright, metallic hair, rustling it with bluish fingers. "Very good indeed. Yes, yes, this should impress them."

"Thank you, Maestro," he said. "I hope it impresses. I just have to make a scabbard."

"Mmm, hurry, we leave in an hour."

"An hour?" he gasped. "The night's over?"

The maestro chuckled as he walked out of the room. "You are in for a long day. Good thing you are young. It'll be hours yet before you can find your bed."

He didn't feel tired as he picked up his knife. He smiled. He had made this on his own. Amiollea had to be impressed. He imagined what she could look like. A young face emerged, his age. Only, it was a Taechizian face. He struggled to remember what Karadrisans looked like. They had that rich, brown skin, not the palish blue he had. Her hair would be probably red. Probably. He pictured her with red hair cut short.

That felt right.

But, now, how would she cut her hair if they don't have knives? Is it just a wild tangle? A matted mane?

He knew she went naked, his fingers remembering the brush of her nether hair. He found himself thinking about her figure. From overhearing the gossip of wardens, he had a good idea about Karadrisan women. They were tall but lacked the curvaceous beauty of Povazian women. No overflowing bosoms, but modest breasts.

He didn't know when he crossed into sleep, but his dream version of Amiollea was there. Clean, standing in the light, her hair a fine shower of red. She let him touch her nether hairs this time. And do more than that. This warmth suffused the dream. A wild urgency and a fiery burst of passion.

A hand shook him as he struggled to hold onto the sweetness of the dream. He came awake, his cheek resting on the square leather he'd worked on. Drool had cemented it to his face. He blinked, seeing his maestro over him, shaking his head.

"No time for that scabbard now," he said. "Come on, nap is over."

"Nap?" he asked. "I . . ." Then Maegwirio felt the stickiness in his britches. A flush of heat washed through him. "I need to change my clothes."

"What's wrong with what you're wearing?" the old man asked.

"Nothing!" he gasped, his voice squeaking and breaking. "I just . . ." He fought the urge to cover himself. Then he fled to his room while memories of that sweet dream lingered in his thoughts. He couldn't wait to speak with Amiollea again.

He looked forward to it more than meeting the Glowers and showing off his rune-carving skill. Even more than unraveling the mystery of what his maestro did atop the Spire every day at noon.

CHAPTER
FOURTEEN

"I don't want you to go muckraking," Zhee whispered worriedly to Ablisio. He was setting out with one of their few burlap sacks. They were valuable since they survived longer in the rot and mold than other cloths. But they didn't last forever. "It's too dangerous."

"Stepping out to piss is dangerous," he muttered. "I'll be fine."

Zhee bit her lip. It was the next "morning" since Amiollea had vanished and come back excited by her new Runecarver friend. She'd been moping ever since, needling her brother, begging to go see the boy. Their arguments would flare up every so often, making the cramped shack feel even tinier.

The walls closed in on Zhee.

"Why don't you come and gather dung with Amiollea and me?" Zhee pressed. "If we all work together, we can get enough to feed us in a day or so."

"You don't know that," he said. "This is *certain*."

"If you come back," she said, her heart aching. She held her belly. Her monthly hadn't arrived. She had a child growing in her. A mix of her and Ablisio. Would this one survive, or in a month or two would she have a heavy flow?

Did she want to bring a child into this nightmarish world? A part of her was desperate for a piece of Ablisio. She could feel how tenuous was the tether between them. It had to snap one day. He would finally be forced to choose Amiollea, casting Zhee aside to keep protecting his sister.

Assuming he didn't die today trying to feed them.

She feared being alone, but if she had a child, a little bit of him to hold when she was lonely and starving...

We'd both just die together, she thought. *Or some muckling would find me again. They wouldn't waste time on a squalling babe.* Maybe a Ratter would let his "wives" keep a few children around, but most others wouldn't. She was certain Ablisio would, but not if he left her.

Dread froze her belly.

She wanted to cling to him but knew that would only make him shove her away. Amiollea was the key. She had to win the girl's support. If they were allies, Ablisio would never have to make that decision.

"I can go muckraking with you," Amiollea said. "Watch your back."

"I am not taking you a step toward Phosphor Lake!" snapped Ablisio. "You'll go with Zhee and help her find dung. I'll keep us fed until then."

"If you let me go—"

"I don't want to hear about that blue-stained bastard!" Ablisio's words thundered through the shack. Zhee flinched beneath their intensity. "You are never going that far alone. You are not going to be some Runecarver's whore. His people will never let you past their walls. They hate outsiders. If you're not born with sapphire in your blood, they don't give a dog's testicle about you."

"Maej does," muttered Amiollea. "He's going to give me a knife."

"Sure he is!" Ablisio spat. The saliva splattered on the ground to Zhee's right. "After he's enjoyed you, I'm sure he'll hand over a knife worth two weeks of food to some muckling girl he's just met."

"Yes, he will!" Amiollea stamped her foot.

"If you sneak off on Zhee, I will stalk across this city, find you, and drag you back by your hair. I mean it, Amiollea, I didn't spend seven years keeping you alive so you could get your head bashed in begging for scraps from a Runecarver."

"Don't we always just beg for scraps? I want to do something bold! Something to help us survive. We can use him!"

"I'm being bold. I'm muckraking!"

Zhee shuddered. Stealing from Runecarvers, using this boy, sounded far, far safer than muckraking or even collecting shit to trade to the dispensaries for algae. She'd rather let a Ratter rut on her body for food than for Ablisio to head to the lake.

But he had made his decisions. And she made hers.

"Come on, Amiollea," Zhee said, brushing the girl's wrist. "Let's gather something useful and hope that the Wise Owl and Cunning Fox watch over your brother and keep him safe."

"Fine." The girl ripped her hand from Zhee's grasp. "Let's go, leech."

Zhee sighed. This had better work.

She hugged Ablisio, clutching tight to him, fearing she would never see him again. Twice he'd muckraked. She'd rather him climb the Rubble and steal from Glowers. Who knew what Death did to a person they killed. Did they steal their souls? Glowers would just stab you with a spear or ram a sword through your heart.

"Don't get too close to the lake," she whispered. "We can go a day or two without food."

"I'll be fine. Don't let her out of your hearing."

"I'm not going to sneak away," Amiollea muttered. "I won't give your leech the satisfaction of tattling on me."

Zhee beat down that rush of anger. She understood Amiollea's bitterness. The anger that fueled it. Amiollea wasn't a child any longer, but she wasn't quite an adult. She hovered between them and needed an outlet. Her emotions were boiling like crazy.

Zhee only had sympathy for the girl.

However, some days, her patience wore perilously thin. How much more vitriol could she swallow before it drowned her?

She gathered up one of the clay urns they used to collect the algae, Amiollea her own. As Ablisio headed southwest toward the lake, the women went east to the Povazian slums where the shadow painters had their latrines. They didn't like to contaminate their work. It was dangerous searching for them. The mucklings in the surrounding neighborhoods could be violent.

Still, if the two women were quiet, if they moved with skill, they would be fine. Zhee had braved it alone many times to keep them alive. She knew the terrain. She never precisely felt comfortable without Ablisio and his runed-wood club close at hand, but she wasn't terrified.

She wasn't as brave as Amiollea. The girl had crossed half the city on her own. The idea bewildered Zhee.

And she couldn't believe she was about to allow the girl to do it again. Her stomach twisted. She waited until they were far enough from Ablisio so that he couldn't possibly hear what she had to say. On the edge of the rotting orchard, she whispered, "Go see your Runecarver. I will tell your brother you never got out of my earshot."

"What?" Amiollea gasped. "Why? What are you scheming?"

"You're right. This Runecarver is useful. That knife can be traded for food or kept for protection. If you can get him to get us food or other items, that would be a boon."

"So you're sending me across half the city so *you* can have a better chance of survival?"

"So *we* have a better chance," Zhee snapped back, her frustration mounting. "Don't you want to see the Runecarver boy?"

"Well, yes."

"So why are you arguing with me? Give your brother time to realize the strength of this plan, and until then, you keep up your contact with your friend. We can't lose this. Flirt with him."

"Flirt?" Amiollea choked.

"Yes, flirt. Be friendly. You're a girl, he's a boy. It'll come naturally enough to you."

"I've never talked with a boy before."

"You talked with him yesterday. You must have made an impression if he's making you a knife to show off."

Amiollea shifted. Her scent changed, a hint of excitement. "He's showing off?"

"Of course he is." Zhee laughed. "Oh, Amiollea, boys enjoy showing off.

They love it when girls appreciate what they can do. Even when they're being stupid."

"My brother does that a lot?"

"Yes, he does. We all are stupid from time to time. That's living. Now go. But don't spend too long. You have to get back to me so we can return. If your brother finds out, he's never letting you out of earshot again."

"Thank you," Amiollea said after a moment, her tone softer than usual. "I—"

"Just go," Zhee said, smiling. *And you better come back. Please, Wise Owl, watch her through the night. Clever Fox guide her steps. Don't let my selfishness get her killed.* "Hurry, but be safe. And trust your heart about this boy. I listened to my heart about your brother."

The girl set down her urn and headed off to the northwest.

∽

Zhee did something nice.

The thought rippled through the shocked, bemused, and excited turmoil of emotions roiling inside Amiollea as she headed west. She took the same path as she had when going to the escarpment, the steps memorized. She couldn't believe Zhee would defy Ablisio. If he found out, he would be furious with them both.

As much as she would love to have her brother *finally* turn on Zhee, she couldn't betray the Povazian woman. Not now that she had a chance to speak with Maej again. To learn about runes and caravans and ways they could get food. Real food. Not slimy algae.

But how do I flirt with him? Maej was the first boy beside Ablisio—and he didn't count—that she'd spoken to. This nervous heat billowed through her. This tingle awakened parts of her body she didn't know could feel such sensations. It scared her and drove her to move faster all at the same time.

She had this yearning deep in her core to be united. An itch that had her skin feeling alive. Reminding her that she was dirty. She reached the sluggish waters and, instead of crossing on the bridge, she sank into the current. She felt it around her, cool on her dirty body. She scrubbed the grime off her skin as stood half-floating with her head just above water.

She was making noise, but she wanted to be clean when she saw him. As clean as she could be considering she had to wade through the Slithering Pit to get to him. She felt the layers of muck on her dissolving as she rubbed her hands over her body. The gentle current carried it away. She imagined a dark streak flowing down the river from her.

Do I remember what water looks like? she thought. *Was it really clear? Mostly. Did dirt stain it like a cloud? Is my skin really brown? And what's blue? Is the sky the same color as Maej? Is his skin really blue like people say?*

Suddenly, she missed light. That bright and sunny world where the scariest thing was being chased by her brother when she broke one of his tin soldiers. That had always been more a fun game in another lifetime. The joy of an innocent and happy girl who had no worries. Who knew Mother would make her breakfast, lunch, and dinner. That when she slipped into her bed, she would wake up to the sun shining through her window in the morning.

Was that world ever real?

Is there only darkness?

No!

She panted in the water, her head snapping to the Spire. To where the Light flared every "noon." It was proof there was something like the sun. Something that shone bright. A beacon in this dark and twisted world. She would learn about it through Maej. She scrubbed harder at herself, the excitement to see him growing inside of her.

He held such promise for her.

Knowledge. A chance for a better life with her brother and even the leech. A way out of this foul pit of mud and muck. To experience light again, even for just a moment, was a startling thing.

She finished her scrubbing and knew—*knew* in the very depths of her soul where that hope shone so bright and dazzling—that this was the beginning of something better.

Her brother would see that.

Ablisio would be proud of her.

Fear warred with worry.

Ablisio approached Phosphor Lake. The deadliest place in all of Hamiocho. The reason why the Rotting Orchard made such a good place to hide. Most avoided coming even *that* close to what had once been the heart of the picturesque park in central Hamiocho. A place of green and life in the middle of brick buildings and cobblestone streets. An escape from the crushing bustle into pastoral nature. An orchard of pleasant apple trees and gardens of flowering plants.

The rich wives of the Glowers had sponsored the park for reasons Ablisio couldn't fathom.

The lake's green glow bled through the rotting foliage at the edge of the Rotting Orchard. He'd passed deep through the trees, the glow spreading in intensity. Already, it hurt his eyes. Branches appeared, reaching like skeletal fingers into the darkness.

The flesh of the dead earth oozed beneath his bare toes.

The same algae that grew beneath the roof of the Slime Fields festered in the lake. The stringy gunk in the lake provided the only natural light source in the city. Nothing scared Ablisio more than its radiance. Light revealed everything. It painted all with its illuminating brush.

Death...

It was easy for Ablisio to forget that chthonic horrors sailed through the air above his head. Sometimes, he might catch a faint whisper from them. A rustling of wind when the air was calm. The soft sigh when no one else was near you. Luckily, Death was blind. They didn't learn to see with their skin like Ablisio. They didn't have acute hearing and noses nearing the sharpness of bloodhounds.

Death only saw.

And if they witnessed life, they savaged it. The why didn't matter to Ablisio. Nor the how or the what. Survival meant staying out of the light.

Muckraking meant getting perilously close to it.

He stepped out of the last of the rotting orchard. What used to be a sweeping lawn leading to the lake was now oozing sludge, the grass long since rotted away and mashed into the muck. The lake was a brilliant sheen that illuminated the beach around it. Enough for Death to see you.

The waters rippled. No one knew why—questions were for people who had time to think and not to scrounge and fight and run—the water moved. Perhaps some hoary thing existed beneath all that algae, agitating the surface and sending waves to wash up the slope. Perhaps whatever fed the lake, some hidden spring, released water haphazardly, causing a sudden surge to increase the level of the lake and spread the algae across the shore. It was almost like a tide.

Whatever it was, it spread algae onto the shore. He could see the patches of fresh algae. It had spread recently. The freshest algae you could find that was safe to eat if you had the courage to rake through the muck to gather it. It would be good for a few days before it rotted and dissolved into the mud.

Ablisio's entire body trembled. Zhee and Amiollea were gathering dung. He should be with them, his cudgel ready to swing and defend them from attackers. He shouldn't be here. Only a fool would do this.

A fool with two women needing to eat.

The terror churning his stomach didn't stop him from taking the first fateful step out of the rotting orchard onto the muddy slope. The shadows were still strong here. He was still safe. He kept his ears pricked for whispers as he crept out.

His shoulders itched. He could see the shape of his feet now, the black mud oozing around the sides and between his toes. His arms moved with him, the burlap sack swinging from his grip. The ground had contours, divots full of water, and little rises of muck thrusting above the other. The closer he came to the lake, the more distinct things grew.

He had toes.

Fingers.

Hairs on his arms poked out of the grime.

He could see too much. He felt the weight of eyes upon him. His knees buckled. Terror boiled away in his belly. He tasted acid burning up his throat. The pain in his stomach intensified. His worry for his sister and Zhee. They needed to eat. They had to survive. Another day. Maybe, just maybe, this punishment would end.

Whatever ancient force or dark malevolence who'd cursed Hamiocho would relent. Hell would be lifted and they could be free in the sun. There had to be a way out of this. A way to make things better. They couldn't just fester in this rotting pit of a city.

Zhee and Amiollea didn't deserve it.

He crawled now. His fingers splayed in the mud. Touches of color highlighted his skin. Blue reflected on the highlights of mud, catching on bulging mounds and crumbling protrusions. His heart thundered. His body shook.

Could Death see him?

His fingers landed on something wet and clumpy. Not mud. Algae. A patch had washed up here and lost its glow, but it hadn't started rotting. He could feel the freshness. Despite the pain in his gut, the burning hole drilled by fear, a hungry rumble growled out of him. The impulse to shovel the algae into his mouth hit him.

He clutched it tight and thrust it into the sack instead. His fingers raked through the muck, gathering more of it. Life for his sister and Zhee. His shoulders itched. He wanted to flinch against the slashing talons of Death. He could feel the malevolence gathering above him.

A sigh.

He fell to his belly on the mud, squeezing his eyes shut. This was it. The hot stab of pain. The end of his life. Had he made Amiollea strong enough? Would she have the smarts to survive? The intelligence not to do something as stupid as this?

Would she look after Zhee?

Death didn't come.

He opened his eyes, his face rubbing into a sticky mound of algae. To his right, a shadow moved. He wasn't the only one muckraking. Another had crept out to gather the bounty and take the chance. The person appeared to be stuffing it straight into his mouth, feeding on it like an animal.

If Ablisio stayed on his belly, he would look like the mud. He could escape Death. If he just didn't move, he could survive.

So long as he worked with care, he would be fine.

He smeared algae off his cheek and shoved it into the bag. Followed by more scooped off the ground. He raked through the mud and found more of it. A large clump that he shoved into the bag.

He crawled forward, sweeping his hand out before him. He was coming close to the lake, but he was finding more food. Algae just as good as what the Glowers sold at the dispensary. He didn't have to kneel to get it. He was his own man.

He worked forward on his belly, his stomach rumbling.

A loud rippling drew his attention to the lake. The center bulged like something had broached the surface for a moment. Like a sea monster he'd heard in stories. A vast beast of rubbery tentacles that swallowed dolphins whole and cracked the hulls of ships that ventured out on the deep waters.

The lake rippled outward from the displacement. The wave grew as it approached the shore. Then it broke and sloshed the algae across the shore. A new band of glowing blue-green spilled onto the mud. The world grew a little brighter.

He worked his way to his right now, fearing coming any closer to the shore and the new glow. Ears pricked for any alien sounds, he gathered more and more algae. He piled it into his burlap sack. Knees dug furrows into the muck as he scooted forward. The bag grew heavier and heavier. His stomach burned with fearful acids. The bile vapors tickled the back of his throat.

Did he have enough?

Maybe a few days worth.

He could get more. There was so much algae. More than he'd ever found. The lake must have been particularly active the day before. He swept through it, gathering up more algae. He had a large patch. Another day's supply. It should last three days. He didn't get too close to the lake. He was fine. Death wouldn't get him.

A loud gurgle burst from the lake.

The waters in the center heaved upward and then splashed down. Three waves washed out in a concentric rings, the one in the center the largest. They churned through the algae. The blue-green glow intensified as the slimy growths rode the swell of the waves rushing to the shore. They broke in a triple crash of surging water.

It rushed at him, glowing with frothy brilliance. Ablisio's arms became stark, painted in the greenish radiance. Grime coated the beds of his fingernails. Stringy green wrapped about his fingers, algae clinging to him.

He could see a blurry nose at the bottom of his vision.

Whispers rushed above him.

Death can see me!

CHAPTER
FIFTEEN

Noon approached as Amiollea leaned against the wall around the Runic Door. She had found the small door that Maej had described with ease. She waited, feeling mostly clean. Her legs had streaks of muck on them from crossing the Slithering Pit, but her hair didn't feel as weighed down. She trembled, waiting for him to appear.

Footsteps whisked closer. The thud of leather-clad steps. She stiffened, slowing her breathing. Her skin became hyperaware, feeling every divot and protrusion in the stones that made the wall. The mortar between the large bricks. The air lightly moved about her body, the gentle stirring created by an open space. She could feel the echo of empty air before her. The wall didn't go all the way to the edge of the escarpment, but three steps would take her to the edge.

It was a long drop to the Slithering Pit below.

The whisk of cotton robe over skin. Heavy breathing muffled by a barrier. The scratch of fingernails against linen. Another whisper. A loud clink of metal on metal. A clatter. The door groaned open.

"Amiollea?" hissed Maej, his clean scent brushing her nose. Beneath the aroma of his clothing, she could smell that salty musk of a man, different from her brother's scent or Zhee's. "Are you here?"

Can he figure out if I am? she wondered.

He stood within arm's reach of her, standing in the open doorway. His clothing rustled. She pictured him leaning out, searching the dark with his useless eyes to see her. He should smell her. Hear her breathing. Maybe even the fast beat of her heart.

It thundered in her chest.

"Amiollea?" Maej called again. He edged out of the door, hesitant. "Are you here?" Then came a heavy sigh.

Disappointment.

"Probably has no idea what the time is," he muttered. "How could she without a watch? I'll just wait for her, talking to myself in her tongue like an idiot." Then he switched to his own language, this liquid sound she couldn't understand.

It made her smile. He *was* eager to see her.

"Hi, Maej."

He gave a loud shriek, a sound that almost hurt her sensitive ears. His feet scrambled beneath him. He stumbled back before catching himself. His clothing swished over his body, a riot of sensory data she had trouble interpreting. Wind stirred over her naked body from his flailing arms.

"Amiollea?" he asked. "*Nokwill zihzil!* Were you there the whole time?"

"The whole time," she said, amusement in her tone. "You are blind."

"Of course I'm blind. I can't see at all."

"I can see that you're waving your hand in front of your face to prove how blind you are."

He froze. "How?"

"Your robe makes so much sound it almost hurts my ears. It's scratching all over your body."

"Is that why mucklings go naked?" he asked. "I mean, I guess there's no point in wearing clothes to be modest since no one can see your . . ."

"Breasts?" she asked.

"Er, yes, I mean, those are . . ."

She giggled, delighting in the flustered sounds he made. It was *fun* to provoke him. She moved closer to him. "You have no idea what they look like, do you?"

"I know what breasts look like," he muttered. "I mean . . . When they're clothed and . . . Why are we talking about this?"

"You're the one who brought them up." She grabbed his hands. "For us mucklings, we use our hands to see details. Our fingers." She lifted his hands, a big smile on her face.

"What are you doing?" he asked, his voice strangled. A mix of hope and fear all at the same time.

"Why, helping you to see." She brought his hands to her chest. "Don't you want to feel them?"

"I mean . . . That is . . . Are you . . . ?"

She jerked his hands hard upward, pressing them into her face. He froze for a moment. Then his fingers twitched. They swept out, thumbs brushing over her nose and lips. His fingers quested, touching her ears. Her hairline.

"That's your face."

"You didn't think I was going to bring your hands *there*, did you?"

"I didn't know what to think," he said.

"Disappointed?"

His fingers twitched. "I . . . well . . . um . . . Is there a safe way to answer this?"

"Nope." She giggled again.

Maej's fingers traced across her face. He brushed her cheekbones. Her nose. Then her lips again. He caressed her chin and ran up to her temple. She had never felt anything quite like his touch. It spread a warmth down her face to her neck. Her shoulders. Her heart pounded.

"I'm trying to picture what you look like," he said as he kept touching her. "This is difficult."

"You have a big nose," she said. "I remember that." She reached out and brushed his chin. A tingle galvanized down her digit as she touched him. She slid higher, caressing up and down his features. She felt a fine fuzz beneath her touch. "You have facial hair. My brother can't grow a beard at all."

"I'm told Karadrisan men rarely have facial hair. Sometimes a mustache."

"Mmm, but you shave, don't you?" She paused. "That's what it's called, right? I think my father had a mustache he had to shave off."

Pain swelled in her. Her father must be dead. Her and her brother gave up searching for him years ago after they found their home ransacked. He probably died in the dark, looking for his family.

Retreating from the pain, she said, "Mother hated it."

"Yeah, shaving." He pulled his hands from her face. "You have a small nose. It's . . . cute. Dainty. And your cheekbones are delicate. You have a refined face. I think you'd look beautiful as a statue. That classic Karadrisan visage found on all those statues and reliefs of young maidens."

Warmth burned through her cheeks. This intense, giddy joy rushed through her. "Really?"

"Yes."

"Well, you have a large nose. I think that's good on a man. Bold, you know, but comforting."

"I have never thought that about my schnoz before."

"What a funny word," she said. She brushed his cheekbones. "You have a rectangular shape to your head and . . ." Her fingers brushed his hair. It was so silky and fine. She ran her fingers through it, feeling it fall to his shoulders. "What lovely hair. It's not like mine. It's always matted and a tangled mess."

"I, uh, have a comb."

"I used to have a brush. Mother would comb my hair." She let her hands fall from him. "I can remember sitting on her lap every morning while she hummed and ran the brush through my hair. I think she was happy."

"I'm sure she was," he said. "My mother liked to hum while she painted."

"Is she . . ." Sadness choked at her voice.

"My family is still back in Taechiz. They're still . . ." He cleared his throat. "I don't mean to sound like I'm gloating."

"No, no, it's good. You have something to hope for if this ever ends."

"*If* is a good word—"

"It's about to happen!" she gasped. "Light!"

"My maestro's work," he said, sounding wistful. "Cover your eyes. It can damage them."

She closed her eyes, remembering how much it hurt seeing the Light this close. It was so bright, it bled through her eyelids as a red glow. It *still* hurt. She savored the pain. It reminded her that she still lived. She grabbed his hands, clutching at them as the brilliance washed over them.

Then it faded. Died. Gone for that day.

She blinked, a blur smeared across her vision.

"I hope you didn't look at it," Maej said. "There are a few in the Runic Ward who are permanently blind from staring at it. Not a problem, I'm sure, for a muckling, but when they return to their homes, they can't see the lights from the runed lanterns. They're denied a bit of the world."

"I closed them," she said. "Yesterday, it almost overpowered me. Why does he do it?"

"I really don't know. He won't tell me. I'm 'not ready.'" A bitter sigh. "I keep studying. Keep practicing. I want to know. It must be important. He does it every day. Maybe it's just to give hope to the city. It can't be to keep back Death."

"No, they're still around," she sighed, voice tight with the terror of the fire yesterday.

"Oh, I made you the knife," he said. His hand jerked from hers. Cloth rustled. "I didn't have time to make you a scabbard. I fell asleep. I was working on it all through the night, then we had to take the caravan to the Glowers to get food."

"No Sun Ravagers attacking you?"

"Blessed runes, no," he said. "Those madmen are being hunted. A group of Glower soldiers are chasing a thief. One of the Sun Ravagers. They marched out to teach them a lesson."

"Chasing a thief?" she asked, her stomach tightening. "Since when do they do that?"

"Have you stolen from the Glowers?"

"My brother has. It's dangerous climbing the walls, but it's the only way to get good food, weapons, and supplies we can't get out there."

"Like daggers?"

A cold handle pressed into her hand. She closed around it and felt the weight of the knife. "Is this really for me?"

"Yes," he said. "Runed so it'll never rust or grow dull."

A shudder ran through her. It was a precious item, metal, sharp, deadly, and enchanted. And he just gave it to her like it was nothing. This would show her brother. Ablisio would want more like this. He would have to recognize the good in this.

Have to let her keep seeing Maej.

～

Zhee found one of the shadow painters' latrines. She could smell the sour flavor of fresh shit leading her through the warren of streets. She used to live in this part of town. She wasn't exactly sure which building she'd lived in with her parents and her ol' gramma, but it was nearby. She didn't see much point in finding it. It would have long since been looted, any wood taken for weapons or to make fires deep inside buildings where no light could escape.

Her home had been defiled.

Nothing in this city remained clean.

She closed her eyes as she tried to imagine the baby inside of her. She wished there was a way for her to deliver him or her into a clean world. Maybe it would be better, though, if she lost this one like the other two. What was the point of bringing something so pure into this world only to suffer?

What's the point of me climbing into the latrine to gather shit to trade for food? she asked herself. *Hope that one day things will change.*

Did she have hope growing in her? Like when a little jackrabbit burst out of her burrow and braved the talons of desert hawks to find roots for her babies, she had hope that she wouldn't be snatched up. That her child could grow strong and leave behind the burrow to find their own family. To spread far and wide.

Maybe something could change in this city like Ablisio wanted, Zhee thought. *If we had a Runecarver with us, someone who'd create tools to help us survive, maybe something stable could spread. An alternative to the Glowers' cruel grip on the food supply.*

They can't keep grinding us into the muck, pretending we don't exist.

She shuddered at the foul mud she sank into. She never grew used to the stink. It was wet from their piss and squishy from their mud. It was just what she needed. Fresh dung would go a long way. She reached down and ignored the revulsion as she slid her hand around, searching for the excrement.

Survival came at a cost in Hamiocho.

She had a strong stomach and would wash herself in a small pond near their home. It was full of the wrong type of algae to eat, the water undrinkable, but they could use it for washing off the muck. For drinking, they went to the sluggish waters a few times a day to drink their fill.

She kept her ears pricked for anyone moving through the buildings as she worked through the latrine. The mad ascetics were fastidious. They always used a latrine for a week or so before creating a new one. There must be a dozen or more of them, lost in their own world of creating art. Maybe they did it in worship to Death or to another god. The Karadrisans had gods, if barely remembered and not well revered.

Their people had replaced faith with wealth. Their arrogance had led them to worship themselves. They didn't listen to the guidance of Wise Owl or Cunning Fox. To Hopeful Jackrabbit or Fierce Desert Hawk. She followed in the wake of Industrious Honeybee who made his honey in holes in the rocks near patches of spiny cacti.

This is no different from Hungry Scrub Bear digging open a hive for sweet honey, thought Zhee in a fit of amusement. *Same consistency. My hard work will pay off. If I can find another latrine, I can get half a bag. Combine that with our own . . .*

It wasn't enough to feed them. Not with the price increase of algae, but what else could she do but hope things would get better? She kept working through the sludge, feet sinking into the filth of the world, her fingers muddy and dripping. She scooped up what she found by touch and added it to her bag.

The reek filled her nose, deadening her senses. It was dangerous without having Amiollea to listen for mucklings while she worked, but she wasn't *too* close to where the cannibals haunted. If they even were still alive. How long could they prey on each other before they ran out of people to eat? They mostly lived farther east and south in the Reek, the place where the dead were all taken after Darkfall.

Back when everyone tried to pretend that society still worked.

That had only lasted a few months before full anarchy reigned.

She kept working, reminding herself that she was safe here.

Probably.

~

EMMAIT STILL HADN'T FOUND the perfect spot to squat in. He was in the ruins east of the Rotting Orchard, the Povazian Slums. It wasn't in the Reek but was far enough away from Phosphor Lake. After the brush with Death the day before, he found himself unwilling to get too close to the lake. The Rotting Orchard were out even if the dead trees might provide something.

He was poking through the buildings when he smelled dung. The sour musk filled his nose. Sun rubbed against him, whimpering softly. He turned his head in the dark, stopping himself from entering the next building to see if it was the right place. The scent was drifting on the wind eddying through the buildings.

It was confusing in here. The streets were narrow. His mother might have lived in this place as a child before her beauty attracted the lust of Lord Achogear.

"Seek," he whispered to Sun.

His sense of smell outstripped Emmait's. He kept a hand resting on his dog's fur at the shoulders. The dog padded forward, snuffling. He moved with him, the scent of shit growing as they reached an intersection.

The wind came from his left now. The scent grew stronger. With it, the faint pad of footsteps. Someone was walking. He could hear the faint shifting of something wet inside of a ceramic jug. A muckling carrying shit to trade to the dispensaries?

The footsteps grew louder. Walking right for Emmait.

He gripped the hilt of his sword. He'd converted the satchel into a makeshift sheath, a baldric, and let it hang from that. He backed around the corner, gripping Sun's matted fur. The footsteps whisked closer.

Scents beneath the sour smell of shit filled his nose. The aroma of a person, dirty but with this exciting undercurrent. A woman. Alone. That was two in as many days. It wasn't the same one. He could hear the sway of large breasts. She sounded a tad heavier, more flesh on her frame.

A Povazian like him?

She passed him and this strange tingle raced through his body. A stirring in his nethers. A twitch to his penis. It was wholly unlike any sensation he'd felt before. It filled his nethers with hot iron. He became so aware of his phallus. It seemed to pulse and beat with his heart, growing turgid, lifting before him as the scent of the woman lingered.

He gripped his sword and followed her as she moved through the buildings. She paused at the next intersection. He could hear her breathing in deeply. She was searching for something, too. More excrement?

He wasn't one for stealing shit, and they were far from any group he'd feel comfortable selling her to, so why did he follow? Why did she stir this warmth in him? This excitement? *Is this why men want women?*

He knew about sex, but he never had seen the appeal. So much wasted effort to pump away on a woman. This wasn't like the world before, when you could spare resources on feeding the woman, in keeping her in your home and taking care of her son. And yet others in dark Hamiocho did. They put their own survival at risk to take care of a woman.

It wasn't the same with Sun. He was useful. He could fight and dig and find food.

This woman's being useful, he realized. *She's collecting dung. Did her man send her out? Is he around?*

He didn't hear anyone else. Sun surely would. He swallowed against the ache seizing his phallus. He grabbed it, shocked by how engorged it had become. He bit his lip against the urge to keep exploring it.

The woman walked to the left, making her decision.

He followed. Now he could only smell the shit she collected, but that brief inhalation of her aroma stayed with him. It filled his memory as he rounded the corner. She had gotten farther ahead, her footsteps a bare whisper. Then she paused. He froze. Her feet shifted. She set the jug down. He heard a sucking sound, foot stepping into thick mud.

Must have found another latrine, thought Emmait.

He grimaced at the thought of this Pavlovian woman digging through it while her man was probably lying on the ground taking a nap. He made her risk her life to gather the shit to pay off the dispensaries. This strange anger boiled through Emmait. He drew his blade slowly, wanting to find this lazy man and put his blade through him.

He wondered what she looked like. His mother filled his mind, smiling, her brown hair falling as fine as silk. His left hand gripped his hard phallus. This woman was right there. He could march up to her. Claim her.

What will I do with a woman? he asked. *It doesn't do anything to help survive.*

Sun stiffened. He let out the lowest of growls. Emmait froze and listened for what his dog had sensed. Breathed in for any new scents. He could only smell the excrement. It was so strong. It almost overpowered his nose...

No, there was something beneath it. Rotten. The putrid reek of dead flesh.

The woman's movements stopped. The foul scent grew in his nose as the brush of feet on stone reached his ears. Men were moving, converging. But not on Emmait.

They rushed for the woman. Someone laughed, wild and mad.

The woman gasped and scrambled out of the latrine as the cannibals swarmed for her.

CHAPTER
SIXTEEN

The whispers surged over Ablisio. The light had to illuminate him. He pressed his belly as tight into the muck as he could. Cloth fluttered through the air. A chill rippled down his body. He clenched his eyes shut, picturing Amiollea and Zhee as he saw them in his mind.

As he'd seen them with his touch.

"NOOOOOO!" screamed from his right.

A sickening crunch. Shrieks gibbered. A loud, wet tearing cut off the frightful man. Two heavy thuds hit the ground. The flutter of cloth whispered above him. Ablisio trembled, pressing his face into the muck.

Don't see me! Don't see me!

"Mother!" another man shouted. Footsteps pounded up the mud for the edge.

A whispered shout of exultation. The final, breathy gasp of the dying. Death swooped over Ablisio. The man racing for the cover of the darkness gibbered. Air rushed. A sickening crunch. A thud hit the ground followed by a heavier one. The coppery scent of blood filled Ablisio's nose.

I'm just the ground. Just mud.

The glowing water retreated to the lake.

The fluttering of rotted cloth faded. Ablisio trembled on the mud, his breath bursting from his throat in ragged gasps. The muck grew warm beneath him. He'd pissed himself and didn't care. Death hadn't come for him.

His entire body shook. He lifted his face, muck dripping from his cheek. The lake's surface looked calm. A patch of glowing algae had washed up a body length from Ablisio. He shuddered. Death hadn't seen him. He'd stayed on his belly and lived.

Two halves of a body lay to his right, the mud slick around the severed stumps. Ablisio jerked his gaze away. He twisted around on his belly, too scared to stand. He grabbed his burlap sack full of algae. He had enough.

He had food for Amiollea and Zhee.

He crawled slowly up the bank. He didn't care if he spent an eternity wiggling on his belly through the muck. He wouldn't let Death kill him. His sister and Zhee needed what he'd gathered. He'd bought them a few more days of life.

His knees slid through the muck, pushing him forward. He slid the burlap sack across the mud and pulled himself along. A dark mound lay before him. A shape like a rock he didn't remember passing. He came closer and closer to it, inching his way forward bit by bit.

The shape had a strange protrusion. Like a nose and . . .

Ablisio's stomach quivered when he realized what it was. It was the head of the poor man who hadn't been so lucky. Another dark shape lay a few paces away. He breathed in the scent of spilled life. Ablisio pushed the head to the side. He wasn't hungry enough to become a cannibal.

He feared ever becoming so hungry he'd feast on a corpse.

He kept crawling. Darkness lay ahead. A profound curtain that would embrace him like his mother's arms.

The slope grew steeper. His hands grew indistinct. His arms became the mere suggests of limbs. Now when he reached out, his hands merged into the black. Ragged breaths burst from his mouth. He had never been so glad to be wrapped up by black.

Even once the darkness swallowed him, he kept crawling. He couldn't stand. Not until he was in the trees. He couldn't take the chance. Terror whipped at the soles of his feet.

Never muckraking again! He had to find another way to help them survive.

Another way to feed his sister and his woman. *Robbing others? Why couldn't I have known a Ratter or a blind fisher?*

Those groups were all so clannish. Families who had stayed together instead of turning on each other. They had prospered for it. Yes, they traded with outsiders, but they didn't trust. The Ratters only took in women.

And then rarely.

I could rob people crossing the Kneeling Dark, he thought. *Just bash their heads in and take their food. Be a disgusting thug. It's not like they're Zhee or Amiollea. They're not my family.*

His stomach roiled at the thought. He had never done something that despicable. Seven years in the dark, and the only group he'd attacked unprovoked had been those bastards raping Zhee. Her cries had stirred this righteousness in him.

Just imagining his sister in Zhee's place had sent him into a bloody rage. He beat those men to death.

The Glowers . . . I have to be more daring than ever. Find ways around their guards. Their dogs. Find reliable ways to get food.

And the Runecarver runt? another voice asked.

A silky, nauseated writhe twisted through his guts. It meant putting Amiollea in danger. Trusting that the Runecarver boy didn't just want to use his sister's body was too much. He hadn't fought and bled and suffered to keep her from that fate only to sacrifice her to a Runecarver.

He wouldn't fail his mother.

Well, he had bought a few more days to figure out a plan. Something bold. Something that would change their fortunes.

∼

THE SMELL of rotting death froze Zhee. She trembled in the latrine. Footsteps moved around her. Three, four, maybe five men. Their stench rose over the shit she stood among. Fear melted her bowels. Piss ran hot down her leg.

A mad cackle burst out of the darkness before her.

Panic shot through her. She scrambled out of the latrine and bolted toward the street that ran mostly straight in that direction. She abandoned her jug, not caring. Her dirty feet smacked on the cobblestones. Her hair flew out behind her. She wouldn't be captured. She would get back to Ablisio. Hope grew inside of her. She couldn't—

A hand seized her hair.

She screamed at the sharp jerk of pain. Her run came up short. Her feet left the ground. A heartbeat later, she slammed down on her back. The cloying scent of death spilled over her. Bones rattled around the cannibal who seized her.

"Don't you smell pretty," the voice growled. "Even if you are covered in shit. I heard them big bouncers heave. You got them Povazian sacks, don't ya? Lots of fat in 'em. Gonna take care of all of us."

"Please," she sobbed, horror from two years ago rising in her. They wouldn't just rape her over and over. After they'd finished, they would eat her. She had to survive long enough for Ablisio to save her. "You don't have to kill me. I can be very friendly."

She would say anything to survive and escape.

His hand grabbed her breast. He squeezed her and chortled. "Oh, yes, lot of meat on 'um. Maybe I should just cut 'em off first and then enjoy you."

"No, no, no!" she gasped, her fear knifing through her attempt to be seductive. Panic consumed her. "Ablisio! Ablisio!"

She knew he wasn't near, but she had abandoned rational thought.

She lashed out with her hands, striking at the darkness. She hit the cannibal's chest. His arms. She kicked, lashing out at anything. Laughter echoed around her, mocking her futile struggle. They moved around her, their foul stenches assaulting her nose.

Strong hands seized her flailing arms and pinned them above her head. Grubby hands with iron-hard nails seized her legs and wrenched them apart. One inhaled deeply as he crawled between her thighs.

She thrashed, picturing the cannibal's member aiming at her. She had to get free, but they were too strong for her. She couldn't get free. Tears spilled from her eyes, cutting hot tracks through the grime. Their rotten stenches clogged her nose. Bones clattered as if they wore necklaces of fingers and toes, of ribs dangling down their chests.

"Please!" she sobbed. She couldn't die. Not with Hope growing inside of her. "You can't kill me. I'm too good! You'll enjoy me too much. You'll miss me."

She had to live.

"Doubt you got a cootch that good," said the one between her thighs. "But let's find out, eh?"

"Ablisio!" she screamed as she fought with hopeless desperation against the hands clutching at her body.

∽

DON'T DO THIS, Emmait told himself as he padded forward to the screaming woman. Five men gripped her. Two pacing back and forth while the other three had her pinned. One shuffled forward. Her scream echoed through the streets. *You don't know her. It's her problem. There are five of them. Just let them have her. Move away. Live.*

"Ablisio!" she screamed, a voice of such helpless fear. "No, no! You can't!"

"Ablisio!" mocked one of the cannibals. "Is he 'round? We can eat him first."

"Or second," said another cannibal. "Maybe he'll be better to poke than you. Probably tighter. You Povazian's got coochies that've been used too much. Got no good grip."

"Please! Please" she sobbed, her cries tearing at Emmait's soul.

Just run away, he snarled at himself as he came closer. One of the pacers was just in front of him. *Flee!*

"Sun!" he shouted and sprang forward.

"Who dat?" snarled the cannibal, giving Emmait a good fix on where he stood.

Emmait swung the runed sword before him. It hissed through the air and struck flesh. The ensorcelled blade bit deep. The cannibal screamed. Hot blood splashed across Emmait's face and chest. He ripped his sword free of the rapist who fell on his back, gasping out in gurgling pain.

"Muck and shit!" snarled another cannibal. "You're going to fill my belly, muckling!"

Sun snarled and slammed into the other bastard, tearing flesh. The cannibal screamed in agony. The three holding down the woman snarled and stood, their feet smacking on the ground. Bones rattled about them, making so much noise.

Emmait darted forward, blood burning in his veins. He thrust the sword forward; felt the fleshy impact of burying in a belly. He wrenched the blade to his left. The man screamed like a little girl as something wet and slimy splattered the ground.

"He cut out my guts!" screeched the cannibal. "He got him a sticker and—"

Emmait's next swing took off his head. The body landed with a thud, the head bouncing and rolling into a wall. Emmait leaped over the corpse and slashed into the next, burning with fury. These men were foul and disgusting. They didn't deserve to live and spread even more misery.

Hamiocho inflicted enough of it already.

Confusion beset Zhee. Her attackers were being killed. The one between her thighs shouted in fright as gurgling pain burst around them. Her body shook with relief at this sudden reprieve. The cannibals howled in pain.

"Mercy!" gibbered the one who had wanted to violate her.

He scrambled to his feet, and she screeched with a fury. Maybe Ablisio had come for her after all. She shifted her weight, heard the panicked flight, and threw herself at those feet. She reached out through the dark and seized a bony ankle and a heel thick with callouses caused by years of walking barefoot. She landed with a painful smack on her belly and breasts.

But she kept a hold.

Her rapist fell to the ground with a hard smack. His legs kicked, but she didn't care. She scrambled up to him, hissing with fury. She fell on his back and grabbed a tangle of hair, greasy with something rotten.

"No, no, mercy!" he shouted.

"Who are you!" screamed one of the rapists behind her. "Have the woman! Take her! Nooooo!"

The sickening sound of a metal blade plunging into flesh answered her.

That wasn't Ablisio. Someone else murdered these men. She didn't care though. She focused her fury on the man squirming beneath her.

Strength born out of helpless despair metastasized into fury, she gripped the hair and slammed his face hard into the cobblestones. He grunted beneath her. She screamed as she drew back again and slammed down hard.

"Bleease!" blubbered the cannibal squirming beneath her. "Donjjj . . . hurzzz . . . meee!"

CRACK!

She heard the skull fracture. She screamed and drew back, driving the head into the cobblestones again and again and again. She didn't let up as the corpse spasmed beneath her. Zhee howled her helpless fury into the dark, screamed it all out of her as the others died.

Tears poured down her cheeks. Her entire body shook. She leaned over the corpse, her hands rubbing at herself, wanting to wipe their filthy touch from her body. She rolled off the corpse and onto her back. She sobbed as the fright bled from her.

She lived.

A gurgling moan cut off suddenly. Metal ripped from flesh. Footsteps stalked toward her. A beast snarled and tore at meat. The snarl of a hungry dog? She trembled as the attacker approached her. Not Ablisio but another man.

"Please, please don't hurt me," she whimpered to the unseen killer before her, the scent of blood thick on him. She wasn't safe. He had fought to claim her.

She had to submit to survive.

∼

EMMAIT SNARLED WITH EACH SLASH.

He became Death, delighting in killing these filthy beasts. They weren't men. They were jackals.

Pigs!

They rooted through their own shit to find whatever scraps they could, not caring what it used to be. They saw the woman as nothing more than a walking meal who'd wandered into their territory. One they could use to satiate all their disgusting hungers.

There were more of them than he'd thought. Others lurking in the darkness. One screamed in the background, the sound of a skull pounding into the pavement. The woman screamed out her righteous rage at her attacker.

Emmait slew the rest.

Blood painted hot across his body as he growled, as wild as them. His blade found them while the woman gasped and trembled. His sword held no mercy for them. He swung until he silenced their croaking pleas for mercy.

Mercy? These wretched, slimy, shit-stained creatures demanded *mercy?*

He laughed as he impaled his blade through the last one, twisting it in the animal's gut. He savored those porcine squeals ending in a gurgling groan. He wrenched his blade free and turned to the crying woman.

Emmait stared in the woman's direction, breathing heavily. Sun tore at one of the bastards. He *was* an animal. Meat was meat to a dog. He was a good boy and deserved to glut today. Why should he starve?

Blood ran hot down Emmait's body as he approached the woman. It sounded like she rocked on the ground near the man she'd killed. He could hear the way her teats swayed with her heaving chest. The heat boiling in his blood pressed at his phallus and hardened it. This aching need to release all this energy throbbed through him.

He just had to fall to his knees and take the woman.

"Please, please don't hurt me," she sobbed.

He froze, his manhood turgid and throbbing.

CHAPTER

SEVENTEEN

"Don't hurt me," Zhee moaned, trembling before the killer. She reached out her hands before her, brushing a thigh. Strong. Muscled. "You don't have to kill me, too."

The man didn't answer her. She could hear the slight rustle of his weapon moving through the air to her left. He held it low. A drop of blood fell from it and splashed on the cobblestone. He had a sword. A weapon. Where did the muckling get that?

He could kill her with ease. He'd dispatched the cannibals without effort.

"I'm useful," she begged. She had to protect the Hope in her. She could stand her body being soiled if it meant Hope could live. Maybe she'd even return to Ablisio. This man might just use her and let her go. Or she could escape after they fell asleep after a good rut. "I'm young. I have . . . I can . . ." The tears flowed as she forced herself to say these words. Her hands slid higher.

She found him hard.

She grasped him. Stroked him, feeling so dirty. Fouler than a day spent trudging through a latrine.

"I can do . . . do things . . . Just don't hurt me . . . I'll be good to you . . ." Her body shook so hard. Ablisio flashed through her mind. She wanted to return to him so much. She hated herself but ached to live and return to her family. She wanted to be with him more than it made her stomach crawl to do this.

Hope needed her.

She leaned forward. "I can . . . I can take care of you."

Bile bubbled in her throat as her lips neared the tip of his phallus. She would swallow him. Men liked that. Her last owners, the ones Ablisio had rescued her from, never hit her in the face. They didn't like her having split lips.

It spoiled their fun.

She closed her eyes even though she couldn't see a thing. Her mind retreated from what she was about to do. She would survive. The mad rage that had consumed her fled with the cannibal's death. Now only cold fright stayed with her.

She'd learned how to deal with men. Ablisio was different. She couldn't count on that mercy ever again in Hamiocho. Tears fell down her face as she forced her mouth to open wide.

∼

Emmait didn't know what to do.

Her hand felt incredible on him. He loved her hot breath washing over the tip of him. He couldn't imagine why she brought his cock to her mouth, but his body wanted to find out. That ache needed the release. She would give it to him, but . . .

She cried. He could hear her shoulders shaking. Though her voice had this throaty excitement to it, there was also this . . . disgust to her tone. Self-loathing. She forced herself to do this out of fear. She didn't want to. He hadn't come here to force her. He didn't do that.

He might have sold her to the Ratters or other mucklings, but he'd never do it himself.

She was Povazian. Had his mother done this with Lord Achogear? Was that how she'd fed herself and Emmait? Yes. She'd kept the nobleman happy with her body. Now this woman wanted to do the same, and it sickened Emmait.

It overcame the boiling lust.

"No." He put his hand on her. "You don't have to do that."

"What?" she croaked in surprise.

"It's fine," he said. "You don't have to do those things for me. I didn't kill those men to claim you."

"Why did you do it?" she asked. "Is this your territory?"

"I guess so," he said. "But . . ." How could he explain it? "They offended me. Now go. Gather what you've been collecting."

"Thank you," she said and now she sounded genuine. "Thank you."

"It's fine. My dog needed food."

She moved back from him. He heard her grab a clay jar, the container scraping on the paving stones. She stood and headed back the way she came. She went a few steps and paused. "I'm Zhee."

"Emmait."

"You're Povazian, too?" He imagined her smiling, using his own mother as the basis. "Thank you."

She hurried off, feet rushing down the street, moving faster than she should in the dark. Not that he blamed her after this. He listened to her leaving, that ache remaining in his phallus. He groaned, wondering if he could have gotten her to stick around a little longer. Not forced her, but . . . Maybe . . . She could have been a little more welcoming.

Her scent lingered around him. Filled his nose.

"Sun, stay," he ordered and drifted after her. He didn't understand it, but . . . Zhee . . . *A beautiful name. She must be gorgeous.*

If she was willing . . .

∽

AMIOLLEA ENJOYED her lesson on runes.

They sounded so complex. She couldn't imagine drawing sentences with hundreds and hundreds of little pictures. It was a number so big it held no meaning for her. But listening to Maej talk about them was so stirring. He had such passion for them.

His arms waved before him as he talked, his robe rustling. She pictured his hair flowing around his handsome face, his bold nose darting right and left as he turned his head. The air whispered around her, caressing her face, stirred by his gesticulations.

"And that's the problem," he was saying, "it's so complicated. All those clauses have to be in perfect, logical harmony."

"I really don't get that," she said.

"What?" he asked. "Clauses?"

"Yeah."

"Sentences have parts to them."

"No, they don't." She frowned. "And what's a sentence?"

"That!" he exclaimed. "'And what's a sentence?' is itself a sentence. A sentence is merely a group of words that convey an idea. They need to have a subject who is doing the idea, a verb to describe what the subject is doing, and an object that the subject is acting upon. That's a basic sentence. 'What' is the subject of your question. The S you contracted on the end is the verb 'is' and 'a sentence' is the object. So, a clause is a part of a sentence that has a complete idea, but not necessarily a complete sentence. Sentences can hold multiple ideas with multiple clauses that are all working together. Like the one I just spoke about. I linked the clauses with the conjunction 'but.'"

Amiollea furrowed her brow. "That sounds complicated."

"It is." He laughed. "People with far, far too much time on their hands figured all of this out. But it holds true for my native Taechizian, your Karadrisan, Povazian, and even other languages out in the world. Some sentences only imply a subject or an object, but they all need those three things to work. Anything else is a fragment. Now, my master has created a sentence that is as long as an entire paragraph of words. It's a masterpiece of crafting that keeps going on and on, adding all sorts of ideas but all of it simultaneously focused on *one* idea. I have a hard time doing three clauses like that."

"So until you can wrap your head around it, you can't get through the lock on his door."

"I'm trying." He sighed. "If anything happens to Maestro Kozonio, no one will be able to get into his office."

"And the Light dies?"

"Yeah. He's old. I don't want him going on the caravans. It's dangerous." Amiollea shuddered. "Yeah."

"That's why I'm going. The Glowers need to get used to me and understand I can do all the work he used to do for them. They trust him as the maestro but settle for using other Runecarvers. However, his work buys the most food."

"So you have to work for the Glowers, too," she said.

"In a way. The Glowers, of course, couldn't maintain their lifestyle without us."

"Would it be such a bad thing if they had to wallow in the mud with the rest of us?" she asked, anger flaring in her.

"It would be better if no one had to wallow in a pigsty, but they have the resources to keep the city alive. The materials and the livestock. Saving those cattle and feeding them in the first few days was vital. Creating the pasture so they could live was an immense undertaking. Every Runecarver had to work fast to erect the ceiling over the Abattoir Fields. To protect the food source, we then had to create the Rubble because things were getting worse. People were getting impatient. Several dozen cattle were killed, including some prime heifers. Good breeding stock. That gave us time to figure out other food sources."

"The algae."

"One my maestro designed." Pride resounded in Maej's voice as if it was also his work. "It's why the city is so healthy."

"Healthy?" Skepticism rang in her voice.

"You should be dying of cholera, dysentery, or a host of other diseases in the conditions you live in, but the algae boosts your body's healing. It's a modification of a strand of yeast we use in Taechiz to treat the sick. By making it into the food source, everyone is more resistant to diseases that should have killed most of the mucklings."

"Oh." She gripped the dagger tight. "But why don't they give it to us? We have to scrounge up shit to pay for it. Shit! They want to debase us."

"The algae need their own food." His robes shifted. "Shit, as you put it. They feed on it, break it down, and transform it into more algae that are safe to eat. All the Glowers dump their chamber pots in the Slime Fields."

"Then why is the price going up?" she asked. "It's nearly doubled."

"It has?" She could *hear* him blinking. "Perhaps there is a shortfall driving up prices?"

"You're saying all those rich glutting on meat and other delicacies aren't full of enough shit?" Amiollea asked, anger burning through her.

"Ah, fair point," he said.

She sighed. It wasn't Maej's fault. It was those Glowers. She shifted beside him. "So . . . how often do you Runecarvers go on caravans?"

"Every three weeks," he said. "We start to run low on food. We have to feed several hundred. Always a few more mouths to feed every year, too."

"You're having children in there?" she gasped.

"You don't have children out there?"

"Well, I mean . . ." She flushed. "I've never met a new child. I hear they die. It's hard out there on babies."

"Ah, well . . ." He shifted, robe rustling. She pictured him rubbing at the back of his neck. "Anyways, every three weeks. We have the guides lead us. We take care of the Glowers, and they trade us the food. Salted beef, fresh algae. We supplement it with food we trade cloth to the Ratters to obtain."

"So you eat slime and rat, too," she said grimacing. "But also beef. I haven't had that in a year. It's so delicious."

He shifted. "Yeah. Uh, maybe I can give you a bit. Next time."

She swallowed, realizing she'd been here too long. She had to get back across the city. It took an hour or so. "I'd like that." Her stomach growled. "I'd like that a lot."

"And maybe next time, I'll realize you're standing beside me." His tone sounded light, friendly, but also forced. Like he was trying to drown out her hungry belly.

"Just use your nose," she said. "I know I cleaned myself, but you should still smell me."

He breathed in deeply. "There is something . . . charming about your scent. Something exciting. Beautiful, even. I never thought a smell could be beautiful."

"It can be," she said. Her brother's scent when she was scared. "I should go. My brother worries."

"Right. My maestro will be wondering where I am." He paused. "When should we meet again?"

She thought about it. "How about in three days?" *That will give me time to badger Ablisio. Maybe Zhee can help.* "Same time?"

"Sure! I'll make a scabbard for your knife."

She smiled. "Thanks." She had this sudden urge to plant a kiss on his cheek. A flush suffused her body. "Well, uh . . ."

"Yeah, um . . . Goodbye." His robes rustled like he was opening his arms wide.

For a hug? she wondered. *Should I hug him?* She was suddenly aware of being naked. It had never bothered her before, but now . . .

"Bye!" she gasped and darted away, her heart pounding.

"Be safe, Amiollea!" drifted after her through the dark.

She felt so warm on the way back. She positively floated as she gripped her knife in her hand. It was metal but wouldn't rust. She could defend herself with it. She felt incredible as she crossed the Slithering Pit, making more noise than she should.

Not caring one bit because she would get to hear and smell and talk to Maej in three days.

∽

ZHEE CROUCHED in the algae pool by the shack. She ducked her hands beneath the slimy surface to the water beneath. She scrubbed her body, needing to get clean. This water was undrinkable, poisoned by the non-glowing pond scum, but it was still cleaner than those foul cannibals.

Their words still echoed through her mind. Their desire to rape her and eat her had her stomach churning. If it wasn't for Emmait coming to her rescue . . . He'd swooped in, saved her, and didn't even ask for anything.

Like Ablisio, she thought as she scooped up cleanish water from beneath the scum and rubbed at her breast where the cannibal had groped her. She feverishly cleansed herself, wanting to erase every trace that they had touched her body. Her stomach churned.

Zhee knelt in the pool, her knees sinking into the scum. She batted away the worst of the algae and plunged her hands into the depression she made. She scooped up the water and splashed it across her face, mouth and eyes sealed shut. Her hands worked over her body, wanting to rid herself of every bit of their touch.

I'm alive, she thought. *Hope's alive and I can return to Ablisio. Emmait protected me.*

She still shuddered as she tried to forget this encounter by focusing on the good. If Emmait lived to the east of them, and since he was like Ablisio, it made it even safer for her to venture into those neighborhoods and collect from the latrines. She didn't have to worry about cannibals or others moving around.

Did she have a new friend in Emmait? That eased her disgust as she washed away those cannibals. She scrubbed away the awful memories of today like she had done with the worst of the memories she had of her past. Of what those bastards had done to her before Ablisio had killed them and saved her. The cannibals couldn't hurt her again. They did not matter. She grew calmer with every breath as she splashed more water over her body.

"Zhee?"

Amiollea's voice drifted out of the dark.

"What are you doing?" she asked. "Are you in a pool?"

"I found a fresh latrine," Zhee said. "Just getting it off of me."

"I can understand that," said Amiollea.

"How'd it go with Maej?" Zhee asked. No one needed to know what happened. Ablisio would only worry. Amiollea might even feel guilty.

∾

Who is this Amiollea? Emmait wondered. Did this Ablisio have two women? He remembered Zhee crying out for an Ablisio when the cannibals came.

Emmait listened to the two women talking.

"He gave me a knife," the new girl said. "Runed steel."

Runed steel? Emmait touched the hilt of the sword dangling from his makeshift baldric. *What could she have possibly traded for* that?

"Did you do anything?" Zhee asked, a playful tone to her voice. Water dripped off her as she climbed out of the pool. It rippled for a few heartbeats.

"We talked."

"Just *talked?*"

"What are you implying?"

Zhee breathed in. "Well, your brother will be happy."

"That I have the knife?" The girl sounded confused.

Zhee laughed. "Amiollea, you know what I'm talking about."

"I'm not a *leech!*" hissed Amiollea. "Maej just wanted to talk. He told me about runes. About how he makes them."

Emmait's brow furrowed, the muscles tightening across his face without him even realizing it. He did not need to control his facial expressions. His mind spun at those words. There was something familiar about the girl. Her scent. Was this the girl he tracked to the Runecarvers the day before?

"He wants to meet again. I suggested three days."

"Then we'll have to find an excuse to get you away from your brother," Zhee said, her voice fading as the two walked away. "Your Runecarver must be interested in us mucklings."

"He's a nice boy," she said. "He told me when the next caravan's going to be."

Emmait trailed after, following Zhee's lingering scent. The other girl's musk mixed with Zhee's, but it wasn't as mature and exciting. Hers was riper and more inviting. He listened to the sound of her body moving, picturing her hips and breasts in his mind.

He followed them into the Rotting Orchard.

～

It took some time before Ablisio could move.

His near collision with Death had him rooted in the deep dark of the Rotting Orchard as if the skeletal canopy would shield him against the hoary evil gliding through the deep night above. Finally, he forced himself to move through the trees. He pressed through the decaying limbs almost in a daze. He had to make sure Amiollea and Zhee were safe.

That Death hadn't somehow claimed them.

He moved with familiar ease through the trees. He knew their roots and how they would trip him, where the decaying limbs reached to brush his face. He wove through them, his insides pure muck. The bag of algae he'd collected swung from his hand, the weight equal to the value of his life.

Soft sounds drifted through the darkness. Talking. Muted. Two voices. Both feminine. He smiled at the sounds of his sister and Zhee chatting. Relief ripped fear from his heart. They were safe. Of course, they were. They were just to the east. Compared to Phosphor Lake, they had been gathering shit in paradise. They could traipse through those winding mazes of buildings searching for latrines without any fears.

Cannibals hardly came west.

They might even all be dead by now, he thought.

He moved closer to them when he caught a faint odor. He froze. A prickling danced across his skin. Though he couldn't see, he still turned slowly, scanning the heavy black before him for the source of the scent. He inhaled deeply...

He didn't pick up any strange aromas.

Still...

His hand tightened on the burlap. He listened for sounds. The breeze rustled through the rotting branches. Distantly, one snapped and fell to the muck. It happened from time to time. Nothing to be concerned about. The faint flow of the Sluggish Waters drifted from his left. The women chatted in the cabin.

Just being paranoid. Death can't find me in the dark. No one's out here. Just head back to the shack. They're waiting for you.

He resumed his trudge to his home. He could visualize its shape in his mind, a featureless box with a door that was coming up. He skirted a tree and walked right for it. The two inside stopped talking for a moment.

"Ablisio!" Zhee's excitement surprised him. She rushed out and threw herself into him. Her soft body felt wondrous against him, her skin so much cleaner than his. The mud on his belly smeared onto her as she nuzzled into his neck.

"I'm safe," he told her. "It was nothing too dangerous. I stayed clear of the lake. Didn't even hear a whisper. I'm fine."

"I'm just glad," she whispered, her arms like a vice around him. "I thought I was never going to see you again."

"It's only muckraking," he said, forcing the bravado he didn't feel. "I got enough food for two or three days. You don't even have to go collecting dung. You can stay here in our little home. We don't need Runecarvers. I can feed us."

He rocked her as she held him tight. This was what he risked his life for. He had to muckrake again. Amiollea couldn't go out to the Runecarver. He wouldn't let that blue-skinned rat paw his sister. He would protect her from all of that.

"Come on, let's get inside and eat," he said.

CHAPTER
EIGHTEEN

"*We don't need Runecarvers...*"

Her brother's words resounded through Amiollea's mind. She couldn't escape them as she scooped up another handful of the stringy algae he'd collected from muckraking. It had an earthier flavor from what the dispensaries handed out, stained with mud. It was drier, too, which made it chewier.

She sat in silence, that one sentence resonating through her mind again and again. How could she convince her brother that *using* the Runecarvers, letting her see Maej, would only help? Why did he have to be so blitheringly stubborn? She could do things with Maej if she had to.

Leachy things.

But Maej hadn't wanted her to do those things. He'd just wanted to talk. He'd given her a knife. She had hidden it beneath a rock outside the shack. She couldn't explain where she'd gotten it. Besides, she had no way to hold it without a sheath, and he'd just smell the iron anyways.

She couldn't jeopardize her next chance to see Maej. Just three days away, and she'd get to talk to him again. Who knew what he's give her? What he'd tell her? She could help him figure out how to get through that lock on his maestro's door.

No, I can't do that, she said, honest with herself. All his talk about parts of grammar and sentences and all was nonsense. Objects and subjects and verbs. Words were just words. They didn't have any special parts to them, right?

And even if they did have special parts, she didn't understand them enough to do anything with them. But she could listen to him talk. She could tell him stories, and she could find out more about the caravan. The wealth and ease it promised her family made her quiver with temptation.

Beef. Real food. Supplies like good rope and weapons.

So long as Maej wasn't hurt, then what was the harm in stealing from his people? She just had to convince her idiot brother and that stubborn lump of rock he had in his head instead of a brain. It was the only explanation for why he couldn't see how amazing this opportunity was.

Stony-headed idiot!

Currently, he was eating with Zhee. The leech was sucking even harder than usual, clinging to him like she didn't want to let go of him. Couldn't be parted from him. Muckraking couldn't be *that* dangerous. Ablisio knew how to sneak about and avoid Death. Nothing could harm her brother. He was the best thief, best fighter, and best survivor in all of Hamiocho.

She had learned so much from him. She wanted to prove her skill to him.

"Mmm, you were so brave to go down and get all that algae," cooed Zhee. "Here."

Her brother slurped some algae into his mouth. Was she feeding it to him? Then they were kissing. Their lips smacked. A tingle prickled through Amiollea from a hot ache in her nethers.

Maej filled her thoughts.

Would he kiss me like that? she wondered, hearing the passion between her brother and the leech. The smack of lips and the wet dueling of tongues. It sounded disgusting as usual, and yet . . . She pursed her lips, imagining Maej kissing her. He would press her down like her brother did with Zhee.

She shuddered, the heat between her thighs growing wet. Her cheeks burned now as she could hear the sounds between her brother and Zhee increasing in their passion. The leech whimpered and moaned. The greasy caress of his hands roaming her body filled Amiollea's ears.

Would Maej caress my breasts while kissing me? Would he touch me in other places? Would he want to enter me?

She heard the moment her brother united with Zhee, the wet plunge. Amiollea bolted to her feet and burst out of the shack. She couldn't listen to that. Not up close. It made her feverish to find Maej and see just where a few kisses could lead.

To satiate this itch she felt more and more inside of her. This raw, pulsing ache she didn't know how to soothe.

She found the rock with ease and lifted it. She grabbed the knife, clutching the gift Maej gave her. Behind her, Zhee's moans rose in passion. Amiollea wanted to deafen herself so she didn't have to hear the rhythm of flesh smacking flesh. Her brother grunted.

Amiollea slashed at the darkness with the knife, letting out a frustrated growl. It fit in her hand, the handle smooth metal. The blade whistled through the air. She stabbed forward, imagining her brother for one vicious moment.

She didn't want to hurt Ablisio—she loved her brother—but right now, she wanted to see Maej without sneaking behind Ablisio's back. How could she prove she was an adult and not a child? She was a woman and had the breasts to prove it. Maybe not Zhee's bountiful mammaries, but hers were moving as she thrust and slashed and snarled her anger.

Why does he have to be so stubborn about Maej?

The sounds from the shack only grew louder. She hissed and stalked farther off in the dark. With her knife, she could set out on her own. She could defend herself from any man who thought her being a woman meant she could be seized and claimed. Like that shit-filled thug who'd made that mistake grabbing her in the Kneeling Dark last week.

If I'd had this, your entrails would have been spilling on the ground, and it wouldn't have been my brother ripping off your cock and feeding it to you! Her toes curled into the muck as she slashed the air before her in punctuation to her thought.

She spun around, the knife whirling around her, slashing at all the unseen foes that would harm her. She grew dizzy, swaying, and stumbled into the rotting bark of a fruit tree. It creaked as she pressed against it.

Something crashed above. A branch came down with a wet splat on the ground.

I could just leave. Strike out on my own. Why do I need Ablisio at all? I can find my own place. Survive. Use Maej for resources and follow the caravans and thieve food from them. Sneak right past their guards, grab a sack of meat, and dart back into the maze of streets before they knew what happened.

The prospect of freedom was so enticing. To abandon her stifling brother and the leech. Ablisio could spend all his time rutting atop the Povazian cow. He could enjoy her big udders; Amiollea would help Maej with his runes. They'd figure out why his maestro made the Light.

Wouldn't that be wonderful?

So why didn't she just go?

She glanced toward the sounds of the muffled grunts and groans. Her brother and Zhee neared their climax. Soon it would be over. Now was her opportunity to flee from her brother and find her own place in Hamiocho.

He'd be terrified for me. He'd tear the city apart looking for me. He wouldn't rest until he found me, the great, big idiot.

She sighed. How could she be mad at him for loving her? Guilt swallowed her rebellion. She would get to see Maej in three days. That gave her time to work on her brother. To convince him to stop being stubborn and trust her. If she ran away, he would never know that she could be useful. He would just see her as a girl he had to chase and drag back home.

Like a lost puppy.

She hoped she didn't have to sneak away again.

She sighed, squirming against the tree. The bark scratched at her back. She gripped her knife, wanting to use it to do something important. There was no food that needed cutting into smaller bites, no wood to carve into useful items.

The blade was only good for killing now.

And there was no one around to fight.

If Maej had given me rope, we could do something useful with it. We could make it safer to cross Treacherous or trade it for fish or rat. If it was a fine cord, maybe we could set traps for rats. There has to be a way to catch those slinking creatures. They infested Hamiocho.

The sounds from Zhee and Ablisio's passion ended abruptly. Soft kisses and...

Something shifted the brush. Reflexively, her gaze shot down the side of the cabin. She gripped her knife, a sudden tightness in her chest. Was someone there? She smacked the flat of the knife against her thigh, the metal cool on her flesh.

She had her weapon. If she killed an intruder with Maej's knife, that had to prove his usefulness.

Amiollea marched forward, clothed in the certainty of her success because she had sharp steel.

～

Emmait cursed in his mind as Amiollea padded toward him.

He pressed down on his belly, ignoring that ache in his nethers. He shouldn't have moved so fast, but hearing Zhee and Ablisio sent this strange rage through him. It wasn't fair that Ablisio was enjoying Zhee. Emmait should have taken the woman up on her offer, but...

She'd offered out of fear. With Ablisio, she willingly shared herself. She wasn't a woman paying a man for protection. She was something almost mystical, something his mother never was: a wife.

Emmait wanted that. Sun was an amazing friend, kept Emmait alive through so much, but he was just a dog. He couldn't give Emmait everything he craved. Now he had all these confusing aches inside of him. Things had been simple when women weren't different from men.

Amiollea stopped so close to him. How sharp was her nose? Had he covered himself in enough mud? He hardly dared breathe. He could hear her toes flexing in the muck. Smell the iron she held in her hand. Would he realize there was more iron before her?

She had sharp senses like her brother, who had almost uncovered Emmait earlier. His heart pounded. He counted the beats. Whenever he reached thirty-nine, he started over. He didn't know what was beyond that number. After five counts to thirty-nine, the girl turned around and returned to the shack.

The frantic, panting, almost grunting sounds of passion were over. Ablisio and Zhee were chatting. They sounded happy. Comfortable with each other. There was an ease Emmait hadn't heard since Darkfall.

He used to talk to his mother like that. Not afraid to say anything. Not worried about offending her like he would Lady Achogear or her children, the *true* sons and daughter of Lord Achogear. Emmait was the extra. The sloppy leavings dumped in a Povazian slut's womb, as Alechio, the oldest son, would say in mockery.

Amiollea entered the cabin and the conversation broke off. Emmait closed his eyes and pictured Zhee snuggled up to Ablisio. The ache in his heart was stronger than the throb in his loins.

∽

ABLISIO FELT RELAXED, the last vestiges of his fear fading away. Confidence built in him. Zhee had a remarkable ability to swell that feeling in him. It was more than just the release of his seed. There was something about her that challenged him to do better. Be stronger.

To succeed against the odds and brave any danger.

Maybe any woman could do this for him, but he liked to think this was how his father had felt about his mother. He stroked Zhee's hair as she giggled against his chest. She felt relaxed, too, like he'd done something similar for her. Given her something she needed.

"The way the water rippled was beautiful and terrifying. The glow . . . It was like moonlight. You remember that? Ethereal. Elusive."

"Yes," she said. "Wise Owl's great eye watching us."

"Maybe the lake's moon piss." He chuckled. "Or owl piss."

She giggled again. "Wise Owl doesn't piss glowing algae."

"How do you know?" He smiled even though she couldn't see it. "Just flying above us with his shining eye. Everything's got to pee. Why wouldn't his urine glow? Maybe that's why the lake suddenly has those large waves."

"If the Wise Owl peed on the world, don't you think it would happen more often?"

"I don't know what's outside of Hamiocho. Do you?"

"When I was a baby, my parents crossed the Drylands with me as just a little bundle strapped to my mother's breast." Zhee shifted. "They came to find work with my grandmother. They told me stories about . . ." She trailed off. "Hi, Amiollea."

Amiollea grunted as she stepped into the shack.

He hadn't even noticed her leaving, but he wasn't worried about her wandering off again like she had two days ago. He had impressed on her why it was a bad idea. She had this strange notion of the Runecarvers, but she always listened to him. She knew his word meant survival.

I survived the muckraking. Death didn't see me lying in the mud. The further removed in time he was from the event, the more his fear felt so alien to him. He'd done something risky and survived, which proved he had the skill to do it again. When Death had come, he'd done the right thing when the other man panicked. They idiot had stood instead of blending in with the muck.

Death found the fool, not Ablisio.

He was about to say something when he caught a faint whiff of something metallic. "Are you bleeding, Amiollea?"

"What?" she asked.

"I smell metal," he said, breathing in again.

"Oh, uh, scratched myself," she said. "It's nothing. I'll go wash off."

"Is it bad?" he asked as she headed outside.

"No, no, just a little one. It'll be fine."

A little one probably would be fine, but anything deep could fester. He'd heard the screams of those rotting from gangrene. It devoured flesh, bloated legs, and burned through the veins. Some people could go years with ulcerated wounds while others died in days. They said if your stomach went rigid, you would perish soon.

Best to just put them out of their misery.

"I'm sure she's fine," Zhee said, stroking him. He heard his sister padding outside the hut. Not concerned. A rock shifted. Was she playing with it? Then she headed to the algae spring.

When his sister returned, she sat on the other side of the shack, the wall creaking. She must have leaned against it. "You said we don't need the Runecarvers."

"That's right," Ablisio answered. He nudged the burlap sack full of algae. "We got enough food in there for a few days. We can relax again."

"But . . . wouldn't it be a good idea to take advantage of them?"

"They're too dangerous. They use magic. It's unnatural."

"What is natural in this city?" Zhee asked.

He scowled but didn't speak his annoyance.

"I don't mean I'm going to do 'Zhee stuff' with Maej," Amiollea added.

"'Zhee stuff'?" Zhee asked, sounding amused.

"Well, I just don't think Maej wants to do that with me."

"He does," Ablisio grunted. "Every man wants the same thing."

"Mmm, that's true," purred Zhee. "But he's a Runecarver. He's soft, and she's a muckling. You trained her."

"What are you saying?" he asked, shifting and sitting up.

"Well, what if you were nearby when she met with him? Close enough to stop him if he tried to do 'Zhee stuff' with her? You know, chaperon her."

"No," he said flatly. He stood and leaned against the wall. "We'll get by on muckraking for a while. I have it pretty much figured out. I know how close I can get and what to do."

"The algae in the lake isn't as good as the dispensary's," Amiollea said. "The Glowers' crops are healthier for us."

"What?" He snorted. "That sounds like rumors the Glowers started to make sure we're dependent on them. Muckraking makes us independent."

"And risking our lives," Zhee said.

"What doesn't? In three days, when we're out of food, I'll do it again. I'll do it better. Prove how safe it is when you know what you're doing." He pushed down that twinge of fear. He'd done it once, he could do it again. And again.

"Fine," Amiollea said, "then Zhee and I will go collect more shit from the latrines. Right?"

"Right," Zhee agreed.

"Fine," he grunted. He feared another argument with his sister. "I'm glad you're seeing sense, Amiollea."

Zhee was in a good mood as she snuggled beside Ablisio later on to sleep.

His sister would keep seeing Maej, and she would cover for the girl. Things would get better. Ablisio spoke of muckraking with such confidence. It was dangerous, but he seemed to understand it a lot better.

And he had brought home three days' worth of food. She hadn't managed to bring home enough excrement to pay for that much food from the dispensaries. Not enough to take the risk of being attacked in the Kneeling Dark.

She wouldn't have to worry about being alone collecting shit. Emmait wouldn't hurt her. She could relax around him and be safe. He had his sword and his dog. He would protect her because he was a good man, too.

As Zhee rested her head on Ablisio's chest, she wondered if she should tell him about Hope. Should he know he might be a father? She knew he would be a good one. Amiollea was proof of that. Many fathers had sold children after Darkfall just to get scraps of food. Their wives, too. Anything to survive.

Weak men. Not like Ablisio or Emmait.

But maybe it was too soon. How would he react to the news? Would he become more protective of her? Would he keep her in the shack, chained here until she gave birth? What if she lost it? She hadn't told him about the last two. There was no guarantee Hope would survive.

But she wanted Hope to. The child in her felt so important to her now. She'd accepted his or her existence. Things had to be better. They had to improve. Using the Runecarver was a great start. Even if they didn't rob the caravans, maybe they could get out of the muck and into their ward . . .

It was all on Amiollea. Maej wanted to see her again. Give her more gifts. He was a young man, and she a young girl. It was only right. Things could work out between them. All these thoughts danced through Zhee's head as she drifted down into sleep.

It was wonderful to dream of a future again. Her, Ablisio, and Amiollea found safety and happiness.

CHAPTER NINETEEN

Talking with Amiollea drove Maegwirio to study the lock on his maestro's study door again. He had to crack it. He imagined how impressed she'd sound once he'd done it. If he could figure out the right sentence to unravel all the clauses and variables of the large runic sentence.

He sat in the workshop. He gave a nervous glance at the door. He had the parchment with the lock's runes copied onto it. They spiraled out from the doorknob with his keyhole in it. They were each scribed with care, rotating as they spread across the circle. The spiral felt important. He almost felt like the runes would spiral for eternity, incapable of being unraveled.

But they had an end. A beginning. He could tug at that.

He read the runes again. "This door can only be opened with negation, the door is impervious to all tools, the door is impervious to all flames, the door can only be opened with the correct idea delivered with elegance, the door is warded against those who do not belong, the door is impervious to all acids, the door is a nexus of belief, the door's beliefs cannot be rewritten."

He studied it for the hundredth time. The book *The Shades of Meaning for the Seventy-Five Key Runes* lay ready to be slid over the parchment to hide it should his maestro enter. The book itself was opened onto the rune for Nexus.

It was a complicated word. It meant the center, the convergence, the heart of the spiral.

It felt important to Maegwirio.

Much of it was straightforward, runic clauses to stop the door from being damaged with tools, fire, acid, and even other runes. "This door's beliefs cannot be rewritten." To the runes, the door itself was alive. It had a personality set by the runes. It needed that perfect clause to open it. The key clause his maestro had crested. The entire lock needed to be negated with a single, elegant phrase.

Something that could strip away all its protection.

"How to do that?" Maegwirio asked himself again.

He shifted in his chair, the growing bangs of his silvery hair spilling over the bluish skin of his forehead. It was said his people had skin as pale as the Povazians, but the bluish glow of runes had impregnated the pigment of their skin. They were the only people to discover the secret of tapping into the power. Thousands of years ago at the Rune Heart, the great Taedeocha had been struggling to save his daughter.

He'd failed, but what he had discovered changed Taechiz and, through his people, the rest of the world.

He glanced at the shades of meaning of Nexus. *Xhofig* it was called in his tongue, the rune itself a stylized spiral made of six lines rising from a dot in the center then enclosed the simple rune for Wall. Many runes were compounds of simpler ones. Wall enclosed many ideas, implying they had boundaries. Limits.

Nexus was a single point, the birthplace of an idea that then spiraled out into the world, changing everything.

"Nexus of belief," he repeated. *Could I inscribe a key to believe that it was a part of the door? Would that get around the rules?*

He glanced at the phrase again. It required an elegant key with the correct idea on it, the belief that it belonged to the door, enough to open it. To negate the rest of the clauses as the first sentence said. This excitement gripped Maegwirio.

He had time to make a key before Amiollea would visit. When he saw her in three days, he would impress her with his skill.

∽

Hunger growled through Emmait as he lay on his belly in the mud outside Ablisio's shack.

It was his second full day of spying on them. He couldn't help himself. Just listening to Zhee, Amiollea, and Ablisio talk stirred something in him. That jealous longing for what he'd lost with his mother's death.

The one thing Sun had failed to give him.

He loved his dog. He managed to pry himself away to check on Sun while they were sleeping. His dog was restless but stayed near the corpses. Sun was trained well. He understood that following Emmait's orders meant food and survival. The corpses were growing ripe, but that didn't seem to bother Sun. He had glutted on them, gnawing on bones.

Emmait was glad Sun seemed happy. He wanted to stay longer, but after a few hours, enough time to sleep with Sun's furry body beside him, he had to return. He hadn't eaten. Hadn't even thought about food. He just had to spy on them.

Ablisio, do you even know what you have? Emmait wondered for the thirty-ninth time. Well, more than that, but he didn't know what to call bigger numbers.

The growling in his stomach gnawed at him. His innards were hollow. He should get food, but they were laughing in there. Zhee was telling a story about Wise Owl and how she tricked Swift Desert Hare into finding the largest pearl in the ocean.

"And Swift Desert Hare said, 'Of course, I can run so fast that the water won't touch my fur. After all, I outrun Fierce Desert Hawk all the time.' And Wise Owl ruffled her feathers. 'So you claim, but you have never even been to the great bitter lake. How do you know you can do it?' Swift Desert Hare thumped her back foot repeatedly in annoyance."

THUMP-THUMP-THUMP echoed from the shack.

"How can she really be that fast?" Amiollea asked.

"Because she once made a bet with the South Wind, which is the fastest of the four winds," answered Zhee. "I told you that story."

"Yeah, South Wind claimed she could blow so fiercely, she could knock over anything," said Ablisio. "Even a big pile of buffalo shit."

Amiollea burst into giggles as Zhee huffed. "It wasn't buffalo scat but Hungry Scrub Bear's droppings."

"Shit's shit," said Ablisio, and Amiollea laughed louder.

Emmait shifted at the sound. Laughter. When had he last made that sound? Even with Sun, he hardly ever talked. Here these three were. They had something he had never heard anywhere outside of the Glowers. They had a family.

His finger idly traced into the mud.

"Anyways, Swift Desert Hare boasted she could run so fast she could dive into the great sea, all the way to its unfathomable bottom, and come out dry. 'Prove your speed,' said Wise Owl."

Emmait wasn't even sure what an owl was. He understood what a hare was, though. A rabbit. He'd eaten rabbit before Darkfall. He traced in the mud as he listened about how Hare had darted down into the ocean and returned so fast Wise Owl hardly noticed her gone. As the Swift Desert Hare boasted, she was dry.

"'But how do I know you did it?' asked Wise Owl. 'You could have merely run out of sight and come back.' 'But can't you see all the night world from flying up high, Wise Owl?'"

The story continued as Wise Owl claimed she couldn't because her eyes grew tired. She needed proof. Something from the bottom. Something unique. Swift Desert Hare didn't know what was down there that could be unique. Emmait shifted as he heard how Swift Desert Hare darted down to the ocean floor and found rocks and strange plants. But those were all found above the ground or washed up on the shore. Finally, she found a large clam. It was the size of a house.

"And in it was a pearl," said Zhee with such breathy excitement. "The biggest pearl any had ever seen. It was smooth and gray-white. Swift Desert Hare was entranced. She knew this was it. So she darted up, running so fast the water still hadn't touched her, and snatched it."

"But didn't the clam try to stop her?" asked Amiollea, sounding as breathy as a little girl.

Emmait wanted to know, too. He knew clams and pearls.

"Oh, Angry Clam did. He tried to snap his jaws down tight, but Swift Desert Hare was too fast for any of those nasty things that lived in the sea. That is where the dark creatures dwell. Ravenous Shark and Pinching Crab and Gnashing Eel. Where Grandfather Whale thrashes and sends his mighty waves to crash into the shore and drown those who live by the sea. Angry Clam could shut her jaws so fast, nothing could escape them."

Emmait's breath caught.

"Nothing beneath the sea, that is. Swift Desert Hare ran so fast, she snatched up the pearl and was gone before the shell even began snapping shut. Swift Desert Hare ran across the sea floor. Angry Clam shrieked in anger and her friend, Devious Octopus, answered. He shot after Swift Desert Hare and fired his black ink at her. He missed her, but splattered half of the pearl."

Emmait sat up. Swift Desert Hare brought the pearl out of the water, but it was permanently stained black on one side. Wise Owl wasn't happy, but the proof was there. So Wise Owl used the new pearl as her new eye so she could see everything. But it slowly rotated in her socket, going from full brightness to murky darkness.

"Wow," Amiollea gasped. "I remember the moon changing shape. I didn't know why. Mom just said the moon was Goddess Celia's gift to women, but she wouldn't say why."

"I have no idea," Zhee said. "I didn't know any of your people's gods."

"They weren't important," Ablisio said. "It's not like they've helped us out since Darkfall."

"Maybe they are," Zhee said. There was something wistful. "Sometimes, those we need come upon us at the right moment to save us."

She's talking about me. Emmait smiled.

"Exactly!" Amiollea said. "Just like when I met Maej. That had to be one of the gods helping us. Nudging me to be there! So I should do it."

"The gods have no power here," grumbled Ablisio. "I don't want to hear about that Runecarver. I won't see you used."

Amiollea would fetch a good price to the Ratters, thought Emmait. He had planned on selling the girl to them anyways before they'd stumbled on the

Runecarvers. *I could go in there, kill Ablisio with my sword, and take Zhee with me . . .*

He sighed. Zhee would hate him. He would never get to hear those wonderful sounds she made for Ablisio. He had to find another way. He had to be kind to her. Tomorrow, she would be heading off to his territory. While Ablisio gambled his life muckraking, he would guard Zhee.

Talk to her.

And if Ablisio didn't return from muckraking . . .

"Why won't you let me?" Amiollea demanded, her voice shrill. It hurt Emmait's ears. His stomach rumbled. It was hard to ignore his hunger without Zhee talking. "Huh? What's wrong with my ideas?"

"I have already made the decisions. A way we *know* will get food. This Maej . . . You don't know what he's after. What he wants. There are Runecarver girls he can pursue. He probably just wants . . ."

"What? Say it! He just wants a muckling to poke for a laugh? Like those despicable things that lurk out there who pass women around until they get bored of them and sell them to the next group. Swapping minge, right? That's what it's called."

"Maybe," Ablisio said. "I'm not letting you be used like that."

"If he did, you'd kill him for me," Amiollea said. "Or I would."

"Just drop it," he said. He walked to the door. "Where's the urn? I have to make dirt."

It would be so easy to sneak up on Ablisio as he squatted over the urn outside the shack. One slash, and Emmait would have Zhee all to himself. He sighed. It wouldn't work. She'd hate him. Talking would work.

Hopefully. And until then, he could listen to her voice.

∼

Maej quivered with excitement.

Two different delights beat through him. He would meet with Amiollea tomorrow and, almost as important, he had finished his key. He had carefully shaped it to fit into the lock. He had carved the runes he was certain would unravel it. He would slip in there and find all the secrets his maestro didn't think him ready for.

All the mysteries that could be solved by reading his journals. He needed to know why his maestro created the Light. What it did. If he could help.

His ears picked up the labored steps of Maestro Kozonio ascending the spire. The clunk of staff. The creak of aged joints. Key in hand, Maegwirio stepped out of his study and listened as the maestro climbed higher and higher, spiraling upward to another door as secure as the study door

The roof door.

The metallic rattle of key sliding into a lock. The click of the mechanism disengaging. Then the maestro stepped out onto the roof. A loud boom. The door closed. Locked behind the old man.

Maegwirio sprang into motion.

His robes swished around his legs. He raced up the steps two at a time. Soft-soled shoes whisked on the stone runners. His heart pounded as hard as it had during the ambush. He stood before the door, the tension squeezing at his heart.

Maegwirio inspected his creation. The brass key gleamed a dull amber in his hand. The runes, inscribed as small as he could make them on the teeth, read, "*Akolianoll ball zoheddin nof sorabaez.*"

"*This key will always belong to the impervious door.*"

He brought his key to the keyway. He pressed forward. It clicked into place. He fought against his heavy breath. His hand trembled on the key. He drew in a deep inhalation through his nose to calm his jitters.

Twisted and—

The key refused to turn. No smooth click of the lock disengaging. He jammed it deeper, pressing the round base into the palm of his hand. He squeezed about it, applying all the torque he could. His forearms bulged with the strain.

"Come on," he muttered. "That has to be it."

The material had to be right. He'd seen his master's key in brief flashes from pocket of the robe to the keyway. He recognized the gleam of brass. So it didn't have to be the same material as the door.

"What did I do wrong?" he muttered as he pulled the key out. Shoulders crushed by his failure, he trudged down the stairs and entered his lab.

He had to dissect his mistake and figure out where his logic went wrong. He didn't hear his maestro unleashing the Light nor the sound of his return. Maegwirio lost himself in his study of the phrase and how to overcome it.

CHAPTER TWENTY

Amiollea woke up early.

Her internal timepiece was rarely wrong. She could usually guess when the Light would appear within a few heartbeats. It wouldn't be for seven hours or so. She sighed, rolling over onto her back. Her brother and Zhee slept.

She tried to return to sleep, but her stomach quivered with giddy eagerness to see Maej today. *Maybe if I meet with him a few times and tell my brother that he hasn't tried to bed me, he'll relax. Maej doesn't trade for minge or plunder honeycaves or sheath his sword in every slimy scabbard possible.*

She closed her eyes as she lay on her back. She had long grown used to no pillows or blankets. Nothing soft to lie upon but hard ground. She hardly reflected on how a human could get used to almost any deprivation.

To find normality in any horror.

All she cared about was that excited flutter in her stomach. A nervous dance of butterflies swirling around inside of her and made sleep impossible to find. She felt tired. Knew she *could* sleep more. Normally, she could sleep away a day when there was nothing to do.

But now...

When she had hours and hours to pass with nothing to do before she could leave, she couldn't find it. Sleep had eluded her. It fled from Hamiocho like sanity. Taken away from her by Death. She rolled onto her side, struggling to find reassuring comfort in Ablisio's regular breathing while he slept.

Only Zhee's faster breath ruined it. The leech spoiled everything.

Amiollea rolled the other way, facing the wall. She listened to the sounds outside. The rotting trees rustled in the wind. A distant branch crashed to the ground. One day, the trees around them would collapse.

Everything would. The city would be nothing but mud and muck and the Runic Ward. They would survive. They had the magic. Why shouldn't she meet with Maej and get all she could from him? He was smart and fun. Safe. He would help her and all she had to do was talk to him.

She might even do more, but he wouldn't push her.

Though if he did push a little, she might enjoy that. The heat in her built and built. That wet itch that grew harder and harder to ignore swelled in her. She bit her lip and stayed on her side, listing to her brother's breathing.

"Maej," she whispered, almost a prayer.

She started to finally drift off into sleep thinking about kissing Maej. Her brother loved kissing Zhee, and she seemed to make appreciative sounds. Amiollea felt like she would enjoy it. Those fantasies drifted through her thoughts as she descended closer and closer to that point of oblivion.

Her bladder had other ideas.

She realized how full she felt. She groaned and set up, groggy now from her near sleep. She stepped out of the shack and squatted in the appropriate spot. She stared at the darkness as she passed her water, humming beneath her breath.

She didn't return to the shack. She found her knife and slashed it in the air, practicing fighting with it. She flailed wildly before her, grunting and snarling. Trying to sound ferocious. She felt so powerful with it. So safe.

She could march out across the most dangerous parts of Hamiocho. Cross the Sun's Ashes to where the Sun Ravagers were, or head beyond the ruins outside their grove to the Reek and fight cannibals.

She could even sneak into the Glowers' territory and let them fight back with their own weapons. No one could stop her. The fantasies danced through her head of all the amazing and daring deeds she would accomplish with her knife and whatever else Maej was kind enough to give her.

Slick with perspiration, she sat on her rock and stared up into the dark. She had five hours to go.

Finally, her brother and Zhee stumbled out to pass their own water. Ablisio let out such a satisfied grunt like peeing was the best thing in the world. Or the second best. Then he grunted, "What are you doing, Amiollea?"

"Being bored," she said. "I've been up forever. I couldn't sleep."

He grunted and headed in. "What are we having to break our fast?" he muttered to himself. "Yep, that's right, algae!"

"Nourishing algae," said Zhee, joining him. "Have you eaten, Amiollea?"

"No," she muttered. "I'm fine." Her stomach fluttered too much to eat. Or so she thought, because a moment later, it growled in hunger. She felt it now. She sighed and rose. In Hamiocho, you should always eat when you had the chance.

You never knew how much effort it would take to seize your next meal.

She walked into the shack, knocking off mud from her rear. She joined her brother and Zhee scooping up the stringy algae from the bag. She piled it into her mouth. It was drying out, but still good. She chewed on it. It had a bland flavor. A little like grass, she thought. It was . . . fine. It would never be her favorite food, but it didn't make her sick.

It sustained her. That was the best most days.

"So," she asked her brother as she scooped out more. "You going to go muckraking today? Soon?"

"Naw," he said.

She stiffened. "What?"

"We have enough algae to get us through the day. I can go tomorrow."

"But . . . but . . . you said you were going today." This fluttering panic skittered around her heart. "That's what you said. Right, Zhee?"

"You did," Zhee said.

"I gathered more than I thought," he said.

Her mind struggled to think. Zhee didn't sound concerned. She was picking at her algae, the tearing sound echoing through Amiollea's ears. Her stomach writhed. Maej would be expecting her. She had to go.

She whimpered.

"What?" Ablisio asked. "I thought you'd be happy I'm not risking my life."

"It's just," she said, almost babbling, "I thought you were going to go today. Zhee and I were going to go collect excrement. She found those new latrines. We could get enough to buy algae. So, I mean, you have to go."

"I don't *have* to go. I'll go when we need me to. But we can still go scout out those latrines. It'll be safer if I'm with you."

"No!" Amiollea shrieked.

"Uh . . ." Her brother's shock rumbled out of him. "No? You *don't* want me going with you? It's safer if I'm with you. If we're together."

"It's just . . ." Amiollea floundered. She thrashed her thoughts for an excuse. "I needed to talk to Zhee."

"About what?"

"Girl stuff."

∽

"Girl stuff?" Ablisio asked in shock. He stared into the black in the direction of his sister. "Uhh . . . ?"

"Yes, girl stuff," said Amiollea. "Things between girls. Not boys. Even brothers and sisters."

"Okay," he said. "I can go out for a bit. Give you two some privacy here." His brow furrowed. "But what girl stuff? I don't smell either of you bleeding. So it's not time for your monthlies." *Shouldn't Zhee have had hers by now?* Of course, he couldn't be sure. The days all sort of blurred together. "So you can talk about your . . . girl stuff."

"Never mind," she muttered.

"Uhhh . . ." He was utterly baffled. "Did I say something wrong?"

"No, you're just an idiot! You ruin everything!" Amiollea burst to her feet and darted for the door. She rushed outside and raced around the shack.

His ears tracked her footsteps. It took him a moment to realize she was moving *away* from the shack. "Don't go far, Amiollea!" he shouted. "You hear me?"

She stopped and let out a frustrated shriek that rose to a shrill screech.

"What did I do?" he muttered. "I thought she'd be happy I wasn't risking my life."

"I thought you said muckraking wasn't as dangerous now that you figured it out," Zhee said.

"It's still dangerous. Just manageable. It's dangerous crossing the Kneeling Dark. Or just living in Hamiocho."

Zhee sighed. "True."

"So, what was that about? Girl stuff?"

"She just wants to see her Runecarver."

He groaned with annoyance. "So she planned on sneaking away from you out there? No wonder she didn't want me along."

"She can try," Zhee said. "I won't let her. Unless . . ."

"Unless what?"

"We could still do her plan."

"We're not letting her do *that* no matter what it will give her."

"She's turning into a woman, Ablisio," Zhee said in a patient tone. "She has ur—"

"No!" he snarled, refusing to hear anything like that about his sister. "I'm not letting her do that. She'll stay away from him if I have to tie her up when we leave to make sure she doesn't wander."

"With what rope?"

"I'll figure that out," he grumbled. It sickened him. She was still a child. She wasn't in need of what he shared with Zhee. Right?

∼

Stupid brother! hissed through Amiollea's mind as she dug out her knife. *Why does he have to be so dumb and worry about me?* She slashed the air before her with the blade. *He doesn't think I can protect myself!*

SWISH!

He'll never trust me if I don't prove it!

She faced out in the direction of the Spire.

Toward Maej.

She marched forward, feet stomping on muck, stepping over the familiar roots and branches. She sliced the air before her, cutting through a rotten branch. It landed on the ground. She stepped on it, the moldering crunch of it splitting in half bursting through the air.

"I can hear you, Amiollea," Ablisio called. "I'll drag you back in here."

She threw back her head and shrieked out her frustration. Maej was *waiting* for her. "I hate you! You're an idiot! I know what I'm doing! He won't hurt me!"

"I know what's best," he answered.

She had to go right now. Maej wouldn't wait forever. She could feel it. The moment was almost upon them. It would happen at any second. She just had to rush off. Defy her brother. Her big, dumb brother who just wanted to protect her and love her and keep her safe.

She wanted to just flee from him, but something tethered her to him. This knotted cord about her soul that wouldn't let her just defy him so blatantly. He would do anything to protect her, including dragging her back and sitting on her to keep her from leaving. He'd find *something* to tie her up and keep her there.

He didn't trust her, and that was the most galling thing. "I hate! Hate! HATE YOU!"

Her voice hurt. She gripped the knife, wishing she could slash the cord and free herself from him. To get away from him. But she couldn't. Blood bound them together. That warm, hot splash of their mother's life across their faces when Death killed her.

She sank onto a rock, pressing her elbows into her thighs, and shook. Her emotions poured hot down her cheeks. It was so unfair. Her toes dug into the muck before her. She squeezed her eyes shut, forcing out more tears.

The Light flared.

She didn't care to look at it.

∾

Ablisio beat down the pain. *She can hate me all she wants.*

He'd endure it. Had endured so much to protect her. He'd take every one of her slashes. She could rip his soul to pieces so long as she stayed safe. His chest tightened. His throat burned, but he fought back the tears.

"Ablisio," Zhee whispered. Her hand touched his arm. Then her head rested against his shoulder.

"It's fine," he said, listing to his sister sob. "She's not going anywhere. She'll get over this. Grow up."

"She has. That's the problem."

Ablisio nodded. He knew it to be true. It would be so much easier if she just stayed that scared little girl huddled on his lap. Too frightened to talk back. To argue with him. More terrified of being alone than questioning his orders. Maybe if he'd never taken in Zhee, Amiollea wouldn't be so rebellious.

Why couldn't Amiollea just understand that he knew what was best for her?

***

THE SPIRE VIBRATED.

Maegwirio gasped. He looked up from his notes. The maestro had finished setting off the Light. Which meant he was supposed to be out there meeting with Amiollea. She would be waiting on him. A surge of panic rushed through him.

He jumped to his feet from his study, abandoning his notes and speculations on why his key had failed. He bolted out of his study, not even caring to cover it up. He slammed his door shut and hurried down the stairs. He burst out the door and into the dark.

Rancid fear congealed in him. He so rarely came out here alone. His heart thundered, drowning out his hearing for a moment. It disoriented him. This nothing around him. Not an iota of light reached his eyes.

The shouts from the ambush opened a cold pit inside of him. Footsteps echoed. He pressed back into the door, expecting the screams. The scent of blood. One had almost killed him and stolen his satchel, taking his favorite pen and a stack of papers with his last set of notes on the lock.

Gone forever out there in the muck.

He swallowed it down. He had faced this to see her last time. He could do it again. He'd memorized the route. It wasn't too far. He trailed his hand along it. He wanted to run, but he couldn't. He reached the end of the octagonal base. He took a deep breath and struck out blind.

His hands waved before him as he fought to keep a straight line. It should be twenty-three steps to the corner of the nearest building, a house occupied by an ink maker and his family. He counted each one, fingertips straining.

"Twenty."

Almost there.

"Twenty-one."

Where is it?

"Twenty-two?"

I should be touching it, right?

"Twenty-three."

Where is it?

"Twenty-four."

I went in the wrong direction. It should be right in front of me.

His arms swept out wildly before him. He reached as far as he could in all directions. A complete circle. His robes swished and swirled about his lanky frame. He felt nothing. His feet shifted in place. A growing dread swallowed him.

"No, no, no, I should be here. It was easy last time!"

He fought the panic. *What will Amiollea do? She strolls around the entire city it like it's nothing. She can't see anything and walks with impunity.*

"*Your eyes are a crutch,*" Amiollea's voice whispered through his mind. "*They make you weak. Without them, you have to learn other ways to see. I can feel you moving on my skin. I can smell how close you are. My ears are picking up echoes. We have buildings around us, but there is an alley to our right. The sounds don't echo back from there much.*"

Maegwirio lowered his arms. He had to do that. He closed his eyes. It would do nothing for him, but he needed to concentrate. He took breaths, fighting his heart's pounding beat. He concentrated on his face. His hair.

A slight breeze flowed almost straight at him. He extended his right arm and pushed up his sleeve. He felt the air spilling over it, jostling the fine down of his hair. The air blew back toward the direction from which he'd come.

This must be flowing down the street. It can't come from a building.

So he faced the street. He was aiming for a building on the left side. So if he moved to his left, he should find it. He thrust that arm and then took a sideways step in that direction. Then a second, fingertips straining for—

Stone.

He felt the rough texture beneath him. He let out a sigh of relief. He felt the texture beneath his palm. He had found it. Confidence re-surged through him. His robes suddenly felt like a detriment. He had so much surface area of skin that could be used to feel the air.

And it wasn't like it was cold in Hamiocho. It always felt like summer. Humid, groggy summer.

He followed the building to the end of the street. He crossed to the right side and found the building. He followed it around the corner, using touch to navigate. He dragged his fingers along walls, his feet shifting out before him to feel for obstacles. He wanted to go faster, feeling time dragging on and on.

Too long to get there. He should have left an hour ago. But he'd gotten caught up in his test.

She'll be waiting, he told himself. *I'll make it up to her.* He checked his pocket. He had the scabbard in there he'd made for her dagger. Along with a belt to fit her waist. He took a left and moved closer to the wall.

She's eager to see me. She won't leave.

He told himself this as he moved closer and closer to the postern gate. Finally, he reached the outer wall and went left. Three steps later and he found the small gate. He turned the knob and stepped out onto the edge of the escarpment.

"Amiollea," he called. "I'm so sorry I'm late. I tested the key to get into my maestro's office. It was a failure, and I got caught up in . . ."

No one answered.

"Amiollea?"

He didn't hear her. He breathed in deeply, trying to find her scent. He smelled his robes. His own sweat. Mud. Not that feminine musk that wreathed her, that exciting scent that had filled his dreams the last few nights.

"Are you hiding again, Amiollea?" he asked. He reached out and found the wall. He swept his hands down it.

Nothing.

He swallowed. *She's just late. That's it. She'll be here.*

He leaned against the wall and settled in to wait.

And wait.

She didn't come. His sense of time was distorted. Wrapped up in darkness, in nothing, all he had was the feel of a wall behind him, the near-still air around him, and his robes on him. He squirmed and fidgeted.

Dark thoughts started intruding. *She's not coming because she just used me for the dagger,* warred with, *She waited and waited, but I was so late she thinks I don't care about her.*

He didn't know which was worse. That she had used him for a weapon, or that she thought he didn't value her. Both twisted up his guts and kept him waiting and waiting, hoping that both ideas were wrong.

The ideas skirmished in his mind. They hacked and slashed as he slouched against the stone. His knees slowly buckled. He slid down the wall until he sat hugging his legs. He rested his chin on his knees. A hot bitterness stung his eyes.

She just used me for the dagger won the fight.

He felt sick. It hurt more than he could have thought possible. He wanted to see her with such fervent need he almost set off into the dark. But he had no idea how to even find her. He had arrived in Hamiocho as a boy of nine mere hours before Darkfall. What little he remembered of the city was seen with awe as he was led through it by the caravan who'd brought him from the mountain vastness of Taechiz.

Finally, he stood. He slouched to the postern gate. He stumbled back to the Spire, his shoulder rubbing against the wall. His heart beat against the pain squeezing it. He wanted to rip it out.

He hardly paid attention to his return, retracing his steps without much focus on it. When he reached the octagonal base of the tower, he sighed. He opened the door and stepped into the lightlock. He closed it shut behind him before opening the interior door.

Light stabbed into his eyes. He winced against it. He closed his lids and fumbled his way inside. He could find the table by memory. He sat at it, his eyes still stinging from the light. He fluttered them open, pupils dilating.

"You look like a boy whose girl promised to meet him beneath the kissing tree and never showed up," Maestro Kozonio said.

Maegwirio started at the sight of the aged man sitting across from him, a bowl of steaming algae before him. The old man spooned up the stringy substance to his lips and slurped it into his mouth.

"Basically," Maegwirio grunted.

"Well, if you have time to mope, you have time to help me make new swords," the old man said. "Once I'm done, we'll be off. That will keep your mind off her. Is it Iahzachea's daughter? She's your age, right?"

"She's ten, Maestro," he muttered, wanting to lie on his bed and sleep away the pain.

"Huh?" said the older man. "I thought she was older than that."

"You're thinking of Nexohachea's granddaughter. She's my age. And, no, it's not her."

"Is it Nachiotzea?"

"She's married!" Maegwirio shook his head. "I'm not having this conversation with you."

"When did she get married?" the maestro asked.

"Three years ago. We attended her wedding." Maegwirio gave the old man a look. "You fell asleep during it."

"Did I?" The maestro shrugged. "Boring things, weddings. Why I never bothered." He frowned. "How did we get talking about weddings?"

∼

Hunger drove Emmait from the shack. He settled on muckraking. If that whiner Ablisio could do it, so could he. Making his sister cry. Just wanting to lie in there and be lazy. Doing *it* with Zhee. Emmait didn't need to hear *that* again.

Not when she made those noises for Ablisio.

I'm brave enough to do it, Emmait told himself.

He reached the blue smear of the lake. He drove down his fear. He'd never been so desperate to get food before. In the past, he'd climbed over the rubble for food. He'd robbed other mucklings or traded favors to Blind Fishers or Ratters for meat.

He stepped out onto the slope leading to the water. The large lake glowed, the surface serene. The color hurt his eyes. He looked at it askance, keeping it at odd angles while he moved around it, searching for algae. When he came across it, he piled it into his mouth. He fed his hunger. He moved fast, scampering over the mud, on the edge of life and death.

It didn't seem that hard. He stuffed his face with the algae. He didn't hear a whisper of Death. The chthonic horror couldn't get him. He spat out bits of mud and crawled forward. He found another pile and shoved it into his mouth.

He fed one hunger, but another grew in him.

He had to get back to Zhee. To listen to her. Be near her.

CHAPTER
TWENTY-ONE

Ablisio woke to dread squeezing his guts.

It felt early.

Zhee still slept beside him. Her body, normally a comfort, felt almost a burden this morning. A vast weight like he was a Povazian laborer laden with sacks and sacks of grain, his back bowed from the strain as he staggered through the market.

Amiollea, sleeping nearby, was another weight.

He had to feed them. He had to keep them alive. Normally, it never weighed on him, but . . .

Why did I claim that muckraking was easy?

A few days ago, in the giddy reunion after his survival, he'd felt invincible. He had faced Death, escaped the hoary entity's notice while it had ripped apart the other muckling who wasn't as smart as him.

I wasn't smart. I was scared. So scared I didn't move. That's why I'm alive. And yet he'd boasted and lied about it, a merchant promising the high quality of his jugs that couldn't hold water for more than an hour. Now he had to go. He had to feed them.

They'd finished off all but a handful of algae yesterday. Muckraking was the only sure way to eat today, tomorrow, and the next. He pulled away from

Zhee, hating this resentment building inside of him, this barrier against the rising flood of fear filling his guts.

He stood. Zhee shifted in her sleep, rolling onto her side. He marched outside into the hot dark. It was night. Probably. If the world existed out beyond the Darkfall. If it hadn't constricted to a single bubble around one damned city.

He rubbed his hand across his face as he stared toward Phosphor Lake. A faint, bluish lightning to the dark. A band of almost imperceptible color verging on deep violet. He had to go there and risk it again. He had no choice. He moved through the orchard the short distance, a few blocks, and stopped at the edge of the slope, staring at the waters.

I could have used the last few days to prepare going over the Rubble. To find a good break in the wall. A place where the runes aren't as closely placed as they should be.

Those were getting harder to find. He could have helped the girls collect more excrement or scrounged through ruins picked over a thousand times in the hopes for a miraculous bit or rope or clothing or even wood that wasn't rotten. An overlooked kitchen knife. Something that could be traded to the Ratters or the Blind Fishers.

Instead, he had stayed safe. Kept to his home.

Now he had to march out and risk his life. Come close to Death's touch. Memories of the glowing water surged at him. How the lake had bulged upward like something had risen out of the water. Something that hated him and wanted to kill him.

And he had no choice. He'd given his word. His sister and woman counted on him. He had to do it. That was how the world worked, right? The man marched out into the dark. To hunt. To break his back in the field or the mines. To bring back the resources so that his women could be safe and raise the next generation who would repeat the entire cycle again and again and again.

Only here, the cycle had been broken. It had been ground into muck. In the chaos, so many had died, and those who survived had shattered. It was the rare man who hadn't betrayed them for survival. Those who'd tried to keep their families were preyed upon by those who didn't care, their wives and daughters taken to be used in new ways.

Ablisio had clung to those old ways. He wanted to be a man. He didn't think much of his father. It was his mother whose death had so dominated his dreams, but every day his father had worked in his shop and created the furniture that fed their family another day.

He'd work for hours and hours with his tools. Sometimes he'd come home with cuts, his back aching, wearied by his long days of labor. He'd suffered every day to provide for them while his mother suffered to cook and clean and clothe them.

Darkfall had stolen away normalcy.

Out there in the black, his father had died. Ablisio knew his father had ran out into the chaos to find his family. How he died . . .? Ablisio didn't know the particulars, but he knew in his heart Darkfall orphaned him and his sister.

Ablisio tried his best to cling to it. And that meant he had to march out there and muckrake. He had to get the food for them. He would. No matter how much fear liquefied his bowels. He battered down his terror.

No cowards in Hamiocho! he growled at himself. *No cowards in damnation! They're the ones who get preyed upon. Their lives are taken. Their women stolen.*

He would march out there puking his guts out if he had to.

∽

ABLISIO HAD SPENT a long time just standing at the edge of the orchard before the slope leading to the lake.

Emmait had been asleep when Ablisio marched out of his shack. The youth had woken up, grabbing the hilt of his sword, worried that Ablisio had discovered him. He was *eager* to defend himself, only . . .

Ablisio had marched past Emmait toward the lake and . . . stood there, muttering to himself, the words too low for Emmait's keen ears to hear. He'd waited halfway between Ablisio and the shack, it wasn't too great a distance. He tracked both.

Finally, the women stirred. They embarked on their normal ritual. Urination. Filling their water jar from the nearby spring they used. Eating the last of the algae. The spoke with the casual boredom of those who spend too much time together so knew what topics were safe.

Laughter from Zhee's jokes.

Talks of collecting excrement and muckraking. Ablisio didn't seem to be in a hurry to go. Nor did Amiollea. Venturing beyond their domicile, hidden in the rotting orchard, opened them all to risk.

Emmait waited until, finally, he heard them leaving.

"Let's go collect some shit," Amiollea said. There was something utterly girlish about her tone, like saying the word so boldly was itself a joke because she giggled. "Come on, Ablisio, that always used to make you laugh."

"You're not eight any longer and enjoying swearing for the first time," he grunted. "Are you two going to be safe?"

Emmait wasn't happy about Amiollea going with Zhee. He'd hoped she wouldn't want to leave the shack since she'd missed her meeting with the Runecarver. *Now how can I speak with Zhee alone?* How could he just enjoy being around her? He ached to talk to her.

Impress her.

He kept his frustration bottled up as he backed away from the shack. He moved through the darkness with careful steps. Their sounds dwindled so he hurried along, soon leaving behind the orchards and entering his new home territory. He hardly knew it other than the fact those strange ascetics, the shadow painters, used it for their latrines. He'd never met a muckling who interfered with them. They were supposedly holy.

Beings supported by the Old Gods.

That word always felt nebulous to Emmait. He had a vague idea of something up there, above the clouds, watching him. Like there was some sort of old man peeking over the clouds to spy on him when he was peeing behind a tree in the garden. A father waiting for his child to be disobedient.

Such a critical being didn't seem like someone who should be worshiped.

No one knew how the Shadow Aesthetics fed themselves. Or defended themselves. People avoided them for similar reasons they avoided the Sun Ravagers: those considered mad to the suffering denizens of Hamiocho were truly alien beings.

The smell of death drew him to Sun. The corpses Emmait had slain four days ago were growing bloated and rotting. Sun abandoned the bone he gnawed upon, dropping it with a clatter, to pad toward Emmait.

"Hey, Sun," Emmait said, guilt rippling through him. Sun had been his companion for all these years. Every day, the dog bounded up to him with the same loyalty and love. Never wavering. *And I've been ignoring you, but . . .*

He didn't quite understand the urges Zhee inspired in him, but they were powerful. As strong as needing to eat. He could be lost just listening to her while darker impulses demanded he just take her. That was how Hamiocho worked. Women were just things to use.

But Zhee wasn't a thing. A thing didn't have a name. Didn't laugh and tell stories and make those cries of passion in Ablisio's arms.

"Your breath stinks," Emmait said to Sun and laughed. His stomach rumbled. He'd glutted while muckraking the other day, but he hadn't eaten since then. "I guess we should figure out how we're feeding ourselves today. We could do another Glower raid."

There was a part of him that wanted to raid Lord Achogear's pantry again. If the man had his soldiers still quartering the dark, then Lord Achogear's house was open and vulnerable. The perfect time to strike.

Besides, if he did run into trouble, he had his new sword.

"Let's get these bodies cleaned up, okay?" he said. "We can't just let them stink up the place. I know you don't mind, but I do."

He broke from Sun and searched for the corpses. He found one, grabbing bloated flesh. He lifted it and something scurried away. Instincts screamed through him. He drew his sword from its makeshift baldric and swung it down at the ground.

He hit something. He smelled blood. His hands reached out and he found a fat rat. He grinned and lifted it. "I've been feeding you, too, huh?" He swung the dead thing by its tail. He'd managed to get just the head. "Now you got to pay. Nothing's free in Hamiocho. Right, Sun?"

Sun whimpered and nuzzled his thigh. The entire dog's body rubbed past him, ending with a wagging tail thumping into his knee. He grinned and set about cleaning his home, his stomach rumbling.

Some fresh meat would be perfect.

Amiollea had kept everyone from leaving too early. She had this mad hope inside of her that Maej would be there today. That he would come out and meet her even though she had stood him up. He had taken the risk to step outside the wall alone.

He wouldn't do that again, but...

He must think I just used him for the knife. And she had, but she wanted more from him. Not just food, but knowledge. To talk to him. To be around him. He was so unlike anyone else. A man who didn't try to rape her. He wasn't like her brother who wanted to leash her. And he definitely felt different from Zhee.

So he had to be waiting for her today because she needed to see him. She needed to know if he had unlocked his maestro's door and learned the secret behind the Light.

"Be safe," Zhee whispered to her brother. Amiollea could hear them hugging, skin pressed on skin. "Don't take risks. We'll collect enough excrement to go to the dispensary tomorrow. We could even go a day hungry."

Amiollea stiffened. "But why risk going a day without food? Skip too many meals, and you end up a sleeper."

"Your brother's life is worth more than... than... filling your belly," Zhee said and there was a sharp warning in her voice.

Amiollea winced. *She knows what I'm going to do.* "Sorry. You don't have to risk yourself."

"It'll be fine," he said, sounding so noble. "I'll get us food. You two be safe. Don't let those shadow ascetics catch you stealing their crap."

"I was planning on holding the jar for them to squat in," Amiollea quipped. "Get it nice and fresh."

"Better than digging through the muck for it," muttered Zhee. "Come on, let's get going."

"I'll be safe," Ablisio said. They kissed, the wet smack of lips reaching Amiollea's ears.

She rolled her eyes without even knowing she did it. She hardly paid any attention to her eyes and how much they moved. She listened to her brother march off into the dark with powerful certainty, so full of confidence in what he was doing.

"Be safe!" she cried out, sudden fear knifing through her.

"I thought you wanted me to die," he answered her, still walking away.

She winced. "Of course not. You're my brother. Why are you so stupid?"

"I'm your brother, so if *I'm* stupid..."

A smile played on her lips.

She waited for him to get farther away before she darted to her rock and grabbed her knife from beneath it. She wiped the muck off the blade on her thigh before dashing over to Zhee. The Povazian held an empty jar.

Her brother's steps paused. "And Amiollea, don't even think of sneaking off from Zhee. If you do, I *will* find a way to stake you to the ground whenever I go out."

"I'm not going to sneak away!" she hissed, anger flaring through her. "Even though Maej is just what we need, but you're too dumb to see it."

"We're not having this conversation," he growled. "I warned you. Disobey me and regret it."

"There you go again, being an idiot! Go and risk your stupid life muckraking! You don't have to! I found us a better way! Keep being a shit-for-brain! Once you're dead, I'll do it! I'll—"

"Enough!" Zhee snapped. "He's risking his life to feed you! Don't be a brat! If you want him to treat you like an adult, then don't be a spiteful rat."

Amiollea spat at Zhee and hissed in frustration. Her brother's footsteps receded. She stamped her foot. Why did he have to go and ruin everything? She had *almost* forgiven him only for him to remind her how much he deserved her anger.

"Why do you do that to him?" Zhee muttered, fury thick in her voice. "He loves you."

"I know," muttered Amiollea. "That's what makes it suck. If he just wanted to use me, I could run away. Escape him, but I love him, too. And I know he just wants me safe, but he's being too *stubborn*. He doesn't trust me."

"You're not going to earn his trust by wishing his death."

"Sorry." Amiollea squirmed.

"You're going to have to bring him something. Some proof." Zhee shifted.

"I think it's the only way to get through to him that you're a woman. You really trust this Maej?"

"Well . . ." Amiollea hesitated. "I don't think he's ever hurt anyone in his life. He's *soft*, Zhee. Like . . . in his soul or something. He was terrified when the Sun Ravagers attacked. Flailing blind. He's helpless in the dark. When I was eight, I could have handled him."

"Then go," Zhee said. "That knife you have is a good start. Show your brother the advantages of it, and maybe he'll agree, but . . ." She sighed. "He believes muckraking is the best way for us to survive."

"I'll do it!" Amiollea declared.

Before Amiollea even knew what she was doing, she was hugging Zhee. She threw her arms around the woman and held her tight. She rocked Zhee, this giddy rush shooting through her. Zhee stiffened for a moment before returning the embrace with Amiollea.

"Thank you," Amiollea said. She hesitated. "For a leech, you're not terrible."

"There's those spiteful, childish words again," Zhee said, her tone almost . . . motherly.

Amiollea's cheeks warmed. Before she could say anything stupid, she broke away and hurried through the Rotting Orchard, hope beating beneath her breast. Lapping at its heels was the turbulent flood of dread.

Was she about to cross half of Hamiocho for nothing?

Please, please, please be there, Maej.

∽

Z<small>HEE SMILED</small>, a little shocked by the hug. *She's finally growing up.*

That was good. An Amiollea who had an outlet for her affections that wasn't her brother was a good thing. The girl clung to him tight because she had no one else, and now Zhee hoped something beautiful could blossom in Hamiocho.

Something normal.

She rubbed her belly before hefting her jar and heading in the opposite direction. As she left behind the Rotting Orchard to sniff out the latrines, she wondered if she'd run into Emmait again. It had been only four days, but that was a lifetime in Hamiocho.

People died so easily here.

But he had that sword. I wonder where he got it. That must be a story.

She entered the neighborhood, muck giving way to cobblestones. She followed her mental map to the nearest active ravine. She kept her ears peeled for sounds, every breath through her nose for any scents.

She smelled a faint rot coming from the latrine she refused to check. The ascetics would never use it again, and she didn't need to think about what had almost happened.

I didn't get taken. Nothing happened to me.

The click of claws on cobblestones drifted out of the dark. Soft but approaching her. She turned down a street and said, "Hello, Emmait."

"Zhee," he said in surprise. "You're back."

"Well, I bet those shadow painters have taken a few more shits."

He chuckled, his excitement echoing through the buildings of her old neighborhood. Once, this sound hadn't been alien here. It had echoed with the delight of Povazian children who didn't know just how poor they were. It was a welcomed sound.

"They probably have," he said when he stopped.

"You don't know?" she asked in surprise. "I thought you lived around here now."

"Oh, well, I've been busy." He padded closer, his footfalls sounding louder than they should. Like he was letting her hear him. "Survival, you know?"

"Hence why I'm about to get ankle-deep in crap." She breathed in. "Do I smell blood on you?"

"I caught a rat."

"Impressive. I don't know how the Ratters do it. Those vermin scurry away so easily."

He chuckled again. "Well, we all have our skills."

"Mmm, I'm good at finding shit, and you're good at finding rats. In any other place, those would be poor skills, but here . . ."

"We're so blessed," he said wryly.

She laughed as they headed down the street toward the sour reek.

Emmait was so different from the other men who lived in Hamiocho. He didn't want to harm her. Didn't want to use her body. He just wanted to help her. A decent person. She was glad another one existed in the city.

"I bet you'd like to meet Ablisio," she said.

He stiffened. "Your man? The one who lets you come out here alone?"

"He's doing something even more dangerous. If he wasn't watching out for his sister, I bet you two could be friends."

"Why does his sister matter?"

"He's protective. And you're, well, male." She laughed again. She liked that about Ablisio. "You two might be the last decent men in the city. At least mucklings. That's rare, you know? Precious."

"It's been a long time since anyone's called me precious."

∼

I'm precious!

A thrill bubbled through Emmait. The emotion rose through him. Like the springs scattered throughout the city that brought clean water to the people, their sources too deep to be corrupted by the rot of the surface.

"Maybe it's best if he doesn't know about me," said Emmait. "I don't want to trigger any protective feelings."

She giggled, causing those fleshy bits of hers to slap together and ripple. The sound stirred that heat in him. He ran his hand through Sun's fur to fight the urge to grab them. Squeeze them. They must feel so soft. *Ablisio is so lucky.*

He definitely didn't want Ablisio to learn of his existence. If he killed the man *before* he'd won Zhee over, she'd hate him. And he would do anything to avoid that. Even if it meant sparing a man who had what he wanted.

He violated the earliest rule he'd learned from Hamiocho: the strong preyed on the weak. It was better to be strong.

∼

Ablisio stood on the edge of the muddy shore. Phosphor Lake hurt his eyes. He stared at it from oblong angles. His knees quivered. The fear liquefied his bowels and threatened to spill out of him. He clenched his sphincter.

He couldn't step out there. Death whispered in the air. He could almost hear the ancient horrors flying above. There was too much light. He would be exposed. Naked and vulnerable. It didn't matter how strong he was. The greatest fighter in the mightiest armor had died on Darkfall. Death couldn't be harmed. You couldn't argue with it. Fight it.

All you could do was die.

Ablisio didn't want to die. He wanted to live. For his sister. For Zhee. For himself most of all. Hamiocho wore at his soul. Existence wearied him day after day, burying him further and further into the muck, but it held moments of sweetness. When his sister didn't hate him. When he held Zhee. Not just the lovemaking, but the kisses, the tenderness of her embrace.

His stomach rumbled.

Right now, Amiollea and Zhee dug through latrines to get them food that was only marginally safer. They soiled themselves because their bellies growled with that same need. There was no escaping it. He had to go out there.

For them.

For the scared girl who'd clung to him soaked in their mother's blood.

For the sobbing woman he'd rescued from her rapists' cruelty.

If it was just himself, he would never have found the strength to push past his terror.

Ablisio edged out onto the muddy shore. He fell to his knees after two steps. It squished beneath him. His hands planted onto the slime and he crawled forward, every step battling against dread's net yanking him back toward the safety of the darkness.

He ventured closer and closer to the blue-glowing lake. His arms became distinct. His fingers separated from the darkness of the mud. Light painted his flesh and exposed him to the uncaring vitriol of Death.

He quested for food.

CHAPTER
TWENTY-TWO

Amiollea dripped with water. She did her best to clean herself after crossing the Slithering Pit. She found that same pool she used last time that wasn't *too* covered in scum. She scrubbed off the mud while remembering her mother's perfume.

The scent of flowers distilled into a spray.

A memory, startling in its vibrancy, struck Amiollea as she climbed the hill beside the Escarpment. She was sitting on her mother's lap at her dressing table. Mother had a smile on her face as she held up the delicate bottle of crystal full of an amber liquid.

"Perfume from across the Drylands and beyond even the Povaz Protectorate," Mother whispered with obvious delight. "From the burned lands of Maleki'z where everyone has skin even darker than ours. Not brown, but *black*."

"Wow, Momma," young Amiollea had answered. She had been maybe six. A year or so before Darkfall.

"This is the scent of flowers that can't grow in Karadris. Not even here in Hamiocho. It had to cross all those thousands of miles to reach here." She pulled off the glass stopper and pressed the mouth against her wrist. She turned the bottle up and down, letting the liquid come in contact with her brown skin for less than a heartbeat. "Smell it."

She'd brought her wrist to Amiollea's nose. The child had breathed in. Joy burst in her soul. "It's sweeter than gardenias. Than tulips or fuchsias."

"The flower's called a southern rose," her mother continued. She inhaled it herself. "Your father bought it for me."

"Why?"

"Because he's a good man." A radiant smile spread on her lips. "One day, you'll find one. It's the eyes. You'll see it in his eyes. In the moment that you're united, the truth is there. What he truly feels."

Even now, she didn't quite understand that last part. She thought it had to do with "Zhee" things her brother did with the leech. As a child, she hadn't even realized her parents did things like that. She thought they played in their bedroom when she heard weird sounds. Like how she wrestled with her brother.

Amiollea smiled as she reached the top of the bluff and the wall of the Runic Ward. She didn't have perfume, but she smelled as nice as she could considering where she was. It would have to be good enough for Maej. It was a shame she could never see into his eyes.

She would have to trust his voice. It was gentle. Sweet. He had a shyness about him. An innocence that she'd lost so many years ago. He had stayed safe while she had endured so much. She hated the Glowers and the Runecarvers for hiding behind their walls, but not Maej.

He wasn't just *a* Runecarver.

He was . . . special. Different. He wanted to speak with a muckling.

And not why you think he does, Ablisio! she thought angrily to her dumb brother. A flutter of fear then washed through her confusing emotions. He was doing something dangerous, and she didn't want him to get hurt.

She just wanted him to trust her. To know she could handle things. Was that too much? Anger swept through her again, the urge to lash out with her knife building in her. She gripped the handle, the metal reassuring.

She reached the top of the Escarpment with trepidation. He wouldn't be here. Why would he? He had to think she didn't care about him. He had to think she had just used him for the knife like all the other mucklings would.

What could she do to change that? To prove to him that she wasn't *only* interested in the knife?

Break into the Runic Ward?

Her hand ran along the outside of the wall. Going off her memory, she knew she'd reached the right spot before she even felt the postern door. She leaned against the wall and trembled. She didn't even realize she'd closed her eyes as she struggled not to let doubt and fear destroy her hope.

Like the Glowers in their houses with every conceivable wall and door and crack sealed tight, she hid her hope in a strong shelter. She wouldn't let the darkness see it. She breathed slowly to calm herself as she fought against her doubts.

The moment of the Light flashing came closer and closer. He should be here if he were coming. She rubbed her head into the wall, her matted hair rasping about it. She needed to cut it short again. She had a proper knife instead of gritting her teeth while Zhee hacked at her tresses with a piece of stone they'd managed to make passably sharp.

It was more tearing than cutting.

Her toes flexed. The moment swelled and swelled. She stared out at the city, not looking at the Light. It blossomed. For a second, stark white rippled out over her. The Slithering Pit lit up, a thousand mirrors of different sizes and shapes reflecting the flash of light sweeping over the cursed city. She caught a hint of ruined buildings, the stones crumbling from the heat, the humidity, and the spreading mold.

The darkness crashed down on her.

She braced herself against the pain of disappointment. He wouldn't come. This was pointless. She was wasting her time.

⁓

"She's not coming," Maegwirio muttered to himself as he sat at his table. He could hear his maestro coming down the stairs. He should have left already if he were going to meet with her. But that was yesterday.

He had left. She never came.

She made it clear with her actions that she'd just used him.

Maestro Kozonio paused at his office. The door opened, the smooth glide of perfect hinges, then the boom of it shutting. Maegwirio leaned forward and rubbed his hands across his face. Grit clung to the edges of his eyes.

Not enough sleep.

He kept thinking up new reasons why she hadn't appeared, each one worse than the last.

She had been delayed, and he hadn't waited long enough.

Her brother had caught her and prevented her from coming.

She'd hurt herself crossing the Sluggish Waters.

A viper had bitten her in the Slithering Pit.

Attacked by mucklings and raped.

She lay dead in the dark.

Injured and needing to be rescued.

A hundred reasons why he should just go and see if she showed up.

Could he withstand that crushing disappointment again? He stared at the half-formed sword before him. He had shaped the metal. He had to finish carving the runes, but he had no enthusiasm for it. Amiollea was out there.

Somewhere.

A city of darkness and mud and rot. How could anyone survive out there and be as happy as her? How did the unending murk not crush her spirit? She scrounged, hid, and fought for every scrap of food.

What did he have to worry about? How to violate his maestro's privacy and break into his office? Such a burden he had to carry when compared to hers. There were a hundred reasons why she could have missed their appointment.

And only one good reason not to check: *I might be hurt if she doesn't come this time.*

∼

ABLISIO'S TREMBLING hand brought the next pile of algae to his bag. He didn't let the terror control him. No frantic crawl across the mud. No whimpers of fear. He moved with slow deliberation. Going fast in Hamiocho led to disaster. He wouldn't let Death kill him. He had braved it today.

But he couldn't keep doing it.

He had to find another way to provide. Every way to gather food was growing harder and harder. They could scrounge for a week and not find anything useful. Going over the Rubble meant risking the ever-growing competence of the Glowers' guards. The dispensaries kept raising the amount of shit they wanted. Fewer bands of raiders around to kill.

Fewer people around.

That was the sad state of things. Mucklings died every day, but who replaced them? Who had children? Zhee certainly had never conceived. Despite their daily couplings, she had never quickened with child. His fault? Hers? Did it matter? Could they handle a squalling baby in this place?

Would their child even have a chance to survive?

He scooped up more algae and thrust it into his bag. He hefted it, judging the weight. Had he collected enough? Did he need to get more? He had at least a day's worth of food already. Enough to get them by and go to the dispensary tomorrow. Zhee and Amiollea would find the excrement they needed.

Should have used the last few days to have them collect it. That's our best bet for food.

He pushed down his sister's plan. A part of him, while he was wracked with terror, wanted to take the easiest path, but it was too risky. Even if Maej wasn't the sort of man Ablisio knew him to be, what about the other Runecarvers? How would they take it to find one of their young men was sneaking out to give things to a muckling girl?

Runecarvers were dangerous. Magic stained their skin blue. Were they even truly human? And why did they unleash the Light every day? He froze and realized it would be coming soon. He didn't want to be out here when it happened.

That's enough food. No more risks. Ablisio crawled back toward the safety of the pure darkness.

∼

"So how did you and Ablisio meet?" Emmait asked as he squatted by the latrine she dug around in. The scent was . . . pungent.

"He saved me," she answered with a pleased tone in her voice. "He saved my life. He's my hero."

"I thought I was your hero," Emmait muttered, his thrill from earlier swallowed up by that word. "You would have died without me."

"You are my hero, too," Zhee said, her words smooth. They flowed off her tongue like honey dribbling from the jar onto a piece of bread. He hadn't had either since Darkfall. "Thank you for saving me."

"If he's your man—your *hero*—why didn't he save you the other day?"

She shifted her position and scooped up excrement. "He was off muckraking. Getting us food."

"He sent you to get the resources for food and didn't come with you to protect you?" Emmait snorted. "And he did it again today."

"Amiollea's supposed to be with me." She moved a step closer to him. "Besides, this isn't a dangerous part of the city. Not any longer."

"Yeah, I noticed."

"Last time was a fluke. I was surprised to find any cannibals still alive."

"Still, if you were my woman, I'd make sure you were safe."

"He does his best."

"And his best was working out so well when I saved you."

∽

She swallowed at those words. If Emmait hadn't come along, she would have suffered greatly the last few hours of her life before she filled the cannibals' bellies. She pushed down those thoughts along with the fear. The helplessness. Those emotions didn't help.

She buried them deep in her.

"He couldn't have known," she said, her voice tight. "He thought I would be fine. Besides, he trusts me to go out of his hearing. You know how many men allow their women to do that?"

"I don't know," Emmait said. "I don't normally interact with people. I stay away. Just me and Sun."

The dog, as if hearing his name had caused it, yawned. Then his tail thumped into the ground. Zhee smiled. She didn't think any dogs had survived those first weeks of hunger. Cats, horses, donkeys, chickens. Anything that could be eaten, was. She remembered two weeks after Darkfall. That was when the hope that she and Father would find Mother alive had faded. Father had found a dog. A cur that had growled at them. With patience, he'd coaxed the dog to them.

Then snapped its neck. She had wept even as she filled her belly with the meat. So she was glad at least one dog lived.

She felt the warm sting of tears on her cheeks. "Ablisio doesn't make me his prisoner. He doesn't use me. He trusts me to come here because he thought I would be safe. We can get more done when we split up. But nothing is without risk in Hamiocho. I'm not his prisoner. I think I love that about him the most."

"Still, I'd keep you safe," Emmait said, something sullen and boyish in his tone. He suddenly felt younger than she thought him to be. He felt like he was Amiollea's age.

"You are keeping me safe," she said, nervousness sweeping through her. The way he was talking, he almost sounded . . . bitter. Like he resented that she was another man's woman. Would he ask her to do things for that protection? He had let her go last time, but . . . "Thank you."

He had that sword and a dog. If he wanted her, she wouldn't have much choice. It would be easier to surrender and suffer the pain that would come later. Wounds to her soul wouldn't kill her.

"I'll watch over you," Emmait vowed. "When you need it, let me know. I'll protect you from anything."

Relief flooded out of her. He didn't make any conditions. No demands. "I'm glad you're my friend, Emmait."

∽

He's not coming. *You should just go.*

Amiollea sighed. The Light had come and gone. She had a city to cross. How long would it be before her brother would realize she'd slipped away? How long could Zhee stay away from the house waiting for her? She didn't have a knife. Even in a relatively safe part of the city, she could still be assaulted.

Maej must hate me for not showing up, she thought. Anger at her brother swelled in her. She'd had this one chance, and he'd stolen it from her. Why should she go back? She could live out here. In the Slithering Pit and hunt snakes. No one else did it. No one else had an amazing dagger made by Maej.

She slashed the air before her.

She panted, her emotions tearing at her in a dozen different directions. To stay. To go. To return to her brother. To find her own way to live in Hamiocho. To climb the walls of the Runic Ward and find Maej.

Ablisio will worry. He'll search the city and do something dumb and get him and the leech killed.

Whatever bound her soul to her brother tugged at her. She sighed and surrendered to it. She didn't have Maej any longer, but she still had her brother and Zhee. They would find new ways to survive. She had the knife. She would tell him everything. It wouldn't matter now.

She took two quiet steps when the shuffling of feet reached her. She glanced behind her. Someone approached the gate. A patrol? It wasn't a guard. No metal jangled. The steps were unsure. Not the confidence of someone who lived in the black.

They had a cadence to them.

Joy burst through her heart as the postern gate opened. "Maej!"

∽

ABLISIO DROPPED off his algae at the house then entered the Povazian Slums to find Zhee and his sister. They would be in the northern part, near where the shadow painters dwelt. He moved on soft feet, gripping his club. The rune-cast wood had a sturdy weight about it. The elements didn't affect it.

It had saved his life a dozen times.

The ruins rose around him. The close-packed streets of the Povazian Slums. The Trudgers, as his father had called it. The men who broke their bodies for Karadrisan coins. Who'd brought their families from distant lands for the promise of something better. Did they find it?

They had brought Zhee here.

Ablisio breathed in and caught the scent of bodies. That disturbed him. But they weren't fresh. Days old. If he'd known killing happened around here, he wouldn't have let his sister and Zhee venture here to collect shit without him.

At the next intersection, he caught a whiff of Zhee's scent. It was almost buried under the sour reek of shit. He paused, feeling the wind on his skin. It was a slight breeze, but he found its source and followed it, footsteps hardly making a whisk on the dirty cobblestones.

He heard her voice drifting. He relaxed as he approached, not hiding the sounds he made. Her voice cut off. Movement. Something almost like a low growl that made him hesitate for a second. He shifted his grip on his club and breathed in again, but it was hard to smell anything over the latrine.

"Ablisio?" Zhee asked. "What are you doing here?"

"I gathered enough food for us to eat today and get us to the dispensary." He paused, listening. "Amiollea? Are you still sulking?"

"Ablisio..." Zhee's words came out tight.

"Come on, Amiollea," he said. *Maybe I've been too hard on her. Maybe... Maybe this Runecarver idea isn't as mad as I thought. It has to be safer than muckraking.* "Come on, Amiollea, I want to talk."

"Ablisio, she's not..."

The tone in Zhee's voice stiffened him. He marched forward on the street and stopped right before where Zhee's voice came from. She stepped out of the pit, her feet smacking wet. The foul aroma filled his nose, but he had grown a strong stomach.

"Where is she?" he demanded. "I heard you were talking with someone. Where is she? Tell me, Zhee!"

"That is... She—"

"Did she sneak off?" His hand shot out toward her. He brushed her arm. Seized it. He pulled her to him. "Huh?"

"She didn't sneak off."

His stomach chilled. "You let her go? Alone? You let my little sister march out across the city where any diseased muckling could seize her?"

CHAPTER
TWENTY-THREE

Zhee trembled in Ablisio's grip. She flexed her dirty fingers as he shook her. The anger washed off him, a heat that swept through the darkness and buffeted her. She didn't know what to say. How to answer him. The fear in his voice struck her to the core as she realized what she had done.

I sent her alone, she thought. *Just so she'd like me more. So I could stay and... and...*

"She's safe," Zhee choked out, terror for Amiollea squeezing about her chest.

"Safe!" he snarled.

The slight sound of movement came from her right. From Emmait. He had that sword. If he attacked Ablisio in some noble attempt to protect her... Sun must be bristling in the dark, ready to pounce.

"She's *safe?*" growled Ablisio. "She crossed half the city by herself. Again! And you let her go this time?"

"Yes," she whimpered. "This isn't the place to discuss this, Ablisio."

"Not the place? Where is the place to learn that you'd let my little sister traipse across this cesspit with nothing to guard her?"

"Someone could be listening to us," she said. "Attack us. We're making too much noise."

"Oh, so you're concerned about *us* being attacked, but not my little sister scurrying across the city. Passing nests of vipers and dens of starving maggots!" Spittle splashed across her face. "What were you thinking, Zhee?"

"That we needed something better to survive!" The anger bursting out of her shocked her. She pressed a dirty hand on her belly and felt that little bit of life growing in her. Hope. She had to be strong. "You're being stubborn about the best opportunity we've ever come across. How much longer can we go on like this?"

"I'm saving us!" he growled back.

"It isn't enough."

His hand tightened on her. She braced herself. He'd never hit her, but after her father died, she had experienced a string of men who followed such backtalk with heavy hands. Men didn't like their accomplishments belittled. They didn't like to be told they'd failed. That they were inadequate. She'd learned that lesson well.

Better to lie.

To praise them, flatter their egos, their cocks. Let them think no man was better. She had used those lessons with Ablisio. She had disagreed with him but never attacked him like this.

"I'm sorry, but it's true," she said, face tensing for the impact. She had to do this. Had to hurt his ego. "You have to stop being stubborn and accept the truth. The old ways of survival are dwindling. They're not as effective. We need something new. You're a lot like your sister."

"What does that mean?"

He hadn't hit her.

Emboldened, she continued. "You both love so much." She needed to turn this. To soothe the wounds she caused. "She wants to help us survive. Let her. She's not a child any longer. She's a woman."

"I know that," he muttered.

"No, you really don't." She put a hand on his chest. She hated that Emmait was listening to this, but she had no way of explaining his presence to Ablisio. Not right now. "She wants to save you just like you want to save her."

"She doesn't have to save me! She's the one who needs protecting."

"That's what I'm saying. She doesn't want to be a burden, Ablisio."

"She's not," he protested. "Not really." His hand tightened on her arm for a moment. "I do my best to feed you both. To care for and protect you."

"I know that," she said. "But she found something, and she just wants you to listen."

"Listen, huh?" His voice hardened. "Listen as she throws herself at that boy? She doesn't need to sell herself. There are other ways."

"I don't think it's like that," Zhee said. "I don't think he wants to use her like that."

"There's not a man in the city who wouldn't throw down a woman given half a chance!"

"You wouldn't."

He sucked in a breath.

"You didn't. Not with me." She said those words low. "I came to your bed."

"I didn't turn you away. And he won't turn her away." He yanked her from the latrine.

She gasped as she stumbled to catch her footing. "Where are we going? My jug!"

"You can come back for it later! I'm not letting her do this."

∼

"I brought you some food," Maej said.

Delight burst inside of Amiollea. She could smell the jerky on him long before he produced it from his pocket. The scent of dried meat and pepper filled her nose. Her mouth watered in a flash. She couldn't remember the last time she'd had it.

She took it from him and brought it to her nose. She inhaled deeply and let out a long, low groan of delight. The aroma tickled her nose. She wrinkled it, the scent of pepper lodging in her nostrils. Then she turned her head and sneezed.

"Good health!" Maej gasped.

"Good health?" she asked. "Why would you say that?"

"Oh, well, there's an old superstition that you are sneezing out bad air. If you do it right, you don't get sick. So, wishing you good health."

"Oh, thank you," she said. Her fingers stroked up and down the dried meat. It was a strip longer than her hand from wrist to fingertip. She wanted to stuff it all in her mouth. "And thank you for this."

"It's nothing." His robes rustled. "I probably could have taken more, but we don't keep a lot of excess supplies."

"Still . . . This is a treasure."

Something rustled his hair. Was he rubbing? "It's just food."

"I know," she said. "There's nothing more valuable in all the world than food."

"I know a few Glowers who would disagree."

"Do they still use money?" she asked. "I remember coins. My father was forever counting them, worrying over them. Now food is something to worry over."

"It's a minimalist attitude," said Maej. "It makes sense you would have it. Out there, if it doesn't help you make it one more day, I guess it's useless."

"Mostly," she said, thinking of Zhee. She didn't want to end up like that woman. She had to find ways to feed her and her brother that didn't require being a leech. This was a start. Her friendship with Maej and finding out about the caravans.

She tore the jerky about a third of the way down and popped it into her mouth. She would hold the rest for when she got back to her home. She didn't know how she would explain where she'd gotten it to her brother, but she had to share it with him.

She groaned at how good it tasted as she chewed. And chewed. And chewed some more. She hadn't eaten anything this tough in so long. The algae was soft and wet, and the rat was lean and stringy. Catfish practically melted in your mouth. But this . . .

She whimpered in delight.

"That good, huh?" he asked her. "I guess it must be. I eat algae, too. Not the greatest tasting food in the world."

"No," she moaned through the jerky. It dried out her mouth and she didn't care. The peppers were strong, warming her mouth. She finally swallowed it and let out a satisfied groan, holding the jerky in one hand, the knife in the other.

"I'm glad you came today," Maej said.

"Me, too," she said, loving the feel of the jerky in her belly. "My brother kept me from coming yesterday."

"Oh, I thought I was just so late yesterday you left," he said, sounding relieved. "I kept imagining that you were furious at me. That you'd risked your life crossing all that dangerous land for nothing."

She giggled. "I was thinking pretty much the same. That you must have thought I was just using you and . . ." She trailed off. This strange sensation rippled through her. It made her shift as her cheeks warmed. "Well, I didn't like it. I had to find out if, maybe, you would show up."

"I'm glad you did," Maej said. "Oh, I made a sheath and belt for your knife. I don't know how you're carrying it around since you're, well . . ."

"Naked," she said. "You sound embarrassed. It's not like you can see me. You could strip naked right here, and I wouldn't see your little thingie."

"Little thingie," he said, groaning. "I wouldn't call it that."

"Thingie?"

"The other word." His voice sounded strained. "Oh, never mind. Here you are."

She liked it. The way he grew flustered. With her brother and Zhee, Amiollea never felt like the one standing on firm dirt but on thick muck that slowly dragged her down. But Maej was just so naïve. So adorable.

She heard the swish of a leather strap. She thought he was handing it to her then gasped as he pressed it into her side. His hands slid along her. He moved closer. His robe rustled right before her while her heart exploded into a frantic beat.

His fingers caressed her naked skin as he wrapped the belt around her. He brought it together at her navel and pulled it tight. The leather rasped on her skin. Her breath quickened. His exhalation washed across her face.

He's so close, whispered through Amiollea. The heat in her swelled. Thoughts of kissing him assaulted her. To press her lips against his mouth and make those sounds Zhee and her brother did. *Only, it won't be annoying if I do it with Maej.*

～

Maegwirio's heart pumped blazing fire through his veins as he pulled the belt closed.

She stood so close. A girl. Naked even if he couldn't see her. Then her breath crossed his face. This urge to lean in and kiss her seized him. It pulsed out of his crotch. He stiffened against his breechcloth.

Then panic swept through him. He didn't know how to kiss, and what if she didn't want him doing it to her? What if he leaned in, and she stabbed him with that knife? Or if he missed her lips and kissed her nose?

He stepped back from her in a flurry of rustling cloth. He cleared his throat. "Uh, I uh, I tried to get through my maestro's door."

"Oh," she said, her voice quiet.

Is she disappointed I didn't kiss her? Is she mad at me for putting the belt around her waist? Do girls get mad about things like that? I didn't even ask her. I'd be mad.

"Yeah," he pressed on, feeling the strain growing in the air. He was messing this up. It was clear. He couldn't let that happen. He had to get them away from his faux pas. "Yeah, I made this key. I created it to think it was part of the door."

"Part of the door?" she asked. "How does that work?"

"Well, I told you how language conveys ideas, and that's what magic is. Imposing your ideas on an object. I created one of my best rune sentences ever. The ideas all harmonized. I thought it was perfect, but I shoved it in and nothing happened."

"Oh, well, you'll figure it out," she said. "I've just been sitting in the shack listening to my brother and Zhee."

"Zhee?"

"She's the leech."

Maegwirio listened as she talked about her life. Most of it was boring, hiding in the shack in the middle of the Rotting Orchard, a place Maegwirio didn't even know about. The monotony punctuated by moments of fear and stress when they left it to scrounge for food and resources.

"Only, that's getting harder and harder to do," she said. "The ruins are picked over pretty thoroughly after all these years."

"I bet," he said. "What's the Rotting Orchard like?"

"It's just trees," she said. "They're dead. They still stand, but the ground around them's pretty muddy now. Branches will just drop off them. You can hear them crashing down. And if you brush them, they break easily now. I leaned against one of them, and it cracked. I bet I could have pushed it over without much effort."

"It's so interesting that they're dead and still standing," he said. "I would have assumed they would have collapsed."

"Half collapsed," Amiollea said. "What about you? What have you been doing in the Spire besides making keys?"

"I made a few swords," he said.

"That would be useful."

He chuckled and glanced out to his left. He couldn't see the city of Hamiocho spread out before him, but he could feel it. The festering cesspool was full of dangers, and she lived in it day after day.

"Tell me more about the city," he said. "How do you survive?"

"It's not pleasant."

"I don't care." He wanted to know more about her. He leaned against the wall separating his people from the rot and listened to her speak about blind fishermen, crazy ascetics, the Kneelers, cannibals, and more.

∼

ABLISIO SLOGGED across the Slithering Pit. The muddy water rippled about his knees. He moved as fast as as he dared across the festering depression. He had no idea if he went the right way. He'd never moved through this part of the city, but this was how Amiollea had described her path to the Escarpment and the Runic Ward perched upon it.

Zhee moved behind him, probing ahead with her feet like he did. He'd already found several treacherous pits, sudden drops in the muck that would plunge him into foul liquid. At the same time, he kept his ears listening for splashing or slithering. He wasn't about to get bitten by one of the rumored vipers.

Fury beat in him. He couldn't believe Zhee let his sister move across the city by herself. It was madness. He wouldn't let Zhee travel so far on her own. No one should. Hamiocho was too dangerous, but doubly so for a woman.

The filth would just kill Ablisio. They wouldn't use him for pleasure for as long as they could. They wouldn't abuse him day after day. *Zhee! You should know better! I saved you from that, and you send my sister out here!*

"Ablisio," Zhee said.

"I don't want to hear it!" he growled.

She sighed. "I don't care. Something has to change. I can feel it. We're not going to last another year. Hamiocho is dying."

"What can I do about that?"

"Listen to your sister."

He growled out his anger. Dark thoughts stirred through him. Shameful thoughts. It would be so easy to throw Zhee out of their shack. Keeping Amiollea alive would be so much easier if he had one less mouth to feed. His sister would be happier. She wouldn't be running off, acting rebellious.

What sort of man thinks these thoughts? he demanded of himself. It sickened him. His father wouldn't do that. *Ablisio* wouldn't do that.

He would find a way to keep them all alive. He had to.

The ground changed as before him, air washed over a wall. They climbed out of the muck onto dry land and found the Escarpment. He went to his left and, like Amiollea had claimed, the ground sloped up at an angle. Zhee panted behind him as he pushed up the slope, feet sliding before him over the crumbling road.

It leveled out and he paused. He didn't know where to go now. Where was Amiollea meeting this Maej? He cocked his head. Zhee pressed up behind him, her hands resting on his hips. They trembled. Afraid.

Some of his anger dwindled.

He was about to ask her opinion when footsteps approached.

CHAPTER
TWENTY-FOUR

"I'll see you in three days," she said, giving Maej's hand a final squeeze.

"Yes," he said, his voice brimming with excitement.

The urge to kiss him swelled in Amiollea. With it came this great fear that she would do it wrong. She had no idea *what* her brother and Zhee did when they pressed lips. She just heard the wet smacks and the increasingly sloppy sounds. It often sounded so *messy* to her ears.

But now it was a messy sound she wanted to make with Maej, but if she did it wrong...

But what if she did it right? This breathy, nervous exhilaration washed through her. If she did it right, would he want to do *other* things she'd heard her brother and Zhee enjoy? A confusing welter of desire and dread bubbled through her.

"Bye!" she gasped and broke away from him because it was the easiest thing to do.

For a moment, his hands clutched to her like he didn't want to let her go. Their fingers parted. She shivered and turned her back. She heard him breathing, his robes rustling about his frame, as she hurried down the side of the Runic Ward's wall. She ran her hands down it, not wanting to step off the cliff.

As bewildered as she felt, she couldn't trust her navigation until she calmed down. And she couldn't do that until she didn't hear Maej any longer. Smell how clean and fresh he was. *I'm so dirty. Why would he even want to kiss a muckling? There must be beautiful Taechizian girls he could kiss aplenty. Girls that have access to soap.*

Amiollea remembered soap in her dreams. Father would bring the copper tub out and mother would spend hours boiling the water to fill it. Amiollea had splashed the soapy surface in delight as her big brother washed her hair from behind.

She didn't want to hate Ablisio. He just had to stop being so stupid. With Zhee. With her. *If he just listened to me, then everything would be smooth. I wouldn't have to sneak out here and trust Zhee not to tattle on me.*

She leaned against the wall, struggling to regain her composure. Maej had all sorts of random thoughts invading her mind. She needed her focus. She clutched the piece of jerky in her hand, her knife secure at her side. Deep inhalations soothed her. Put her in the right mind to cross half of the cursed city and find Zhee searching for excrement.

Why does she let me sneak off and leave that disgusting job for herself to do? Amiollea asked herself. She shuddered, not wanting to think of the answer. She didn't want to start *liking* Zhee. That would be a disaster.

She fixed her prejudice in her mind and took a step forward.

The rattle of metal caught her attention. The thud of boots. Soldiers approached the Runic Ward. She instinctively crouched low and pressed against the wall. She felt the slight vibration in the ground from their steps. They stopped and banged hard on the gate, the blows trembling through the wall.

"Who's there?" barked an accented voice, not unlike Maej's refined tone.

"Lord Achogear's men," answered a booming voice. "Captain Fhaaghin and five men. We need to speak with Maestro Kozonio."

Glowers, thought Amiollea with disgust. She listened as the gates opened and waited for them to swing closed before she continued her travel. She reached the corner and broke away to round the edge of the Escarpment and find the road that led down into the Slithering Pit.

"Amiollea."

She jumped, her hand squeezing on the jerky. Her heart leaped into her throat.

She knew that voice.

~

"That's you!" Ablisio growled. "I can smell you no matter how clean you scrubbed yourself."

He moved to the sound of quickened breathing and shuffling feet. He thrust his hand out into the dark. His sister gasped as he brushed across her chest. His hand shifted right and found her left arm. He yanked her close to him.

"What are you doing?" he demanded.

"Zhee tattled?" demanded Amiollea. She stamped her foot. Her hot breath spilled over his face. "She let me go! I didn't sneak off!"

"I know that!" He shook his sister, bringing a gasp of pain from her. "I went out to help you collect shit after getting us food and found you missing! So don't get mad at her for anything other than being an idiot for letting you traipse across the city alone!"

"Idiot?" Amiollea gasped.

His anger burned hot. At his sister. At Zhee. They both exasperated him. After he risked his *life* to keep them alive, they thought they could go behind his back and live out this fantasy of theirs? How delusional were they to believe the blue-skinned Runecarver wasn't trying to prey on Amiollea?

He wouldn't let his sister be hurt. He wouldn't let his sister out of hearing range—scent range—again.

"What were you thinking, Amiollea?" demanded Ablisio. "You could have gotten that moldy head of yours split open if you weren't spit-roasted on by some mucklings. Probably both!"

"Well, I wasn't!" she snapped back. "I'm not an idiot."

"Wandering the city alone isn't the dumbest thing you could possibly do?" Ablisio tightened his grip. "Please, tell me, Amiollea. Why isn't it dumb?"

"Because I have this!" she hissed.

His sister moved. He heard leather rustling and, before he could understand what she did, something sharp poked him in the stomach. A stillness seized his body. His skin recoiled from the tip of a metal knife. He sucked in his guts. His breath quickened.

"This is why!" she snarled.

He hadn't felt something this sharp in years. The metal daggers they found in the first few years had slowly corroded to uselessness in the harsh reality of Hamiocho. This was fresh. New. He could smell how bright it was, that metallic tang, and mixed with leather. A sheath. Fresh, cured. Not something that had been moldering in a missed corner of a building.

"Runed steel?" he asked, keeping his voice calm.

"Yes. Enchanted to never rust. To never grow dull. It will last forever just as sharp as it is now. It can disembowel any muckling that thinks to seize me and make me his. I'll spill out their guts before I cut off their manhood. Maej gave it to me."

"For nothing?" Ablisio growled, his stomach twisting now. The idea of his little sister submitting to a male's lusts, pleasing that blue-skinned rat to get the dagger, churned his stomach. Bile burned up his throat.

"He gave it to me for *nothing!*" she hissed. "No kisses or other Zhee stuff. He also gave me some jerky, which I was going to share with you, but you're being stupid!"

"Nothing?" Ablisio said, the words shocking him. They whirled around him. That wasn't how things worked in this broken city. He might still cling to the old traditions, but the rest of the men in this cursed city were monsters. They killed their women when bored of them or traded them for food. If they didn't outright eat them.

Generosity didn't last long in Hamiocho. Not after Darkfall. If he hadn't had his sister to protect, what would he have done? How would he have turned out? Would he have found a woman like Zhee by killing her last man and making her his? Beat her until she submitted? Raped her when he desired pleasure?

His hand slipped on his sister's arm. Not even he would give a dagger away for nothing. Not something that priceless.

He let go of her arm as she spat more words at him, the dagger poised to hurt him.

"You're going to listen to me," spat out Amiollea. He had let go of her arm. He finally realized she wasn't a little girl, and she would make sure he didn't forget the lesson. "I'm not helpless. I'm not a child. Maej isn't trying to take advantage of us. He's trying to help us! So why are you being so stubborn?"

Her brother didn't make a sound save for ragged breathing. Zhee trembled beyond him, the sound of her feet shifting nervously on the ground reaching Amiollea's ears.

"Huh?" Amiollea demanded, pushing her dagger a little harder against her brother.

He took a step back, but she kept up the pressure.

"I understand you don't want me to be used—raped—I do. I love you for that, but I'm not that little girl any longer. I'm strong. Because you made me strong." Emotion stung her eyes. She trembled; despite her words, she felt like that little girl. She just wanted her brother to hug her. To be appreciated by him. "Tell me, Ablisio, why can't you respect that I've grown up? That I have ideas? Good ones! I can help us survive as well as you or Zhee or anyone else in this shit-filled city!"

"Because," Ablisio croaked, his mind whirling. He struggled to understand it himself. Why had he rejected her plan? He had rejected Maej using her body, but if they were careful, they could have used him. They could have taken advantage of these caravans. Something that could change everything for them.

A new way to survive.

But he wouldn't listen. He was stubborn. *I went out to muckrake again even though it almost got me killed!*

"Answer me!" Amiollea snarled, her voice choked by emotion. A hot, salty scent wafted from her. Tears. "Please!"

Why was he so scared to let her help? What did he fear about using her plan? This pit sunk in him. Understanding found the problem. Examining his soul, he found something festering, a fuzzy mold that clung to him. Choked him.

He feared losing her, but not just to death.

"If you are strong enough to survive without me," Ablisio whispered, "then you won't need me. You don't need me. You have this Maej. He gave you a knife. Jerky. He can help you survive better than I can."

A strangled sob burst from Zhee.

Amiollea lessened the pressure of the knife poking his stomach.

"I've been protecting you since Mom died. I just want to hold onto you, to keep you safe, but the stronger I do that, the harder I clutch to you, the more it drives you away. Now you have an option, some way to survive that isn't me. I can't keep you, can I? I don't want to lose you, Amiollea. I want to keep protecting you, but . . ." He grabbed her hand holding the knife. He pushed it against his stomach. "That blade is a better gift than anything I've given you."

"How can you lose me?" she asked. "You think I'm going to abandon you? After you didn't abandon me? You're my brother. I love you, even if you can be so stupid and infuriating and make me want to scream. You kept me alive all this time."

She ripped her grip from his hand. Steel rasped against leather before she hugged him. Her arms went around his neck. She clutched him tight, her face buried into his neck. His arms trembled at his side. He feared hugging her even as he slowly embraced her.

"We're family!" she sobbed. "Me and you and even the leech. I guess. If you still like her."

Those first words shifted something inside of Ablisio. He ripped at that fuzzy mold covering his soul. He hugged his sister tight. He crushed her against him, squeezing and rocking her. She trembled in his arms, shaking as she sobbed.

He had been so stubborn. An idiot. Her encounter with Maej was fortuitous. He could see it. He smelled the jerky in her hand, the leather wrapped around her waist, the metal tang of her blade. Supplies. Food. All they needed to improve their lives. They could buy food from the Blind Fishers and the Ratters. They could defend themselves. No longer hide, but conquer.

They could raid the Glowers with more success, stealing more of their food. This was the change he had been looking for. Zhee was right. Hamiocho was dying, and he couldn't see how he could keep his family alive for much longer.

"We need to learn about the caravan," he said. "Who will have the food. How many guards. What we have to do to rob them."

His sister stiffened against him. "What?"

"Your plan," he said. "We have preparations to make. We have, what, two weeks?"

"Yes," she said. "We have to survive that long before we try to steal from them. We'll probably only get one chance."

"That's fine," he said. "We can get a month's worth of food. More. Salted beef keeps a while. We'll get weapons. Resources. This is it, Amiollea. We have a chance. We're going to find a way to prosper. Those shit-stained Glowers can't keep us down. We'll show them all."

"Yeah," she said. "Yes, we will!"

"We just have to survive for two weeks," Zhee said, her voice soft.

"We'll figure that out," he said, breaking the hug. The last of his anger toward Zhee dwindled. Evaporated. He reached out and found her hand. He pulled her to him. He felt a hesitancy from her. His arm went around her. A tension stiffening the muscles of her shoulder beneath his hand dwindled. Her head rested on him.

"Well, food should be easy," said Amiollea. "We can muckrake."

A shiver ran through Ablisio. "That's too dangerous" He hastily added before she could question that,. When do you see Maej again?"

"In three days. He promised to bring some rope."

Ablisio nodded. He felt hope beating through him for the first time. He didn't dread the next day. He didn't have to fear for his sister. She had grown up strong, but that didn't mean she didn't need him. You didn't stop needing your family and friends just because you became an adult.

Sometimes, you needed them more.

As Amiollea tore her jerky in half, giving him and Zhee a piece, he began to organize his thoughts. What they would need to ambush the caravan and rob them. He chewed on the meat, energized by the peppery flavor.

CHAPTER
TWENTY-FIVE

Maegwirio floated through the darkness, buoyed by his wonderful meeting with Amiollea. He hadn't realized just how dreary his life had been. He lived in light inside the Spire, and yet felt like he lived in a murk. In the pure black, everything seemed more real. More alive. He couldn't see her, but he could touch her, smell her, hear her.

Three days...

It felt like an eternity. He'd fill it with work. He'd have to make her rope. He'd have to ask her what other things could make her life better. Maybe a runic lantern if they had a light-proof home. Or a net. She mentioned something about catfish. After, he'd have to finish his own work. Study new ways into his maestro's office, figure out what the old man was hiding, and make some swords. Weapons to replace those lost in the darkness, stolen by slinking thieves like the one who'd killed Eddakwio.

A flash of anger swept through Maegwirio's joy.

That thief had left a dagger in his throat and taken his sword. He probably used the blade to butcher others. It was in the hand of one of those crazy Sun Ravagers. Madmen deliberately summoned Death and left countless people dead.

Maybe if something prevented our valuables from being stolen, then they wouldn't have a reason to rob us.

He followed this line of thought as he retraced his steps back to the Spire. He moved with greater ease, not even realizing he'd become used to not seeing, adapting to it. His robes rustled and his shoes smacked on the cobblestones.

It wasn't the only sound he heard.

He lifted his head to hear the jangle of metal. He breathed in and smelled the oil greasing the metal to keep it from rusting and beneath it, the scent of sweat and leather. The men and their clothing wearing it. A group of soldiers tramped in the dark.

"Hello?" he called out without fear.

"Who's there?" a familiar voice said. It was Fiaxhazio, one of the wardens.

"Maegwirio. Just out for a walk. Who are the soldiers?"

"Lord Achogear's men," the guide said, heading closer to him. "Why are you out for a walk?"

"I was bored. Needed to stretch my legs."

The man sniffed. "You smell a little dirty."

He flushed. Amiollea did her best to wash herself, but it was filthy beyond the walls. Cheeks burning, he said, "Yeah. I fell."

"What's going on?" a gruff voiced asked in Karadrisan.

"Just speaking with the maestro's apprentice," Fiaxhazio said, switching to the tongue with fluent ease.

"Your maestro best be able to see us," the gruff man said.

"I'm sure he can," Maegwirio answered in fluent Karadris. *"Uh, we're almost there."* He peered through the black. *"I seemed to have lost my bearings."*

Fiaxhazio sighed, muttering in Taechiz, "Boy, you should leave the darkness to the wardens."

Maegwirio's embarrassment deepened as Fiaxhazio led them the last dozen paces to the Spire's entrance. They opened the main door and crowded into the lightlock. The warden closed the door. When it latched heavily, Maegwirio, pushed up against the interior door by a brawny man in mail, found the knob and twisted it.

Light flooded around them. Everyone blinked against the bluish runic light. Maegwirio stepped into the entrance room and wiped his feet on the mat. He called out, "Maestro, guests!"

In short order, Captain Fhaaghin, leader of the guards, sat at the dining table across from the maestro. The other guards lounged on the stairs. It was too small to fit them all in the kitchen with their gear. Maegwirio pulled out an earthen jug of mountain rice sake, one of the few that had been kept for guests. He broke the wax sealing the cork and popped it.

He sniffed it. The strong scent burned his nostrils, but it wasn't vinegary. He poured the white alcohol into two porcelain cups patterned with blue-breasted robins. He carried them to the table and set a cup down before his maestro and the guard.

Captain Fhaaghin had the broad shoulders and short stature of a Povazian, his skin milk-pale. Gray, thinning hair covered his round head while a haze of stubble covered his cheeks and jaw and brimmed on his thick upper lip. He looked only a few years younger than the maestro, but the difference in stamina was apparent. Captain Fhaaghin still possessed the strength of a younger man, wearing his coat of mail with ease.

"Pour one for yourself and join us," said the maestro. "Just the other day, I was reminded that he's not a boy any longer. Not that lost child I found waiting for me after Darkfall..." The old man swallowed, grief shadowing his face. "My other apprentices..."

"We all lost good people that day," Captain Fhaaghin said, raising his cup. "To those lost. May the Wise Owl look after their souls and Clever Fox keep them from being swallowed by the darkness."

"And may Cunning Jackal never find their souls and devour them," Maestro Kozonio finished.

It seemed to be the right thing because the two men tapped their cups together then tossed back their shots. Maegwirio joined them, throwing back his cup, eager for his first taste of alcohol. His eyes widened.

His mouth burned.

He coughed, the vile stuff blazing all the way down into his gut. He bent over, wanting to get the taste out of his mouth. The captain burst into laughter, amusement dancing in his eyes. The maestro chuckled.

"It's fortified over the years," he said. "An aged sake is always a delicacy."

"It's . . . liquid . . . fire . . ." wheezed Maegwirio. He sought out the bucket of well water brought to them every day. He dipped his cup in the cool liquid and tossed it back.

It did little to soothe him.

"This is better than the piss we brew from algae," said Fhaaghin. "Make it into beer or distill it into whiskey, and it's still nasty."

As Maegwirio sat, anger blazed through him. *They make alcohol out of food while people are starving out in the dark?*

Before he could launch into a passionate scourging of such behavior, his maestro said, "What does Lord Achogear need so badly that he has sent his soldiers from his estate?"

"We need a way to track that muckling thief," Captain Fhaaghin answered. He leaned back in his chair, the wood creaking beneath him. The delicate legs seemed to bend, like they sagged beneath the weight. "He wasn't with the Sun Ravagers."

"Really?" Maestro Kozonio rested his chin on folded hands, elbows perched on the table. "He attacked us with them."

"Killed Eddakwio and took his sword," muttered Maegwirio.

"We found the Sun Ravagers and killed a fair number. Took more prisoner. Cinder got away, but we learned from the survivors that they never had a half-Povazian youth with them. Not one that would be the thief's age." He glanced at Maegwirio. "Your age, boy."

How do they know the thief is half-Povazian? Maegwirio wondered.

"I'd need something connected to the thief," the maestro said.

"Like?" grunted Fhaaghin.

The maestro glanced at Maegwirio, arching bushy, white eyebrows.

Lessons flooded Maegwirio's thoughts. "Well, we would need something from the thief. Not a belonging, but a part of him. Hair or skin or blood would work, but the hair has to be plucked. It needs the root still attached to be useful. Fingernail or toenail clippings are no good. His waste is not ideal, but . . ." He shuddered at the thought of using it. "Fecal matter works better than urine."

"Why's that?" asked Fhaaghin.

"There's more of you in it. The little bits of you that build you up. They're too tiny to see, but they exist. Fingernails and hair isn't you."

"Sure looks like me," said Fhaaghin, glancing at his fingernails.

"It's not alive, but when you excrete, some of you is spilled out. You get more with blood and skin."

"Well, what if we don't have that?" asked Fhaaghin. "Don't even have a bit of shit from him. Anything else?"

"A close relative. A mother is great. Siblings are good, too, especially if they share the same mother."

"Why?"

"Well, uh, then you know they are actually related by blood," Maegwirio said. "You know..."

"Ah, got you. I fathered a bastard or two. Never can be sure if they're yours."

"But you're always sure of the mother," the apprentice said, his ears burning. He shifted. "Anyways, the father will work if you're sure of the connection. It's difficult using a relative. It takes longer to calibrate the divination. We have to isolate the part of the mother or father that's in the target."

"If we have samples of both, it's faster still," said the maestro.

My books didn't mention that, Maegwirio thought, but he could see the logic of it. If half of a person came from a mother and half from the father, having both would give you the make-up of the person.

"I can bringing you something of the father's tomorrow," Fhaaghin said. "If you can really do this."

"How do you have that?" blurted Maegwirio in shock.

"His father's a servant to Lord Achogear. The boy stole Lord Achogear's favorite dagger. One that was runed to be tracked, though that could only get us close to the boy. He kept slipping away into the murk."

"I can make it, maestro," Maegwirio said, wanting to help find the man who killed Eddakwio.

"No, no, I can handle it. You need to keep working on those new swords the Glowers want."

"So some thief can steal them," Maegwirio muttered. He itched. His idea prickled at him. "Maestro, could we bond swords to their owners?"

"Hmm, it's not something that's been done in, oh, a thousand years. Not since Taedeocha first discovered runic power beneath the Rune Heart." The maestro leaned back. "They used to do that with runed swords. For the first knights. That was when only a few people knew the skill and they were so valuable."

"Better than worrying about one of these rats," muttered Captain Fhaaghin. "There've been twice as many mucklings going over the wall. They're getting careless. No skill, just rampaging. One kicked open a door that wasn't supposed to ever be opened. It had no lightlock. Death flowed into the house. Nineteen people killed. If one of them got a good blade . . ."

Maegwirio shuddered. Had there been any trying to break into the Runic Ward?

"It will give my apprentice something to occupy his time when he's not cloud counting with a girl."

Captain Fhaaghin gave Maegwirio a sly grin. "I always found tickling a girl's ears made her ripe and open."

"He must have done something right. Yesterday he moped about for hours, but then he came in with you with a bounce. Though he won't tell me who she is."

"His first?" Fhaaghin asked. "Remember my first. Tits out to here." Held his hands out before him while Maegwirio's face burned so hot he was surprised he wasn't setting his robes on fire. "A Povazian washer woman who gave me an education." The guard laughed, coarse and hearty before it trailed off. His face darkened. "Well, I should be going. I don't like being away from Lord Achogear more than I have to. I'll have the sample delivered tomorrow."

"And I shall bring the diviner with the caravan," said the maestro. "Deliver it to Lord Achogear himself."

"Good, good." The man stood, chainmail rattling. "If your apprentice can figure out bonded swords, I guarantee the Council would be interested in it. See if we can't spare more food even if algae production is down."

"Oh?" asked the maestro.

"The mucklings ain't bringing as much shit as they used to. Less fertilizer or something. We're not sure why. Maybe they found some way to eat without it. Those fishermen I hear about, maybe."

"Or maybe there are just fewer of them," said Maegwirio. The way

Amiollea talked sounded harsh. How did small children, infants, survive in these conditions?

Something to ask her.

"Well, if they are, it will only mean better odds for the rest of us living longer. We're not ever getting out of here. This hell is our new life."

"I cannot figure out any way to bring down the Darkwall," said the maestro. He sounded weary. Strain appeared over his face.

The guard grunted and marched out.

Maegwirio studied his maestro. "I could help with the problem. Maybe a fresh set of eyes could find a way to undo it."

"I don't think that's possible." The old man leaned back. "Something broke, Maegwirio. Something precious, and there doesn't seem to be any way to repair it. How can you inscribe runes in the air?"

"Still," he said. "You're getting old. At least, tell me why you make Light every day."

"For hope," he said. "Nothing more."

"Hope?" Maegwirio studied his maestro. "You told me it was none of my business before."

"You're becoming a man," he said. "I wanted to preserve hope in you. It's important, but, my boy, I'm afraid there is no escape from this place."

"There has to be." A sudden, powerful homesickness for the mountains of Taechiz swept over him. For his older brother swinging a wooden sword at his friends while Maegwirio watched, too small to join them. He'd chased his brother across alpine meadows in the shadow of Atzuchaeb Hzachit, wanting to play with him. Was his brother married now? Did Maegwirio have nieces or nephews? Were his parents alive? "This can't be our world."

"You'll understand when you're older," the maestro said. "I'm tired. I'm going to lie down. I want you to research the bonding. I expect a report delivered along with supper on your theory about how to form the runic clauses on the swords."

"Yes, Maestro," he muttered, slumping in his chair.

Ablisio needs to go, Emmait thought as he lay beside the latrine. Dirt still clung to his hands from wiping himself clean. *He's too possessive of Zhee.*

And she doesn't want to be free of him.

Like anything in Hamiocho, you couldn't expect what you wanted to fall in your lap. You had to seize it. Food. Supplies. Territory. The woman you loved. It made sense to Emmait. They were both Povazian. Mostly. He would treat her better than Ablisio. He could provide for her and protect her with greater skill. She cared for him; he could see it.

She would do things for him if he seized her.

But he didn't want to seize *that* from her. That one thing. He wanted what she gave freely to Ablisio. And she wouldn't give it to him so long as Ablisio lived. It was a horrible loop. Emmait felt a twinge of pity. Ablisio wasn't a cannibal. He didn't prey on others. He didn't abuse his woman or sell his sister for a few day's worth of food. He cared for them. Fought for them.

He was admirable.

If Emmait didn't love Zhee, he could see making an alliance with them. But he didn't need Ablisio. Amiollea could fend for herself or use her Runecarver, and Zhee would find a new protector to care for her. Love her.

"You'll like her being around all the time," Emmait said to Sun. The dog padded over and lay his muzzle across Emmait's stomach. He petted the dirty fur, gnarled and snarled and glued together in places. Despite that, it was still soft. Comforting. "She's a good person."

Sun licked at his belly for a moment.

Emmait smiled, idly stroking down Sun's back. "The three of us will have a good life here. It's safe now. Especially with the sword. She won't have to worry about any dangers. No one will ever hurt her again. Only problem is Ablisio. I can't *kill* him."

That was the problem. He had to find a way for Ablisio to die without Zhee suspecting anything. Even better, if he could charge in and "rescue" her from whatever danger had killed Ablisio, he'd be her savior twice.

She would have to love him after that. He deserved her love for saving her from the cannibals. For protecting her.

Maybe there's another group of cannibals out there, he thought. *They can have Ablisio and Amiollea while I'll save Zhee. I just have to kill enough for her to think I did all I could. Too bad for the brother and sister, but she'll have me. I'll help her forget.*

A stirring formed in his nethers. That new itch she always sparked in him. He had found a way to deal with it. It was something amazing. No wonder men wanted women if they made them feel half as good as he'd learned to make himself feel.

The idea swelling in his mind hardened him. That itch to take care of it swelled. He stirred, wanting to get away from Sun so he could concentrate. He'd almost gotten to the point where he couldn't ignore it when Sun lifted his head.

But he didn't growl.

He bounded to his feet. "Zhee?"

"Emmait?" Zhee gasped, her voice nearly a block away. "How did you hear me from that far away?"

"Sun told me."

"Your dog talks to you?" she asked in amusement.

"He would have growled if it wasn't you. Sun likes you."

"And I like him," she said. Sun trotted over to her, the pads of his feet and claws whisking and clicking on the cobblestones. "Hey, boy. I still can't believe you're real. You must be the only dog left alive."

"A few of the Glowers keep some," Emmait said.

"Is that where you got him?"

"I found him on Darkfall. He was just a puppy." Emmait stood, aching hard. "I collected the last of the excrement for you."

"Oh, you did," she said and a nervous catch entered her voice. "What do you want . . . for it? I don't have much . . ."

"No, nothing," he said. "We're friends."

She released a sigh. He knew what she was prepared to offer, not out of desire for him, but fear of angering him. It was rare for such a lopsided trade in Hamiocho. It stung a little that she didn't *desire* him.

You will. Once you realize I'm perfect for you.

"You're such a nice man, Emmait," she said. She moved toward the latrine. He heard her feet sliding across the ground then the tap of ceramic. She'd found her jug. "You and Ablisio should meet."

"What?" he asked, this nervous twinge rippling through him. That was the last thing he wanted.

"I think you two would work great together. We could share resources. Have a better chance of survival. The Ratters and Blind Fishers do it."

"Because they have a stable source of food," said Emmait. "I don't need to work with another guy. I have Sun. Now, if I had a woman . . ."

"Sorry," she said, voice tight. Nervous. "But you're my second hero," she added hastily. "And . . . maybe I can get you some food. We've found an opportunity. Another person helping us would be beneficial."

So Ablisio has come around to robbing a caravan . . . Dangerous.

"I'm fine," he said. "I'm skilled at muckraking."

"Can dogs eat algae? I thought they needed meat."

"He catches rats, and I have other ways of feeding him," Emmait answered. "Don't worry about us. Just visit us. I get lonely with just Sun."

"I can do that." He could hear the smile in her voice. "I hope you'll change your mind. This is an exciting opportunity. Something that will change things."

CHAPTER
TWENTY-SIX

Three days later, Emmait lounged in the Rotting Orchard listening to Zhee, Ablisio, and Amiollea talking as they prepared to visit the Runecarver. Amiollea's excitement echoed through their shack. She bounded back and forth, feet smacking on the dirt.

"You need to get all the information you can about the caravan," said Ablisio for the dozenth time.

"I know," Amiollea said for equally as many. "I haven't forgotten it since the last time you told me."

"It's just . . . you can be forgetful."

"When?"

"That time," Ablisio said. "A year ago."

Zhee giggled. "You did forget you were supposed to be triggering the alarm on the wall north of where your brother crossed, not south."

"I got them mixed up," Amiollea answered. "It's a dumb way of thinking of things. Should have told me to go top."

"Top?" Ablisio asked. "Climb the wall?"

"No, the top of the city. Glowers are at the bottom. We're in the middle, and the Runic Ward and Blind Fishers and the Dark Lee are at the top."

"Also known as north." He shook his head. "What do you use for east and west?"

"Well, I remember where the sun rose and set. That's not something you forget. Spire flashes toward sunset. West. I'm not dumb."

"I wonder," Ablisio muttered.

"I think I'm going to stay," Zhee abruptly said.

"What?" Ablisio asked.

"I don't like crossing the Slithering Pit. Slogging through runny soup. I feel so dirty. I think I'll go collect more excrement."

Excitement surged through Emmait. He hadn't spoken to her in three days. She had stayed with Ablisio, leaving with him and his sister to get food from the dispensary.

"We don't need any. Maej is giving us rope. Good length. We should be able to buy enough catfish to last us a few days."

"Let's not be careless," said Zhee. "It's not like shit spoils."

"It's not safe for you to be out there alone."

"It's perfectly safe. There's someone new living in the old Povazian Slums where the shadow ascetics make their latrines."

Emmait stiffened. Alarm shot through him. What was she doing?

"What?" demanded Ablisio. The mirth in his voice had vanished.

"A young man with a dog," Zhee said. "He's harmless."

"And why is this the first time I heard about it?"

"He's scared of you."

I'm not scared of him! screamed through Emmait. He stood, his hand going to his sword hilt as it swung from his makeshift baldric. He wanted to march in there and prove it. Just hack down Ablisio. That would prove how brave he was.

"He doesn't want to meet you. I tried."

"And he didn't try to . . ." Ablisio's voice held all the warmth of a dagger.

"No, no. And he could have. He caught me by surprise and didn't do anything to me. Not every man is like what you fear, Ablisio."

"Most are." Ablisio paced in the cabin, his footsteps heavy. "I want to meet him."

Why is she betraying me? Emmait demanded. *Does she want me to kill him?*

"I'll ask again. You two meet with Maej, and I'll speak with Emmait. He's a nice boy. Amiollea's age."

The sounds of kissing echoed while Emmait fumed. Ablisio would be on his guard. He'd be concerned about this "neighbor." Would it matter to Zhee if Ablisio attacked first? Could he justify murdering her man in self-defense *and* still keep her?

∼

Zhee could tell Ablisio wasn't happy with her, but if she could get him and Emmait speaking, it would cause great things. Another person to help them rob the caravan would be perfect. Emmait had skill in fighting. He had Sun, who had impeccable senses.

She would help him get over his caution. She called him shy, but it was really more the former than the latter. People who trusted easily in Hamiocho had the misfortune of fertilizing the algae fields. Emmait was different. Someone like Ablisio. Noble. He'd kept Sun alive all these years when others would have butchered the dog the first time they began to starve.

It didn't take long before she heard the pad of Sun approaching. Soon, his hot breath rolled over her belly. She petted his fur, sliding over the burs and gnarls. He licked at her stomach before he then hopped up, planting his paws on her stomach to lick her face. She twisted her jug in her left arm, almost dropping it.

She giggled and gasped. "Sun! Ouch. You have sharp claws." She pushed him back. "I'm glad to see you, too, but there are limits."

He'd scratched her, but there shouldn't be a risk of infection. They weren't more than skin deep.

"Emmait?" she asked as she knelt to pet Sun at eye level, setting down her jug beside her. His hot tongue slathered over her cheek. "Emmait?"

"Here," he called. "Sun heard you coming and broke away from me when I wasn't expecting it. He usually doesn't do that."

"He knew I'd scratch him behind his ears. All dogs love that." She did just that. His tail thumped on the pavement, bringing a smile to her lips.

"Hunting more shit?" he asked her.

"That and I'm here to see you. I talked to Ablisio about you."

"Oh?" He sounded tense as he asked, "Why did you tell him about me?"

"I can't lie to him and sneak off to see you behind his back. That's not right. Besides, he wants to meet you."

"And I have no interest in meeting him. Nothing good could come of it."

She rolled her eyes. "You're as stubborn as him. Is that something that afflicts all men?"

"No idea. I just know that when two men spend time together in Hamiocho, sooner or later one puts a dagger in the other's back."

"The Ratters and Blind Fishers get along. And so do the Shadow Ascetics."

"Those monks are crazy."

"They're not crazy. That's the Sun Ravagers." Zhee shuddered, remembering what Amiollea told her. "Cinder and his fools purposefully summoned Death to attack the Runecarvers. Can you believe that?"

"Yeah," Emmait said, his voice flat. "All the more reason to have nothing to do with Ablisio."

"Well, he's my man," she said, standing up. She put her hand on her stomach. So far, she still had Hope growing in her. No heavy bleeding. No miscarriage. With Emmait helping, she might have a better chance for her to carry her baby to term. "I'm not going to hurt him by coming out here to see you. If he doesn't trust you . . ."

"So he'll trust me by meeting me?" demanded Emmait. "And if he just wants to kill a rival?"

"He's not like that."

"You never know."

Zhee sighed, her hand falling away from her belly. "Am I like that, Emmait?"

He was silent for a few moments. "No."

"Then you can trust me to say Ablisio won't do that. You two would make a good team. I believe that."

"I'll think about it," muttered Emmait. He didn't sound happy about it.

"Thank you," she said. "You won't regret it."

He sighed. "It's hard to regret anything when you're around."

"That's sweet."

"I know a better way to get food and supplies than bartering with the dispensaries. It's cleaner than getting your hands dirty in the latrine."

"Oh?" she asked.

"Yeah, it's something I came up with a day or two ago."

"So not muckraking."

"Nope. Come on. I scouted out a place earlier."

Curious, she followed Emmait east through the crumbling buildings that made up her old neighborhood and out into one of the wildest part of the cities. But she felt safe. He had Sun and his sword.

∼

Emmait was thrilled to show off his new idea. His sword opened up so many new possibilities.

Ones he hadn't even considered. His last try had gotten him enough barter to eat catfish the last two days. Now he needed more. He had found the perfect spot. He just hoped they hadn't moved buildings and were still holed up where he'd found them.

"We're going east," she said after they'd gone a few blocks. "That's toward the Reek."

"Yes, it is," he said. "Don't worry, it'll be safe. I'll be there to watch over you."

"Still," she whimpered, her voice tight.

He reached out with his hand, remembering something that had always made him feel safe when he was a child. The clasp of his mother's hand on his. Flashes of tottering behind her as she moved through the marketplace. He was almost shocked by the intensity of the colors in his memories. Greens and reds and blues and even browns.

Something other than *black*.

Zhee's arm flinched when the back of his knuckles brushed her. He slid down to find her hand. She didn't resist him as he took it. He remembered another thing his mother used to do. He squeezed Zhee, his lips curling in a smile.

"I'm here," he said. "You don't have to worry."

She squeezed him back, her hand soft, and he felt almost like that child again. Zhee could be his mother. They both had the same accents, swallowing some of their Rs in words Karadrisans pronounced perfectly. Her Os came out a little longer, her Is verging on Es sometimes. He pictured his mother beside him, naked and voluptuous, wondering how close Zhee looked to her.

"I'll protect you," he added, so stiff now. That part of him led the way.

Sun padded behind them as he followed the route he'd memorized to take them to the spot in the city where they would find what he'd discovered. The building that housed all the supplies he would need. Food for Sun, trade items for him to barter, and safety for Zhee.

He could walk forever holding her hand. So warm and soft. Beneath the dirt and mud, he could smell her natural aroma. He filled his nose with it time and time again. Every step brought him closer and closer to how he could provide for her.

He could give her the luxuries and resources she deserved.

He took them to the right as they left his territory. The character of the city began to shift. The crowded tenements gave way to larger buildings. Warehouses with low roofs that had collapsed. Buildings long picked over. He led her around the sharp glass he'd found buried in the dirt that had almost cut him.

"I've never been to this part of the city," Zhee said, her voice tight. "We're getting too close to the Reek."

"We're almost there," he said. "There's a building by some of the warehouses. It's not a house, I don't think. But . . . I don't know what it is."

"Factor's office?" she suggested. It wasn't a word he knew, but she sounded confident. Just like his mother had.

"Sure," he said. "We need to be quieter. We can't let them know we're going."

She stiffened, her steps faltering. "What?" Her question came as a whisper, a stir of breath so faint he almost didn't register it.

"Just another block," he said, ears pricking.

The laughter echoed from it, coarse and hard. The sound of the harsh mockery savage men engaged in when trapped up in their hole. The noises drifted out the window and spilled through the store.

"You blew your snot so fast," laughed a voice. "Barely had it in her before you were spraying."

"She had her a tight sheath," the other guy said. "Her man must've had 'im a small blade. Besides, I last longer the second time. I enjoyed her for a good while."

"Don't know how you could with her blubberin' for her husband," the other guy said.

Their vile, course laughter rippled through them. The woman was dead, beaten for her sobbing. Emmait despised their cruelty. They were like the cannibals and the other men he'd killed with his sword. This was a better way. The city didn't need men like this around.

Need men like me. Men who protect. I'll keep Zhee safe no matter what.

"What are we doing?" she asked, her voice a whisper. She leaned close, the softness of her breasts rubbing on his arm. "Emmait." Her breath washed hot across his ear. "They're vile."

"They're meat," he said.

She gasped and stumbled back. He winced, but the men inside didn't stop their laughter.

"You can't..." she gasped. "That's what beasts do."

"I'm just going to kill them," he said. "Sun's got to eat. I'm no animal."

Sharp intake of feminine breath. Smack of hands over lips. Feet retreating. Low groan of shock.

"You can't," she whispered. "That's wrong. Murder."

"They're no different from the men who tried to hurt you. I'm protecting you by killing them. Protecting other women."

"Emmait!" she hissed.

"I'll be right back," he said as he drew his runed blade from its improvised baldric. He gripped it in his hand and walked forward.

Sun moved at Emmait's side, fur just brushing his leg. They approached the house, his blood boiling. He felt the shift in the air, the way it moved through the open doorway to his left. He turned his direction and stepped through it. Sounds echoed around him. The men's laughter came more from his left. Stairs.

He took each step with care, ears prickled. His feet slid more than lifted, toes feeling before him for anything that might betray him. Sun moved behind him. This hot anger surged through him as the men laughed again.

"Now that one woman, she was a screamer," laughed the raspy-voice man. Of the three, he sounded like he'd swallowed a handful of nails that lodged in his throat. "I swear, she liked me more than her man blubbering in the corner."

"He weren't blubberin', he were enjoyin' my blade sheathin' in him," the high-pitched one shouted.

"Better not poke me while I'm sleeping," raspy voice said. "I'll bury a real dagger in you."

"That rusty toothpick you got would snap."

Emmait ascended the stairs.

∼

Zhee's stomach roiled.

The acids in her guts wanted to bubble up. She swayed back and forth, torn between fleeing and stopping him. Only, he was already committed. She'd lost track of him. He was inside the building, heading to those disgusting men.

They were vile. They didn't deserve to live, but to slaughter them? With his runic blade, what chance would they have? All so Sun could rip into their flesh. The idea of the dog eating the men sent a rush of burning vapors up her throat.

She muffled her burp, the sour flavor spilling over her mouth. She had petted that dog. It wasn't right for men to eat men. Or for animals to eat them, either. And to just wantonly kill like that. Not out of protection, but to rob them of life and valuables.

Laughter cut off in a gurgle of pain. Shouts. Loud clashes. Sun snarled. Zhee trembled as she listened to it. The wet smack of blade cutting flesh. Men hitting stone floor. Liquids splashing. The metallic scent of blood filled her nose.

She lost her battle.

She fell to her knees and leaned over. She vomited her stomach, forcing out half-digested algae onto the stones. Her stomach heaved while the men screamed. One begged for mercy, the other howling as Sun growled and savaged.

Flesh ripped.

Zhee gained her feet and raced from the horror into the dark. She couldn't wait for Emmait. Had she utterly misjudged him? She believed he was like Ablisio, but the man she loved would *never* do something that evil and cruel.

CHAPTER
TWENTY-SEVEN

Maegwirio felt the time approaching for him to go out and see Amiollea.

He sat at his desk, staring at his notations. He believed he'd figured out how to bind an object—like the sword he'd created and lay across his desk—to a person. He had to tie the identity of the person onto the blade, make it think it was a part of a body.

Humans, like other creatures, defended their bodies. Inside them, mechanisms launched to fend off diseases, parasites, and other foreign invaders. If the sword thought itself a body part, then someone else picking it up would engage the same response.

He just needed to test it. He had a bold idea. Something that would really help Amiollea. He could lie to his maestro and claim this sword had come out bad, that runic feedback happened and slagged the iron. It was rare—it would be embarrassing—but he was practicing in areas he'd never delved into.

He studied the runes already inscribed into the sword. He had started the sentence, but he hadn't finished it. One last rune was needed to finish the thought and imbue the sword with its newest property.

He thrust it into its leather scabbard. He'd patterned the blade in Taechiz style, the short, stabbing swords favored by the runic knights. With their armor, they didn't need long and heavy weapons. In the mountain forests and glittering grottoes, a long blade could be an issue. No different than swinging blind in Hamiocho.

Less chance to harm a friend. Less chance to hit an unseen wall or strike the ceiling and throw off an attack.

He slung its attached belt over his shoulder before gathering the heavy tarp for his portable lightroom and the runic lamp, its magic off. It was a cylinder of brass with a circular base that would glow when the proper word was spoken. *Aegwik,* the Taechizian word for illuminate. The deactivation word didn't seem to have a good translation in Karadrisans, but deluminate sounded logically correct to him.

Maestro Kozonio headed up the stairs. Working on the sword problem for the last three days gave Maegwirio little time to work on his other project. Or to get lost in daydreams of Amiollea, though sleep was having trouble finding him if he didn't take care of certain needs that always left him feeling a little guilty afterward.

He rushed down the Spire's steps and burst out into the street. He passed into the lightlock with no fear, closing the door behind him before opening the door before him. He had no fear as he stepped into the dark. It was amazing what had once been something he feared now had become... blasé.

Just out for a casual stroll through the city, he thought to himself in amusement. *Blind. Unable to see. No biggie.*

He followed his route to the postern door with skill. He unlocked it with a whispered word and then stepped out of its protection onto the Escarpment. He paused, letting his senses feel the air moving over his face. He breathed in deeply.

Smiled.

"You're here, Amiollea."

"You smelled me," she said in delight. "And what are you carrying? You made so much noise. Cloth rustling and something's thudding on your back. Is that the rope?"

"I have that, too," he answered. It should be wrapped in the canvas. "But I have a sword."

She gasped in shock. "Maej! That's too much."

"Listen, I need to test a new type of runes on it," he said. "A way to bond it with someone. Make it so only they can use it. I can test it on myself, but then I'll have a sword." He chuckled. "When am I going to need that?"

"The next time the Sun Ravagers attack."

He blinked. "Well, I wouldn't know how to use one. But you ... I can only imagine that you could make far, far better use of it than me."

⁓

Amiollea shivered. The idea of a sword sent excitement rippling through her. She thought herself invincible with her runed dagger. Her hand drifted down to it belted around her waist. It felt strange to wear something again, but the irritation on her skin was a small price to pay to have defense.

And a sword...

She felt a powerful hunger for it. A lust that almost had her blood boiling as much as the idea of kissing Maej. Those naughty ideas that sent her sneaking out of the shack in the middle of the night to *do* something about them. Embarrassing things that made her heart flutter.

She wanted the sword, but ... "Could it be for someone else?"

"Who?" Maej asked, a slight tinge of disappointment in his voice. "You don't want a sword?"

"I would love one, but ..." She had her knife.

"Well, I'd need their blood to establish the bond," he said. "To make the sword an extension of their flesh. I'd really like to test this today. Not wait for our next meeting. We'd need your brother's blood."

"I didn't say my brother," Amiollea said.

"But who else would you want to give it to?"

She smiled. "Yeah." She shifted. "So, if my brother *were* nearby, then you could bond it to him?"

Maej stiffened. "Is your brother nearby? Is he listening to us?" He sounded panicked, like a muckling had ambushed him. "I mean ... I ... Well ..."

The flustered sounds he made burst giggles from her lips. "He's not *that* close. Like he wouldn't know if I did this."

She took a step toward him and gave him a quick kiss on what she hoped was his cheek. She felt the corner of his mouth on hers. She jerked back as this heat washed through her.

"But if I scream, he'll hear me," she added, that ache blossoming in her, like a flower of old opening to the sun. She suddenly regretted agreeing to have a chaperon. If Maej and her were to kiss and that led to *Zhee* things, would that be that bad . . . ?

No chance of that with Ablisio stalking us.

"So we can test it on him," she said. "So long as it won't hurt him."

"Just the prick to his thumb for the blood," he said. "Shouldn't be an issue."

"I'll go get him."

∽

Ablisio stiffened at the sound of Amiollea rushing toward him. He heard the murmuring, the pair too far away for him to make out details. He wished to be closer, to make sure this Maej remembered not to try anything with his sister.

Amiollea insisted he stay close enough to intervene but not to hear their talk.

So why was Amiollea rushing back?

Anger boiled through him. *That little muckling worm tried something!* He clutched his club. He'd crack it hard against the blue-skinned slug's head. Spill out his brains. *Touch my little sister!*

"Ablisio!" Amiollea hissed as she stopped. "This is amazing."

"Amazing?" Those weren't the words he'd expected. He had been ready for sobbing tears, for spitting anger. Not giddy joy. His sister's feet smacked the ground as she bounced in place, ragged hair whispering about her shoulders and face.

"Come on!" Her hand brushed his chest, fingernails almost scratching him with her enthusiasm. She darted over to grab his wrist. "He wants to give you something."

"He knows I'm here?" Ablisio demanded as he let his sister pull him along.

"He wants to give you a special sword."

"Why?" The words came out flat. Hard.

"He needs a test subject. Don't be suspicious. He just needs some blood."

"Blood!" he snarled, keeping his voice low, but it was a struggle. "What foul thing is he going to do with my blood? Curse me?"

"Don't be dumb."

"Well, then what?"

"Something about bonding a sword with you. It's a test. Some amazing runic magic he's worked out."

"That needs my blood," he muttered.

"Brother, you said you'd trust me. So, I'm saying relax."

He wanted to spit out his anger at her, to be stubborn, but where had that gotten him? He swallowed those impulses and grunted, "Fine."

Soon, he could smell Maej. The Runecarver had a fresh scent. Almost no dirt, just a little sweat, and mixed with cloth. Fibrous. Dry. The type of fabric that would rot away in weeks in Hamiocho. He smelled . . . normal. How people should smell.

Living safe behind his walls, using his runes to keep him from suffering like the rest of us! The angry thoughts boiled through his mind.

"It's good to meet you, Ablisio," Maej said, his words spoken strangely. They had a crispness about the consonants, almost an over-pronunciation. They didn't quite flow together like they should. "Your sister has told me so much about you."

"I'm sure she has," Ablisio grunted.

"Er, well, I just need a drop of your blood and . . ." Robes shifted. "I hope that will be okay."

Incredulity rippled through Ablisio. The man he feared taking advantage of his sister had as much strength to his spine as a strand of wet algae. A soft, weak man who would be crushed the moment anything dangerous happened.

Ablisio relaxed. These Runecarvers were soft. They lived behind their walls, safe and protected with their magic. He could feel the magic. At the top of the wall, the barest line appeared, the boundary. The runes glowed so dimly you had to be right on them to see them at all. They didn't draw Death.

A lot of mucklings believed the Runecarvers had brought Death upon them. He didn't know how. Death didn't operate like runes. It wasn't an object inscribed and given new properties. Not wood transmuted into steel or walls runed to crackle with alarms or inflict damage on those sneaking over.

Those sorts of runes were covering more and more lengths of the Rubble, the gaps between them narrowing to keep out thieves like Ablisio.

"Sure, just a drop," Ablisio said. "Prick my finger, right?"

"Yes, that will do."

More cloth rustled. Something moved before Ablisio. Fluttering. He snatched a piece of soft, absorbent cloth. His brows knitted tight, but he didn't ask any questions.

"If you would be so kind as to cut your brother's finger or to lend your dagger," Maej said. "Ablisio, sir, if you would let the cloth absorb your blood and return it to me."

"Not going to put a curse on me that makes me bend over in pain if I don't obey you?" Ablisio asked while his sister drew her dagger.

"What?" gasped Maej. "That would be a horrendous thing to do to someone. What sorts of stories do they speak about us out there?"

Amiollea burst into giggles. "I know, brother. They're not the danger we always believed, are they?"

"I'm sorry for not living up to unrealistic expectations of being a monster," Maej muttered.

Ablisio took the dagger from his sister, feeling the subtle shift in the air around it, a slight coolness. He carefully pricked the tip of the little finger on his left hand, the one he could spare in case infection set in. He pressed the cloth to it.

"My thanks," Maej said when he returned it. "Now, I just need to get set up. Please, don't touch my canvas."

~

"Canvas?" the rumbling tones of Ablisio asked.

The man's presence radiated through the darkness. Powerful waves that nearly overwhelmed Maegwirio. With it came a potent musk that stung the younger Runecarver's eyes. He fought to betray any weakness and show fear. This was a true muckling. A man who'd fought and killed to survive. The one who'd kept Amiollea alive for seven years out in the abyssal darkness.

He couldn't show a hint of weakness. He had to project calm and confidence, earn the man's trust. Ideas already nibbled at the back of his mind. Feelings and emotions that swirled around in him. He wanted to say things to Amiollea, but he wasn't sure if he could uphold those promises.

If it was too soon. If she even felt anything for him.

She might be using you, was a thought that never strayed far from his mind, but he fought against it because she was a delight to be around. Fun and flirty, keeping him off-balance. He never quite knew if she was making a jape or if it was an honest invitation. And her kiss . . .

He still felt it on the corner of his mouth.

"What's this about a canvas?"

"My portable lightroom," Maegwirio answered the man. "I am sure you can understand why you don't want to disturb my cloth."

"You're going to make light?" Amiollea asked, true dread in her voice. She moved back from him, her bare feet whisking on the stone ground.

"With my sister present?" demanded Ablisio, rage in his voice.

"None will escape my cloth," I said. "So long as it's not disturbed. So, we all agree not to disturb it while I work?"

"Yeah," Amiollea said. Her skin scraped on stone. A soft rasp.

Maegwirio realized she had pressed against the wall. His senses seemed to sharpen out here. As his eyes grew dull, everything else swelled. Hearing, smell, even his taste when he breathed in through the mouth. His skin felt alive, his robe almost scratching at him. He was missing out on so much of what Amiollea and Ablisio "saw" in the dark by covering his body.

Maegwirio didn't think he was ready for public nudity yet, even if they couldn't be seen. He slipped beneath the canvas and felt the heavy weight around him. Suffocating darkness engulfed him. Sweat instantly broke out across his forehead and ran through his scalp. It dribbled down his face and the back of his head to the nape of his neck.

A wave of fear rippled through him as he grasped the runic lamp he'd set out, the brass cool to the touch. If there was a gap, if the runes stitched onto the cloth didn't work the way he'd been told, he would kill them all.

"*Aegwik.*"

The whispered word activated the lamp. The pillar of brass rising from the base glowed with a bright, blue-white light. It stung his eyes. He blinked against the glare, his retinal nerve protesting the sudden stimulation. He squinted against it and shifted in his crouch, the cloth moving over him.

"Is the light on yet?" asked Amiollea, her words muffled.

"Yes. Can you see anything?"

"Nothing," grunted the brother.

"Good, good, I knew this would work!"

"You don't sound sure it would have," Ablisio said, his words harsh.

"Well, the theory was sound. Others have done it, but I have never made my own. It had to be tested."

"You could have done it in a dark room *indoors.*"

"Something to consider next time," Maegwirio said, pulling out his tools from his pocket. He had to scratch on the final rune. He smeared the muckling's blood from the cotton onto the runes already carved into the steel, leaving a streak of red behind.

When finished, the sentence would read, "*Zaebbim agw uxhun nof xokawniz baez, iak yazigif porra agw kinaz soratzuxi ab zocha teoni.*"

All Maegwirio had to do was carve in the final rune, *teoni*, which meant *to touch*, and complete the sentence.

He pressed his diamond-tipped tool against the metal and slowly scratched in the rune, drawing it with care. He had to get it perfect so the magic would work. So his will could direct the energy into the proper configuration.

Sweat poured down his brow as he worked. The air stifled him. He wanted free of the heavy blanket. It trapped not just light, but his body heat. The temperature soared with every scratch he made.

A bead of sweat dangled at the bridge of his nose. It fell and splashed onto the metal of the blade. He wiped his brow with his sleeve, soaking the cotton. Breathing grew heavier. It was harder to bear than the darkness.

"Almost done," he muttered, his freedom at hand. Whether or not the runed sentence worked, he would be able to cast off the blanket and breathe.

His tool made the final scratch, the grating sound stabbing into his ears. He completed his stroke.

The blade rippled with blue energy as the sentence focused the power bleeding into this world to his will. The runes shaped it. His heart pounded in his chest. He was about to be free. With a sticky palm, he grabbed the leather-wrapped—

Heat seared into his palm.

His hand sprang open, releasing the season's hilt. The burn throbbed down his hand as exhilaration surged through him. He was free and, even better, the defensive spell had worked. He shouted his triumph as he sat up.

"I did it!" he cried out at the top of his lungs, the canvas spilling down his body. "It worked!"

The light from his runic lamp spilled over Amiollea. Her naked body flinched back, raising hands to ward against the brilliance. She shouted in horror, crashing into the wall and sliding down it like a little girl cowering before an angry parent.

Or a devouring monster.

CHAPTER
TWENTY-EIGHT

"Shut that lamp off!" Ablisio roared, the blue-white light stabbing into his eyes.

Pain plunged down his eyes and into his mind as he reached for his sister cowering on the ground. He grabbed her and pulled her to her feet, dragging her away from the bright brilliance. The robed Runecarver fumbled, his youthful face painted by the harsh glare of the lamp, his skin as azure as the half-remembered sky.

"Turn it off!"

Whispers hissed through the air. Ablisio's skin crawled. He threw himself to the ground atop his sister, covering her with his body as Death surged down at them. He braced for the slashing pain, hoping she would be spared.

A rustle of thin cloth, a shroud sliding over a corpse.

A hiss of hatred.

The wind stirred.

"*Baegwik!*" shouted Maej.

Darkness engulfed them.

The whispers rustled in frustration. Ablisio shuddered, imagining scything blades of invisible hatred ripping through the air above them, so close to killing them and thwarted. Amiollea sobbed beneath him. His own body trembled.

"I'm so sorry, I'm so sorry," Maej babbled. "That almost . . . It was . . . I didn't . . ."

The sky above them exploded in white light. Ablisio screamed as a new pain assaulted his already hurt eyes. He squeezed them shut against the searing agony racing to his mind. He snarled through clenched teeth as the Light from the Spire announced noon.

"I'm so very sorry," Maej said again.

Ablisio groaned, blinking. A bright, blue smear stretched across his vision. It lay in every direction that he looked. Tears spilled down his cheeks as he climbed off his sister. Fury brimmed through him. He wanted to march over and seize the little worm by the collar and throw him off the edge of the Escarpment.

"I didn't think," Maej said.

"Really?" snarled Ablisio.

"It's okay," Amiollea said, her voice hoarse. "We're alive."

"Okay?" Fury exploded out of Ablisio. "He almost killed us."

"And he made you a sword!" His sister climbed to her feet. She drew in a ragged breath, still choked by emotion. "Did you think there wouldn't be a price?"

"I didn't think a Runecarver's stupidity numbered among them!"

"I almost killed us," Maej said.

"Oh, Maej, that happens to everyone in the dark. We all made mistakes when we started out. Did dumb things. If my brother stayed angry with every person that almost got him killed, he would have abandoned me years ago. *Right?*"

Her last word struck him. He drew in a deep breath. "Always a mistake to break something useful. But if you *ever* bring a muck-smeared lamp near my sister again, I will wring that scrawny neck of yours, death curse or no!"

"Death curse?" Maej asked weakly. "We don't have death curses. I . . . I . . ."

"Maej," Amiollea whispered.

~

AMIOLLEA'S ARM slipped around Maegwirio's shoulder. Trembles shuddered through the Runecarver. He hardly felt the burn in his hand. *I almost got us killed*, he thought. *Death came down so fast. I heard those whispers just like at the raid.*

Screams echoed in his mind. Bodies tearing. Blood splashing hot on the ground.

That was almost Amiollea because of me!

"I'm sorry," he croaked, his hands trembling. "I just . . . I got carried away . . . It worked . . . the sword burned my hand and . . . Then I just wanted out . . . And there was . . . You see . . ."

"It's okay," she said, her voice gentle. "My brother will calm down in a while. He won't hurt you."

"This time," Ablisio growled.

Maegwirio believed him. There wouldn't be a next time. They were out in the darkness. It seemed so safe with Amiollea around, but you couldn't relax out here. You had to be vigilant. He didn't have the runed walls around him to protect him.

"So it worked?" Amiollea said.

"Lucky we're not dead over a dumb sword," Ablisio muttered.

"Oh, just pick it up and back off! Don't whine that you had to risk your life to get a *runed* sword, Ablisio. And it has a scabbard. I can smell it. Right, Maej?"

"Yes," wheezed the Runecarver. He drew in deep breaths. "My deepest apologies, Ablisio, for the—"

"Stop saying those damned pointless words!" Ablisio growled. He swept his hands around the ground. A steely rasp echoed. He had the sword. "'I'm sorry,'" mocked the man. "Empty words. The air you waste on them won't make up for what you did. Next time, don't do it! Think! You Runecarvers are supposed to be smart, not children playing in the mud!"

"He's not a muckling," Amiollea shot back. "He grew up safe."

"That's the problem. He'll get you killed if you're not careful!"

"Just go! You have the sword. Back off. Okay? I can keep us both from doing anything dumb."

Ablisio spat. Then he stalked off, his footsteps heavy.

"I'm sorry," Amiollea said, resting her head on his shoulder.

"Your brother has every right to be angry." Maegwirio couldn't help but take some delight in the sensation of her head on his shoulder. "I did almost get us killed. You killed. That is something I would never forgive myself for."

"Hard to forgive yourself if you're dead."

A nervous chuckle burst from his lips. "True, true."

"You'll do better next time, won't you?"

Her words shocked him with their simplicity. The open forgiveness in them. "Yes. Yes, I will."

"Good."

They sat in silence for a long moment, Maegwirio's heartbeat drumming faster and faster. He became more and more aware of it pounding beneath his chest. He breathed in deeply, struggling to think of anything to say.

She still leaned against him. She wasn't saying anything. Maybe she wanted him to do something else. He couldn't imagine she wanted to kiss after what just happened. His body still felt clammy from the shock.

Does she just want to lean on me? It was nice. More than nice. In fact, he didn't want to say anything because of how pleasurable it was. Relaxing. The fright bled out of him as they sat on the canvas.

"So . . ." Amiollea said, breaking the silence. "That was exciting."

"Is that the word for it?" asked Maegwirio. "Perhaps my knowledge of your language is not as complete as I thought. I found it to be terrifying. I *heard* Death."

"Yeah." She shifted her head against him. "But . . . I mean, coming close to any death, even *the* Death, is exciting. My heart was beating so hard. I'm shaking now."

"Me, too," he said. "That's the chemicals your organs secrete to help your body deal with stressful situations."

"How do you know that?" she asked.

"Books."

"And how do the book makers know that?"

"The authors did research or interviewed those that did."

"Ah." She lifted her head and more silence weighed down on them. "I almost don't know what to say now. After..."

"Yeah," he said.

⁓

Amiollea couldn't let the silence stretch on. Maegwirio couldn't stay here forever, and her brother would grow impatient with her. As much as she wanted to cling to him and lean her head on his shoulder, she needed to ask him questions.

Questions that made her stomach feel weird. Slick like rancid oil.

It almost seemed harder to ask after their brush with Death. She should be angry with him—and, honestly, there was a small spark of annoyance in her—but mostly she was just relieved he was alive. Terror had gripped her the moment the Light flashed over her and she saw his scared, young face as he realized what he'd done.

She sighed and let her arm drop from his. He shifted beside her, the robe rustling against her side. "Amiollea?"

"Let's talk about..." That rancid grime coated more of her. "Caravans."

"Oh, sure," he said.

"They're fascinating how your people go to the Glowers. I would have thought you'd move into the Rubble. You built it for them."

"We've always been strangers in Karadris," he answered, his voice gentle. "We know that we... unnerve people. With our knowledge, it makes people jealous."

"Jealous?"

His robes rustled. "Yes. Karadrisans have tried to take our knowledge before. They need our runes but resent having to pay us to make them. In centuries past, there have been pogroms that have driven out my people or harmed them."

"Really?"

"So when Darkfall came, we already had our own walled-off enclave in the city. It was easy for us to just stay here. We worked with the nobles and merchants to save the city from utter collapse by creating the Abattoir Fields and the Slime Fields. We made the walls and traded our skills for food. That's hard to make in great quantity with runes."

"You made the algae." She shifted. She was supposed to be talking about caravans, but this was easier. "That's what you said."

"Modified an existing strain that naturally grows in the waters of Hamiocho. To make them healthier and boost the immune systems of those who eat it. Most of the city's population would have died to a number of terrible diseases from the poor sanitary conditions without that algae. It's simple to make, breaks down waste products to make food, and keeps producing oxygen so we can breathe."

"Oxygen?" She stumbled over the foreign word.

"What's in the air that our bodies use when we breathe in," he explained. "Anyway, you were asking about caravans. That's why we need them; because we don't trust the Glowers, as you call them."

"At least that's wise of you," she said. She drew in a deep breath. "So, do they happen every three weeks?"

"Yeah."

"So the next one's going to be coming soon, huh?" Amiollea tried to sound casual. Making conversation.

"It is. Two weeks away, I believe."

"Same route?"

"Why would we change it?"

"Sun Ravagers ambushed the last one."

"A fluke." The air fluttered against her face from his waving hand, his robe flapping. "They were punished. Most were butchered."

"Oh, good." That sent relief flooding through her. "By who?"

"Glower guards."

A shiver ran through Amiollea. "Why were they outside the Rubble?"

"They were after a thief. A servant. He ran away with something valuable. They're hunting him down."

"I . . . see . . ." She furrowed her brow. "I've never heard of them coming after a thief before. They don't like to leave their walls."

Maej chuckled. "I guess it must have been something Lord Achogear wants back bad enough. He's having my master make a way to track him. They delivered a sample of blood from the thief's father."

A chill ran through her. Before she could open her mouth, Maej pressed a cloth into her hand. She felt a sticky portion. The tacky sensation of drying blood. She shifted against him.

"You and your brother don't have to worry," he said.

Pain slashed through her. "Maej, I didn't mean to —"

"It's fine." He laughed. "I want there to be trust between us."

"Me, too," she said softly, her stomach roiling. She suddenly felt so terrible and then the impulse to kiss him rose in her. To give him *something* back for what he was doing. Her heart pounded as the sensation seized her. She felt him against her. The warmth.

She leaned her head in and brushed his cheek with her lips. When she felt him, a soft roughness of stubble, she kissed his cheek. Not a quick peck, but lingering, feeling him. Her heart beat faster and faster.

"Amiollea?"

She pulled her lips back, cheeks blazing with heat. "I'm not trading kisses, I just wanted to—"

He moved before she could react. Cloth rustled. His breath caressed her cheek. His lips found her chin and went up to her mouth. When he found it, she closed her eyes and whimpered against him. His lips were soft and warm and wet. Her mouth moved against him by instinct. Tears stung her eyes. The pain swelled in her.

It didn't make her feel better at all. She was *using* him. In the pit of her stomach, in the throbbing wounds in her heart, she knew the truth. She didn't want to use him. She wished she could just come here and trade kisses with him. Talk with him.

But she had to survive out in the terrible city with her brother and Zhee. They needed more and . . . and . . .

He's enjoying it, she thought as she kept kissing him. *I'm not lying lying to him. I just . . . We need help, and he's giving it to us.*

The tears spilled down her cheeks. She broke the kiss, wanting to hide her turmoil from him. He panted beside her. He sounded . . . happy. Joyful. She wanted to share that with him. In another world, before Darkfall, she could have just been a girl kissing the boy she liked.

I have to eat tomorrow, and the next day, and the day after. I don't get to sell my abilities to the Glowers.

She didn't hate Maej for that—envied him, yes—but she didn't hate him. She was happy he didn't have to think like her. She rubbed her cheek into his robed shoulder, wiping away her tears as his ragged breathing slowed.

"Well, I . . . That is . . ." He swallowed. "The rope! I have the rope. You needed that."

"We can trade it to get food," she said. "Blind Fishers always need rope."

"Probably to make nets," he said.

"Nets?" she asked.

"Something fishermen use out at sea to catch fish."

"You know a lot," she said, her tears passing.

"So do you. We just know different things. Doesn't that make it all interesting?"

"Yeah." She lifted her head. "I should probably be going."

Maej chuckled as he shifted around and felt on the ground. "Now you have my rope, you're ready to run off."

He said it playfully, but the words pummeled her heart, battering fists leaving her more bruised. She tried to sound jovial back, saying, "All I'm here for."

It came out bitter.

Maej didn't seem to notice as he handed her a bundle of rope, the fibers rough on her fingers. She stood, reflexively brushing off dirt from her rump. He rose with her, standing before her, robes rustling. The warmth from him almost seemed hotter than the air.

"So . . ." he said. "Three days?"

"Three days," she agreed. "I . . ." She hugged the rope to her. "Thank you, Maej. You've been a good friend."

"This city hasn't ruined everything good, has it?" he asked.

"No, it hasn't," she said, visualizing that flash of his face she saw, skin blue, eyes wide, at once triumphant and then terrified. Innocent of his actions. Despite the pain in her heart, she smiled.

CHAPTER
TWENTY-NINE

Emmait had ruined things with Zhee.

His anger at her for leaving had died to a simmer. He had a belly full of meat—*and that is all it is,* he kept telling himself, *meat!* —driving back the hunger. He lay outside their shack, listening to the return of Amiollea and Ablisio from meeting with the Runecarver they were tricking.

Using him like you wanted to use me! snarled through Emmait.

The desire for Zhee battered down that thought. He couldn't believe that. He had pushed her too far. He had to ease her into his idea. She was a gentle creature. Her loving nature hadn't been beaten out of her by the last seven years. That was remarkable.

He listened to the three gorging on catfish. It appeared Ablisio had swung by the Blind Fishers and traded something the Runecarver gave. The scent of the fresh fish, their oily scales and rich flesh, drifted through the rot of the orchard. The three sounded happy. Laughing, joking, the family Emmait yearned for.

It's just meat! he thought to himself, rubbing his stomach. He could feel it in him.

Heavy.

He closed his eyes, running from the turmoil in his guts, to thoughts of

Zhee. She was important. Soft hands. Gentle words. And though he'd never seen it, he knew she had a sweet smile. A loving smile that would be only for him.

As the trio enjoyed their dinner, his thoughts drifted to a memory from his childhood. Sitting on his mother's lap, her soft brown hair falling about her laughing face as she ran a comb through his "unruly mane."

He sank into it...

She smelled so fresh and sweet. He was in her bedroom, the sunlight spilling through the open window, the scent of lemon blossoms drifting through it. She hummed as she ran the comb through his hair.

"My handsome boy," she said, a dreaminess to her voice. "Oh, all the girls will be smiling at you when you're older."

His face contorted with disgust.

She laughed. "You won't think so when you're older. You'll find yourself a pretty girl to love. I know it."

His mother kissed his forehead and he smiled at her. "I can love you, mama."

She laughed. "But I already have someone who loves me. Your father. And you're going to be just as handsome as he is."

His good mood almost evaporated, but then she ran the comb through his hair again. She hummed and he closed his eyes. He was safe in her room. Away from the others of the house. No teasing. No sneering hatred from Lady Achogear, no servants only tolerating him if not outright mocking him if the lady was around. The indifference of his "father."

He was safe here. With her.

A shadow filled the doorway.

"There you are, my little fox," she said. She kissed his brow. "You go and play. Your father and I have to talk."

His father stood in the doorway and...

Emmait's eyes snapped open. The sounds of laughter rippled through the air. The smell of fish and rot filled his senses now. The young him hadn't understood the looks Lord Achogear and his mother had shared, but he did now. The hunger in the man's smile. The invitation in his mother's eyes.

It poisoned his memory of his mother. She'd sent him off to play to dally with *him*. She'd have rather writhed beneath Lord Achogear than comb his hair. Just like Zhee would rather be with Ablisio.

Now Emmait was a man. He had a sword. He could kill Ablisio. Cut him down. He could regain Zhee's full attention. Even if he couldn't see her, he knew she would smile at him like that. That invitation. He ached for it. He would have it.

But he had to be smart. He wasn't a boy in another way. He'd learned that impulsiveness killed. He had to think. Plan. Scout. So many ways to kill Ablisio, but what was the way that would keep the blood from Emmait's hands?

How could he be Zhee's hero again?

"Amiollea knows a good two-thirds of the route the caravan takes," Ablisio was saying, his words pricking Emmait's ears. The joviality had dwindled. They spoke of serious matters.

"Oh," Zhee said. "They never deviate."

"Nope," Amiollea said, her voice not as bright as usual. "Always the same way. Maej says so."

"So we're really going to do this."

"You pushed me to this, Zhee," Ablisio said. "Don't be a cat fearing the puddle."

"No, no, I'm committed. It's just . . ." She laughed nervously. "It'll be dangerous."

"We have two weeks to plan," he said. "We're going out tomorrow to scout the route. Learn it. Memorize every bit of it. We'll find the perfect spot to slip in and rob them."

Dangerous, thought Emmait, rubbing his bloated stomach. He'd eaten too much meat. *If things go wrong for them during the caravan . . .*

Zhee would need a savior. She would need Emmait again. It was his chance to show her he wasn't an animal—*It's just meat! No different from the catfish she's eating*—but the caring hero who protected her.

Like Amiollea, he also knew the route. He would be lurking in the dark. Following them. Listening. They weren't the only ones who could do an ambush. His hand gripped his sword as fantasies of Zhee's gratitude played out in his mind.

A SPARK IN THE NIGHT

~

A FULL BELLY FEELS GREAT, Ablisio thought.

Lethargy had settled on him after they'd talked about their scouting. He had all that rich catfish in him. Fatty and juicy. He'd sucked at his fingers for an hour, nursing out every last bit of flavor. And more hung from their ceiling. A few days' worth if they were lucky. By then, Amiollea would have another meeting with Maej.

Things had changed. He had a sword. He could defend them even better than before. He stroked Zhee's hair as she lay against him. She seemed quiet this evening. She had gushed over the fish, but something felt off about her. Guarded.

"What happened with your friend?" he asked, keeping his voice neutral. He didn't like this "friend" out there in the dark. What sort of man helped others for nothing in return? For strangers? What did Zhee pay him?

That sent an oily writhe through his guts.

"Badly," she said, heat in her voice. "I . . . misjudged him."

"Oh." The oily slick burst into happy flames that then became anger. "He didn't hurt you?" He had a sword . . .

"No, no, he's just not the man I thought him to be. He isn't like you."

"Oh. What did he do?"

"He's a beast," she hissed, snuggling up. "I don't want to talk about him. I want to forget about him. He might be nice to me, but he's not . . . The things he did . . . It was horrible what he did to them."

"Them?"

"A group of mucklings. Rapists. Vile men, but still . . ." She shook her head. "I won't go near him again."

"Maybe I should find him," Ablisio said slowly. "If he lives near us and frightens you . . ."

"He's not going to hurt me. Us." She pressed tighter against him. "I know that much about him, but I just don't want anything to do with a man who just *murders* when he doesn't have to. It wasn't about self-defense. It wasn't about protecting someone else in danger. It was cold. For *meat*."

"A cannibal."

"For his dog."

"He has a dog?" Amiollea said. "I haven't heard a dog in years."

"Not since we ate that one," Ablisio said. That was before Zhee.

"He just went in and slaughtered them," Zhee said. "I don't want to talk about it."

"Fine," he said, stroking her hair. "We'll just be on our guard. I won't go hunt him down."

"That's it?" Suspicion crept into her voice. "Where's the Ablisio who doesn't listen to good advice?"

"He was starving on a diet of algae. This one's fed with catfish. Too stuffed to do anything but lie here beside you."

"You two aren't going to do *things,* are you?" Amiollea asked from across the room.

"Oh, yes, we are," purred Zhee, shifting onto Ablisio. "The things you want to do with Maej."

"I don't," his sister said, but her protest sounded weak.

She is growing up. Is she going to leave? Not because she doesn't need me, but because she found her own man to love. Found safety in the Runic Ward...

No, they would never let her in there.

She would be hurt by this eventually. Maej wouldn't stay their friend forever. They had to use the boy for as much as possible. They'd get one, maybe two raids on the caravan, but it had to be enough. A foundation to do something bold.

To take the fight to the Glowers. They couldn't horde the food forever. It had to break. Someone had to do something about it. He had the sword. He would get more supplies. Maybe they could get Maej to make armor. Chainmail, runed to protect him.

His hands slid down Zhee's body to cup her rear. He pulled her onto him, the heat building between him.

"You *are* doing those things," moaned Amiollea. "Can't you control yourself one night?"

"Nope," Zhee said. "Don't pout, Amiollea. Think of it as practice for you and Maej."

"Don't talk about her and Maej," Ablisio protested. "Not right now."

"Now you understand how I feel," his sister muttered. "Maej isn't like that. He's just sweet."

"He sounds like it." Zhee rubbed her nose on Ablisio's. It was almost as intimate as a kiss. In some ways more so. It was playful. Exciting. "He's like boys used to be, giving gifts to spend time with a pretty girl."

Something sour congealed in Ablisio. Did she want him to give her gifts? "That's not a luxury I have."

Zhee kissed him on the lips. When she broke it, she purred, "You have other gifts to give."

"I'm going for a walk!" Amiollea gasped and darted out of the shack.

～

LATER, after Amiollea had slunk back in and Ablisio had fallen asleep beside her, Zhee stared up at the darkness. She absently stroked her stomach. Hope grew inside of her. Their child had a chance.

Trust me, you have given me a gift, Ablisio, she thought. She wondered when she should tell him. *Not now. Not while we're preparing to rob the Runecarvers. After. It'll be two more weeks. I'll be even more sure that Hope will survive.*

Emmait crept into her thoughts as she lay there. He worried her. She didn't think he would hurt them, but . . . The way he had marched in there and slaughtered those men held such a casualness about it. He hadn't seen them as human. They were just things. Meat to feed his dog. He'd butchered them with the sword.

Would he be angry that she had rejected him? Men didn't like that.

No, no, she told herself. *He might be mad, but he won't hurt us. He likes me. He's shy. I just . . .*

Those men he'd killed were vile, but it was hard not to turn putrid in Hamiocho. If Ablisio didn't have Amiollea to protect, how would he have turned out? Just as wild? Zhee had her father sheltering her for years before bad luck had landed them in the midst of the wrong group of mucklings.

You would have liked Ablisio, Dad, she thought. She hoped Wise Owl and Clever Fox had led him to join with her mother's spirit.

What did Emmait have? Sun. His dog. That proved there was good in him.

That she didn't have to worry about him. He protected his hound like Ablisio protected Amiollea. So she could trust that he wouldn't come for them.

She told herself that over and over as sleep eluded her.

~

Amiollea led her brother for once.

They moved from the gates of the Runic Ward the following morning after their catfish feast. They scouted the route. She remembered ghosting down the street after the Runecarvers, curious about their caravan. She felt so wicked, a naughty ghost in the dark. They had no idea she was there.

A moment of fear flashed through her of the Sun Ravagers' attack. She pushed it down by reminding herself if that awful thing hadn't happened, she wouldn't have met Maej.

Something good that came out of something dark and bitter. She liked thinking that.

"The road goes mostly straight," she said as they descended the slope. "There must be a turn, but I don't know where it would be."

"We're sort of heading toward the Rubble," said Ablisio. "I have a building here."

"Tall," said Zhee. "Does anyone live around here?"

"I didn't hear anyone," Amiollea answered. "We're close to Ratter territory. They might have their traps around here."

All three of them ran their hands around the outside of the building. Amiollea felt the texture of the stone. It was well-constructed, made of a hard stone, the bricks large. It wasn't the cheaper construction like the buildings by where they now lived. It had three doors, one facing the street, one behind it, and one in an alley.

They went inside, searching for any signs that people squatted here. For anything of use. They had to memorize the route. They had to learn every bit of it. They couldn't afford to pick the wrong spot to rob the Runecarvers.

With only three of them, they had to slip in and escape. They couldn't afford to get lost, to trip over an unseen obstruction. They had to build their mental maps of this region. It was something Amiollea didn't even think about any longer. She dimly remembered how hard this had been in the early times, but like anything, if you practiced enough, you gained skill at it.

She could almost see it in her mind. Not quite a real image, but a shadowy impression of the building's shape and how it fit into the street. The neighborhood. The entire city of Hamiocho she had in her mind. And it wasn't just the shape. It was smells. Sounds. Tastes in the air. The bit of musk in one corner. The dusty aroma to the right. The sound of air moving through a crack in the wall.

She had four senses to use. She drew on them all.

Fed on catfish for breakfast, they had the entire day to spend on the project. They kept quiet but with her dagger and Ablisio's sword, Amiollea felt emboldened. Zhee carried Ablisio's club, ready to use it, too.

They worked building by building, counting both sides of the street. They felt every cobblestone with feet, mesmerized rubble and depressions. They had to find the perfect spot to slip in to meet the Runecarvers. The buildings grew more compactly built. Taller. They were tenements, a residential neighborhood.

Many of it had been picked over by scavengers, but it seemed abandoned. They were close to the Fire Break, the part of the city torn down to stop the fire the Sun Ravagers had started. As they headed south, those cultist lands lay to their right. To their left was the Rubble surrounding the Slime Fields. Those who lived in the shadow of it dwelled in an area called the Hungry Shade. It was a lawless place like most of Hamiocho, but she'd heard it had its share of violent thugs, roving bands who preyed on any who tried to get food from their territory.

"Is it strange that *no one* lives on this street?" asked Zhee.

Amiollea furrowed her brow. It did seem unusual.

"Runecarvers?" Ablisio asked. "There were signs people have squatted here."

"Years ago. I could hardly smell them. These are good buildings. I can't believe no one is holed up in them."

"The Runecarvers unnerved them," he repeated. "Wouldn't you if they came down here every three weeks? Maybe they drove them out. What did they call their guards?"

"Wardens," Amiollea said, pride swelling in her. "They spend all their time in the dark in the Runic Ward, wandering around in it. They have decent senses. But they didn't detect me."

"It makes this easier for us," Ablisio said. "Come on, I want to know every bit of this street. Every stone and puddle of muck."

By midmorning, they reached the battle spot. At the first scent of drying blood, she stiffened. The burning smell lingered, the smoke from the dreaded fire. A spark of dread flared in her. She'd almost died in that madness. Shouts rang in her mind. Screams. The bright light.

The whispers of Death.

She didn't realize she'd drawn her dagger. She felt it in her hand as her brother walked past her. His footsteps slow. Zhee made disgusted sounds nearby. Amiollea trembled. She suddenly felt how full her bladder was. How much she just wanted to release her water in a spurt of fear.

"I don't smell any bodies," said Ablisio. "But the blood's soaked into the streak."

"The fire was over here," Zhee said. "Soot on the ground. Oily. Those Sun Ravagers really attacked them."

"Called them . . . something. Monsters. Evil." Amiollea trembled. "I don't remember."

"So this is as far as we know they go," her brother said. "I'd love to track them all the way to the Rubble. They must be making for one of the gates, but they need to make a turn."

"Probably taking this main street to another," suggested Zhee.

"Does it matter?" Amiollea asked. "This isn't the place to attack them. We shouldn't be anywhere near this place."

"No," her brother said. "This will remind them of the danger. We should hit them closer to the Runic Ward. At least halfway between here and their gate. Let their guard relax again before we slip among them and steal what we can."

"It'll be hard to drift in among them," Zhee said.

"Most of the Runecarvers are blind in the dark," Amiollea said, her voice tight. "Just the wardens we have to get by. They're in armor."

"Easy to avoid," Ablisio said, sounding pleased. "This will work. We just need the right spot to wait."

"Yeah," Amiollea said. She rubbed her belly, hating the sour ache there. She was stealing food from Maej and his people. She was using him. This was her idea, but she was liking it a whole lot less.

How could she keep giving him kisses when she would betray him? What did that make her?

CHAPTER THIRTY

Maegwirio set another sword on the stack. When he wasn't meeting with Amiollea every third day, he was making swords. The days passed in his workshop, shaping, transmuting, and imbuing the blades with all the standard runes, laboriously scratched into the sword's metal, but also his new idea. They were all ready to be bonded to their owners. He just needed their blood and to scratch in the last rune.

It was tedious work. Time consuming work. It was different from his studies or pondering how to break into his maestro's study and find the secrets the old man refused to divulge. Secrets that might be important. If anything happened to Maestro Kozonio, then who would make the Light? Manufacturing swords had become repetitive. He found little ways to improve his efficiency, but it still took him more than two days to produce one because of how difficult it was etching the metal. And if he made a scratch wrong, he had to undo his mistakes and start again.

But the swords would be valuable. Earn food for his people. He told himself that over and over again.

In between making swords and meeting with Amiollea, he squeezed in the time to make her rope to trade from leather straps. He was eager for his next meeting with her. They would have one more before the caravan headed for the Glowers.

Another chance to kiss her.

They did that between her questions about life in the Runic Ward, about how the wardens trained, on what it was like living in light instead of dark all the time. Every time he wanted to ask her a question, her lips found his.

They were distracting lips, but he didn't mind. He enjoyed the feel of her mouth on him too much to care. The heat it sparked.

He wanted to do more. He started touching her. In chaste places. The knee. The arm. He stroked her side while they kissed. He was all too aware that her brother was nearby, ready to swoop in if he thought they were doing something else.

"Who is she?"

The question shocked Maegwirio out of his reverie. He almost dropped the sword he held and fell out of his chair. He glanced at the door to his study and found his maestro in it, the old man chuckling in amusement.

"Who, Maestro?" Maegwirio asked, his cheeks burning. He hastily set down the sword.

"The girl you're thinking about so hard. The one you sneak out to see every few days." The old man took a few steps toward him. "Unless drooling over the sword is a vital step in the manufacturing process."

"I don't sneak out," Maegwirio said. "I leave normally."

"Just when I happen to be busy at the top of the Spire?" The maestro chuckled. "I'm old, not senile."

"She's . . ." How to explain her? "Wonderful."

"Of course she's wonderful, but she's not a Taechizian girl, is she?"

Maegwirio's back stiffened. His stomach lurched and then fell out of him. "I, uh, what, sir?"

The maestro's smile turned sly. "You are going out through the eastern postern gate. Right? Don't deny it."

He squirmed.

"I wondered how you got back on your own after the cultists attacked us. It didn't seem possible."

"I'm not that hopeless," Maegwirio muttered. He swallowed. "You don't think I could have done it?"

"No, not alone. Not how fast you returned. You might have found your way on your own, eventually—much like a lost mouse following the edges of a wall to find his hole—but you arrived at the gate before everyone else did. You ran into a muckling girl. She—"

"Don't call her that," Maegwirio said. The sudden anger surging through him shocked him. "She's not a muckling girl. She's a person. Yes, she led me back, and I'm seeing her."

"You're giving her gifts." The old man's gaze slid to the coil of rope on the desk.

Heat suffused Maegwirio's cheeks. The anger simmered in him. "I am. And? I know she might be using me, but I don't care. I like spending time with her. She's exciting. Alive. She makes me feel . . ."

"How does she make you feel?"

"Doesn't matter," the youth muttered. He shifted. "So I don't mind giving her some gifts. They're easy to make, and if they make her life easier, then it's worth it because she makes everything brighter. Out there, in the dark, she almost glows."

The maestro studied him. "You fear she is just using you."

"A little, but . . . I don't want to let that stop me from spending time with her. Everyone doubts things. I'd rather hope and take a chance."

"Powerful thing, hope." The old man's gnarled hand rested on Maegwirio's shoulder. The maestro squeezed and added, "We all use each other, Maegwirio. But that doesn't mean we don't care about those we use."

"What?"

"Relationships are all about giving and taking. Using and being used. So long as it's honest, that what's being given and taken is understood by both parties and the feelings and motivations are out in the open, there's really no harm in it. After all, you used me to survive after Darkfall."

"You're my maestro," Maegwirio protested.

"And? Did that mean I had to spend effort in raising you? Did it mean you weren't using my generosity to survive? It doesn't make you a bad person. I gave it to you willingly. See, we understood. It was honest and open. So if your, er, friend is using you to help her survive, does that bother you?"

"No. I want to help her survive."

"Has she given you any other reason?"

"She likes meeting with me. She's excited. Inquisitive. She asks me all sorts of questions about life in here."

"Good, sounds honest. Now, you don't have to sneak in and out anymore because you are lousy at it. You make such a racket trying not to make a racket."

He blushed. "That's it, Maestro?"

"Did you want me to say anything else?" The old man gave him a piercing look. "Do you understand about sex?"

"Yes!" he gasped, his voice choked. "I mean, you're not going to object? Forbid me from seeing her?"

"Why?" The old man chuckled. "Wouldn't do any good. You'd just be *more* motivated to see her if I forbade you. Sheer youthful stubbornness would drive you to rebel. No different than black-horn rams crashing heads together to win the females. Besides, you're still doing your work. Even better. You've had some particularly good insights."

"Oh," he said, squirming.

"You've been worrying I'd be mad for catching you sneaking out, and now you're disappointed I'm not." He put on a stern look. "Maegwirio, I am very, very disappointed. See my disappointed face."

A smile broke across Maegwirio's lips.

"There's too much suffering in this corner of damnation," the old man said, his eyes growing distant. "Embrace what you've found. It's certainly provided you motivation to hone your runic craft by making her things."

And kept me from thinking about breaking into your office. The guilt swirled through his guts. He knew he shouldn't, but if anything happened to the old man, who would continue his work? Who would light the beacon? It must be important. It had to be more than hope.

"I do like making things for her," Maegwirio said, the itch to ask building in him.

"And give her a kiss or three." A fond look crossed his face. "Or more.

We're all dwindling. We're just putting off death for as long as we can. So enjoy your life."

Death . . . Spurred to confidence, he asked, "Good enough to learn what you're really doing on the roof?"

The old man looked away. "Well, uh." He cleared his throat. "No. One day, I promise. When you're older."

"I'm a man."

"You're, what, fourteen?"

"Sixteen."

"Keep working on your runes." He turned. "I'm tired. Going to take a nap. Have to keep my eyes rested, you know. How you keep your mind sharp when you get as old as me."

"Maestro," he called, but the old man closed the door behind him.

∼

Nervous energy danced through Ablisio. He felt more and more restless the nearer and nearer the day of the caravan came. Sleep came with difficulty. He wanted to just get there while his mind worried over every possible thing that could go wrong.

The Runecarvers would change the date.

The time.

They would go *before* his family was ready.

They would use a different route.

They would have more guards.

The items would be cursed to burn any who touched them.

The Sun Ravagers would attack and summon Death.

Zhee or Amiollea would bump into a guard and be killed.

The three of them would be heard making their approach.

Smelled.

Felt.

Other worries gnawed on Ablisio's soul. It was dangerous crossing the city. Twice, he'd used his new sword to kill mucklings who'd come across them crossing the city as they either were memorizing the caravan route in painstaking detail or when Amiollea went to spend her hour every three days with the young man.

The gifts he gave of rope or wood or cloth had let them purchase rats and fish to feed them. He felt stronger than he had in a year. His belly was full more often than it was empty. The increased vigor had few outlets.

Zhee was one of them.

Their couplings had a frenzy about them as they both sought to contain their anxiety. They clutched each other with fierceness while his sister scowled and muttered and went for long walks with her knife.

They were even keeping some of the supplies. The last section of rope Maej had given them they had kept. Now they were trying to weave it into a net. Maegwirio had explained the principal to Ablisio's sister, but the execution was difficult. How to knot them together. How big to space them apart. They only had so much rope. If they could do their own fishing...

They needed more rope.

Every day, Ablisio reminded himself that they were careful. That they were not taking risks. That they would succeed. They had to. Things were growing too hard. He had his sister and woman to care for. And he would do it.

"This is the spot," he said as they stood on the route for their dozenth walking of it. They stood by a building that had water dripping through it. The sound echoed out of the building. There must be a cistern on the roof that had cracked and the water had been dribbling out for some time. Enough that he hoped the Runecarvers should be familiar with it.

"We'll use the noise to give us some added cover," he said. "I'll be on the left side, Zhee, right forward, Amiollea, right rear."

"You're sure?" Zhee asked.

His stomach lurched. "You're not?"

"It's not that," she said quickly. "I can't think of a better spot, I just mean, we're not getting another chance. So let's be sure."

"Okay." He glanced through the dark in the direction his sister stood. He heard her breathing, the press of skin sliding on skin. Her fingers stroked herself, making noise. "Amiollea?"

"I have no objections, it's just... Maej's waiting." Her eagerness to see her friend—Ablisio couldn't stomach using the word "lover" in conjunction with his little sister—was palpable in her tone. "It's almost time."

"Okay," Ablisio said. "We'll rehearse when we get back."

The sound of Zhee padding to Amiollea whispered in his ears. More skin rubbing on skin. Ablisio pictured Zhee putting her arm around the slenderer girl's shoulders. "You're going to kiss him just like I told you. He'll like that."

"With the tongue?" Amiollea asked as they strolled up the street.

Ablisio's stomach lurched even harder. *What are you teaching my sister? And since when did you two get along?*

He trailed after. Two days to go. Two days, and this would all be over. They would have their supplies.

CHAPTER
THIRTY-ONE

Zhee leaned into her place against the wall along the route. She sank to her knees and sat there. The stone was rough against her back. The water trickled through the building behind her.

PLOP! PLOP! PLOP!

The steady sound echoed through the darkness. They only thing she heard as she settled herself. She breathed slowly. Waiting was something you grew used to in Hamiocho, just letting the hours drift by with nothing to do but stare into the impenetrable dark.

She stroked her belly, Hope growing inside of her still strong. She wanted to tell Ablisio. After they had their success and had returned to their home with their spoils, she would tell her man that he would soon be a father.

You're going to make it, little one, she thought to herself as she stroked her greasy belly. She smiled, struggling to picture what the baby would look like. *I don't really know what your father looks like. I know what my father, your grandfather, looks like, but not your father. I know the feel of his face. He has a bold nose. Strong and thrusting out before him. His face is square. He feels handsome. He doesn't have a heavy brow like your grandfather, but he's as broad in the shoulder. He's still strong. You will be, too.*

She smiled in the dark as she pictured Hope growing up day by day. Learning to walk. To talk. To sneak through the dark. Ablisio would be an amazing teacher. He would instruct Hope in all he or she needed to know to survive in Hamiocho. To thrive.

A new beginning for them stretched before her. Zhee and her family just had to take it.

PLOP! PLOP! PLOP!

She let her thoughts drift.

~

"You have your inscriber?" asked the maestro as Maegwirio cinched up the pack that held the seven swords he'd made.

"Yes, Maestro," Maegwirio responded for the dozenth time. "And two spares. They're in my pocket. Along with the amulet."

"That's worth an extra bag of food," his maestro said. He sat at the kitchen table.

"I'll be fine, Maestro," Maegwirio said. "The wardens will keep us safe. The Glowers will be impressed with the swords."

"Yes, yes, I know." The old man sighed. "You never expect it to happen to you."

"What?"

"Growing old. It creeps up on you. It's a subtle thing. You feel a little more sore. You accumulate all these aches. Pains. Twinges in your back. Individually, none of them are that burdensome. You could ignore any one of them, but in total, they wear on you. Weaken you. Your body gives up to the frustration of your mind."

"I'm sorry, Maestro," Maegwirio answered slowly. He had no idea how to answer his maestro's somber tone. "I wish I could do something."

"I just mean, enjoy being young. Don't waste it. This girl . . . Don't let her go. If you can hold onto her, do it."

"I will." He smiled. He'd seen her two days before and would see her again the following day. He was excited for that. He would have something special for her. He couldn't wait to give it to her. He didn't care about the cost.

He just wanted to hear the delight in her voice.

He gathered the sack of swords and headed to the door. The wardens and the rest of the Runecarvers awaited to make the short trek to the Glowers. In a few hours, he'd be home with the food eager for time to pass to see Amiollea.

Is there a word sweeter than her name?

○○○

Emmait listened to the clink of metal, the rustle of robes, the scent of something clean. Soap. The Runecarvers marched down the street, slipping past his hiding place. He held Sun to him, the mangy fur rubbing on his chest. The dog stayed still.

The blind Runecarvers had no idea he was here.

He counted them as they passed, picking out the five armed wardens surrounding the party of twenty-two softer Runecarvers. They held sacks that jingled with metal or had the rasp of coiled rope. The sounds of goods produced in exchange for real food.

Salted beef. Maybe even *fresh* steaks or cow's tongue. A stomach stuffed with liver and kidneys. All those glorious dishes that he used to get the scraps of when he'd lived at Lord Achogear's house. He had a different meat in his belly, raw, filling.

Would Zhee adapt to eating the new meat? he wondered. He didn't see why she wouldn't. Not after he showed her the truth of it. He didn't kill people. Just monsters. Things that prowled through the corners of Hamiocho looking to prey on those weaker. Parasites that had to be cleansed from the host.

Never a person like her.

He hid two blocks from where Zhee, Ablisio, and Amiollea crouched. He would let them slip into the crowd of the Runecarvers before he made his move. He would kill Ablisio in the chaos. Zhee would think the Runecarvers got him, then he would appear to save her, fending off the enemy, cutting to get her free and to safety.

My hero, sang through his mind along with imagined kisses. He closed his eyes as he imagined how she would feel against him. Around him. He would rescue her from Ablisio.

He had the man's scent. Memorized it from their home. He would find him in the dark, tracking him like Sun could. His sword would ram right through his back. A single plunge, and Ablisio would no longer be an issue.

"I'll save you, Zhee," he said under his breath, lips moving.

I know you will, she said in his mind.

～

THE RUNECARVERS PASSED Amiollea's hiding place.

In the midst of them, the familiar steps of Maej. She recognized his stride, heard the grunts he made as he shifted what he carried. Metal clattered, the swords he was making for the Glower guards. Ones like her brother's. Maej was near the front. Hopefully, she would go nowhere near him when the robbery happened.

The clank of a warden passed before her. Almost within her arms' reach. He had no idea she was there. She had rubbed herself in the dirt of the area, masking her scent with the surrounding muck. She barely breathed, kept herself still.

Part of her wanted to disturb a pebble. To make a single noise different from the PLOP-PLOP of the dripping water coming from the building behind her. She could apologize to her brother, take his disappointment, and not betray Maej's trust.

It wasn't supposed to be like this. She was supposed to learn from him and use it, not feel like her stomach had more knots in it than an Autumn Rain Feast pretzel, the warm dough contorted and wrapped and twisted about itself until you didn't know where to start with it. The footsteps retreated farther and farther away.

He could never know. She could never tell him. He would hate her, and Maej loathing her was almost more than she could bear. It dug this pit in her belly. This depression that drew deeper and deeper. She felt almost sick.

But her family needed this more. Resources. Food. An ease of their burden. A chance to change things. She had to put Ablisio before Maej. As much as it hurt her, she couldn't let anything come between her and her family.

They have plenty, she told herself. *They'll never miss if some is taken. They can spare some. And he has his runes. He'll be fine.*

She told herself that while the pit in her belly deepened.

Now she had to wait for the caravan to come back laden with food for her family to steal.

CHAPTER
THIRTY-TWO

The gate in the Rubble opened. Maegwirio could feel the heaps of torn building material, an amalgam of bricks, wood, cut stone, and plaster all piled together and bound with runes to erect the wall as fast as possible during the days after the fall while the riots raged and roared, the survivors dying by the scores in the chaos of Darkfall.

The wardens didn't enter with the Runecarvers. They passed into a building. He heard his fellows moving around. They sounded nervous, like they had the entire walk. Unsure. Porresio bumped into Maegwirio and muttered an apology.

None of them knew how to *listen*. To feel the air. To smell. He could tell several men were near him from the rustle of cloth and the scent of their sweat. They shifted the air in small currents that brushed his hands and face.

The door boomed closed behind them. A door opened and light flooded in. It wasn't bright but after an hour's walk in pitch black, he winced against it. The scent of algae and sour mud flooded the air. Air more humid than anything out of the city, stifling and stuffy and bleeding through his robes, afflicted him.

He followed the others out into the Slime Fields.

The roof stretched over their heads was held up by pillars as cobbled together and rushed as the Rubble. An irrigation canal from the Sluggish Waters brought water to the vast pools of algae thrusting out like long fronds from a central stalk. Workers, mostly Povazian, moved among them, scooping out the algae with wire-mesh shovels and dumping them into large jars. Others were dumping waste into the other pools to feed the next crop.

This was the heart of the food in the city. Most people survived off it and nothing more. That was how the Slimers, as those who worked here, were known. They and their families were kept fed, living in houses along the edges. They were safe, protected by the Glowers' guards from intrusions.

So long as they worked and obeyed the rules. They wouldn't want to be thrown out into the darkness.

To the right lay the meeting building. It was one of the two ways to leave the Slime Fields and enter the Glowers District proper. To the unlit but well-maintained streets where the rich and powerful lived with as much comfort as they could, using their control of the food to buy the Runecarvers' loyalty.

The negotiations would begin as the Glowers listed their needs. Runecarvers like Maegwirio would head out into the Glowers District to effect any work they needed, add new defensive runes to tighten gaps in the Rubble that had been exploited by thieves, or repair damaged items. Anything to pay for the food to keep their people alive for another three weeks.

Captain Fhaaghin and other guard-captains grinned when they saw him spread out his pouch of swords. The men were all eager to get theirs, Captain Fhaaghin lining up first. He grabbed a sword, holding it up.

"You need my blood?" he asked, pressing the tip of his left thumb to the razor-sharp edge. He pricked it. Crimson welled on his pale skin. It was so colorless, the pattern of blue veins beneath his hand bled through.

"Smear it on these runes," Maegwirio said. He pulled out an inscriber, like a diamond-tip pencil he could scratch into the hardened metal. "Oh, also, this is for your search." He produced the amulet. "Whoever wears it should feel an echo that draws you to the thief and his father. And any other siblings or close family members."

"He should be the only one out there," growled the captain as he donned it. Then he smeared his blood on the sword.

Another captain sank a bag of salted beef onto the table. Maegwirio smiled. That was his payment for the swords. All that meat for this. It was beyond what his people would need, and he knew what he would do with the excess.

Amiollea could feed her family for a month off it. They wouldn't have to take risks. All he could do was supply them with more rope and help them figure out how to fish for themselves. Excitement brimmed in him, glad he could transform their lives. Do something for those trapped out in the dark.

Things had to change.

He scratched the final rune into the blood smeared on the sword. Each stroke was precise, digging into the metal. Fhaaghin waited, arms folded across his chest. The sword burst with blue light for a moment as the runes channeled the power with his will and made it something useful.

"It's yours, Captain," Maegwirio said with a big smile. "Any but you who touches it will get a nasty burn."

Maegwirio continued his work. He would be here all morning. He went slowly, worked with sure strength, and carved the runes into them, making blades no desperate thief could loot and use to kill a warden in the dark.

∽

The hours dragged on and on. Maegwirio had said they would be there all morning, but the waiting devoured Ablisio's patience. The muscles in his leg cramped from squatting. His fingers fidgeted on the scabbard he had hanging off his left hip, the sword's weight pulling on him. The belt dug into the flesh on the right side.

Doubts and worries crept into his mind, poisoning him with whispered thoughts. What if they didn't come this route? What if they detected their presence and would go two or three blocks right or left to avoid this patch?

Had Ablisio wasted the last two weeks planning a raid that would never happen?

He couldn't talk to his sister or Zhee. He wanted to. Itched to pass the time in idle chitchat, but they had to be alert. Anything could spoil this plan. What if another group of mucklings had the same plan and decided *today* they'd attack the Runecarvers?

The Sun Ravagers had. Those madmen might have all been butchered by the Glower guards, it didn't mean others wouldn't attack. What if a Ratter just came here to lay some traps and detected them? They sold most of their captured quarry to the Runecarvers. They would rush to tell them.

So many things could go wrong *before* the Runecarvers arrived.

And after...

Ablisio took deep breaths. Slow breaths. He fought to control his jitters. He rubbed his hands together, his legs spasming. The waiting dulled his senses. Paying attention grew harder and harder as he found himself sinking more and more into his worries.

A whisper.

His head rose.

A shuffling sound. Distant. A clink of metal. Movement. The Runecarvers? It came from his right. His hearing focused on it, his sense of touch and taste and smell dwindling as he focused on the aural information.

Boot steps.

Heavy sacks.

Jangle of chainmail.

Robes rustling.

Hope surged through him. The rush of energizing cold that rippled over his skin had him rising. His knees popped from the crouch. A faint sound came from across the road. Amiollea rose. Zhee shifted. The Runecarvers approached.

It was almost over. His hands flexed. He rubbed sweaty palms into thighs covered in the local dirt. His chest rose and fell, fighting against the tension squeezing around him. The boot steps grew into twenty-eight distinct pairs of feet wearing everything from tar-coated slippers to soft-soled shoes to hobnailed boots. With it came the swish of heavy sacks. The slosh of algae in jars.

The scent of meat. Salted and fresh.

Saliva spilled over his tongue. A rumbling growl rose from his stomach. His breath quickened as they came closer and closer. The Runecarvers talked in their language, babbling louder than the dripping water. They sounded relaxed. Unconcerned. They were nearly to their runic walls, a quarter hour or so to safety.

Ablisio turned in place, facing the same way they traveled. The leader, a warden with heavy boots, said something. A person laughed behind him. In Ablisio's mind, he pictured where they stood, the sounds of all their footsteps and rustling clothing. He had memorized this block by touch, knew all the contours of the stones. The guard approached the cobblestone that thrust upward, buckled up from the road.

A crunching thud. A curse and a stumble. Words in Taechizian. More laughter.

Ablisio kept his breathing even now. The warden passed him. The Taechizians followed. The hard clink of the two guards on his side. He let the first one pass and then moved out, walking at a diagonal to cut through their numbers. He drifted, an unseen wraith, every footstep bringing him closer and closer to the gap between the guards. He didn't rush it. He took his time, keeping his footsteps soft.

No mistakes now.

He passed between the two guards, armor jangling before and behind him. His shoulder blades itched. The guard held a runic blade like the one strapped to his waist. If he was heard, a quick stab into his back and he'd drop. Bleed out if they didn't finish him.

He edged closer. A Runecarver grunted, his steps suddenly rushing forward a few, moving past Ablisio. The air of his passage washed over the young man's naked body. He shifted behind him, falling into position.

The sack the man held sounded full of food. The impact of hunks of beef. The salted, savory flavor bled through the burlap. Ablisio itched to snatch it now. But he needed to give his sister and Zhee time to move in. He matched the Runecarvers' slow pace, hardly breathing.

He was just one more in their dark caravan.

∽

AMIOLLEA PASSED INTO THE GROUP. The first man she heard held a sloshing jar of algae. Many of them did. She focused on the heavy thud of a sack of meat. She paused in the middle of the caravan, letting two Runecarvers slip by her without pausing in their conversation.

To her relief, Maej marched farther forward. She wasn't close to him. Didn't have to risk stealing from him. Just another Runecarver. She could steal from this man. She itched to grab the bag as she ghosted behind him.

The Runecarvers were all around her. Someone could trip, bump into her naked body, and realize a muckling had infiltrated the group. She trembled with nerves, a mix of fear and exhilaration. Her dirty hair rubbed on her shoulders, making too much noise for her comfort.

She itched to strike. But she had to wait for the signal. Two coughs. Ablisio would give it. They had to act together. Grab their prizes and dart for the alleys between the buildings. She had her mental map firm in her mind, pictured her various ways she had to escape with every step. Her soles felt the familiar terrain she had memorized, the feel of the cobblestones letting her know her exact position.

Her brother just had to give the signal.

Why wasn't he giving the signal?

A man behind her shouted. She tensed, her shoulders tightened. Her hands tingled to spring. His tar-coated sandals slapped on the stone. He hurried forward in a rush of robes. He swept by her, his sleeve brushing her arm.

She squeezed her eyes shut, bracing for the alarm.

Only he laughed and began speaking to the man she followed in rapid Taechizian. The language blurred into a melange of alien sounds. She shivered as the tension melted out of her.

Give the signal, brother! screamed in her mind. *Even Zhee must be in position by now. Her big breasts don't slow her down* that *much.*

～

Sun crouched, waiting for Emmait's signal. Taking a breath, he crept out into the midst of the Runecarvers, sword out and in hand. He ghosted past the one warden on the right side of the party and into the scents of all the robed figures. He breathed in deeply, his nostrils cataloging the various aromas around him.

He caught a whiff of Zhee's scent. She was near him.

He ached for her, but pushed down that twinge of heat in his nethers. He focused on the other scent. It was masked by dirt, but Ablisio's stink drew him on. Emmait moved with confidence among the blind Runecarvers stumbling down the road. They talked and laughed at their ease, unaware that death stalked among them.

But you're not monsters, thought Emmait as he approached his quarry. *Only one here. And I'll deal with him.*

It was noisy in the middle of the Runecarvers. Sounds of the outside world were hard to hear over all the rustling wool of their clothing. The thud of sacks. Smack of footsteps. He didn't hear Ablisio moving at all.

But his scent grew stronger until...

It passed him, following a man carrying a sack of meat. Emmait smiled and moved behind his quarry. The faint disturbance in the air let him know someone was closer to him than the sounds of heavy footsteps of the Runecarver.

Emmait raised his weapon to make the fateful plunge and save Zhee.

∽

Now has to be enough time, thought Ablisio. He drew in a deep breath. His instincts screamed against him.

He had to be loud over the cacophony of the Runecarvers. They talked like careless birds, not caring if the entire city heard them. It almost hurt his ears being among them. He realized he could just shout out, "Now!" and they wouldn't realize anything was amiss.

He coughed. Hard. An explosive burst of air. Then he did it a second time, the signal to strike. His hands lunged for the bag. He grasped it when a ripple of commotion burst through the Runecarvers. Sounds echoed behind him. Ablisio turned his head to pinpoint the sound behind him.

Heavy boots. Jangling metal. A party of guards approached the Runecarvers in a hurry, their footsteps rumb—

Hot pain sliced across Ablisio's lower rib on his left side. Something lunged past him and rammed into the back of the Runecarver he followed. The man screamed in agony. The hot scent of blood filled the air. The man stumbled.

Collapsed.

Confusion spilled through Ablisio. Shouts broke out amid the Runecarvers. A figure moved right behind Ablisio. A man he hadn't noticed. He smelled of the local dirt, but there was a tinge of sweat beneath. And the tang of metal.

A sword.

The attacker growled in frustration.

Ablisio ripped his sword from his scabbard and it struck into a blade slashing at him. Sparks flared for a moment, exposing a snarling face, a naked body. Screams shouted. Men drew weapons. The wardens bellowed.

Ablisio's heart thundered, blood trickling down his side, as he fought for his life against his assailant.

CHAPTER
THIRTY-THREE

"Chiddeffio has collapsed!" shouted from behind Maegwirio. "Broken runes, he's bleeding."

Metal clanged on metal. Maegwirio threw looks behind him at the dark. Shouts burst amid his fellow Runecarvers. Footsteps charged in every direction. The wardens bellowed the alarm. Mucklings attacked *again*. The heavy sack of food hanging off Maegwirio's shoulder pulled him off-balance.

"Follow my voice," Fiaxhazio shouted from the front of the party. "Don't run! Move calmly! Don't get separated."

Swords clashed together, ringing in the darkness. Shouts in Karadrisan drifted from the back. *"The thief's here, Runecarver! He's among you!"*

"Captain Fhaaghin?" Maegwirio gasped in shock.

"A muckling just grabbed my sack!" Akozogwio shouted.

"Sun Ravagers!" shrieked Xhozobbio as he raced past Maegwirio and crashed into someone. They both hit the ground. A jar of algae burst open, dumping the contents across the road.

Maegwirio clutched Amiollea's food to his chest as he backed up, his bowels turning to liquid. Would light flare? Would Death come whispering down to rend and kill?

She wasn't here this time to save him.

"Don't panic!" he found himself shouting. "Move toward my voice. We're going to get out of this! Keep moving!" He could "see" in the dark, not as well as a muckling, but he was better than most of his people. He had to help them.

He couldn't fall into fear.

∼

Everything exploded around Zhee.

In a frightened panic, she yanked a sack from the man before her, not sure what was going on. Shouts in Taechizian echoed about her, full of fright and panic. The Runecarver she'd just robbed shouted and whirled around. His angry cries only made it harder for Zhee to make sense of all these sounds.

Metal clanged. Sparks flared from clashing weapons for moments, the light hurting her eyes. She flinched and stumbled. All the noises disoriented her. She couldn't pick out who was moving where. Footsteps thundered. Armor jangled. A rush of metal and boots came from behind her, these men shouting in Karadrisan.

"He's in there! Find him!"

Who was in there? Ablisio?

Panic surged through her. She had to get clear of the madness. The man she'd stolen from grabbed at her arm, his robe rustling about her. She thrust her elbow into his throat. He stumbled back. She scurried from him, sack clutched to her body. She struggled to regain her mental map and find her escape path.

It was so hard to think. Fear for Ablisio clawed at her. The ringing of metal burst to her left. Blood stained the air. Who was hurt? What had gone wrong? Had one of the wardens realized what the cough meant?

Metal jangled before Zhee.

Air rushed. She gasped and ducked out of instinct. Something slashed over her head. Her shoulder struck a man's solid torso, the links of his armor bruising her skin. She stumbled off him and fell onto her backside, the sack clucked protectively to her, full of the food.

"Muckling!" a voice snarled. Boots thundered at her.

～

Amiollea ripped her sack from the Runecarver and froze as the pandemonium rang out. The man she'd robbed shouted while her brother grunted in pain. Sparks burst and illuminated his face. She hadn't seen him since he was a boy, but she had never forgotten his face. Through the dirt, the grime, the years that had matured him into a man, she saw her brother.

And he fought.

"Ablisio!" she cried.

Shouts echoed all around her. She had to get to her brother. She slung her sack off her shoulder and rushed to his defense. Metal burst again and illuminated her brother for a moment. He fought against another muckling, naked, his body streaked in dirt, his hair a wild mess.

Men behind her were shouting about finding someone. Runecarvers fled in every direction. Maegwirio shouted from the front, his voice, even in his language, prickling her ears. She gripped her sack to swing it.

"Ablisio!" she shouted, coming closer.

A man growled in Taechizian to her right. She stumbled as armor rushed at her. Heavy boot steps. She squeaked and swung her sack before her. It struck the man in the shoulder. He grunted and staggered. Her hand went for her belt knife.

She whipped it out.

The man swung. She felt the air pressure shifting. She darted to her right and thrust her knife. His blade slashed past the left side of her body, a breeze rippling over her. She thrust her dagger right into where she felt his body, that large presence rattling before him.

She struck metal. Her knife scarped across it, unable to penetrate it. She gasped and drew back her weapon. Her foot stepped on her fallen sack. A hunk of salted beef rolled beneath her. She lost her balance, struggling to fight it.

Air hissed.

The sword punched into her stomach.

She gasped at how cold it felt inside of her. She trembled in disbelief. It was so deep in her. She felt no pain for the first two heartbeats. Then he ripped the blade away. She fell onto her back, her warm blood spilling over her stomach.

"Ablisio!" she shouted in pain. She clutched her guts. "Ablisio! Maej! Zhee! Help!"

Terror squeezed about her. Stabs were bad. Wounds festered, and the sword went so deep into her abdomen. She shuddered on the ground. She thrashed, eyes squeezed shut. She pressed both her hands against the wound. The blood almost scalded her fingers as they went numb.

"Ablisio!"

⁓

"Amiollea!" Ablisio shouted, hearing his sister's pain-filled cries as the attacker forced him to retreat from her.

His side burned. Blood trickled down it, slicking his side in the warmth. He swung his blade wildly before him, fending off the maddened strokes from the muckling ambusher who wanted his life. Who'd almost killed him.

Sparks flared between them, the fires stabbing his eyes. He closed them. Didn't need them. He felt the air before him, the sounds of his opponent's bare feet shifting on cobblestone. He focused on it over everything else as he fought for his life.

And his sister needed him.

"Who are you?" Ablisio snarled in frustration.

"She's mine!" the muckling answered, his voice higher pitched, a tenor, youthful and vicious. "I'll save her!"

"Who? Amiollea? Then stop fighting me!"

Blades clashed in the dark. It was all Ablisio could do to block the attacks he couldn't see coming. They dueled in the boiling chaos of the fleeing Runecarvers. Soldiers moved through the dark. They were advancing, shouting about finding someone.

This muckling?

"Over here!" Ablisio snarled in desperation. "He's here! The one you're looking for!"

The man he fought snarled in fury. "Just die! Die! I'm tired of you having her! Touching her! She's mine! Sun! Sun! Attack!"

Boots jangled in the darkness as all Ablisio cared about was his sister dying. She needed him. Her voice rang with pain and fear. Everything had gone wrong because of this muckling bastard. Fury swelled through Ablisio.

He screamed and attacked.

CHAPTER
THIRTY-FOUR

The woman screaming in pain arrested Maegwirio in his retreat. In helping his fellow Runecarvers. The wardens were advancing up the street, herding the others. A shiver ran down his spine. The woman cried his name.

Ablisio. Zhee.

"Amiollea!" croaked from his throat. The sack he clutched fell from Maegwirio's hand.

He rushed around his retreating brethren. A warden shouted at him and seized his arm, yanking him short.

"What are you doing, boy? There are mucklings fighting."

"There's one hurt!" Maegwirio struggled to break free.

"I know. I stabbed the bitch," Akozogwio growled. "Come on, Maegwirio, let the Glower guards mop them up."

"Glower guards?"

He heard the other soldiers. Captain Fhaaghin and his men searched for their thief. Was it Ablisio? Was he the thief? And what was Amiollea doing here? Her cries of pain tore at him.

"Come on!" Akozogwio jerked him toward the others. "We have to get out of here. Things are getting dangerous."

Maegwirio jerked hard and broke from his grip. He charged out into the darkness, running without care. He tripped and fell near the two men fighting. He rolled on the ground, stumbling past them as they shouted at each other and traded blows. Pain burst across his knee, a hot flash of pain.

"*Brother!*" sobbed Amiollea. Her voice sounded twisted by pain. The scent of blood filled his nose.

"*What have we here?*" a hard voice said in Karadrisan. "*A muckling squealing like a pig.*"

Hoarse chuckles rose from several men.

"*Best put her down before her bleating scares off Emmait,*" said Captain Fhaaghin.

Fear shot through Maegwirio. He roared in Karadrisan, "*NOOOO!*"

He threw himself forward, ignoring the pain in his knee. He scrambled, knowing he was so close to the whimpering and wounded Amiollea. His hands planted in hot blood, then he was over her. Covering her.

"*STOP!*" he shouted. "*Captain Fhaaghin, stop!*"

He heard metal jangling and squeezed his eyes shut for the blow that would slam into his body.

"Maej?" croaked Amiollea beneath him. He wouldn't let them harm her.

∼

"Sun! Sun!"

Emmait's shouts over the chaos shot new fear through Zhee as she scrambled back from the warden. She didn't understand why he was here. It had become a disaster. Amiollea was hurt. How had this all happened?

She threw her satchel at the warden. It crashed into his face. He grunted and she rolled to the side. His blade came down, striking the cobblestones where she'd lain. He barked something in his language as she gained her feet.

A dog snarled. Claws scrabbled from behind her. The sound of Sun rose above the clamor reverberating around her. Panic honed her senses razor sharp. Everything grew slow as her mind sorted through the cacophony of inputs assaulting her senses.

Her head throbbed as she gained a partial mental map. Ablisio fought with Emmait to her right. They traded blows. Beyond them, Amiollea sobbed in pain while someone, a Runecarver, threw himself over her shouting out in panic. Armed men were around them. Sun ran toward the fighting pair.

The dog rushed for Ablisio.

She knew what Sun could do. She'd heard the terrible screams and the tearing of flesh when Emmait butchered the group of mucklings. The man she had trusted, thought could be their friend, now fought to kill her Ablisio. The father of little Hope growing inside of her.

"No!" burst from her lips as her body lurched into motion.

Sun hurtled closer, snarling as he rose to his owner's aid.

"She's dying! Let me get to her!" shouted Ablisio.

Emmait roared, "I'll save her! She's mine!"

Zhee's legs stretched out. The warden shouted behind her as she raced to cut Sun off. The dog snarled to her right, almost to the fighters. But so was she. With desperation, she threw herself at the sound of the dog, arms reaching before her.

"Ablisio!" she shouted. "Dog!"

Her arms seized the body of Sun, grabbing him as he lunged at Ablisio. Her arms slipped down his hide and caught his hindquarters. She hit the ground on her belly, pain bursting across her stomach and thighs. She grabbed the dog.

Sun snarled and attacked Ablisio.

∽

ZHEE'S SHOUT twisted Ablisio around. He turned, his leather scabbard swinging on his left hip. Something growled in the dark. She hit the beast, her body smacking the ground. The sounds were confusing to him. Hot spittle splashed his buttocks moments before the dog bit.

The creature clamped jaws down on Ablisio's scabbard and yanked him off-balance. He stumbled back, sword swinging wildly before him. He stumbled and fought to keep his balance. The dog growled with savage fury, head jerking from right and left, tugging on the empty sword scabbard he'd grabbed.

"Get clear, Zhee!" he snarled. Zhee had told him about Sun. About what the dog could do to a man. Which meant he fought Emmait. Ablisio thrust his sword down at the beast savaging his scabbard.

His blade slammed into its body. It bit deep. The hound yelped in pain and released the scabbard. A moment later, whimpering, the dog collapsed, the body sliding off his sword blade. A fresh scent of hot blood filled Ablisio's nose.

"SUN!" roared Emmait.

The sword swung hard and fast. Ablisio felt it coming. The twisted his body and struggled to bring his sword up. Their blades impacted, but his grip was wrong. The force shivered up his hand. His fingers went numb. His sword fell with a clatter.

Emmait's blade buried deep into Ablisio's thigh. It cut into muscle. He snarled against the agony bursting up his body. His leg quivered. His hands shot out, grabbing Emmait's wrist. He wrenched the blade free from his grip, fighting with him.

"SUN! SUN!" the furious muckling shouted as the pair fought over the blade.

The dog whined on the ground.

"Ablisio!" Zhee shouted.

"I'm fine!" Ablisio snarled, blood flooding down his right leg. He couldn't put his weight on it. He squeezed his hands tight about the wrist holding the sword.

"She's mine!" roared Emmait. "You can't have her! You can't have everything! Kill you! Eat you! You'll be meat! Sun will devour you!"

Ablisio dug his fingernails into the bastard's tendons. Emmait gasped in pain as his fingers sprang open. His sword fell from his grasp, falling onto the ground between the two men. Ablisio groaned, his leg quivering.

He tried to stay upright, but . . .

He collapsed, pulling Emmait down atop him.

∽

"STOP!"

The attack halted before striking Maegwirio.

"What are you doing?" Captain Fhaaghin growled. "That's a muckling."

"And?" he demanded. "She's hurt. She's not who you're looking for."

"Maej," the wounded girl croaked.

"Captain?" a guard asked.

"He's right. Not who we're here for. He's close. Up the street farther."

In the distance, a dog whined in pain. Men fought. Another woman shouted in fright. Wardens yelled to gather any straggling Runecarvers. Maegwirio had to get Amiollea to help. It was her only chance. He pulled off his robe, not caring about stripping to his breechcloth—who would see him?—and pressed into her belly where the blood seemed to be coming from.

"Just hold it tight," he said, voice cracking.

Blood pumping terror through his veins, he lifted Amiollea with ease. She felt so tiny in his arms. She whimpered, the sounds of her pain whipping his heart. He staggered up the street with her, moving as fast as he could. She writhed and shuddered in his arms. The smell of her blood filled his nose.

"You're going to be okay," he said, speaking Taechizian without realizing it. "You're going to be just fine."

He passed the whimpering dog and the men screaming at each other. Nothing mattered but getting Amiollea to safety. She would be fine. She *had* to be fine. Tears stung his eyes as he carried her toward his retreating people.

∽

Fury gripped Emmait.

Sun was dying, stabbed by this bastard with *Zhee's* help. He pummeled Ablisio in the side of the head. With a snarl, he grabbed the monster's throat and squeezed. Men moved around them, their armor jangling.

"Which one is it?" drifted through his awareness.

"Careful, careful. Can't risk hurting Emmait."

"You can't have them!" Emmait raged, his hands squeezing. "Give back Sun! Zhee! You can't have them!"

Sun's dying whimpers slashed Emmait's soul to ribbons. Tears poured hot down his cheeks as he strangled Ablisio. The man thrashed beneath him, striking Emmait in the torso. A hard punch but he didn't care. Those pains were distant.

"GIVE HIM BACK!" he snarled while memories flooded his mind.

That small ball of fur huddled on his lap. Wet nose. Warm tongue. Wagging tail. Caring for Sun when he starved. His only friend. His protector until he grew stronger. They had spent seven years surviving.

Now he perished.

"SUN!" His fingers dug into Ablisio's throat. "TAKE IT BACK!"

"Emmait!" Zhee shouted. "Let go! Release him! Stop it!"

She threw herself onto his back, so warm and soft. Her arms went around his throat. He gasped as she jerked his head back to save that bastard from being choked. She wrestled with him. Why would she do that?

"NOOOO!" he roared. "I'm saving you!"

"You're killing my man! You're killing my Ablisio!"

Men laughed around them. They had spectators. Who were they? It didn't matter to Emmait. He threw his elbow back, slamming into her face. She screamed and tumbled off him, landing on a heap on her back.

"Stupid bitch!" he growled.

Ablisio's fist crashed into the side of Emmait's head, rolling him off the muckling. He landed on his side in sticky blood. Sun's blood. His dog whimpered beside him, claws scrabbling, struggling to reach him.

He would murder Ablisio.

"EAT YOU!" Emmait roared.

Metal scrabbled. Ablisio had grabbed one of the swords. Emmait swept his hands out before him. He brushed the edge of a sword and gasped at a flare of pain. Did he cut himself? He hit it hard enough to rattle it across the pavement. One end clanged and clattered. The handle. He grinned in triumph and darted his hand toward the sound of the hilt.

Ablisio roared and attacked.

He grabbed the handle. Fire burned across his hand.

∽

Zhee's sobbing pain swelled Ablisio's anger.

She had given him a moment to breathe, and he took it. He knocked Emmait off him. He rolled over and felt a sword. He picked it up and gained his feet, facing the direction of the foul, disgusting thing. Pain throbbed in his quivering thigh. He put all his weight on his left foot and lunged forward.

"She's not yours!" he growled. "She's Zhee!"

Emmait snarled in agony. Flesh sizzled. A blade clattered on the ground. Ablisio understood as he slashed the blade before him. He had grabbed Emmait's blade, and the muckling bastard had picked up Ablisio's enchanted one.

"SUN!" sobbed Emmait.

Ablisio's sword ripped across flesh. The blade bit deep into his enemy. Blood spurted hot. Then came the slapping sound of guts and entrails hitting the ground. Emmait screamed in pain and collapsed on the back.

"Who just got stabbed?" growled one of the men watching around them. "Is it Emmait?"

"Seize them!" another shouted.

"Ablisio!" Zhee shouted and raced forward toward him. He fought to stand as the armored men advanced on them.

～

Zhee rushed to Ablisio.

The sound hurt Emmait's ears as he fell on his back. His guts had fallen out. He reached out and found Sun. His dog licked his palm. He seized the fur. With the last strength left to Emmait, he pulled his pet to him. He hugged Sun's dying body to his chest.

"I'm sorry," he whispered.

Sun gave a last whimper. His spasms ended. Emmait buried his face into the dirt-matted fur and howled out the pain and agony. His body grew colder. Men advanced on Emmait, and he didn't care.

Zhee chose Ablisio, and he'd gotten Sun killed.

Nothing mattered.

Emmait hugged his dog. They had been in this together from the beginning. He'd forgotten that because of his obsession with Zhee. Who was she? A thing that had aroused him? An object he'd lusted to possess? She didn't love him. She didn't protect him.

Hadn't died for him.

"I'm sorry, Sun," croaked Emmait.

"That you?" a voice growled over him. "Emmait? Your father sent us to find you. It's time to go home."

Emmait didn't care. He held Sun. That was home. He closed his eyes, ready for it to end when a voice cackled with glee. A bright light burst to life. A mad voice howled, "POISONER!"

The burning fire landed near Emmait, exposing the Glower guards standing over him. They flinched and screamed as Death came whispering down.

~

Zhee staggered with Ablisio toward where she'd dropped her sack. The armored men were moving in, coming for them. They couldn't escape, but what else could she do? If she dropped Ablisio and ran on her own, she might have a chance.

Grab the food.

Live for Hope.

But she couldn't leave Ablisio. Hot blood spilled down his thigh and soaked her own leg. The soldiers cut them off. Their armor rattled before them. She smelled how clean they were over the iron of their armor and weapons.

"Who you got there, girl?" one asked. "You going to be as frien—"

Light exploded behind her.

The brilliance spilled around her and struck the two guards in the face. It illuminated them. They had pale, milky skin and the broad builds of Povazian men. They screamed, one dropping his sword to cover his eyes blinded by the brilliance. The other cursed and charged past her.

"Douse that mucking light!" he roared.

The air whispered.

Urine spilled hot down Zhee's thighs. A paralyzing fear rushed through her. She flashed back to that terrible day as she'd walked beside her father. The unseen claws and talons ripped into the others in the street, her father tackling her and crushing her to the cobblestones.

"*Close your eyes, Zheemhaidi,*" Father had shouted, smothering her with his weight.

Ablisio cried her name and twisted in her grip. The guard covering his eyes screamed. Blood burst from his chest. Chains shattered, rent by an unseen force. A weight shoved her to the ground. Pressed her into dirty cobblestones.

Ablisio covered her.

"Amiollea!" he howled as he protected her and little Hope.

Death whispered in the air above them. Men shouted in horror. Zhee squeezed her eyes shut. The light shone so bright it glowed red through her lids. A spiderweb of veins traced dark across her vision. She trembled, sobbed.

Waited for Ablisio to be ripped off her.

CHAPTER
THIRTY-FIVE

"Amiollea!" Ablisio roared. Through the blinding light, he looked for his sister. His eyes hurt, cut bloody by dancing flames. The pieces of the Povazian guard landed nearby in a clang of metal. Zhee sobbed beneath him. The hot stench of urine filled his nose. He pressed tight over her, covering her, his heart sick for his sister while the pain vanished from his leg.

"Get that mucking light out!" howled the soldier racing for the others.

A sickening crunch. A loud thud and then a heavy rattle of a body being crushed. Something rolled into Ablisio's thigh. A fine thatch of hair, the feel of a nose. Terror filled him for his sister. For Zhee. He needed to protect them both.

Couldn't.

Up the street, a Runecarver howled as bloody lines ripped into his back, tearing through the gray cloth of his robe. Death lifted him into the air, revealing another Runecarver farther up the street. He wore only a breechcloth and staggered away at the edge of the shadows. He carried someone, legs dangled off one side, a head the other.

"Amiollea!" Ablisio roared as the Runecarver carried his injured sister away.

The light snuffed out with a sizzle of smothered flames.

A man cursed in Povazian.

The blessed darkness was all around them again. Death retreated, unable to find them. He rolled off Zhee, the pain howling through his leg. The wound pulsed and throbbed. A sudden, woozy weakness swept over him.

"Ablisio," Zhee asked, voice tight with worry.

"Just the stab . . . to my leg . . ." He panted. "Need a moment."

"The soldiers," she gasped. She stood and grabbed his hand.

The surviving guards, a pair of them, cursed at the Sun Ravager. They were still looking for something.

Why did one of those madmen spark a light now? Ablisio wondered as he grunted to his feet on his good leg, his right dangling. He leaned on Zhee, blood spilling down his thigh. "They took Amiollea."

"What?" Zhee gasped as she staggered them away from the Glower soldiers.

"The Runecarvers! They have her! They captured her!" Frantic fear fought through the spinning dizziness. "Crap-damned leg! We have to go after her."

"You're not going after anyone," she said. She bent over and picked up a sack. Her posture shifted as she adjusted to carrying the heavy burden. "Come on, the alley's this way."

"No!" he groaned. "Amiollea."

"We'll save her," she said, her voice thick with worry. "You're *bleeding*, Ablisio. Bad. Real bad."

He grunted and nodded, fighting against the dizziness. He felt the air change. Buildings rose around them. The safety of the alley, away from the shouting guards. They were crying out the name of that bastard.

"Emmait! Where are you, Emmait?"

Zhee leaned Ablisio against a stone wall. He slid down onto his rump. He just needed a moment to catch his breath. Then he would save his sister. His eyes closed. He grunted, his feet growing colder.

Only a moment.

He slumped into unconsciousness.

Maegwirio held Amiollea in his arms as he staggered after the rest of his people in their mad flight from the light. She whimpered in his arms, the pain-filled sounds growing softer. He had to get her to his maestro now. He pushed himself to go faster.

"You're going to be fine," he said, still babbling in Taechizian. "You're going to be okay, Amiollea."

"Maej," she whimpered, her body trembling.

"Just hold on. You're going to be fine."

Ahead, he heard the creak of gates opening. Shouts for help. His people would save her. His maestro would save her. Amiollea wouldn't die. She couldn't die. He would get her back in time. He pushed himself into a heavy-stepped jog.

"I need help!" he shouted. "She's stabbed!"

"She?" a deep voice of Fiaxhazio growled. "Who do you have there, Maegwirio?"

"Someone dying! I have to get her to the Spire!"

Something dragged Emmait away from the light. He clutched Sun's corpse to his chest. He stared up at a face covered in a shaggy beard streaked in filth and gunk. Gleams of silver peeked through, bright and reflective in the dancing light. Someone had carved thick scars into his chest. They formed patterns.

Runes? the dying Emmait thought. A mad look gleamed in bloodshot eyes. The man's skin had a bluish tinge to it.

"Those poisoners won't get you," the man cackled. "Oh, no, they fear the light! And well they should! Death judges them, boy. They're sinners, one and all. The great lie has poisoned this city. It must be purged."

"What?" croaked Emmait. His body felt cold. His heart labored to beat. His head lolled.

The light snuffed out.

"Won't find us," the man cackled. "Oh, no, the poisoners won't find Cinder. No, no. He escaped. They think to butcher the faithful, but the faithful rise and rise. The Sun, boy, the Sun always rises."

Before unconsciousness claimed Emmait, he groaned. He was in the hands of the madman who had burned down a quarter of the city. He clutched onto Sun's fur, holding tight to it while a crazed thought danced through the dying fumes of his thoughts.

Sun... rise... Come back... boy... I'm sorry... Come back...

The madman cackled as he dragged the dying youth away from those who wanted to bring him home.

The END of Book One

BOOKS BY JMD REID

What Darkness Hides
A Spark in the Night
A Gleam of Hope
A Heart of Pain

Shadows of the Dragon
Foundation of Courage
Lady Shadow's Ire
Guilt of Sacrifice
Sands of Loss
Wyrms of Regret
Madness of Light
Blood-Stained Shadows
Sailing the Ashen Seas
Lady Shadow's Promise
The Golden Trees Burn
Maelstrom of the Gods
Paradise Found

BOOKS BY JMD REID

Jewels of Illumination
Diamond Stained
Ruby Ruins
Obsidian Mind
Emerald Strength
Amethyst Shattered
***
Jewels of Illumination Box Set

Mask of Illumination
Mask of Guilt
Mask of Vengeance
Mask of Hope
Mask of Betrayal
Mask of Redemption

The Storm Below
Above the Storm
Reavers of the Tempest
Storm of Tears
Golden Darkness Descends
Shattered Sunlight

The Storm Below Box Set

About the Author

J.M.D. Reid has been a long-time fan of Fantasy ever since he read The Hobbit way back in the fourth grade. His head has always been filled with fantastical tales, and he is eager to share the worlds dwelling in his dreams with you.

Reid is long-time resident of the Pacific Northwest in and around the City of Tacoma. The rainy, gloomy atmosphere of Western Washington, combined with the natural beauty of the evergreen forests and the looming Mount Rainier, provides the perfect climate to brew creative worlds and exciting stories!

When he's not writing, Reid enjoys playing video games, playing D&D and listening to amazing music.

You can follow him on twitter @JMDReid, like him on Facebook, visit his **blog**, and sign up for his newsletter.

Printed in Great Britain
by Amazon